Prais...

David Weber, Chris Kennedy, and

TO CHALLENGE
HEAVEN

"This is thrilling and philosophical military science fiction, in which vampires become saviors and aliens become allies. It will appeal to fans looking for a more fantastic take on what Star Trek could have become."
—*Library Journal* on *To Challenge Heaven*

"Audacious . . . Keeps the pedal to the metal."
—*Publishers Weekly* on *Out of the Dark*

"Marvelously entertaining."   —Vernor Vinge on *Off Armageddon Reef*

"Ambitious."   —*Kirkus Reviews* on *By Heresies Distressed*

"A fun and entertaining space opera."   —*Locus* on *A Call to Vengeance*

TO CHALLENGE
HEAVEN

DAVID WEBER
AND
CHRIS KENNEDY

TOR

TOR PUBLISHING GROUP
NEW YORK

TO CHALLENGE HEAVEN

Copyright © 2023 by David Weber and Chris Kennedy

Maps by Jennifer Hanover

A Tor Book
Published by Tom Doherty Associates / Tor Publishing Group
120 Broadway
New York, NY 10271

www.torpublishinggroup.com

Tor® is a registered trademark of Macmillan Publishing Group, LLC.

The Library of Congress Cataloging-in-Publication Data is available upon request.

ISBN 978-1-250-90741-7 (trade paperback)
ISBN 978-1-250-90740-0 (ebook)

Our books may be purchased in bulk for promotional, educational, or business use. Please contact your local bookseller or the Macmillan Corporate and Premium Sales Department at 1-800-221-7945, extension 5442, or by email at MacmillanSpecialMarkets@macmillan.com.

First Tor Paperback Edition: 2025

Printed in the United States of America

0 9 8 7 6 5 4 3 2 1

For Sharon and Sheelah, the ladies in our lives

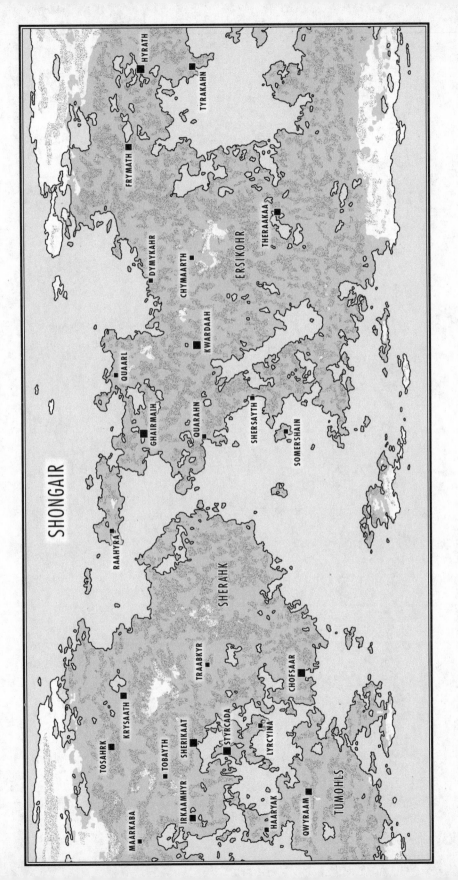

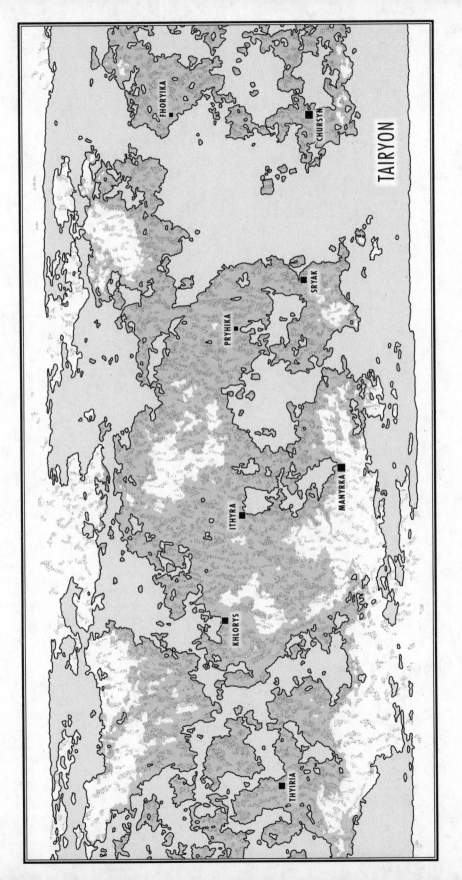

I

The Way of Honor

I find myself, as I rather suspect you expected, surprised to see you," Vlad Drakulya said.

"No! Really?" David Dvorak smiled as he extended his hand to the man history knew as "Vlad the Impaler." Among other things.

The boat bay gallery in which they stood was somewhat larger than the one Vlad had left behind aboard the dreadnought *Târgovişte.* Not unreasonably, perhaps. *Târgovişte,* which Vlad had captured from the Imperial Shongair Navy four decades earlier, was over five kilometers long . . . but that was barely twenty percent of the Planetary Union Navy ship *Relentless*'s length. What *was* surprising—aside from the fact that the Planetary Union hadn't existed when Vlad left the Sol System—was that, despite the absence of any spin section, the boat bay's up and down were as firmly established as they would have been on the surface of Earth itself.

A half dozen or so men and women—and three other . . . beings—stood behind Dvorak in that obviously artificial gravity. Most of the humans wore military uniforms, although not that of any military which had existed when Vlad left Earth, and all of them smiled in obvious amusement as he and his companion took in their surroundings.

The nonhumans among them weren't equipped to smile.

"Whyever should you be surprised?" Dvorak continued. "I mean, be reasonable, Vlad! You *did* leave a planet full of humans with the entire tech base of the Galactic Hegemony. What did you *expect* us to do with it?"

"Obviously, very much what you did do," Vlad replied, shaking the proffered hand, "although you appear to have applied rather more . . . vigor to the process than I had anticipated."

Dvorak chuckled and extended his hand in turn to the very tall, very black, former-Marine who had followed Vlad from the shuttle into the boat bay.

"It's good to see you, too, Stephen," Dvorak said, gripping his hand firmly. "Your dad and mom asked me to tell you they miss you."

"You told them about me?" Stephen Buchevsky sounded much less amused than Vlad had, and his eyes darkened.

"I did." Dvorak met those dark eyes levelly, still gripping his hand. "I know you didn't want them told you were a vampire. Things changed, though, and you know I never liked lying to your dad, even by omission, about that. And before you get too bent out of shape people's attitude about the vampires is one of those things that have changed—changed one hell of a lot—since you left."

Buchevsky looked at him for several more of Dvorak's breaths—Buchevsky didn't breathe anymore—and then released his hand.

"All right." He still wasn't happy about it, but he nodded. "I wish you hadn't. But maybe things have changed enough for them to handle it. I hope to hell they have, anyway."

"Believe me, they have." Dvorak laid a hand on Buchevsky's shoulder and squeezed. "That's why Pieter and Dan both agreed I should tell them. So did Jasmine, for that matter."

"Even Jasmine?" Buchevsky's lips quirked. "I'm starting to feel ganged up on!"

"But only in the friendliest way!" Dvorak assured him.

"Yeah. Sure!" Buchevsky drew one of the deep breaths he no longer really needed. "Dad . . . took it okay?"

"He not only 'took it okay,' his sermon the next Sunday was about the mysterious and miraculous ways God moves to achieve his purposes, and he used *you* as an example." Dvorak smiled as Buchevsky's eyes widened. "Not much worried about the 'vampiric taint,' your dad. And he and your mom also asked me to tell you they look forward to seeing you again a bit sooner than you probably anticipated."

"I guess 'a bit sooner' is probably one way to put it." Buchevsky shook his head with a smile of his own, obviously grateful for the opportunity to change topics. "Just how *much* 'sooner' did you have in mind, though?"

"Well, when we say 'a bit,' we mean 'quite a lot,' actually." Dvorak's smile segued into what could only be described as a grin. "The monkey boys and girls came up with a new way to break into phase space, and we can go a lot higher than the Hegemony."

"How *much* higher?" Buchevsky asked.

"Gamma bands . . . for now," Dvorak replied, and watched Buchevsky's eyes widen. The phase-drive aboard *Târgoviște,* which represented the Galactic Hegemony's best hardware—as of eighty years or so ago, which wasn't even yesterday yet for the Galactics' glacial approach to technology—could break only into the upper reaches of the alpha bands, which allowed them a maximum apparent velocity of a little more than six times the speed of light, and explained why it had taken forty years for *Târgoviște* to reach the Shong System from Sol. But if *Relentless* could go as high as gamma. . . .

"That means you can pull damned near *twenty* lights!"

"A tad over twenty-four, actually, because the Gannon Drive doesn't need particle screening." Dvorak's expression would have filled the Cheshire Cat with envy. "We can get all the way up to point-niner-niner cee, nineteen percent better than anything the Puppies or the Hegemony can pull. We dialed that down a bit, though. We didn't need that much speed to beat you guys here, and it seemed like a good idea not to push things to the max on our very first extended gamma-band voyage. So we held it down to twenty-two cee. Made the trip in just over twelve years. Well, a smidge under six, subjective. If we *had* pushed it all the way up to point-niner-niner, we could've done it in just over ten years . . . and only fifteen *months,* subjective."

"Gannon Drive?" Buchevsky repeated in a rather shellshocked voice.

"The actual official name is the Gannon-Jackson-Nesbitt Drive, but shorthand—" Dvorak shrugged. "Chester gets a little pissed with us over that, but Warren Jackson and Trish Nesbitt are fine with it. They insist he did most of the heavy lifting."

Buchevsky opened his mouth again, then closed it firmly before he could parrot the names of people he'd never met.

"Look, the Gannon Drive's only one of the things we need to bring you guys up to speed on. Why don't we take the two of you to the flag briefing room where we can talk about that. Among other things."

"Quite a few other things, I suspect," Vlad said, glancing at nonhumans in the greeting party.

Their heads were distinctly saurian looking, with high, pronounced crests covered in a fine down, and they were built on a lean, slender model. They appeared to be toe-walkers, and although those heads were shaped quite differently, they reminded him strongly of the velociraptors from one of his favorite science fiction movies. All of them were at least twenty centimeters shorter than he, which made them over thirty centimeters shorter than Dvorak or Buchevsky, but two of them were noticeably taller than their companion.

"Oh, definitely," Dvorak told him. "Definitely."

· · · · ·

THE INTRA-SHIP CAR ride was quite a bit longer than it would have been aboard *Târgoviște*. But it came to an end eventually, and Dvorak led the way down a softly lit passage. A brown-haired uniformed woman, her sleeve bearing the single rocker and three chevrons of a staff sergeant, stood post outside it and braced to attention as they approached.

"Annette," Dvorak said with a nod.

"Good morning, Mister Secretary," the staff sergeant replied.

"'Mister Secretary'?" Buchevsky repeated with a quizzical expression.

"It's a long story," Dvorak replied.

"Secretary of what?" Buchevsky asked.

"State," a voice said from the rear of their party before Dvorak could answer.

"Secretary of *State*?" Buchevsky said in a careful tone.

"Yes," Dvorak sighed, and turned his head to glare over his shoulder. "Gee, thanks, Rob!"

"What I'm here for," the voice assured him, and Dvorak rolled his eyes, then looked back at the staff sergeant.

"Open her up, Annette. And if you could just sorta shoot your commanding officer as he goes by, I'd take it as a personal favor."

"Sorry, Mister Secretary. No can do."

The staff sergeant tapped the smart screen to open the door and Vlad and Buchevsky followed Dvorak through it, then came to an abrupt halt.

"Well, *there* you are! About darn time!" The short, red-haired speaker threw her arms around Vlad. "What took you guys so long?" Sharon Dvorak demanded. "We've been waiting around for you for *ages*!"

"Don't believe her," her husband said. "We actually only got here a month or so before you did."

"Which still represents a stellar, if you will pardon the adjective, accomplishment," Vlad replied, returning Sharon's embrace a bit cautiously.

She'd been less than fully comfortable with the whole notion of vampires when he, Buchevsky, and the crew of *Târgovişte* departed the Sol System. Any hesitance she'd felt then was clearly a thing of the past, now, as she opened her arms to Buchevsky, in turn.

"Well, we needed to catch up with you and explain how there have been . . . a few changes." Dvorak waved toward the huge conference table at the briefing room's center as his wife released Buchevsky. The table's surface appeared to be a single enormous flatscreen, and names glowed on its surface, indicating which chair was whose.

"That much, I had already surmised . . . Mister Secretary," Vlad said dryly as he and Buchevsky found their illuminated names and settled into the proper seats.

"*Former* Secretary," Dvorak corrected.

His expression was a bit pained, and Vlad chuckled. The Dave Dvorak he'd left behind on Earth had been a wounded, ex–shooting range proprietor, part-time survivalist, resistance leader who would probably never use his left arm again. He'd also been at least a decade older, physically, than the man across the table from him, and he had *not* been the Secretary of State—well, *former* Secretary of State—of the Planetary Union, which had *also* not existed at the time of Vlad's departure.

"I suppose," Dvorak continued, seating Sharon before he took his own place, "that we should begin with introductions. Everyone here knows who you two are, but let me run through our motley crowd for you before we dive into any deeper explanations.

"These two, you already know."

He waved at a squarely built red-haired man who bore a strong family resemblance to his wife and the smaller, more compact dark-haired man seated beside him. The name tape on the redhead's black uniform tunic said "WILSON, R.," although—like Dvorak himself—he looked substantially younger than he had when last Vlad and Buchevsky had seen him. The smaller man wore virtually the same uniform, but with what appeared to be different branch insignia. His name tape said "TORINO, D.," and like Buchevsky and Vlad himself, he no longer breathed unless he needed the air for his vocal cords.

"Rob is back on active service now," Dvorak continued, "and that monkey suit he's wearing belongs to the Planetary Union Space Marines. Longbow here is still an Air Force wuss. Worse, those starbursts on his collar say he's now a major general. And worse yet, Rob's a *lieutenant* general." He shook his head mournfully. "Oh, how standards have slipped in your absence!"

"Forgive him," Lieutenant General Rob Wilson said. "He still thinks he's clever, even after all this time and despite all evidence to the contrary."

Vlad chuckled again and looked at the woman seated on Wilson's far side.

"Admiral Josephine Mallard, Planetary Union Navy," Dvorak said. "She's the task force CO."

Vlad took note of the words "task force"—and the implication *Relentless* was not alone—as he nodded to Mallard. The admiral was brown haired, brown eyed, and petite. There was nothing fragile about her wiry frame, and she carried herself with a springy, athletic grace. Despite her surname, she looked more Middle Eastern than European. Especially beside the taller, clearly Nordic officer in the same uniform sitting beside her.

"Captain Ignats Pavlovskis," Dvorak said. "*Relentless*'s skipper and Admiral Mallard's flag captain. The fellow sitting next to him in Marine uniform is Brigadier Branson Fitzgerald, Rob's XO."

Fitzgerald, a chunky dark-eyed and dark-haired man about midway between Dvorak and Vlad in height, nodded in respectful acknowledgment, and Dvorak moved on to the man beside the brigadier.

"Alex Jackson," he said, "my chief of staff. He kept me from screwing up too badly on my first foray into interstellar diplomacy, so the President sent him along to keep an eye on me this time, too."

Jackson was tall and almost as dark complexioned as Fitzgerald, although he seemed younger. Of course, *all* of the humans in the briefing room, including Dvorak, seemed preposterously young. Not one of them looked like he or she could be more than thirty. Obviously, Earth had figured out how to apply the Hegemony's antigerone therapies to the human race.

"Seated next to Alex we have Fikriyah Batma, my official XO on the diplomatic side," Dvorak continued.

"Prince Vlad." Batma smiled. "I was Abu Bakr's deputy on what Ambassador Dvorak's fond of calling his first foray. Abu is . . . otherwise occupied at the moment, but he asked me to pass along his greetings. And thanks."

"He is most welcome, of course," Vlad replied.

"And beside Fikriyah," Dvorak said, "is Bai Guiying. Guiying is with the Department of Industry, and she's here to ride herd on the industrial side of our mission."

Bai was obviously Chinese. She was also the only human in the room who was shorter than Sharon Dvorak, and unlike Admiral Mallard, she was fine boned and delicate, with an almost ethereal elegance.

"Salutări, Înălţimea Voastră," she said, bending her head in greeting, and Vlad chuckled.

"Nǐ hǎo, huáitè fūrén," he replied. "But while I appreciate the courtesy, I have not been 'Your Highness' in quite some time in *any* language."

"I understand that, Prince Vlad," Bai said serenely. "My mother, however, made me promise to greet you properly in your own tongue. She was visiting family in the United States when the Shongairi attacked us. She was only in her twenties at the time, and she lost her own mother and two brothers there . . . and all the rest of her family when the Shongairi K-struck Guangzhou. But she was also among those you and your fellows rescued from Ground Base Two Alpha."

"I deeply regret my failure to act sooner," Vlad said in a rather more somber tone, "but I am glad we were in time for her, at least."

"You were 'in time' for a whole bunch of people, Vlad," Dvorak said a bit sternly. "If you hadn't been, none of us would be sitting here aboard this ship, because we'd all be too busy being dead!"

"I realize that." Vlad nodded. "It does not mean I might not have saved so many, many more had I faced the necessity of once again embracing what I became so long ago."

"Hold that thought," Dvorak said. "I need to come back to it. But first, allow me to introduce the last three members of our group." He gestured with an open palm to the first of the nonhumans in the room. "Major Merahl BryMerThor," he said.

The kilted alien was perhaps thirteen or fourteen centimeters shorter than Vlad, with dark red crest down. He and his companions all wore rust-colored cardigan sweaters, despite the compartment's comfortable—for humans, at least—temperature. They also wore kilts, not the uniform Wilson and the other humans wore, and unless Vlad was very much mistaken, those kilts' blue-and-green pattern formed an actual tartan sett. Precisely why aliens might be wearing a human tartan was a bit of a mystery, but he was becoming accustomed to that.

They wore no shirts or uniform tunics, but the very edge of a diamond-shaped pattern of fine, red and black scales showed at the neck of the alien's sweater as he rose slightly from his chair to bow across the table in response to the introduction.

"Captain Thornak BryMerThor," Dvorak continued, and the second alien—this one a centimeter or so shorter, with yellow down and a banded black-and-yellow scale pattern—also rose to bow to Vlad and Buchevsky.

"And Captain Brykira BryMerThor."

The third and smallest alien, with white down and a more muted chevron pattern of white-on-black scales, bowed in turn. They were, Vlad noticed, the only individuals in the compartment who were obviously armed, although the pistol grips looked a bit odd. Probably because their four-fingered hands were so slender compared to human hands—despite, he realized, having not one, but two opposable thumbs. That probably also explained why the magazine well was in front of the trigger guard, since the grips were too narrow and too short to accommodate much ammunition. Although it didn't explain *why* they were armed. For that matter, unlike the human members of the group, Dvorak hadn't explained why they were present in the first place.

Vlad pondered that, then raised an eyebrow, and General Wilson chuckled.

"Noticed a slight omission there, didn't you, Vlad?" he asked cheerfully, pointedly ignoring the glare Dvorak gave him or his sister's suddenly resigned expression. "Care to explain to Vlad and Stephen why you guys are here, Merahl?"

The red-crested alien glanced at Dvorak and prominent nose flaps twitched visibly . . . and energetically.

"Oh, stop laughing and just tell him," Dvorak growled, and the alien turned his attention to Vlad.

"My spouses and I are Sarthian," he said. Or, rather, the slim translator on the chain around his neck said it, and Vlad's eyebrows rose once more. The translating devices the Shongairi had brought to Earth had *sounded* like machines, converting the Shongair language into the manifold languages of Earth without any vestige of tone or nuance. Indeed, their ability to handle tonal languages, like Mandarin, had been . . . limited, to say the least. But while it was obvious that Thornak's natural vocal apparatus was poorly suited to forming human words, his translated voice was richly expressive. And what it was expressing at this moment, unless Vlad was sadly mistaken, was affectionate amusement.

"Sarth is the first extra-Solar planet to have joined the Terran Alliance," Merahl continued, "and at least one of us is required to accompany Clan Ruler David at all times as his sherhynas." The last word was clearly in Merahl's native language. That was Vlad's first thought. Then—

"Clan Ruler David?" he repeated.

"Yep!" Wilson sounded delighted. "And that makes my baby sister Clan Ruler Consort Sharon. Actually, their Sarthian names are Clan Ruler David SharDa nar Dvorak and Clan Ruler Consort Sharon SharDa nar Dvorak. Falls trippingly off the tongue, doesn't it?" he added brightly.

"You do realize that even if Annette won't, I have the authority to have Merahl shoot your ass, right, Rob?" Dvorak growled.

"Hey, I'm not the guy who took over half a planet!"

"I did *not*—" Dvorak began, then paused and drew a deep breath.

"I believe I said we had a lot to discuss, Vlad," he said. "I'm not sure Sarth is the best place to begin, but now that my beloved and soon-to-be-deceased brother-in-law has decided it's all just as funny as hell, maybe we should go there anyway."

"Oh, definitely!" Wilson said, while several other people seemed to find it very difficult not to laugh.

. . . . .

"—SO THEN MALACHI personally took Juzhyr's surrender, after identifying himself as my son." Dvorak shrugged, his expression trapped between wry amusement, something very like consternation, and resigned acceptance. "Since Juzhyr had been Clan Qwern's clan ruler when Clan Qwern attacked the Terran mission, and I was the head of that mission—although, of course, I was still unconscious in the regeneration tank at the time—that meant the entire *clan* had surrendered to me. Or, rather, to Malachi as my agent. And that," he sighed, "meant that Clan Qwern and the entire Qwernian Empire no longer existed."

"So if I have this straight," Stephen Buchevsky said in a careful tone, "you basically acquired an entire empire by right of conquest?" He tipped back in his chair and looked at Vlad. "Bit of an overachiever, wouldn't you say?"

"I must acknowledge that it surpasses my own modest accomplishments as Voivode of Wallachia," Vlad replied, clearly suppressing laughter. "I feel a certain degree of jealousy!"

"It's not like I set out to do it!" Dvorak protested. "And I gave that . . . impetuous youngster a good talking-to, too!"

"And just where do you think *your* son acquired his 'impetuosity'?" his wife asked sweetly. "Imprinted on his male role model early, didn't he?"

"I never—" Dvorak began, then stopped himself as Thornak BryMer-Thor's translator produced an extraordinarily human-sounding laugh. Dvorak glared, and the Sarthian—who, Vlad had discovered, was the female member of the tri-sexual union of Dvorak's sherhynas—nodded her head, in what Vlad had also discovered was the Sarthian gesture of negation.

"Yes, Thornak?" Dvorak said just a bit repressively. "You had something to add?"

"I fear I must stand at your wife's back in this matter, Clan Ruler," the captain replied. "Your son is very like you. And—" her translator-produced tone became much more serious "—it was a very good thing for the Empire that he is."

"I must agree," Batma said. Vlad looked at her, and she shrugged. "With all deference to Thornak and her spouses, I had a rather closer proximity than most members of our mission to Juzhyr and the Qwernians. There was much to admire about their culture, but there were . . . downsides, as well. And among those downsides was the fact that tradition, personal rule, and personal *loyalty* played a much greater role than the rule of law among them. They found the very concept of international *law* . . . arcane, which had unfortunate implications for things like diplomacy and formal, binding treaties."

"And we still find it—the concept of international law, I mean—rather bizarre," Thornak inserted. "We are making progress as a clan, but it will be some generations, I fear, before we match Dianto in that respect." She gave a very human-looking shrug.

"For that matter," Batma said, "there truly is much to be said for the Qwernian—well, the Dvorakan, now—traditions. And even if there weren't, Dave really couldn't have renounced the clan rulership, as badly as we all knew he wanted to. It would have completely destabilized their empire, because there would have been no clear line of succession. That would almost certainly have resulted in a civil war between competing claimants and, almost as badly, have prevented Sarth's inclusion in the Terran Alliance. The Planetary Union had already determined that the decision to join must be endorsed by every nation on the planet, not just some of them, and no one could have spoken for what had been the Qwernian Empire if it disintegrated. As Clan Ruler, on the other hand, Dave could simply sign on the dotted line, and it was done. If he were to choose to renounce the treaty, they'd follow his decision to do *that* without a qualm, as well, but as long as his orders are to abide by it, they'll cross every t and dot every i."

"And just who's running the show back on Sarth while you go gallivanting around the stars?" Buchevsky asked.

"I have a very good urizhar looking after Dvoraka," Dvorak replied, using his own translator software to produce the Sarthian title. "It means roughly 'viceroy' or maybe 'vizier,' he said. "Fellow by the name of Abu Bakr. I won't say he turned any handsprings of delight when I offered him the job, but he was a pretty near perfect fit. And he's also the head of our permanent delegation on Sarth."

Vlad cocked his head, then nodded slowly.

"It seems unlikely to me that any human empire could have . . . acquiesced in such a transformation," he said. "But I suppose that is rather the point, is it not? Sarthians—" he inclined his head across the table at the nonhumans "—are *not* humans, are they?"

"I believe we have more in common than one might think," Brykira BryMerThor replied. "There are differences, however. Especially between humans and Dvorakians. Those disgustingly effete Diantians are much more like you, I fear." The neutro's translator voice rippled with laughter.

"They are," Dvorak agreed, "although it was really the way the Qwernians responded that led to our presence here in Shong, in a lot of ways."

"Should I assume that you have come to lend your voices to Stephen's and advise me to hold my hand against these vermin?"

Vlad's tone had turned colder and those green eyes hardened as they met Dvorak's across the briefing room table. In that moment, it was much easier to remember why he was known to history as Vlad Tepes.

"Yes, actually." Dvorak met that agate gaze levelly. "I have. *We* have."

Silence hovered for a long, taut second as their eyes held one another.

"There is such a thing as justice," Vlad said then, softly. "Such a thing as retribution. These . . . *creatures,* these Shongairi, came uninvited into our star system. We had never injured them in any way. And they *announced* their presence with a kinetic strike which killed millions upon millions of humans. Of your own 'breathers.' Of your families." He nodded to Bai Guiying, who looked back serenely. "Your *children.*" He reached out to lay a hand on Buchevsky's shoulder and shook his head slowly, his expression carved from granite. "They followed that up with additional strikes that killed not millions, but *billions,* until not even half the human race survived. Until, dissatisfied even with that, they planned to murder the *rest* of humanity in its entirety. What claim can such as they present upon our mercy?"

"Mercy isn't something you claim from another," Dvorak said quietly. "It's something you extend *to* others. And it isn't solely for the benefit of those to whom you show it, Vlad. It's also the salvation of your own soul."

"Then perhaps it is the Shongairi's misfortune that I *have* no soul." Vlad smiled, and his teeth shifted, extending ever so slightly into fangs.

"That's . . . not as much of a given as you may have thought," Dvorak said.

"I like you, Dave Dvorak. And I admire and respect you. But do not presume to lecture *me* on the loss of one's soul." Vlad's voice was chiseled ice, and his eyes were bleaker than any glacier. "My soul was stained enough even before the curse came upon me. Now?"

He shrugged, and Longbow Torino stirred in his chair. He opened his mouth, but Dvorak raised a hand before the general could speak.

"First," he said, still quietly, "I suspect your soul was in somewhat better state than you thought it was. The man—and, yes, Vlad, whatever else, you're still a *man*—before me wouldn't be here today if you'd truly been the soulless monster history says you were. And that I think you've allowed yourself to be convinced that you were. A hard, often brutal man? Yes. I'll give you that. And even cruel. But I also know the time in which that man lived, the challenges and threats he faced, and I find it difficult to believe that the man who could become the person sitting across this table from me was any of those things because he *wanted* to be. And whatever you may once have been, I don't believe you're any of those things today. I've spent too much time with Pieter and Dan and the other vampires you made before you left Earth to believe they're damned to hell, will they or won't they, because of their monstrous nature. And if they aren't, neither are you."

Their gazes held across the table, and Dvorak inhaled deeply.

"But, second, your 'curse' isn't remotely what you think it is."

Vlad stiffened, a terrible core of anger burning suddenly in the ice of his eyes. The anger of one who had lived for seven hundred years unclean, accursed, cast out into the darkness. Of one who had borne every ounce of his curse's crushing weight for all those years.

"Breather," he said ever so softly, "be very careful. You do not know—"

"No, Vlad," Torino said. "He *does* know." Vlad's eyes whipped to the general, still fiery, and Torino shrugged ever so slightly. "At least, he knows something you don't," he said. "You can't, because we only discovered it after you'd left Earth."

A brief, titanic sliver of silence hovered in the briefing room. Then Vlad sat back in his chair.

"What?" he asked coldly.

"The docs have examined the 'vampires' you left behind to protect and help us," Dvorak said, and Vlad's eyes tracked back to him. "It wasn't easy, even with Dan and Pieter's full cooperation, but they managed it in the end. And what they found, Vlad, is that you aren't dark, supernatural creatures of the night. We can't replicate what you *are*—not yet—but one day we'll be able to. Because what you are, Vlad Tepes, is a creature of science, not the product of a curse."

"Science?" Vlad retorted scornfully. "Science that curses its victims with immortality? Renders them invisible? Lets them pass through key holes and flow through the cracks between shutters? Rip out mortals' throats with fangs and claws?"

"Yes, science." Dvorak nodded. "Nanotech, to be precise. Because that's what you 'vampires' are made of, Vlad—*nanotech*. I brought along the documentation if you want to see it. For that matter, Maighread's one of the task force's senior physicians, and she can demonstrate it for you and Stephen and all the others right here aboard *Relentless*."

Vlad had stiffened, his eyes wide.

"We still don't know where it came from, although I have a few suspicions. And we still don't know how you contracted it. But that's what it was, Vlad. It wasn't God cursing you for your sins. And it wasn't Satan claiming his own. It was . . . well, what it *was* was a fucking industrial accident of some sort. That's what it looks like, anyway. I can't guarantee you that your soul transferred along with the rest of you when whatever the hell happened turned you into a constellation of nanobots, Vlad. I *can* guarantee you that it wasn't a curse designed to punish you for your misdeeds, though. I won't take those misdeeds, those crimes, away from you. You committed them, and they're yours to own. But you weren't turned into a vile monster because of them. And neither were the 'vampires' you made before you left. And whatever you may have done in Wallachia, whatever atrocities might have been yours in the fifteenth century, you've damned well earned forgiveness. You made restitution for all of it the day you and your vampires saved the human race from *extinction*. You're the only reason we still exist. The only hope the galaxy has of breaking the Hegemony's tyranny. So don't you tell *me* you're a 'monster,' Vlad Drakulya! And don't use the belief that you are as an excuse to take vengeance on an entire species."

Vlad flinched at the word "excuse." It was a small thing, scarcely visible, but Dave Dvorak saw it.

"I understand," he said softly, almost gently. "Not all of it. I can't, because it didn't happen to me. But I *understand* the darkness, Vlad. Trust me, I've tasted it myself. I've wanted it *so* badly. You're right. The bastards did kill over half the human race, including a lot of *my* friends and family, and I wanted to see *them* die, instead. And I told myself it would be justice.

And I told myself it was a pragmatic necessity, to prevent them from attacking us again.

"But it wouldn't be justice. Not really. The Shongairi here in the Shong System never authorized the genocide of the human race. The more I've studied the Hegemony's records of their culture and its imperatives, the more convinced I've become that the Shongair Empire *wouldn't* have authorized it, either. Their culture incorporates something called 'Jukaris' that translates as 'the way of honor,' that I'm pretty sure would have kept it from doing that. But even if it might have signed off on what was done on Earth, *it wasn't there,* Vlad. It was never consulted. One Shongair—*one* of them—decided to kill us all, and that was Fleet Commander Thikair. And much as I don't want to, I have to say I question, given how hideously wrong his neat little invasion had gone in the end, how rational he was, even by Shongair standards, when he made that decision. I'm not making excuses for him, but God knows more than enough human commanders—" his eyes bored into Vlad across the table "—have done horrific things in the name of 'military necessity.' On the scale of their capabilities, some of them have done things every bit as horrific as what Thikair intended, really, and you know it.

"But every single Shongair directly involved in the attack on Earth is already *dead,* Vlad. *All* of them, dead. How could killing the Shongairi here, in their home system, when a third of them hadn't even been born yet, be retribution—or justice—on *them?* And, trust me, given how we've already improved on the military capability they brought to Earth, they aren't going to be a threat to our future, either.

"So I suppose what it comes down to is whether or not you choose to go back to the monster you may once have been. And I know which way *I* hope you'll choose for the sake of the soul you thought you'd lost."

Well, *damn*," Stephen Buchevsky said as he and Vlad followed Rob Wilson and Brigadier Fitzgerald into PUNS *Emiliano Gutierrez*'s combat information center. "I sure wish we'd had something like this when *I* was still in the Suck."

"*Is* kind of nice, isn't it?" Wilson acknowledged with what might have been an edge of complacency, and Buchevsky nodded.

The compartment was enormous by the scale of any ship Buchevsky had ever boarded, including *Târgoviște*. Of course, *Emil Gutierrez* was built to an enormous scale. She was every bit as large as *Relentless*, but unlike Admiral Mallard's superdreadnought flagship, relatively little of her stupendous bulk was devoted to ship-to-ship weaponry. She had enough offensive and—especially—defensive armament to look after herself if she had to, but she'd been designed and built specifically as an expeditionary force transport and command vessel. She and her sisters *Michael Wallace* and *Achilles Adamakos* constituted Task Force One's transport element, and despite their mammoth size, they were stuffed to the bulkheads with personnel, armored vehicles, transatmospheric fighters and strike aircraft, and the food, fuel, ammunition, spare parts, printers, hangar bays, and machine shops to keep all of the above in action.

And to provide command facilities like this magnificently appointed CIC.

Buchevsky gazed admiringly at the holographic displays and status boards. The compartment was built around a hemispherical holo display ten meters across. A ring-shaped console circled the display and provided built-in communications and computer stations for the quietly efficient staff clustered about it. At the moment, the display featured a grid of at least thirty individual com quadrants, but only seven of them were actually in use.

Carefully arranged bulkhead and freestanding displays gave instant access to the status of every unit of the Shongair Expeditionary Force and a combination conference table and command desk was placed to allow someone seated at it to see almost any critical display instantly.

No, Buchevsky realized. It wasn't placed to let someone see *almost* any critical display; it was placed to let someone see *every* critical display. What he'd thought at first were less efficiently placed primary displays were actually secondaries or backups, judging from the information duplicated upon them.

"This way," Wilson said, leading the way towards the conference table as the people seated around it rose and braced to attention.

"Sit back down," the general commanded with a rather casually waved acknowledging salute. The same wave continued to indicate the empty chairs at the table. "Pick a seat," he told the visitors.

Vlad and Buchevsky settled into two of the indicated chairs, and Buchevsky looked around the table thoughtfully. There were a lot of men and women with the single starbursts or gold planets the Planetary Union had adopted for its colonels and brigadiers. There were several with the single golden planet of a major, as well, and even a couple with the three white moons of a captain, but he was pretty sure he'd never encountered such a concentration of senior field grade—and flag—officers in his career as a breather.

"We've got a shit ton of people to introduce you guys to," Wilson said, dropping into his own chair, followed a moment later by Brigadier Fitzgerald. "That can wait until we've been able to give you a better idea of what we're thinking here, though. For now, let me just introduce Colonel Mihail and Colonel Boucher." A wave of his hand indicated a tallish, fair-haired woman and the shorter, darker man with a pencil-thin mustache sitting beside her. "Jenny's my S2, and Christian's my S3."

Buchevsky nodded. That meant Colonel Mihail was Wilson's intelligence officer while Colonel Boucher was his operations officer.

"I figure the place to start is with a general background brief on the Expeditionary Force and the basic thinking behind what we're calling Operation Riposte," Wilson continued. "Actually, that's what Dave christened it; here in Marine Country we think of it as 'Operation Payback's a Bitch.' I gotta admit Dave's name is shorter, but I think ours has more pizzaz." He smiled again, thinly. "Admiral Mallard and her people will give you a clearer idea on the Navy's side of the shop when you sit down with them, so we don't have to go into any excruciating details there, but we will have to at least touch on some of her stuff if we want to fit all the bits and pieces together in a way that makes sense."

"That seems eminently reasonable," Vlad said. He shook his head. "From what I have so far seen, alone, it appears that the Planetary Union has been very busy building things since we left."

"One way to put it," Wilson acknowledged. "Of course, as usual, the damned Squids get all the big-ticket items. Still, I guess I have to admit we heroic Space Marines get our own share of shiny toys. I think you'll like them when we get around to walking you through them, Stephen. But for now—"

He tipped his hand in Mihail's direction, and the colonel cleared her throat.

"Prince Vlad, First Sergeant Buchevsky." She nodded to them across the table. "First, since I rather doubt the Boss got around to it—" she smiled at Wilson "—please allow me to formally welcome you aboard the *Emil*. Technically she belongs to the Navy, but we're rather proud of her, ourselves. She's named for one of Colonel Sanders's company commanders who died at the Harirud. In fact, both of her sisters are, as well. We thought it was appropriate."

Given what Lieutenant Colonel Alister Sanders and the men and women of his brigade had done to Brigade Commander Harshair at the Harirud River in Afghanistan, Buchevsky had to agree with that one.

"All right," Mihail continued, and the conference table's smart screen surface came alive with the Expeditionary Force's table of organization. She hadn't touched any controls, and Buchevsky's eyes narrowed at his first demonstration—or the first one he'd recognized, at any rate—of the direct neural interface Earth had developed since his own departure.

"As you can see the 'Transport Element' is listed way down here at almost the bottom of the chart, just ahead of the 'Fleet Train' supply echelon," she said as one of the headings blinked. "But despite our humble place in the pecking order, all the rest of them are really here to support our mission. Not—" she smiled almost impishly at the single Navy officer seated at the table "—that the Space Squids want to *admit* that. But that's okay. We all know the truth, so we can be big-minded about these things."

Laughter rumbled around the compartment. Even the single Naval officer present—a curly-haired, green-eyed commander with severely elegant features and a name tape that read "DENVERS, M."—joined it.

"I don't think you want to put it quite that way to the Old Lady," she said with a grin. "I'd pay good money to see it, though!"

"Jenny wouldn't even flinch," Wilson told her. "She's a Space Marine, and we're totally fearless. Says so right in the recruiting brochure!"

"I don't think you want to talk to me about recruiting brochures—or *recruiters*—and their veracity, 'Uncle Rob,'" Buchevsky said dryly.

"Cheez! Does that *still* rankle?" Wilson shook his head, his expression doleful. "I even *told* you I had a quota to make!"

More laughter rumbled, but then Wilson nodded to Mihail, and she cleared her throat.

"Up here at the top," she said as another heading flashed, "we have BatRon 11: *Relentless, Neobosit, Implacável,* and *Ameíliktos.* They're all *Relentless*-class superdreadnoughts: twenty-four-point-eight kilometers length of hull, four-point-three-two kilometers maximum beam."

An exterior view of *Relentless* appeared on the tabletop, and the more Buchevsky studied it, the less like a Hegemony design it looked. The huge, bulbous "nose" of the Gannon Drive *ought* to have been the most obvious difference, and he supposed it was. But what actually struck him most strongly was the absence of the outer shell of *Târgoviște's* war hull.

Unlike the Hegemony, the Planetary Union Navy no longer required spin sections to produce a gravity humans found comfortable, and its designers had done away with the angular, geodesic baskets of the war hulls the Hegemony wrapped around the central, rotating cores of its warships. All of the fixed weapon mounts, drive nodes, and access points which had been mounted in their individually armored pods on the war hull, like encrusting barnacles, had disappeared along with it. Instead, *Relentless's* flanks were smooth, dimpled with the rows of heavily armored hatches behind which her weapons crouched. And there were a *lot* of those weapons. Despite her relatively slimmer profile, the human ship's mammoth dimensions gave her almost fifty times *Târgoviște's* internal volume. And while the Gannon Drive was enormous as a single system, it took up barely a third of the volume *Târgoviște*'s far more numerous phase-drive nodes required. Not only that, its "energy siphon" effect—which Buchevsky still hadn't wrapped his mind fully around—cut the load on *Relentless*'s internal fusion plants by over seventy percent. Since humans had also reduced the mass and volume of her reactors by better than thirty percent by reducing the multiply redundant layers of failsafes Hegemony technology incorporated, her actual onboard power plants massed barely twenty percent of what a Hegemony-designed ship her size would have required.

Assuming, of course, that the Hegemony could have built a starship her size and gotten her into phase space in the first place.

Which it couldn't have.

But all of that volume had to be used on something, which was why *Relentless* all by herself, could have polished off the entire Shongair Navy in an afternoon. Hell, she could have done it before lunch!

"In addition to the superdreadnoughts," Mihail continued, illuminating another heading, "we have Cruiser Squadron Nine: eight *Sword*-class heavy cruisers—" which, despite their designation as mere cruisers, were a kilometer longer than *Târgoviște*, with almost twenty percent more volume than the Shongair dreadnought, Buchevsky noted "—to screen for the big boys and spread our coverage envelope. And to increase our platform numbers for purely psychological reasons, to be honest."

"Psychological?" Buchevsky asked.

"We'll get to that in a few minutes," Wilson said. "When we get to the ops plan. For now, let Jenny finish building out our force for you."

Buchevsky nodded, and Mihail turned to the final item on her list.

"And here we have the Fleet Train," she said, "although that's actually a bit of a misnomer. They aren't really here to support the Expeditionary Force or the Task Force themselves so much as they are to support our greater mission. Assuming things go according to plan—" she rapped her knuckles on the tabletop's surround, which, Buchevsky realized, was made of actual wood, not a synthetic "—the Transport Element and the Task Force's units should be pretty much completely self-contained. But because certain general officers—" she very carefully *didn't* glance at Lieutenant General Wilson "—believe in a belt-and-suspenders approach, we also have *Armory* and *Waffenkammer*, which are basically really big-assed freighters loaded with ammo and general stores." Her expression sobered. "They're roughly the same size as *Relentless* or the *Emil,* but their complements are a *lot* smaller—less than a hundred people each—and their total engineering and environmental requirements use up less than fifteen percent of their volume. That leaves an awesome amount of cargo space, and the two of them carry enough material to meet our projected needs for a minimum of three years of sustained combat. We have no intention of being caught short like Fleet Commander Thikair did when he came calling. But we've also brought along *Forge, Zhùzào Chǎng, Jujo,* and *Gießerei.* They're all *Foundry*-class industrial ships, each with about forty times the combined capability of the two industrial platforms Thikair had. They have more capacity, even on a mass-for-mass comparison, their robotic and cybernetic support is a lot more efficient than anything the Hegemony has, and Director Bai can have all four of them up and running within four months."

She paused, and Vlad shook his head.

"I am . . . impressed," he said. "Indeed, I grow more impressed with each revelation of your capabilities."

"That's basically the idea," Wilson replied. "Not so much to impress *you* as to impress the hell out of the Puppies, though. Which brings us to the next stage of our little presentation. Unfortunately, you'll have to put up with a Frenchman for this next bit. Christian?"

Colonel Boucher rolled martyred eyes.

"On fait du mieux qu'on peut entouré de barbares," he observed with a deep sigh and a perfectly executed, ineffably Gallic shrug. "Although, I must confess, the task of elevating the cultural level of certain unnamed superior officers does rather remind one of an ancient Grecian gentleman named Sisyphus."

"We don't even need penicillin to cure that anymore," Wilson informed him. "So go ahead. We're all prepared to put up with you."

Boucher smiled, but then he turned his attention to Vlad and his expression sobered.

"Operation Riposte had its origins in Ambassador Dvorak's research into the Hegemony's history, and in his observations and experience in the Sarth System, Your Highness. Before we get into its underlying reasoning, however, a bit of context-setting history might be in order.

"After you left Governor Howell in possession of the captured Shongair industrial platforms in the Sol System, he parlayed that into the creation of the Continental Union, with Canada, Brazil, and the United States as its original members, and the Governor as its first president. His obvious eventual goal was the creation of the current Planetary Union, but achieving that was the classic example of even the longest journey beginning with a single step. It was not until almost twelve years after your departure that the Planetary Union's Constitution was formally ratified, and even at that time, not all of Earth's nations had joined. A few were more . . . recalcitrant than most," he glanced at Wilson, who grimaced in memory, "but ultimately all of Earth's countries, including the successor states of some former nations, such as the People's Republic of China and Italy, petitioned for membership and ratified the Constitution.

"President Howell was, not surprisingly, elected as the Planetary Union's first president by an enormous majority. Given the life spans now available to us, the drafters of that Constitution recognized the absolute necessity of building in term limitations. The last thing anyone wanted—especially President Howell—was a 'President for Life' whose tenure lasted three or four hundred years! Because of that, the Constitution provides for a twelve-year term of office, and a president may serve two successive terms. He—or she—may also stand for reelection for additional terms after two terms out of office, however, and there is no limit on the total number of times one may serve, so long as they are served in no more than two successive terms. President Howell was reelected to a second term approximately eight years before our departure. I would suspect that he has since been succeeded by Jolasun Olatunji, who has served as his vice president and is almost as popular as President Howell, himself.

"During his first term, President Howell initiated what's become known as the Howell Doctrine. In essence, it's the exact opposite of the Hegemony's traditional foreign policy. It calls for the creation of an alliance of star systems and species designed to defy the Hegemony's supremacy, and rather than stultify technology in the name of stability, it aims to stimulate research and development as a way to provide the Terran Alliance with the physical means to resist something as enormous and powerful as the Hegemony." His mouth tightened just a bit. "Despite the size and firepower of ships like *Relentless,* the sheer disparity between the Alliance and the Hegemony in manpower and resources remains staggering. Literally astronomical, in this case. Which is why we're here and why Operation Riposte was first conceived."

He paused, looking back and forth between Vlad and Buchevsky, and there was no humor in his brown eyes. He let the silence linger for a breath or two, then shrugged once more.

"As President Howell's Secretary of State, for both the Continental and Planetary Unions, Ambassador Dvorak played a leading role in formulating the Howell Doctrine, and he left the Secretary's office to lead the first diplomatic mission to another star system: Sarth."

"Where," Wilson interjected, "he damn near got his ass killed." He grimaced, his eyes dark. "It was sheer luck he didn't. And, much as I may rag on him, it's a damn good thing he made it."

"I believe most of us would agree with that." Boucher nodded soberly. "And in more ways than one. The Ambassador's study of the Hegemony's history had already started him . . . rethinking his initial view of the Shongairi. His experiences on Sarth, and particularly with the then–Qwernian Empire, solidified his thoughts, and upon his return to Earth, President Howell authorized Operation Riposte. Convincing the President and Congress to endorse it was . . . less than easy, but he succeeded in the end. And had President Howell not already been into his second term as Planetary Union President, I strongly suspect that *he* would have led this expedition. As it was, it was imperative that we depart the Sol System in time to overtake *Târgoviște*."

"Damn good thing, too!" Wilson snorted. "Dave would've let Howell have Shong, but much as I love my brother-in-law, that man can hold a grudge forever! He would've been like a bear with a sore tooth for *decades*. Hard enough living with him when he's feeling *cheerful*!"

Vlad smiled, but Buchevsky laughed out loud.

"I don't know the Ambassador as well as General Wilson does," Boucher said in a judicious tone, "yet I'm forced to concur in that estimate. On the other hand, at the time of our departure, missions were being planned to several additional star systems, as well, including the Tairyon System."

"Tairyon?" Vlad repeated, forehead furrowed in thought, and Wilson grunted.

"One of the systems the Hegemony handed over to the Liatu about nine hundred years ago," he said.

"Ah." Vlad nodded. "I knew I recalled the name. The Liatu deployed a bioweapon in Tairyon, did they not?"

"One way to put it. Like you say, the Hegemony cheerfully signed the system over to the bastards. But when they arrived, they discovered a little problem. The Tairyonians were only a Level Six civilization, about equivalent to Earth around 1000 BC, when they were cleared for conquest, but they'd moved almost to Level Five by the time the first colony ships got there. That was still slow as hell, by our standards, but it was a scary rate of progress by *Hegemony* standards and suggested that they might become . . . rambunctious. Especially since they were omnivores with a strong carnivorous streak. The Liatu could hardly be expected to put up with something like that!"

The disgust in Wilson's voice was profound.

"Of course, the Froggies—no disrespect, Christian," he continued, flashing Boucher a fleeting grin, "are respectable, morally upright herbivores, not like us aggressive, morally repugnant omnivores. And they're certainly not *carnivores,* like the Shongairi! It would *never* occur to them to genocide an entire species just because it was inconveniently in possession of real estate they wanted. So instead of killing them all, the Liatu whipped up a little genetic cocktail, instead. There are still plenty of Tairyonians, according to the Hegemony's files. Not as many as there might've been, with advanced technology, of course, but probably—oh, as many as four whole million of them, spread across the entire planet. That's what happens when you reduce a species which has discovered agriculture and city building to an intelligence level somewhere between a Labrador retriever and a four-year-old and then just ignore the hell out of them while they die back to a level their 'technology' can support. The Froggies—" Wilson's term for the amphibian Liatu was unflattering but quite apt, given their body form, Vlad thought; it was definitely *not* one of approval, however "—call 'em guharnaks, now. Means 'nuisance animals,' and much as it pisses me off to admit it, from their perspective, it's an apt label, cause there's jack shit the Tairyonians can do about the bastards. They're still social animals, and they even still use fire and flint-tipped spears. That's about it. And that's not worth squat against air cars and autocannon."

"I see." Vlad leaned back, gazing at the stony faces of the "breathers" around the table. "And I understand your anger over what was done. But forgive me for pointing out that if the Tairyonians' . . . mental capacity and numbers have been so reduced, they would not seem promising material for President Howell's Alliance. And there is the minor matter that the Liatu are currently in possession of the system. I suspect that both they and the rest of the Hegemony would not look favorably upon any attempt to dispossess them of it."

"Agreed." Wilson nodded. "But as far as your first point is concerned, their capacity doesn't have to *stay* reduced. The details of the Liatu genetic bomb weren't in the records, but there was more than enough for our medical people to reconstruct what they must've done. And come up with a way to *un*do it that we're at least ninety percent confident will work."

"Ah!" Vlad repeated in a very different tone, and Wilson nodded again.

"This is exactly what the Terran Alliance is supposed to be about preventing . . . or fixing," he said. "We've got a moral responsibility to undo the genetic damage if we can, but to be brutally honest, rescuing the Tairyonians and repairing what was done to them—and *documenting* what was done to them by the 'noble' Liatu herbivores—should give us a pretty hefty bargaining chip when we come calling on any other species at risk from the Hegemony."

"And if I recall correctly, Tairyon is over four hundred light-years— and what? Sixty-five years' travel time?—from the Liatu homeworld," Vlad said.

"More like four hundred fifty light-years and seventy-five years' flight time for a Hegemony phase-drive. Of course, it's a bit closer than that to Earth—only about four hundred and twenty. Even running the current Gannon Drive at max instead of easing off a bit, like we did on the trip out, that's a seventeen-and-a-half-year trip. On the other hand, Gannon and his people were still tinkering with it when we left, and their projections said they were getting really close to the next plateau. God only knows what they'll have by the time we get home! But the distances involved mean it'll take at least seventy-five years for anybody in the Hegemony to realize the monkey boys and girls are rooting around in the

Liatu's back pasture. And that's assuming somebody heads home to tell them about it the minute we get there. So, absolute worst-case, the Tairyonians get a hundred and fifty years—call it six generations, with neural education and modern medicine to reduce infant mortality—to recover from what the bastards did to them and get up to speed on *our* tech before anybody gets back to them from Liatu."

"I see."

"And, assuming things are proceeding according to plan back home, President Howell is now Ambassador Howell and heading the expedition currently en route to Tairyon," Wilson said. "He's got a few bones of his own to pick with people who think bioweapons are a good idea."

"Yes," Vlad murmured. "I imagine that is *precisely* how he would see it."

"Damn straight," Wilson said. Then waved an open hand at Boucher. "In the meantime, though, I think we should probably let Christian get back to Operation Riposte."

"Indeed." Vlad faced the Frenchman squarely. "So I presume that the underlying logic of 'Operation Riposte' depends upon the 'submission' mechanism of the Shongairi?"

"It does." Boucher nodded. "In fact, it depends upon a much deeper appreciation for Shongair psychology than we possessed at the time of your departure. I believe Ambassador Dvorak's already mentioned the Shongair honor code—Jukaris—to you?"

Vlad nodded, and Boucher shrugged again.

"Jukaris can be thought of much like the Japanese code of Bushido, but 'Bushido' is in many ways what might be called an umbrella for a host of variations on a central theme that one might call chivalry. It has evolved as Japanese culture evolved and changed over the centuries, and it is essentially . . . philosophical in nature. It's a code of conduct for the individual, and there have been many what one might call 'schools' of Bushido. And as many philosophies, especially *military* philosophies, over the course of human history, Bushido has sometimes been perverted, as when it was twisted into what amounted to a national suicide pact in the course of the Second World War.

"Jukaris goes even deeper in Shongair history and society than Bushido in the Japanese experience. It evolved out of the nature of the primordial Shongair pack's psychology, and there are far fewer 'variations on the theme' in Jukaris than in Bushido. What variations exist are minor and consist of what might be called differing interpretations of the 'fine print' by individual pack groups. The central core of Jukaris, and its governing tenets, are accepted by the entire Shongair species. Even the variations between pack groups have been adjudicated, with legal precedents to determine which pack group governs in a given situation for literally centuries. *Galactic* centuries, not our own."

"Indeed?" Vlad tipped back slightly in his chair. "And how does this code of honor speak to our present situation?"

"Essentially," Boucher said, "Jukaris codifies the pack's challenge and submission mechanism. None of the xenopsychologists are prepared to offer a definitive opinion, even now, on how much of Shongair psychology is 'hardwired' and how much of it is a purely social construct, but given Jukaris' longevity and persistence, I, for one, incline toward the 'hardwired' thesis. This is a truly ancient part of Shongair culture—its recorded form literally dates back as far as the Shongair Bronze Age, as if the Code of Hammurabi had survived into our own time. And whichever came first, the chicken or the egg, Jukaris is very much central to Shongair thinking. It lays down the moral and philosophical justifications for both the beta's right to challenge the alpha and for the beta's responsibility to submit once the alpha's dominance has been proved."

"Actually," Vlad said, his eyes intent, "one might argue that Hammurabi's laws contributed significantly to the underlying DNA of even modern Western legal thought."

"A valid point, Your Highness." Boucher nodded. "But after four thousand years, that Babylonian DNA has become far more attenuated than in the case of the Shongairi's Jukaris. Unlike Hammurabi's laws, Jukaris is a living, dynamic philosophical code which is directly incorporated into their current legal jurisprudence, not simply social practice. For example, it's expanded to provide for and govern non-combat challenge modes. A Shongair bureaucrat may 'challenge' a superior for promotion into that superior's position under Jukaris, not on the basis of physical combat but on the basis of demonstrated levels of performance. And, arguably, Thikair *violated* Jukaris in his operations against Earth. That's a significant point of which the Shongair *Empire* cannot be aware, since none of Thikair's ships survived to report back to it."

"And does 'Jukaris' enshrine some reason the Shongair should have extended their honor concepts to an alien species it intended to enslave?" Vlad asked skeptically.

"That, unfortunately, is an interesting and as yet undetermined point," Wilson said with a grimace. "It's what the Expeditionary Force is here to find out, really. But it seems pretty clear that whether or not Thikair ever believed the provisions of Jukaris applied to alien species, its concepts and the entire challenge-submission mechanism it rests on were fundamental to his strategy and choice of tactics."

"In what way?"

"Thikair's own memos and an analysis of his actions make it clear that the massive strike on Earth's pre-invasion military forces wasn't prompted solely by his recognition of how powerful they were," Boucher replied. "While it's true that the Shongair psychology and honor code enshrine the principle of submission to a proven superior—and regard *refusal* to submit as a highly dishonorable act—the internal mechanisms are rather more complex than we'd believed. There's no dishonor, in Shongair eyes, to being bested, to acknowledging that one is the beta to another's alpha. But there *is* dishonor—and quite a lot of it—in not first striving to one's utmost to avoid being bested. That is, it is the honor responsibility of the beta to *force* the alpha to demonstrate his superiority before acknowledging defeat.

"Thikair anticipated that, had he not struck our pre-invasion militaries such a devastating blow, we would have fought back—hard—to the best of our capability, as his concept of honor would have required. From the pragmatic viewpoint of securing control of the planet, that would have made his task far more difficult, and that was probably the *main* driver of his strategy. But, in addition, just as the beta is honor bound to resist to the utmost of his ability, the *alpha* is honor bound to demonstrate his superiority by besting the beta as rapidly as possible, and he confidently expected the total destruction of our organized military forces—and the decapitation of our civilian governments—would demonstrate that to *us*."

"Well, *that* didn't work out for him real well," Buchevsky observed.

"No." Boucher nodded in agreement with the observation. "But remember that by his lights, he *had* proved, in the most decisive imaginable fashion, that the Shongairi were the alphas in the equation. However he'd chosen to do it, he'd accomplished that part of the process and proved, both to his own satisfaction and—he believed—to our own, that no effective resistance was possible. And to be totally honest, he would have been ultimately correct in that, had not you, Prince Vlad, and the other 'vampires' been able to intervene. There's a great deal of material buried in the archives to suggest his methodology would have been considered less than honorable against another Shongair, which may indicate that Jukaris *doesn't* apply to an alien species. But as a countervailing point, his own memos and the minutes of his staff meetings make it clear that in his thinking, he and the Shongair Empire would have been obligated to respect our role as betas and treat us as honorably submitted subjects of the Emperor if we *had* submitted after his initial 'demonstration strike.' That suggests that Jukaris *would* have applied to us, at least in his eyes and in his initial planning. It's unlikely that we would have possessed all of the rights of the Shongairi, but the Empire would have been prohibited by its own honor codes and legal framework from contemplating anything remotely like what the Liatu did to the Tairyonians.

"And to the point of how the Empire might have regarded Thikair's actions, another reason Ambassador Dvorak has become convinced the imperial government would never have authorized Thikair's bioweapon is the Shongairi's profound respect for their habitat. They evolved out of hunters, not farmers. When they developed 'agriculture,' it was only so that they might better breed and produce their domesticated meat animals. And, like all apex hunters, in their pre-technic existence, they were dependent upon the habitat that produced the herbivores upon which they preyed. Preserving that habitat—avoiding its destruction or pollution and culling the herd to prevent *it* from destroying it through overgrazing—is imprinted upon the Shongairi at an almost genetic level. One reason they were so shocked by our widespread use of fossil fuels and other non-nuclear means of power generation was because of their negative impact upon our environment. Indeed, I think it's probable that Thikair's best chance to convince his Emperor to accept his actions—at least after the fact—was that our use of fossil fuels demonstrated that we constituted the equivalent of deer or elk overgrazing our range, and if so, our . . . poor stewardship of our world might very well—indeed, probably—have weighed in the balance against us."

"But the point here," Wilson said, pulling Vlad's and Buchevsky's attention back to him, "is that the Shongairi *do* have this alpha-beta submission mechanism, and that so nearly as we can tell from the records, Jukaris and its workings run deeper and are even more decisive than the social tradition that turned the Qwernians into *Dvorakians*. If we can convince them to submit, we may well bring them to genuinely embrace the concept of the Alliance, and that would add all the star systems they've already colonized or conquered to the mix, as well."

"And how does 'Operation Riposte' propose we accomplish that?" Vlad's tone was torn between skepticism and something very like disappointment, and Wilson gave him a shark-like smile.

"I have five entire Space Marine brigades up here," he said. "Numerically that's a good bit less than the strength Thikair had along. In terms of combat power?" He snorted. "Trust me—there's no comparison!

"Now, when we turn up and demand their surrender, their Navy's almost certain to fight. There's that business about 'striving to the utmost,' after all. It's possible that after the dreadnoughts and their orbital defenses get smashed, they'll recognize our superiority and surrender. From our analysis, we don't think that's likely. We think we'll have to go down and demonstrate our superiority on the ground, as well, unless we want to do a Thikair and just blast hell out of them with kinetic strikes. Our current plans call for us to avoid mega casualties to the best of our ability, though, and the xenologists think that once the Shongairi figure out we were 'going easy on them,' doing our damnedest to avoid mass slaughter and ecological mayhem while we proved hell out of our alpha status, it will only deepen their recognition and acceptance of honorable defeat. But no matter how hard we try, it's going to be ugly. Frankly, I'd love to convince them to roll over with a few demonstration strikes. Maybe, I dunno, write our names on their moon, like Chairface."

Buchevsky surprised himself with a bark of laughter at the mention of one of a much younger Stephen Buchevsky's favorite animated villains, and Wilson grinned at him. But then the grin faded, and he shook his head.

"I'd like that, honestly. Truth in advertising, I'm like you guys; I want some of our own back—a *lot* of our own back, really—for what happened to us. But like Dave says, no one in this star system had anything to do with Thikair's decision to kill us all. For that matter, it's been eighty years since Thikair set out. Hell, the Emperor who *sent* him may be dead by now, even with antigerone. But everything we've seen indicates that they'll fight, and they'll fight hard, before they surrender. So whether or not I *want* to kill job lots of Shongairi, I'm pretty sure we'll get a hell of a lot of payback for what happened to Earth, anyway."

T hat smells delicious."

Stephen Buchevsky sounded a bit wistful, and Alexander Jackson smiled sympathetically as the two of them crossed the living room of the Dvoraks' comfortable shipboard suite with Thornak BryMerThor.

The Sarthians, he'd discovered, were more than "just" bodyguards. Specifically, despite Merahl's superior military rank, Captain Brykira was the neutro "anchor" of the BryMerThor triad. And the fact that ou (Buchevsky was still getting used to the Sarthian neutro pronouns) also just happened to be Herdsman Belsorak, which translated into English roughly as Earl Bright Shield, meant both Merahl and Thornak bore the title of Herdsman Consort Belsorak, since Sarthian patents of nobility passed through the neutro parent, in addition to their military ranks. Perhaps even more to the point, Brykira *also* just happened to be the grandchild of Yairka CharYairSha nar Dvorak, Flock Lord Consort Thairlahn, Dave Dvorak's (and Abu Bakr's) Dvorakian chancellor on Sarth. Aristocratic connections didn't get much higher than that, and Buchevsky had already recognized that the triad were Dvorak's Sarthian "sounding board" as well as his bodyguards.

The sherhynas clearly took their protective responsibilities seriously, however, and one of them stood post outside the Dvoraks' quarters whenever one or more of the Dvoraks in question were home. Tonight, Merahl had that duty, but Sarthian custom required that at least one bodyguard have the indoor "close cover" watch on social occasions, as well. And Bektor nar Dvorak, Sharon's personal sherhyna, looked up from his post by the open door through which various delectable aromas wafted.

It was probably fortunate that Qwernian—Dvorakan—custom required only a single sherhyna for a clan ruler *consort*. Buchevsky didn't like to think about how Sharon would have reacted to being trailed around by three of them. For that matter, it was probably fortunate that all four of them had become members of the Dvorak clan in more ways than one.

Stephen Buchevsky knew exactly how the Dvorak "extended family" tended to envelop anyone who crossed its path, and it was obvious that had happened to the Sarthians. Which let everyone *pretend* Thornak and Bektor had just dropped by for dinner rather than admit they were there as the Dvoraks' mandated bodyguards.

And that enveloping process also explained the Sarthians' tartan kilts. The kilt itself was normal Sarthian attire; the tartan was that of Clan Gunn, the clan to which the Irish Clan Wilson was sept. What Buchevsky hadn't figured out yet was whether the idea had been Sharon's or Dvorak's, but he *had* discovered that the Sarthians took it very, very seriously.

"I like a lot of Dave's cooking," Jackson continued now, sniffing appreciatively, "but I really do think I like his spaghetti sauce best of all. Of course, I can't appreciate the aroma the way you guys can." He shook his head. "Until Pieter and Dan started working with the medics, I don't think any of us could imagine what it must be like to control your senses the way you 'vampires' can. And even with direct neural links and built-in sensory boosters incorporated into the wetware, I don't think we can match that even now. We can come a lot closer, mind you, but General Torino can still pull stuff out of his sense of smell and hearing in ways no 'breather' *I* know can."

"Yeah, it does kinda suck at moments like this, though," Buchevsky said wryly. "*Damn* that smells good! And the hell of it is, I've *had* his spaghetti. Lots of times." He grimaced. "That means I know it tastes as good as it smells. I've never been able to decide if it's the sweet Italian sausage or the brown sugar."

"Can you at least sample it?"

"Not unless I want a really serious case of 'indigestion.'" Buchevsky shook his head. "But I can probably at least have a beer while you guys pig out in front of me."

"'Pig out' might be putting it just a bit too strongly," Jackson protested.

"Alex," Buchevsky grinned, "I've seen Malachi eat. For that matter, Maighread's no slouch at the table. I admit, the twins were only twelve when we left, but both those girls have always had hollow legs where their

dad's spaghetti sauce was concerned, and I watched her playing basket-
ball in the *Emil*'s gym with her brother and Raymond yesterday. I sorta
doubt anyone in that kind of shape's worried about calories. And I will
guarantee you no Marine—and I don't care if he's a 'Space' Marine—is
about to pass up seconds or thirds!"

"You know, I forget sometimes how long you've known Dave and Sharon," Jackson said.

"Well, in a lot of ways, you've actually known them longer than I
have," Buchevsky pointed out.

"I thought you'd known the Dvoraks for years, even before the invasion!" Jackson said.

"Oh, I have." Buchevsky nodded as the two of them followed Thornak
into the dining room. "In fact, I've known 'Uncle Rob' since I was about
twelve. And you know my dad's a Methodist pastor, right?" Jackson
nodded, and Buchevsky shrugged. "I'll be more than a little surprised if
Dave's managed to keep up his certification, but he was a Methodist lay
speaker *forever*. He covered Dad's pulpit more than once when I was in
senior high. So, yeah, I've known him and Sharon a long time. But I left
Earth forty years ago, Alex. And you met him—how long ago?"

"I went to work for him in the State Department about five years before
we left for Sarth. So that would've been, um, about twenty-two years ago."

"There you are." Buchevsky shrugged. "I met Dave when I was sixteen.
I was thirty-five when we left Earth, so only nineteen years for me."

"But that was forty years ago," Jackson pointed out. "So you're up to
fifty-nine years."

"No, only forty-two. Only twenty-three years subjective voyage time
for me."

"Yeah, but—"

Jackson paused, his expression a little absent, then shook his head.

"All this relativistic crap really screws with your time sense, doesn't
it?" he said. "So, by the calendar, you've known Dave and Sharon for fifty-
nine years. Subjectively, you've only known them for forty-two, right?"

"Right."

"Well, First Sergeant Buchevsky, allow me to point out that I met
them—calendar wise—twenty-two years ago, and that given the Gannon
Drive, we made the voyage from Earth in only a year and a half, so that

means that by the calendar, you've known them for thirty-seven years longer than me, and by subjective time, you've known them *seventeen* years longer than I have."

"Sure, but you've been in constant contact with them that entire time, whereas I only saw them when I was home on leave. So in terms of *elapsed time—*"

"I hope the two of you will forgive me for observing that Earthians tend to upset themselves over very strange things," Thornak observed. Both humans looked at her, and her nasal flaps quivered in laughter. "May we all simply agree that both of you have known the Clan Ruler for a very long time?"

"You Sarthians really know how to take the fun out of an argument, don't you?" Jackson replied with a chuckle.

"It is a gift," Thornak agreed gravely. "One not given to many, I admit."

"Oh, yeah? You ever seen *Sharon* take the fun out of an argument?" Buchevsky demanded.

"Did I just hear my name taken in vain?" a voice asked from behind him, and he turned as the Sharon in question walked in with an enormous basket of garlic bread. The high-tech basket would hold the bread at exactly the right temperature indefinitely, and she walked past them to place it in the center of the large table.

"Oh, no! Heaven forbid!" Buchevsky said. She turned from the table to arch an eyebrow at him. "I just meant that you've had a lot of practice shutting Dave down when he gets . . . overly loquacious."

"You know," another voice said, "when you hit the bottom of the hole, it's usually a good idea to stop digging, Stephen. 'Overly loquacious,' is it?"

"Damn you're quiet," Buchevsky complained, turning to grin at David Dvorak. "You been taking lessons from Longbow and Pieter?"

"Far be it from me to suggest that your situational awareness could use a little improvement," Dvorak said, carrying the pot of spaghetti sauce across to the table. Brykira followed him with a huge tossed salad bowl, and Maighread Lewis trailed behind both of them with the spaghetti bowl and smiled a greeting of her own as she passed.

Buchevsky laughed and followed the three of them to the table. Dvorak set down the spaghetti sauce and pointed at one of the chairs. There was no place setting in front of the chair; only a beer stein.

"Sit," Dvorak said. "Pieter and Longbow have eaten with us enough that I just set out the beer mugs—or the coffee cup, in Longbow's case."

"Wise of you." Buchevsky held Sharon's chair for her before he settled into the one Dvorak had indicated. "Vlad tells me that in another few decades, I'll actually be able to eat solid food occasionally. That'll be nice."

"Yeah, I'd really miss that myself," Dvorak said a bit more soberly, taking his own place as Maighread relieved Brykira of the big salad bowl and began filling the smaller bowls at each place. Except Buchevsky's, of course.

"Dare I ask where your other two guests are?" Jackson inquired as he sat.

"Malachi and Raymond are running a little late," Sharon said. "Something about someone's son—" she looked levelly at Dvorak "—who talks too much. Can't imagine where he got it from."

"Talks too much?" Jackson repeated.

"He and his company commanders had a simulated exercise yesterday, and the debrief session . . . ran a little long," Dvorak said.

"A *little*?" Sharon snorted. "I suppose you could call an extra three hours running 'a little' long. If you're a male whose last name is Dvorak, anyway."

"They're only ten minutes out now, Mom," Maighread said. "And Raymond says we should go ahead and start without them."

"I think *not*," Sharon replied.

"And give up the opportunity to chew them out for keeping us waiting?" Dvorak shook his head. "You've known your mom all your life, Maighread! What were you *thinking*?"

Sharon made a rude gesture, and Dvorak laughed.

"Well, if we've got ten minutes, can I ask a 'business' sort of question?" Buchevsky asked, and despite his smile, his tone was serious. "I mean, if we've got a window before dinner is actually served."

"Go ahead," Sharon said, and he looked back at Dvorak.

"I've been wondering," he said more slowly. "How well is the notion of not just wiping out the Shongairi really going to play at home?"

"Well, that's a downer," Dvorak observed dryly, sitting back in his chair.

"It's just been bugging me," Buchevsky said a bit apologetically. "Obviously, none of us in *Târgoviște* had the opportunity to see how moods and attitudes were changing back on Earth. But after what they did to us. . . ."

"It's a fair question," Dvorak conceded. "Especially for someone who lost as much as you did. Sharon and I—and the kids—were a lot luckier than you, Stephen. Maybe that makes it seem a little easier to me. Maybe even a little easier than it will really turn out to be."

"Can I take a swing at it?" Jackson asked.

"Of course you can, Alex!"

"Okay." Jackson turned his chair a bit sideways to face Buchevsky fully, and his expression was more serious than Buchevsky had ever seen it. "I know about your wife and daughters, Stephen," he said. "And, trust me, I really do know how much something like that tears the heart right out of you. I lost my mom, my dad, and my sister to a Shongair K-strike. For that matter, I very much doubt there's a single person anywhere in the Expeditionary Force who was born before the invasion and didn't lose *somebody* he loved. But we've had a chance to think about it, come to grips with it the best anyone can, and I think for a lot of people the bottom line is that we're not the Hegemony. In fact, we're pretty damned adamant about that. And that means we can't just go around genociding entire species because they've pissed us off. That's what Galactics do, and then pretend they don't."

"There's more to it than that, of course," Dvorak said. "I have to tell you, I was never all that happy about the notion that Vlad was going to just wipe the Shongairi out, even before we started putting Earth back together. I wasn't part of the decision loop at the time, though. In fact," he grimaced, "if I'm being honest, I was happy I wasn't. It let me hide from the fact that I was a lot less *un*happy about the notion in the imme-diate aftermath of the invasion. Can't pretend I wasn't, if I'm going to be remotely honest. And I've never been one of those 'to understand all is to forgive all' people. There *are* some of them back home, though. More of them than there used to be, as we've gotten farther away from the invasion. The interesting thing is that some of the folks who are willing to argue that we may be misunderstanding the Hegemony are a lot less happy about us 'letting the Shongairi off easy.' I never really understood that bit, since it was the frigging Hegemony that enabled the Shongairi and sent them off to cut our throats."

He shrugged.

"Fortunately, the sunshine-and-rainbows crowd was still in a distinct minority when we left, and I expect them to stay that way. But even people who are less forgiving than I am are willing to admit, by and large, that we can't wipe out an entire species because some members of that species tried to wipe *us* out without becoming just as bad or worse than the people who murdered all the people *we* cared about."

Buchevsky nodded slowly. He'd thought the same thing often enough, even as his heart cried out for vengeance.

"I don't say it's going to be easy," Dvorak continued, his expression grave, "but we've got it to do, Stephen. Either we're different from the Hegemony, or we aren't. And if we are, then we have to prove it. And not just to any allies we might hope to pick up. We have to prove it to *ourselves,* in a way we'll remember. In a way that's definitive enough we can actually believe it. And *not* wiping out the Shongairi is the best way I can think of to start doing that."

IMPERIAL PALACE,
CITY OF SHERIKAATH,
PLANET SHONGARU,
SHONG SYSTEM,
241.5 LY FROM EARTH,
APRIL 19, YEAR 41 TE.

I think it may work better if I have a quiet word with old Shardu first, Your Majesty," Urkal-ir-Dyam said. "The Kyam have been the protectors of the Hyraidyr Preserve for generations."

Haymar-zik-Shayma, Shathyra and absolute ruler of the Shongair Empire, leaned inelegantly back in his comfortable chair, grooming the tip of his tail thoughtfully as he considered his first minister's advice.

As always, Urkal had a point. Shardu-ur-Kyam didn't represent an especially large district, and he wasn't getting any younger. But he was the Kyam Pack's senior Pakyrma delegate, and he'd led the Kyam Quorum for the last twelve years. He'd have enormous influence when the Pakyrma debated the Hyraidyr project—*if* they could get it to, finally—and while the Pakyrma could only advise the Shathyra, only a fool ignored that advice.

"Do you think he'll actually support the idea this time?" Haymar asked.

"If he's approached properly." Urkal flicked his ears in a shrug. "The capital needs the additional water supply, and Hyraidyr is the logical place to put the reservoir. He knows that as well as we do. It'll be the local ranchers who scream about it. Again."

"I think Urkal's right about Shardu," Yudar-zik-Shayma said, and Haymar quirked an ear at him. "He'll understand why we need the water—we started talking about that when *I* was still in your chair. Cainharn! I think we started talking about it when your *grandsire* was still Shathyra!"

Haymar laughed, although he suspected his sire was correct about that. The aversion to destroying habitat—and putting a reservoir fifty-one sheertarni long and sixty tarni deep right on top of prime grassland

and watershed couldn't really be called anything else—ran deep in the Shongairi's genes. So it was entirely possible his sire wasn't exaggerating in this case. He would have liked to ask his grandsire about it, but old Shathyrakym Yurma had died three years ago, which left Yudar as the Empire's sole shathyrakym. Haymar missed Yurma's wise counsel, but at least he and the Empire still had Yudar.

"The question is what choice prey we offer Shardu in return," he said, still grooming his tail. "You're right about the ranchers, Urkal. That river valley is choice pastureland, and Hyraidyr-raised dahrmyk venison commands a high price. They'll scream no matter what we do, and if we want Shardu to pour oil on the waters for us, we need to do something to . . . show him our appreciation."

"That sounds so . . . devious," Yudar said. "One wonders what your sire was thinking when he raised you!"

"Deep and devious thoughts, I expect." Haymar let his chair come upright. "I think what we need to point out to Shardu is the recreational aspect of the reservoir. I know he's already aware of it—as you say, Sire, this proposal's been beaten to death for far too long. But what if we promise to name the reservoir after him? He'd like that, and if he emphasizes all the opportunities for boating and fishing in his addresses to the Pakyrma, and if he can bring the rest of his quorum along, I think we might get majority approval. And that would go a long way to calm the storm when I issue the decree."

"*Very* devious of you," Yudar said approvingly. "The old chighor will like that! Of course, we won't want to tell anyone else about it."

"Not until the decree's issued." Haymar flicked his ears in agreement. "I'm sure everyone will understand when I name it after him in appreciation for all his selfless efforts in helping us move its construction forward."

"I think that's an excellent idea, Your Majesty," Urkal agreed.

"Of course it is." Haymar's ears laughed. "It was mine, and I'm the Shathyra!"

"Odd." Yudar cocked his head. "I remember a few ideas *I* had when I was Shathyra that didn't work out so well."

"I'll make certain your biographers don't mention those," his son told him.

"You were always such a good cub."

"I had good parents." Haymar said it lightly, but his ears were serious, and Yudar made a brushing away gesture.

"That was your dam's doing more than mine, cubling."

"Perhaps. But now that we finally have a plan to deal with the Cainharn-damned reservoir, what's the next item on the agenda, Urkal?"

"Well, the Kajarhn Pack has asked to place a petition before the throne," the first minister said. "It's that dispute of theirs with Hourisha. I think they have a proposal that they believe might finally work. On the other hand—"

W hat in Cainharn's twelfth name is going on here?!" Navy Commander Hyrshi-nar-Urkah demanded as he stormed onto Orbit One's command deck with Ship Commander Frekhar at his heels.

It was hard for even Shongair ears to hear him through the howl of alarms, but Orbit Base Commander Larshal knew exactly what the Navy Commander was saying. It was exactly what *he'd* said when he arrived on the bridge a few shrekari before Hyrshi. And praise Dainthar he'd been in Auxiliary Plot! Otherwise, the Navy Commander would have beaten him to Command One. Allowing that to happen would have been . . . unfortunate, although Cainharn only knew what Hyrshi was doing wandering around the huge orbital fortress at this hour of its onboard evening.

Larshal strode across the deck to a range where he could be heard without screaming even through the alarms.

"We're still trying to figure that out, Navy Commander," he said loudly. Hyrshi glared at him, ears half-flattened. "Tracking is running the transponder beacon now," Larshal continued.

"It's confirmed, Orbital Base Commander!" Squadron Commander Vilkhar-nar-Kyam called. "It's—" someone hit the button to shut down the alarms "—one of ours!"

Vilkhar's ears flattened in consternation as he finished his bellowed announcement in the sudden, ringing silence.

"And what in Cainharn's hell is 'one of ours' doing right *there*?" Hyrshi demanded, jabbing a digit at the blinking light code in the master display.

That light code was barely four light-minutes outside Shongaru's sixteen-light-minute orbit. That put it just under eight light-minutes *inside* Derinar's orbit. At the moment Derinar was most of the way towards superior conjunction, which put it well over thirty light-minutes from the intruder, but any Shongair vessel was required to announce its arrival as soon as it dropped out of phase-space. For a ship to be in that position without anyone's detecting its emergence footprint, it must have reentered normal-space *six days* ago. So where was its arrival notification? And why hadn't System Command's massive sensor arrays already detected it? Had it coasted all the way in *ballistic*?

"I have no idea, Navy Commander," Larshal confessed. Hyrshi had a well-deserved reputation for demolishing anyone he even suspected of incompetence, but it was always better to tell him the truth. Frankly acknowledged ignorance, he would forgive. Sometimes, at least. Posterior-covering evasions? Never. The orbit base commander turned back to Vilkhar. "What do you mean 'it's one of ours'?"

"We haven't verified ID yet, Sir. All we have is the preliminary decrypt handshake. But—"

"Excuse me, Orbital Base Commander. Navy Commander." Hyrshi and Larshal turned as one toward the tactical officer who'd spoken. The young section commander looked perplexed, and Hyrshi cocked an impatient ear at him. "According to our data files, Navy Commander, that's *Star of Empire*."

"*Star of Empire*?" Ship Commander Frekhar repeated blankly, and the section commander's ears twitched in confirmation.

"According to our records, *Star of Empire* is a *Death Descending* assigned to Fleet Commander Thikair."

Hyrshi's ears curled in confusion.

"I have the breakdown on Fleet Commander Thikair's command, Sir," Vilkhar said, looking up from his handheld. "Seven dreadnoughts, a twelve of *Hasthar*-class cruisers, and a half-twelve of *Shorach*-class destroyers, plus transports and industrial support."

"Why does that name strike a chime in my memory?" Ship Commander Frekhar wondered out loud.

"Because Thikair was assigned to command the KU-197–20 expedition." Hyrshi's voice was flat, and Frekhar's ears went equally flat in surprise.

The ship commander was young for his rank. He hadn't even been born when the KU-197–20 expedition departed the Shong System, but he'd heard about it, because so much was hoped for from it. The weed-eaters who dominated the Hegemony might be horrified by the "blood-thirstiness" of KU-197–20's dominant species, but not the Shongairi. A subject species with that sort of potential could prove invaluable. But KU-197–20 was the next best thing to eighteen Standard Years' travel from Shongaru, and Thikair had departed barely thirty-seven Standard Years ago. For *Star of Empire* to be here now, the dreadnought must have started its return voyage barely a year-quarter after its arrival in that system, and Thikair had been assigned at least two additional colony systems. None of his ships should have returned in less than forty or even forty-five Standard Years! And when one of them did, it should have been one of his destroyers, or possibly a cruiser, carrying dispatches, not a dreadnought. And certainly not his own flagship!

"What in—?" he began.

"Status change!" someone shouted, and all of them wheeled back towards the master display.

"Unknown ships. *Multiple* unknown ships!" Tracking announced, and every ear on Orbit One's command deck went flat as four more data codes burned suddenly bright in its depths.

They stared at the preposterous plot, and then a full twelve of *additional* data codes flashed into existence!

"Is that the rest of Thikair's fleet?" Squadron Commander Vilkhar muttered into the command deck's shocked silence.

"No, Sir." The section commander who'd identified *Star of Empire* was tapping on his own handheld, and the tips of his canines showed as data flashed across it. "The energy signatures are all wrong. *Very* wrong!"

"But how did they get that close without anyone's seeing them?" Vilkhar demanded. "Even powered down, radar, thermal—*visual* observation—should have picked up *something* off that many ships!"

"They must have been cloaked, Sir."

"*Cloaked?*" Hyrshi snarled. "Nobody could cloak that many ships this deep into our sensor envelope!"

"I would've said the same thing, Navy Commander," Vilkhar agreed, still bringing up data on his handheld. "But—"

He broke off and swallowed hard, then looked back up at Hyrshi.

"Sir," he said in a very careful tone, "Tracking reports that the biggest of those ships is . . . It's over a kholtarn long, Navy Commander."

"That's preposterous. Nobody could build a ship that big!" Ship Commander Frekhar said. "That's almost *five times* the size of a *Death Descending*!"

"Sir," Vilkhar looked almost desperate, "the *smallest* of those other ships is nearly a twelfth bigger than *Star of Empire*."

"Incoming transmission," one of the com techs announced in a very . . . odd tone.

The senior officers wheeled towards the master com panel, and their ears went flatter than ever as the broad, flat face of an alien species none of them had ever seen looked out of it at them.

IMPERIAL PALACE,
CITY OF SHERIKAATH,
PLANET SHONGARU,
SHONG SYSTEM,
241.5 LY FROM EARTH,
APRIL 19, YEAR 41 TE.

Do you really think the Kajarhns will just roll over and acquiesce?" Shathyra Haymar asked thoughtfully. "The Hourishas' case could be stronger, you know. I admit precedent is on their side, but sometimes precedent is a weak prop when tempers are fully engaged."

"That's very true, Your Majesty," Urkal-ir-Dyam agreed with feeling. "And the Kajarhns are even stubborner than most Shongairi. But they're the ones who brought the case before the throne instead of settling it in a lower court. They may not like your ruling, but since they're the ones who petitioned for it. . . ."

His ears shrugged, and Haymar snorted.

The truth was that, legally, the Kajarhn Pack had no option but to accept his decree. That was sort of the point of being Shathyra. And he had no doubt that—legally—they would obey him. The problem was that the Kajarhn pack leaders were as stubborn as Shongairi came, and as generations of shathyrai had discovered, even the most officially obedient beta could find all manner of ways to passively resist unless the alpha in question was willing to break a few necks to remind the beta in question who was alpha. In many ways, Haymar wouldn't have minded doing just that—figuratively, of course; not literally—but Yudar had taught him that there were times the hammer wasn't called for.

"Well, I suppose we'll find out in a six-day or so," he sighed finally. "And with that out of the way, I think we can break for—"

"Forgive me, Shathyra!"

Haymar looked up as the office door flew open and his senior secretary burst through it.

"Gyrmal?" He let his chair come upright, ears pricked in consternation.

"Forgive me, Shathyra!" she said once more and dashed across the office, her habitual grace nowhere to be seen. She slapped a palm against the smart wall and the communications system's wallpaper came up on it. Then she wheeled back to Haymar.

"Navy Commander Hyrshi just forwarded this to Palace Communications, Your Majesty. You . . . you need to see it."

"See what?" Haymar demanded, and she touched the smart wall again.

The wallpaper disappeared, and Haymar came halfway out of his chair as the face of a species he'd never heard of appeared on it. Whatever the creature was, it had the appallingly flat face of an herbivore, but the forward-set eyes of a carnivore. It appeared to be essentially hairless, from the little he could see, aside from a short pelt atop its head and some sort of facial fur that barely covered its rounded chin. And its ears! Round, flat, set far down on the side of its head. Obviously, they were useless for expressing any sort of emotion.

"Cainharn," his sire whispered, and Haymar's eyes whipped to him.

"You know what that creature is?" he asked.

"It's been a long time," Yudar told him. "But unless I'm mistaken, that 'creature' is a native of KU-197–20."

Haymar's ears frowned. The designation was vaguely familiar, but—

"The Office of Expansion authorized us to colonize the system," Yudar said, never looking away from the alien frozen on the smart wall, and his curled lip showed the tip of a canine. "That was over thirty years ago; you were only about a year old, at the time. The weed-eaters were horrified by what their survey ship told them about the planet's inhabitants. 'Humans,' they called themselves. They were totally primitive, but their 'bloodthirstiness' revolted the weed-eaters even more than *we* do! Obviously, any species the Council despised *that* much was worth conquering, so old Minister for Colonization Vairtha and I authorized the expedition."

Haymar's ears straightened as he realized why the planet designation had sounded familiar. And also why his father was showing canine. The Hegemony Council and its bureaucracy in the Erquoid System sat at the very center of the web of weed-eaters who regarded the "bloodthirsty" Shongair with bottomless contempt. A contempt which Haymar's own people repaid with interest.

"I remember now, Sire," he said. "You and Grandsire told me about it when I first took the throne and you briefed me on our contingency plans. But what in the names of all the devils is a 'human' doing *here*?"

"Sir," Gyrmal replied, "it's . . . it's delivering a message."

"Message?" Haymar repeated, and the secretary touched the screen yet again.

The image unfroze, and the creature's mouth moved. The perfectly enunciated Shongair flowing from the smart wall's speakers had to be the product of a translating program, since it wasn't even remotely synchronized with that moving mouth.

That was Haymar's first thought.

And then he realized what the creature was saying.

"My name," it said, "is David Dvorak. I am a citizen of the planet we call Earth, and which *you* call KU-197–20-III. Forty-two of our years ago, Fleet Commander Thikair arrived in our star system. He announced his presence by murdering our rulers, our political and religious leaders, and our cities. By murdering *us* and our mates and our children. Not just our warriors, not anyone he'd so much as bothered to challenge. Like an urmakhis, he simply opened fire from space, before we even knew he was there. His initial kinetic bombardments killed millions, but they were only the beginning. He continued to bombard our cities and towns and killed millions—in the end, *billions*—more of my people. Less than half a percent of them were warriors. Half were females. A quarter of them were children. It didn't matter to him. We were in his way. But despite his willingness to slaughter us, despite the fact that he'd killed over half our total population, we proved a bit too much for him to subdue. And what was his response? Why, he decided to create a bioweapon that would allow him to murder all the rest of us without meeting us in combat at all."

He paused, and alien or no, the brown eyes looking out of that smart wall were remarkably bleak.

"That was a serious mistake," he said softly, his translated voice colder than ice. "It cost Fleet Commander Thikair his life. In fact, it cost the life of every single Shongair you sent to conquer or destroy us. They're all dead. Every . . . single . . . one of them. We killed them all, and then we captured your technology, and we've improved upon it. I think the size of our ships—and the fact that Fleet Commander Thikair's flagship is our prize—should probably suggest that to you. And, since you were so eager to conquer—or destroy—us, we thought we would return the favor.

"Understand me, all of you. You, and your entire Empire, *will* submit to us. We will not simply destroy you, the way Thikair intended to destroy us. Unless, of course, you force us to. But understand this, as well. In many ways, nothing would please us more than the discovery that you *will* force us to. I am appending Fleet Commander Thikair's own records to this message. I believe, after you've reviewed them, that you'll understand precisely why that's true."

Listening to that perfectly translated voice, Haymar didn't doubt that at all.

"You have two of your days to submit," the alien said flatly. "If you choose not to, then we will move first against your fleet and orbital fortifications, then against your habitats, and—finally—against your planets, until we have *compelled* you to submit. If you wish to initiate combat sooner than that, feel free. But at the end of that time period, we will have your submission, or you will have our response to Fleet Commander Thikair's billions of murders.

"I advise you to make your choice carefully."

Navy Commander Hyrshi-ir-Urkah's ears were somber as he gazed out at the holographic images of his master display. He stood in Orbit One's com center beside Fleet Commander Gysharu-ur-Shyrak, who'd joined him aboard the command station for this briefing. Gysharu's battle squadron and cruiser commanders attended from their flagships' bridge decks. And none of them looked any more cheerful than Hyrshi did.

"All right," he said. "We have a lot to cover, and don't expect any of it to be good."

He met their massed gazes levelly.

"By now, you've all viewed the initial reports about these humans. Thirty-four years ago, we knew nothing about them, beyond what we had from Erquoid in the Office of Expansion survey crews' original reports. Which—" he allowed his ears to prick sardonically "—were obviously less than complete, even for Barthoni. All we've been able to add to that since their arrival is what they've told us and what Sensor Commander Yirak's platforms have been able to glean since they announced their arrival. And, of course, their demands."

His ears flattened once more.

"I realize that so far we've detected only sixteen of their ships, but the largest of those 'ships' are over half the size of Orbit One itself, and they have four of them. Understand me clearly. We have three dreadnought squadrons and five cruiser squadrons in Home Fleet. Some of our people have thought that was overkill, given all we had to fear from the weed-eaters. But those sixteen human ships out-mass all *seventy-two* of ours by a factor of four."

One or two of his subordinates stirred in their chairs, but Hyrshi continued in those same measured tones.

"Worse than that, we didn't see them at all until they chose to *let* us see them. That clearly indicates a cloaking technology superior to anything we have, so we must assume they have additional ships in reserve which they haven't yet shown us. The mere fact that they can build starships more than a kholtarn in length indicates that however they've accomplished it, their technology must be more advanced than ours—than the entire Hegemony's—by a substantial margin. And if a species which possessed *no* advanced technology at the time we contacted them has been able to accomplish what those ships represent in only thirty-four of our years, they represent something entirely new—and utterly terrifying—in the galaxy."

It said much for the strength of the Navy Commander's character that he could admit that in front of his subordinates, and he gazed around the faces of his commanders, letting them digest that for several endless tiskari.

"I've viewed their message," he said then, softly, and bared his canines. "Whatever else they may be, these 'humans' are manifestly *not* weed-eaters. I don't yet pretend to know what they truly are, but I do know this much. If Fleet Commander Thikair truly killed over half their species, then I fear we've awakened the very Hounds of Cainharn and filled them with a terrible resolve."

It was very quiet in the briefing room. Gysharu allowed that silence to linger, then nodded to Sensor Commander Yirak-ir-Limak.

"Tell us what we do know about them, Sensor Commander."

"Yes, Sir."

The sensor commander, the senior officer of the entire star system's sensor net, stood to address the assembled officers, and his ears were folded close to his skull.

"As the Navy Commander just said, we've so far detected a total of sixteen of their vessels, plus *Star of Empire*. We've subjected our sensor data to the most rigorous analysis possible, but I'm afraid that most of what I can tell you is what we *can't* tell you from that data.

"From optical examination of their hulls, they have no spin sections, unless they're completely internal. We've been unable to determine if, or in what way, their normal space drives differ from our own, since they've yet to accelerate while we could observe them, but assuming that there is, in fact, no spin section, we must assume these creatures have discovered a way to create artificial shipboard gravity. If that's true, then we must also assume that it's possible—indeed, my analysts rate it as highly *probable*—that their inertial compensator technology is better than our own, which suggests they can sustain higher acceleration rates. And while we obviously haven't observed their phase-drive in action, either, logic suggests it must be far better than anything the Hegemony possesses, as well."

Jumhyl-ir-Bohzar, Battle Squadron One's CO, stirred in his chair, ears half-cocked, and Yirak looked at him.

"Yes, Battle Squadron Commander?"

"With respect, Sensor Commander, surely we must resist the temptation to assign these 'humans' demonic capabilities. From the survey data, they were using muscle-powered weapons and animal-mounted cavalry barely two hundred and fifty years ago!"

"The Sensor Commander isn't suggesting they have 'demonic capabilities,' Jumhyl," Fleet Commander Gysharu said. "But they're here, in our system, with the ships we've already observed, and they've arrived in little more than a year-half more than one of Fleet Commander Thikair's ships could have reached us if he'd dispatched it immediately upon his arrival in KU-197–20's star system. So either they'd somehow attained this technological level between the Barthoni survey team's visit and Thikair's arrival, or their leader is telling the truth, and they were still substantially less advanced at that time than we are now. Frankly, I would much prefer the former—prefer that in those two and a half of our centuries they'd risen from swords and axes to a level capable of defeating the best Hegemony-level weaponry could do. As the Navy Commander's suggested, the notion that they've accomplished all of this in only twenty years on the basis of technology captured from *us* is terrifying."

Like the Navy Commander, he met his subordinates' eyes levelly.

"Consider this," he continued. "*Star of Empire*'s returned to us, presumably under her own power with a 'human' crew. That means these creatures must have defeated Thikair, killed him, and captured his flagship in no more than nine of our months. That's the *maximum* time it could have taken them for that ship to be here now. Yet frightening as that is, they've somehow—presumably thanks to the capture of Thikair's industrial ships—developed the manufacturing capacity and the technological capability to build these monster starships and somehow gotten *them* here in the same interval. At the very least, their version of the phase-drive must be enormously more efficient than anything our current technology suggests is possible. *Star of Empire* must have started home within nine months, so for the ships they built themselves to reach here *with* her means they must have overtaken *Star* in transit."

"But how *could* they've done that?" Battle Squadron Commander Kythar-ur-Laitair demanded—not of Gysharu so much as of the universe at large—and Sensor Commander Yirak sighed.

"As I told you, Battle Squadron Commander, most of what I can tell you is what we *can't* tell you. Clearly, that peculiar structure on the noses of their ships serves a function—and an important one, given how much mass and volume they've invested in it—but none of our technicians can explain what that function is. Oh, we can tell that it appears to generate a highly localized, very powerful node of gravitational force. Effectively, these creatures can produce an artificial black hole, which is another reason we believe they're artificially generating shipboard gravity, assuming their process permits them to manipulate it with the necessary fineness of control. But even assuming we understood how that was done, the energy requirements to produce the gravitational node we've already observed must be astronomical, which argues that there's some reason these humans have chosen to pay that price. One of my techs has suggested the possibility that those black holes are at least part of the explanation for the preposterous apparent velocities they must have achieved to reach us so soon after Fleet Commander Thikair attacked their homeworld. He can no more explain *how* it does whatever it does than any of my other techs, but I'd say he's almost certainly right that it's part of the explanation. Yet how it *works* is utterly beyond us."

"Then . . ."

Kythar's voice trailed off and he looked around the briefing room.

"Then what are we to do?" Hyrshi finished for him, his tone unflinching and yet almost compassionate, and Kythar's ears flicked in agreement.

"What we are about to do," the Navy Commander told his officers, his ears as steady as his measured, deliberate voice, "is what we took an oath to do when we entered the Shathyra's service. We're about to fight . . . and even with the orbital bases to back us, I believe most or all of us are about to die. But we are *Shongairi*. We will die on our feet, with our fangs to our enemies. If Shathyra Haymar decides we must submit to these creatures, then our entire empire will do just that. But before that day comes, the Imperial Shongair Navy will force these 'humans' to *prove* he has no choice."

IMPERIAL PALACE,
CITY OF SHERIKAATH,
PLANET SHONGARU,
SHONG SYSTEM,
241.5 LY FROM EARTH,
APRIL 20, YEAR 41 TE.

No wonder these 'humans' are so determined to punish us," Sha-thyra Haymar said softly.

He sat in his private council chamber once more, with his sire and his four most senior ministers, and his ears hung.

"Your Majesty, I must point out that we have no way to verify the legitimacy of these creatures' records," Minister of Colonies Kiramar-ur-Pokal said. "All of this—" he waved a hand at the holo display where the humans' download had just finished playing "—could be fabricated."

"It could have been, but it wasn't," Minister of War Timal-ir-Nolar said heavily.

"But we can't be *positive* of that," Kiramar argued. "They captured Thikair's flagship. That means they have all of his computers, and apparently none of them were scrubbed before they were captured. With all of that, it would be cub's play to generate—to *fabricate*—every single piece of 'evidence' they've shown us."

"But why?" Shathyrakym Yudar asked. Kiramar quirked an ear at the shathyrakym, and Yudar's ears shrugged back impatiently. "Why bother? The humans aren't indicting us of anything before the Hegemony's weed-eaters. They have no need to present 'evidence' or to *justify* their demand that we yield to them. If they're the stronger and we're the weaker, then both necessity and honor are clear, are they not? So why spend the time and effort to create this—" it was his turn to jab an angry finger at the holo display "—before they demand that we do?"

"Because they want us to know *why* they're demanding it, Sire," Haymar said quietly, his ears sad. "They aren't indicting us before the weed-eaters; they're indicting us before our own gods and honor. Indicting us for Thikair's violation of every precept of Jukaris."

"They're *aliens,* Your Majesty," Kiramar said.

"And does dishonor become honor when its victim is 'only' an alien?" Haymar's voice was cold, his ears folded tightly. "I think not. And neither do these humans. Their own spokesman, this Dvorak, proved that when he called Thikair urmakhis. And he was right."

Kiramar looked away, his own ears half-furled in fearful confusion . . . and possibly shame. Urmakhis was the worst insult which could be hurled at any Shongair. In modern usage, it was rendered "the dead who breathe." That was a rather more poetic usage than a literal translation— "shit eater"—of the original, ancient Shongarian, yet the insult was just as profound—and as deadly—as it had ever been.

"They've shown us his actions because they clearly intend to hold us responsible for them. They want us to know that. And they prepared their 'records' to punish us by making us watch them. By making us see what Thikair did in our name to their homeworld. To their *people.*"

"Punish us, Your Majesty?" Minister of Industry Yusair-ir-Lokar repeated.

"How can we view that and not be punished?" Haymar demanded. "Females and cubs . . . How many of them died in their beds in Thikair's initial bombardment? Died not even knowing he was there? How many of their warriors were denied the honor of challenge? Any *chance* to fight back? Thikair's own records make it clear why he did it, but his justifications are beside the point, given the human's presence in our star system. Worse, the humans are completely correct; his justifications, his excuses, don't—*can't*—excuse his actions. Let's be clear about that, here in this council chamber. How these creatures could possibly have advanced so far between the Barthoni's survey visit and Thikair's arrival is more than any of us can even guess at this point. Perhaps they truly were given technological assistance by one of the weed-eaters, as Base Commander Barak suggested to Thikair, however bizarre the entire notion sounds. But whatever he thought, he ought to have abandoned the mission when he realized how enormously Survey Command had underestimated the level they would have attained by the time he got there."

He looked around his ministers' faces.

"But he didn't do that, did he? I understand his reasoning about how valuable such a race might have been to the Empire, why he continued the operation. But even assuming he was justified in ignoring the fact that the humans had attained a Level Two civilization, to strike as he did, without warning. . . ."

"Your Majesty, there's nothing dishonorable in a surprise attack," Timal said almost compassionately when the Shathyra's voice trailed into silence.

"There is when you strike without so much as a challenge against an opponent who can't possibly match your weapons and doesn't even know you exist," Haymar said flatly. "And doubly so when your attack kills so many *millions* of them in their homes, in their beds—in their *schools and nurseries,* Timal. And what possible 'honor' is left when you kill *billions* of them with K-strike after K-strike?"

"But they should have submitted!" Kiramar protested. "Thikair's initial strike may have been—very well, Your Majesty, *was*—excessive. I'll grant that. But if they'd acknowledged that they were defeated, there would have *been* no additional K-strikes!"

"In fairness, Kiramar, honor would have demanded that even Shongairi resist so long as they could do so effectively," Timal replied heavily.

"But the fact that they couldn't stop the K-strikes proved they *couldn't* resist 'effectively,'" Kiramar argued.

"Their aircraft and armored vehicles were certainly capable of fighting 'effectively,'" Haymar pointed out grimly, remembering the holo images of what those aircraft and vehicles had accomplished before they—and their crews—died. "And whatever may have been true where kinetic bombardment was concerned, *something* enabled them to annihilate one ground base after another. Yes, and then to capture every one of Thikair's orbiting ships! So I don't think we can argue that Thikair's atrocities, however 'effective' they may have been, proved to the humans that they'd been defeated." His ears twitched sourly. "The fact that they're here, in those enormous ships, would seem to suggest they hadn't been, and if that was true, not even Shongairi could have submitted in honor!"

"There's too much here that we don't yet know," Yudar said after a moment. "Obviously, these humans are very different from any of the weed-eaters, and I suspect they're very different from us, in many ways, as well. In fact, I think it was significant that their download included Base Commander Shairez's memo about the difference between human psychology and our own. Obviously, we haven't had time to study this, and we have no access to her notes and the data on which her conclusions were based, but they clearly wanted us to have that particular memo, and it seems self-evident to me that she was right when she said that by our standards—by the standards even of the weed-eaters—humans are insane. If that's actually the case, then trying to second-guess their decisions when Thikair attacked their homeworld is pointless. Unless it gives us some insight into what they intend to do to *us*."

"I think not 'insane' so much as sane in a very different way, Sire," Haymar said. "But you're right about the implications. And they, obviously, have had far longer to study *our* psychology, at least from the literature, than Shairez ever had to study theirs. Which means they've come to Shongaru with a definite strategy and a definite plan based on their understanding of how we think. Or, at least, of how they *think* we think. Of how our honor concepts differ from their own. And that, I hope to Dainthar, may be the one good thing about this entire catastrophe."

"Why, Your Majesty?" First Minister Urkal asked.

"Because if all they wanted was to repay us in Thikair's coin, you, and I, and everyone else in this council chamber would have been dead before we ever knew they were here," Haymar said flatly. "If they could approach Shongaru as closely as they did without ever being detected, then any one of those ships could have *destroyed* our homeworld." He looked around the chamber. "Don't think for a moment that it couldn't have. So I believe they have, indeed, come to demand our submission, not to destroy us."

"Your Majesty, you can't—!" Timal chopped himself off, and Haymar's ears twitched bitterly.

"No, I can't," he acknowledged. "For myself, I would. I would contact this human—this 'Dvorak'—and submit in an instant, however it tarnished my honor as a Shongair and an individual. But our people couldn't accept that. And the humans have already demonstrated that they're better than we in at least one respect."

"One respect?" Yusair repeated when the Shathyra paused.

"Thikair was right in at least one way," Haymar said. "If Dvorak had done to Shongairi what Thikair did to the humans in his initial K-strike, we *would* have yielded. His attack would have been made without honor, just as Thikair's was, and we would have remembered *that*, as well, yet

there would have been no question in any Shongair's mind that we'd submitted to the stronger. The humans obviously don't think that way, but
that doesn't mean they don't understand us one hell of a lot better than
Thikair ever understood *them*. That much, at least, may not be his fault,
although I'm disinclined to give him much credit, considering how thoroughly he managed to self-fertilize everything *else* that came his way.
But what matters to us is that they do know how we think. They know
that if they did to us what he did to them, we would yield. We would
have no choice if we wanted our people to live. Yet they've refused to
claim that base, contemptible 'victory.' They've challenged us openly, demanded our submission in honor, instead. Challenged us with the honor
Thikair never showed them. And because they have—and because they
aren't him—I suspect they'll fight our warriors, not our mothers and our
young. They won't just slaughter our people the way we did theirs. But
because they won't, we have no choice—our warriors have no choice—
but to fight and die before we acknowledge their right to rule. And how
bitter is it that I have no choice but to ask that of them and be grateful
that 'only' they have to die?"

PUNS *RELENTLESS*,
AND
ORBIT ONE,
SHONGARU ORBIT,
SHONG SYSTEM
241.5 LY FROM EARTH,
APRIL 21, YEAR 41 TE.

A ll right," Admiral Josephine Mallard said, brown eyes bleak as she gazed at the visual display's image of the blue-and-white-swirled globe waiting in space, four light-minutes from her ships, and the last few seconds ticked off the countdown clock. "Let's do this."

"Yes, Ma'am!" Captain Lucas Escribano, her chief of staff, nodded sharply and turned to the com display.

He didn't really need that display. His neural feed could have implanted the imagery directly on his visual cortex. But it turned out that simply acquiring instant mental access to data didn't satisfy some human requirements. People wanted to use their eyes—not to mention their noses and their ears—and they wanted to actually see one another. It was silly, but it was also true, and he looked at the faces of the sixteen ship commanders on the display.

"Execute," he said simply.

· · · · ·

AS IT HAPPENED, Josephine Mallard's information on the state of the Shong System's defenses was far better than Navy Commander Hyrshi's information on her own command. She and her staff had started with the data in *Târgovişte*'s secure memory, which had contained virtually every detail of the Shongair homeworld's defenses as of Fleet Commander Thikair's departure. And, since *Relentless*'s arrival, her recon drones—which were more sensitive, longer ranged, and enormously more difficult to detect than anything the Hegemony had—had probed those defenses bone-marrow deep. She knew *exactly* what she confronted today.

Which was why she knew that whatever else she might call what was about to happen, it wouldn't be a "battle."

· · · · ·

"**THE HUMANS ARE** advancing, Navy Commander!" Ship Commander Frekhar-zik-Charsu, Hyrshi-ir-Urkah's chief of staff, announced, and Hyrshi checked the time display.

"At least they're punctual," he said grimly. The light-speed sensor's report was a fourteen-shrekar look into the past at this range. Which meant the humans had waited two days to the tiskar from the moment they'd transmitted their challenge. "Alert all units. Although—" his ears twitched frostily "—I would suspect they've already noticed."

"At once, Navy Commander."

Frekhar sent out the orders, and Hyrshi sat back in his command chair as the icons of the human ships accelerated towards Orbit One and Shongaru. It was ironic in so many ways, he thought. Ironic that the Shongairi had built this horrific foe for themselves through their arrogance and the stupidity of one fleet commander. And ironic that the enormously powerful fleet they'd built to deter any attack was about to fight the first—and probably the *only*—battle in the entire history of the Imperial Shongair Navy. All those years worrying about the weed-eaters, planning for the day they awakened to the Shongairi's plans for empire, and instead they faced *this*.

The range was fourteen light-shrekari. For a Shongair ship, that meant a three-yirka voyage, with turnover after eighteen myrtarni, and his ears grimaced as he watched the icons gaining speed. For a human ship, he suspected, it would take less time. In fact—

"Sir, their acceleration rate is over a hundred and fifty gravities," Frekhar said in a carefully controlled tone, as if to confirm Hyrshi's thoughts, and the Navy Commander's ear twitched in acknowledgment. That was two and a half times the acceleration a Shongair ship could have sustained.

A tone chimed, and he looked down at a secondary display as Sensor Commander Yirak appeared on it.

"Yes, Yirak?"

"Their compensators are obviously more efficient, Navy Commander, but their normal space drive itself appears to be identical to our own. They can simply sustain a much greater acceleration rate."

"Well, that's good news." Hyrshi tried to sound as if it were going to make any difference. From the set of Yirak's ears, he wasn't very convincing.

$$\cdot \ \cdot \ \cdot \ \cdot \ \cdot$$

MALLARD CLOSED HER eyes, communing with her neural link, as the task force accelerated towards Shongaru. She had to be careful how deeply into that link she dove. There was no real limit to the amount of information a feed could provide, but there most definitely *was* a limit to how much information a human brain could process. She was an old hand at this by now, though, and she focused on the astrogator's station to watch her task force accelerate. A Shongair ship would have needed just over six hours to make Shongaru orbit; her ships could have done it in under four. Not that she had any intention of coming that close while any of those Shongair ships were still in existence.

Actually, she didn't really *need* to close with them at all. Unlike the Hegemony, the PUN had developed a particle beam that was actually practical for a shipboard weapon system. It was huge—almost two-thirds again the size of a ship-to-ship laser—but it was much more powerful and longer ranged. Part of the cornucopia of the Gannon team's breakthroughs in the field of gravitational engineering was a particle accelerator which consisted of an intensely focused gravity field that allowed electrons to make as many laps around the track as they wanted before the projector fired.

It was a light-speed weapon—well, almost; the electrons moved at "only" about .9999c—which made it deadly accurate at shorter ranges, although its theoretical maximum range against maneuvering targets was a moot point. It was capable of handing out devastating damage at up to four light-minutes, but at that range its particles would take 242 seconds to reach their target, and a ship maneuvering at sixty gravities could alter its position by over 17,000 kilometers in that much time. That was why missiles were and probably would remain the weapon of choice at extended ranges. Unlike an energy weapon, they could chase an evading target, even a Hegemony shipkiller had a range from rest of well over 1.5

LM, and it was much faster than any targets its seekers might be trying to run down.

Against fixed targets, like Orbit One and Orbit Two, the particle beams would have been quite effective, and she'd been tempted to demonstrate just that to the Puppies. But while each P-beam hit was far more powerful than a single hit from a laserhead, even *Relentless* mounted only 138 of them. Each of the PUN's Mjölnirs, on the other hand, carried sixteen lasing rods.

And a *Relentless*-class superdreadnought mounted twenty-seven hundred missile launchers. She could bring two-thirds of them to bear in any firing arc, and if all of them were Mjölnirs, that would have represented over twenty-seven *thousand* lasers, delivered at point-blank range.

"Initial launch point in ten minutes, Ma'am," Commander Ulyana Puhach, her operations officer, announced, and she nodded.

· · · · ·

"MISSILE LAUNCH!" SHIP Commander Frekhar snapped, and Hyrshi stiffened in his command chair.

The humans had been in motion for less than seventeen shrekari. Even at their preposterous acceleration rate, they'd moved barely three hundred thousand shrekari closer to Orbit One. The range was still impossibly long for ship-to-ship combat, but Orbit One and the other fixed defenses weren't ships. They couldn't maneuver, and that made targeting them cub's play even from that sort of range. That was the reason bases mounted so much point defense and so many chaff projectors.

It remained to be seen whether or not they mounted *enough*.

"Navy Commander," Frekhar said, and there was something odd about his voice. Hyrshi looked at him, and the chief of staff's ears were flat. "Tracking estimates eight thousand plus missiles inbound."

No, a quiet voice said in the back of Hyrshi's brain, *it* isn't *enough*.

Those sixteen ships had just launched as many missiles in one salvo as all *seventy-two* units of Home Fleet could have fired.

"Initial launch velocity is almost one hundred sixty-five sheertarni per tiskar, Sir," Frekhar reported. "That's forty-eight times our initial launch speed, and they're already accelerating."

He looked over his shoulder at Hyrshi, and the Navy Commander flicked his ears in acknowledgment of the unspoken part of his report. The Hykarlu, the Imperial Navy's shipkiller missile, named for their homeworld's fiercest winged predator, *wouldn't* have been accelerating from launch. Not at that range. If it did, its drive would burn out over ten light-shrekari short of its targets, and the loss of its drive field would have made it easy meat for even chaff clouds.

"But their acceleration is only twenty-seven percent higher than ours," Frekhar added.

And isn't that *reassuring,* Hyrshi thought. *At least that's only* three *percent more acceleration than the Shyrksu.*

The Shyrksu counter-missile, named for the Hykarlu's smaller, fleeter mountain-top cousin, was marginally faster than the Hegemony Navy's shipkillers. Apparently, it was not faster than the humans' missiles, and he wondered just how much acceleration their *counter*-missiles had.

More to the point, if the humans' attack missiles were capable of sustaining that acceleration all the way to Orbit One, their missile drive's endurance had to be at least half again that of his own. That meant their final attack velocity would be almost twice as great, and *that* meant—

"Second launch!" Tracking announced, and the tips of Hyrshi's canines crept into view. At least his launcher cycle time was forty percent faster than theirs. Assuming that represented their most rapid rate of fire, at least.

"Stand by point defense!" he heard Orbit Base Commander Larshal snap. "Fire Plan One!"

• • • • •

"WE HAVE COUNTER-MISSILES, Ma'am," Puhach reported.

"They launched early," Escribano said, and Mallard nodded.

Even the Planetary Union Navy's missiles would take time to cross that enormous gulf. *Relentless*'s launchers were grav drivers, not railguns. Although their launch velocity was far higher than the old electromagnetic launchers, their recoil was far lower . . . despite which, *Relentless*'s multibillion-tonne hull heaved like an old wet-navy windjammer as the stupendous superdreadnought kicked out over seventeen hundred 300-tonne missiles at 600 KPS. Each of her sisters joined her, backed by the *Sword*-class cruisers, to produce a salvo density of 8,100 missiles. Even from that beginning velocity, they would take seventeen minutes—well, just under thirteen, now, for her initial launch—to reach their targets, which was six minutes more than the maximum endurance of any Hegemony shipkiller. The standard Hegemony counter-missile's range was less than five million kilometers from rest, which meant its drive would burn out long before it reached interception range of her birds, unless. . . .

"Have they brought up their drives yet, Ulyana?" she asked.

"No, Ma'am. The drones picked up the energy spikes when they launched, but we're not seeing any drives. And we have a second launch."

"They're trying to thicken their intercept density, Lucas," Mallard said. "They're just kicking them out on a vector to stack them in front of ours, and given our birds' flight time, they can put nineteen out of each launcher before they get there."

Escribano nodded in understanding. Of course, the Puppies had four minutes less engagement time than the PUN did, due to the light-speed lag in detecting their own launch. If not, they could have launched ten more of them per launcher.

"They don't have enough command link redundancy to manage that many birds individually, Ma'am," he pointed out. "Most of them will have to rely solely on their individual seekers, and that means intercept probabilities will suck."

"Of course they will. They would've sucked against Hegemony birds, much less ours. But they'll have a hell of a lot more opportunities, and they *do* have the links to manage almost fifty thousand of them."

Mallard plugged her neural feed directly into Puhach's tactical systems and grimaced. Those orbital bases—especially Orbit One and Orbit Two—were almost impossible to miss, really. They couldn't dodge, and they were enormous, glaring targets for any seeker system. She could have launched against them from any point in the star system and been confident of generating hundred-percent-accurate targeting solutions. Unfortunately, her missiles had to be under power as they closed on their targets, and once a missile went active, it couldn't be switched off and then on again. Missile drives were enormously overpowered by the standards of any starship, or even drone, and they paid for that with a strictly limited lifetime once they were activated. Which had unfortunate tactical implications in a lot of ways, since if missiles *weren't* under power—if they were unprotected by their drive fields—they could be killed with a kid's marble.

The Hegemony's standard last-ditch defense against birds which had gone ballistic was essentially a high-tech chaff projector, one that spewed hundreds of tiny pellets—about the size of a Terran #9 birdshot, but seventy-five percent denser than any lead shot ever made—into their paths, and the math was brutally simple.

Her missiles' maximum velocity from rest was just over 148,800 KPS. If one of them encountered a single "chaff" pellet at that velocity without a drive field, the relativistic energy transfer would be on the order of 1.2 kilotons, and if it hit one, the odds were that it would hit dozens of them. That would be enough to destroy just about any missile in the galaxy, which was why naval tactics dictated missile engagements only within those missiles' *powered* attack range.

She could have launched from a couple of light-hours, if she'd wanted to, and allowed her missiles to coast ballistic until they came within four light-minutes . . . assuming she'd wanted to wait the five and a half weeks that would take. Which she hadn't. And so, just as any Hegemony naval commander would, she'd launched from the longest range by which her birds would still be under power when they reached attack range.

That took chaff pretty much out of the equation, which threw the Puppies back onto longer-ranged, active intercepts. But since they'd known that would be the case even against a fellow member species of the Hegemony, their warships and—especially—their bases had a *lot* of counter-missile launchers, backed by thousands of point defense lasers and autocannon. The autocannon—multi-barreled railguns in quad mounts with a rate of fire of just over eight rounds a second—were basically last-ditch chaff launchers, firing superdense slugs heavy enough to punch even through a missile's drive field. Unlike a chaff cloud, they could be individually targeted, but they were incredibly short ranged. Even if they "stopped" a missile that would have scored a direct hit, the target was still taking massive damage when that missile's fragments—or plasma cloud—hit it anyway. Against standoff weapons, like laserheads, they were useless.

Point defense lasers had more reach—up to five hundred kilometers— and anti-ship lasers, which could also be used to thicken point defense, could reach all the way out to 1,200 kilometers against missiles, half again their range against a warship protected by both drive field and armor. Even at 1,200 kilometers, they'd have time for only a single shot each, of course, given her missiles' closing velocity. But according to the drone reports, Orbit One, alone, mounted better than five thousand point defense lasers and autocannon . . . and in the neighborhood of *twelve* thousand ship-to-ship lasers. Altogether, that was seventeen thousand defensive lasers from each of the two orbital bases, of which 8,500 could be brought to bear on the incoming missiles.

On the other hand, her ships had already put six salvos into space. That was damned near *fifty* thousand missiles. *PUN* missiles, which were one hell of a lot more capable than anything the Hegemony had.

And she would still be launching—and over two and a half lightminutes—outside the *Puppies'* shipkiller missile range when her first salvo arrived.

Well, whatever else, it's going to be interesting for the bastards, isn't it? she thought as *Relentless* and her consorts spat out another eight thousand missiles.

· · · · ·

THE TSUNAMI OF PUN missiles streaked towards their targets. Launched at forty-five-second intervals, there was a 635,958-kilometer gap between salvos, and the blood-red clouds of icons—the Shongairi and humans used the same color to indicate danger, for obvious reasons—swept down upon Orbit One, Orbit Two, and Home Fleet. Had they been distributed evenly, there would have been over a hundred missiles in each salvo for each base and each individual warship.

But they weren't evenly distributed. Every single missile in the initial salvo was targeted solely upon Orbit One, in a hurricane of devastation whose like Orbit One's designers had never envisioned in their worst nightmares.

Twenty percent of that stupendous wall of missiles consisted solely of penetration aids. Two-thirds of the penaids were Aegis birds, nicknamed "Gunslingers" by the PUN's tactical crews. Fitted with twenty-four electronically targeted laser emitters in a double ring, guided by the best sensor systems and fire control the Planetary Union could cram into its 300-tonne body, it was specifically designed to ride shotgun on the actual shipkillers and destroy counter-missiles its onboard computers determined had achieved an intercept solution on one of them. Half of the remaining penaids were Shangos. Named for the Yoruba god associated with capricious, creative, destructive magical power, the Shango was a decoy missile, capable of generating the emission signatures of up to fifteen false shipkillers to lure counter-missiles astray. And the remaining penaids were Yúnzhōngzĭs, named for the "Master in Cloud," from the sixteenth-century novel *Fengshen Yanyi*, and fitted with directional jammers of stupendous power, designed to both knock holes in the defenders' sensor net and to disrupt counter-missile control links.

Altogether, there were 1,600 of them in that salvo . . . which left "only" 6,480 Mjölnirs. The PUN's true shipkiller, the Mjölnir carried sixteen independently deployed lasing rods and a ten-gigaton warhead. In the instant before the detonation destroyed the missile body, an onboard generator produced a powerful magnetic bottle aligned with the deployed and targeted lasing rods. It created what was, in effect, a directional nuclear explosion of incredible power, and the gamma ray lasers it produced as the lasing rods vaporized were devastating.

Of course, that was nothing compared to what would happen if a Mjölnir was able to actually *strike* its target. As a purely kinetic weapon, it would deliver over 980 gigatons to any target, which would be enough to destroy even a Shongair dreadnought with a single hit.

No one was counting on that today, though. There was no need to. Not with the number of weapons Josephine Mallard had brought to the party.

· · · · ·

"SHYRKSU ACTIVATION IN two myrtarni," Frekhar said, and Hyrshi's ears nodded.

The interception point was just under three million sheertarni from Orbit One. That meant he'd have all of nine tiskari to know whether or not his warriors could stop those missiles.

Hyrshi-ir-Urkah looked down at the secondary com display tied into the Imperial Palace, and his shathyra looked back up at him. Hyrshi opened his mouth, but Shathyra Haymar's ears twitched a quick negative before he could speak.

"I heard, Navy Commander," he said gravely. "Our prayers are with you. May Dainthar and Frygahr gather your warriors as Their own."

"And may Dainthar be with you, Your Majesty," Hyrshi said softly. "I fear all our people will need Him."

Haymar's ears nodded somberly, and he started to reply, but—

"Activation!" Frekhar snapped.

. . . . .

THE SHONGAIR COUNTER-MISSILES' drives engaged.

Or, rather, some of them did. Orbit One and Orbit Two each mounted well over twenty thousand counter-missile launchers. Each of those launchers had been given the time to put nineteen Shyrksus into space, and Home Fleet's mobile units had added another 246,000. Altogether, that was well over a million counter-missiles, enough to stop any attack of which the Shongairi who'd designed those ships, those bases, could have conceived. But Josephine Mallard's ships had deeper magazines than any Shongair defensive planner had ever allowed for, and she was still launching salvos. She'd already fired twenty-two of them, with ten more allocated to her fire plan. In the end, that would be almost 260,000 shipkillers, which gave the defenders less than four Shyrksus per attack bird.

And against PUN shipkillers, that was nowhere near enough.

The defenders assigned five Shyrksus to each missile of the first salvo, willing to burn the extra counter-missiles in the outer defensive zone because they had sufficient fire control links to maintain shipboard control on all of them, rather than relying on the missiles' internal seekers. But also because they had no hard projections on how effective their inner, shorter-ranged defenses would prove.

And because if they didn't stop the *first* wave, it wouldn't really matter how well they might have done against the ones following it.

Forty thousand counter-missiles charged to meet the human missile storm, and Navy Commander Hyrshi bared his canines in an ear-flattened snarl as the Shangos came to life and the tactical plot's missile icons abruptly doubled in number.

His tactical officers had anticipated penaids, but no technology they knew could have produced electronic decoys as good as the ones coming at them now. Orbit One's computers did their best to sort out the confusion, hold lock on the already identified shipkillers, but that was why Mallard had seeded her salvo with Yúnzhōngzĭs, as well. Their jammers awoke, tearing holes in Orbit One's sensor coverage. They weren't as effective against the base's sensors as they would have been against the Shyrksus' onboard seekers, but they probably degraded them by at least twenty percent. Worse, the fiendishly effective jamming broke the control links on over nine thousand of the counter-missiles. Without shipboard control, their probability of selecting a genuine missile to target was no more than even, and their chance of actually hitting it would be . . . low.

And if those decoy signatures could be maintained all the way in, they would also double the number of targets his defensive lasers must engage.

·　·　·　·　·

JOSEPHINE MALLARD WATCHED the Shongair counter-missiles speed towards her first salvo. The range was still well over 3.5 LM, so everything she saw had already happened, but she'd spent the last two decades of her life commanding starships in deep space. She knew all about lightspeed limitations. Which made it no less frustrating.

A second wave of counter-missiles activated forty seconds after the first, charging to meet her second salvo. And forty seconds after that, a third wave brought up its drives and streaked toward her third salvo.

She'd plugged her neural link back into Ulyana Puhach's tactical plot, and she watched with the ops officer as the first salvo's Aegis escort missiles opened fire on the incoming Puppy counter-missiles.

There were just over a thousand of the "Gunslingers," and their presence came as a complete surprise to the Shongairi.

·　·　·　·　·

"NAVY COMMANDER!" SHIP Commander Frekhar said. "The Shyrksus—"

"I see it, Frekhar," Hyrshi said harshly.

How in Cainharn's darkest hells did they do that? What are these creatures?

The questions burned in the Navy Commander's brain as over eight thousand Shyrksus—almost twenty percent of his counter-missiles— were torn apart short of their intended targets.

But that still left well over 31,000, and they screamed in on the human missiles, determined to embrace them in suicidal self-immolation. Ninety-six hundred of them had lost their control links, and only a handful of those Shyrksus achieved intercept. Against Hegemony shipkillers, a Shyrksu was rated for a seventy-five percent intercept rate, but these weren't Hegemony shipkillers, and that rating hadn't taken the Yunzhōngzĭs' jamming or the Shangos' decoys into consideration. Instead of seventy-five percent, they achieved an intercept rate of just under *thirty* percent.

That was still 6,472 of the incoming missiles, but 1,294 of the counter-missiles' kills were Shangos or Yúnzhōngzĭs.

Which meant "only" thirteen hundred Mjölnirs broke through the counter-missile zone and charged straight for Orbit One.

The Shongair base's computers tracked them emotionlessly, immune to the fear and tension of their merely mortal masters, and Navy Commander Hyrshi felt hope stir deep within him. Most of the decoy targets had disappeared with the deaths of the Shangos producing them, and tracking had identified most of the ones which were left. Orbit One mounted enough point defense and ship-to-ship lasers to target every remaining missile thirteen times over. Even with only a single shot each, that was an ample margin of overkill, he thought. It didn't matter how good the humans' technology was, that thinned-out hunting pack of missiles couldn't break Orbit One's defenses. And if they could do as well against the follow-on salvos, they might—

. . . . .

THE MJÖLNIRS STOPPED accelerating. Their lasing rods' powerful thrusters carried them into precise alignment, the mag bottles spun up, and the nuclear bombs at the missiles' hearts detonated.

. . . . .

HYRSHI NEVER REALIZED how wrong he'd been.

The Mjölnir's standoff attack range was four hundred kilometers greater than that of his ship-to-ship lasers.

The savage energy stilettos ripped deep into Orbit One, shredding its flanks, destroying its weapons . . . killing its personnel. Not even they had the power—the numbers—to *destroy* the base outright, but the lasers

clawed their way far deeper into it than the Shongairi had ever anticipated.

Like the one that smashed deep, deep into its heart and killed Navy
Commander Hyrshi and his entire staff.

· · · · ·

"GOOD HITS, MA'AM!" Captain Escribano announced.

"I see it, Lucas," Mallard acknowledged, as her second salvo's Shangos
and Yúnzhōngzĭs lit off their EW systems. She couldn't tell how many of
the Puppies' counter-missiles had just lost their shipboard control links,
but she was willing to bet that the number was high.

Orbit One's outer hull was ripped and torn, bleeding air, shedding
wreckage and what were undoubtedly bodies. *Relentless*'s CIC computers projected a twenty-three percent loss of capability, and she bared
her teeth as the second salvo broke through the Puppies' outer intercept
zone. Almost twice as many Mjölnirs reached attack range this time, and
Orbit One shuddered and heaved as the bomb-pumped lasers' energy
bled into it.

"We still have time to re-target salvo thirteen," she said coldly. "Move
it to Orbit Two."

Her smile was even colder than her voice.

"I don't think we'll be needing it on Orbit One."

IMPERIAL PALACE,
CITY OF SHERIKAATH,
PLANET SHONGARU,
SHONG SYSTEM,
241.5 LY FROM EARTH,
APRIL 23, YEAR 41 TE.

So we have no remaining extra-atmospheric defense capability at all, Your Majesty."

System Commander Brath-ir-Horal's ears were grim, but he met his Shathyra's eyes levelly from the display. He was flanked in the display by Army Commander Urdaar-zik-Caylo, the Imperial Army's senior commissioned officer, and three subordinate army commanders, the senior officers of Shongaru's three continental commands. Division Commander Thyrack-ir-Gowan was also present, despite his monumentally junior rank, because he was Habitat One's military commander. All of them were Army officers, and by rights, Navy Commander Hyrshi should have made Brath's report. Unfortunately, he had died with Orbit One. And technically, Brath had been Hyrshi's superior even before the Navy Commander's death. It was simply that when it came to naval matters, the System Commander normally deferred to the Navy's senior officers in conferences like this.

When there *were* any senior Navy officers, Haymar-zik-Shayma reminded himself.

"So far as we can determine," Brath continued, "we failed to so much as damage a single one of the 'humans" starships. None of our own attack missiles penetrated their defensive envelope, and they never entered energy weapon range until all of our orbital offensive firepower had been . . . eliminated."

"Which means they now control our orbital space," Haymar said.

"Your Majesty, they control *all* our system's space beyond Shongaru's and Derinar's atmospheres," Brath said flatly. "Our remaining sensor capability indicates that not even those monster ships of theirs have bottomless magazines. Once they allowed us to see the rest of their fleet, they also allowed us to watch them re-ammunitioning their warships from their freighters. Which—" his ears smiled humorlessly "—appear to be just as large as their warships. And just as an aside, they've now also allowed our sensors to see what I devoutly hope is all the rest of their expedition's support ships . . . which appear to include at least two industrial platforms they're already putting into service. We can't be certain, but we've tentatively identified three more of them as troop transports.

"Whether or not we're right about those IDs, we must assume that their warships' magazines have been fully replenished, since they're now in Shongaru orbit at barely one light-sheertarn."

"But so far they haven't fired on the planet or the orbital habitats," First Minister Urkal observed.

"No, they haven't," Brath agreed. "I rather doubt that it's because of anything they fear we might do to them, however, First Minister."

Haymar gave a small ear-flick of acknowledgment. No reasonably sane defensive planner mounted offensive weapons on an inhabited world. Planets couldn't dodge, which meant they could be attacked from any range an adversary chose, well outside the effective envelope of planetary weapons against mobile targets that could dodge. So the only real "function" of planet-based offensive weapons would have been to serve as bombardment magnets, and what Thikair had done to the population of the humans' homeworld was a hideous demonstration of the casualty totals that would have entailed.

Most of Shongaru's major cities were guarded by *defensive* weaponry, however, if only to protect them against incoming missiles which had strayed from their intended deep-space targets. Their utility against human-level weapons was at best problematical, of course.

"Forgive me, System Commander," Shathyrakym Yudar said quietly, "but should we assume from what you've so far said that we're now effectively totally defenseless?"

Brath hesitated, and Haymar suppressed a bitter smile. He knew what the System Commander *wanted* to say, yet he couldn't. Not yet. Not unless the humans were prepared to inflict the megadeaths Thikair had visited upon them, at any rate.

"I don't think we can say that, My Lord," he said instead. "At this time, we—" he gestured at his fellow Army officers "—have been unable to form any judgment on the power and effectiveness of their planetary combat equipment, yet there are practical limits to what can be achieved in atmosphere. I'm unhappily certain the humans' infantry and heavy weapons are superior to our own—since, unlike us, they do have a very good measuring stick for our capabilities, and they would scarcely have arrived with so few ships if *they* didn't believe that to be the case—but combat on a planetary surface, or even within the confines of an orbital habitat, provides many opportunities to maximize the effectiveness of one's own weapons. Especially for those fighting on the defensive."

"So you believe there's a reasonable prospect of holding our ground effectively?" War Minister Timal pressed anxiously. "After all, the humans managed to inflict significant losses upon Fleet Commander Thikair's ground forces, even with their original primitive weapons and when badly outnumbered. And however enormous their starships may be, they can't possibly have brought millions of their own troopers with them! Surely, with our own combat ability still intact, our warriors should be able to inflict sufficient casualties to give an invading force so far from home and reinforcement pause!"

"I didn't say that, Minister," Brath replied. "I said we have no way to evaluate the relative effectiveness of our own weapons against those of the humans. Not yet, at any rate. And while you're probably correct that they have significantly fewer troopers than our own Army, I would hesitate to invest too much certainty even in that. Their starships are over a kholtarn in length. In cryo, *we* could easily pack up to a million troopers aboard just one ship that size."

"But in that case—"

"In that case, Timal," Haymar interrupted quietly, "we have no choice but to find out from experience." His ears grimaced. "I wish we didn't. I wish I could simply order the System Commander to stand down and surrender. But I can't do that, can I?"

He surveyed his advisors' faces, and for the first time in his life, he cursed the precepts of Jukaris. They made his people what they were, gave them an unshakeable assurance of *who* they were, and that was a source of enormous pride. But now. . . .

"Is it not truly ironic that if they were prepared to emulate Thikair and simply execute a massive bombardment on Shongaru, I could surrender tomorrow, and our people would accept it?" he said. "But if they truly aren't prepared to become mass murderers—as we did—then I must ask our warriors to die by the thousands instead."

"It's the way of our people, Your Majesty." Brath's tone was almost gentle. "And our warriors are prepared to pay the price in defense of our homeworld."

"I know that, and I thank Dainthar that He's granted us at least that much mercy, but that makes it weigh no less heavily upon my heart."

I don't understand, Sir," Master Sergeant Robyn Sottile said. "Why are we doing this? I thought Puppies submitted when they know they're beaten, and our fleet just smashed *all* their orbital defenses." The Able Company first sergeant looked around the compartment. "Why is an assault on their orbital habitat still necessary? Did someone forget to tell them their stuff is shit compared to ours?"

"Believe me, they're *very* well aware of what we did to the defense platforms," Colonel Malachi Dvorak replied from the raised stage at the front of the briefing room. "And that damned well tells them they can't screw with us in space. Doesn't look like their *ground* commanders got the message though. Or not yet, anyway."

"Oh, I wouldn't go quite that far," Brigadier Olivia Ascaso put in, and all eyes shifted to her.

The briefing room just off *Emiliano Gutierrez*'s combat information center was a very large compartment which, at the moment, seemed just a little crowded by the assembled unit commanders and senior enlisted personnel of Ascaso's First Brigade, Second Space Marine Division. Now she nodded to Colonel Dvorak, who commanded 1st Battalion, then looked at the rest of her personnel.

"We haven't actually told them anything, but even *Space Marines* would be a little nervous after what Admiral Mallard did to their fleet!" she told them with a grim chuckle, and smiled as an answering chorus of laughter muttered its way around the compartment. Then her smile faded, and she shook her head slightly.

"I'm sure their defenders are worried as hell about what we're going to do next," she said more seriously. "And I know we all *wanted* them to be ready to throw in the towel as soon as we wiped out their orbital defenses. But we couldn't be sure they would when we put the Expeditionary Force's mission and basic planning together back home. That's why we planned

Operation Can Opener on a contingency basis from the get-go. We all hoped we wouldn't need it; unfortunately, it looks like we do."

She looked around at the assembled officers and senior enlisted of her brigade's three infantry battalions.

"You all know the xenoanthropologists have been tweaking their appreciation of Puppy psychology all along. Well, according to Doctor Ramos and his team, it looks like it's not as simple as showing them we can destroy their *static* defenses, after all. They won't actually consider themselves beaten until we trigger their submission mechanism. We knew that going in. But now it looks like to do that, we need to punch through their defenders and threaten their civilians. To demonstrate that we *can* threaten their civilians . . . and that they can't stop us."

"That's going to make things . . . dicey, Ma'am." Major Alexandre Abbott, CO of 1st Battalion's Alpha Company, shook his head. "Can Opener's original planning all stressed the need to avoid civilian casualties. But if we're now supposed to be getting close enough to actually threaten them, well, accidents happen, Ma'am."

"Let me clear this up," Lieutenant General Wilson said from the back of the briefing room.

All eyes turned to him, as they had to Ascaso, as he climbed out of his chair. He walked up to join her and Colonel Dvorak on the stage, folded his hands behind him, and faced his assembled Space Marines with somber blue eyes.

"You all know Operation Riposte's basic parameters," he said. "We could've come in here the same way Thikair came in. Could've started right out with mass K-strikes and blasted them straight back into the Stone Age. Hell, that's exactly what Vlad set out to do after he and the other vampires kicked Thikair's ass! And I gotta say, when he left, while all of the older people in this compartment were just crawling out of the rubble, counting the dead, hoping like hell that at least *some* of our friends and our families were still alive, I sure as hell agreed with him. I think all of us did.

"But that was then. That was when we'd just crawled out from under the bus that ran over us. It was before we put Thikair's industrial platforms to work, before we figured out how much more innovative we are. It was when we were still the planetbound species that had just had its clock cleaned by ETs one hell of a lot more advanced than we were.

"That shoe's on the other foot now, people. The Shongairi know now that our tech is better than theirs. Admiral Mallard sure as *hell* showed them that! But they don't know how *much* better, yet. Oh," he waved one hand, "like the Brigadier just said, they have to be worried as hell after what the Admiral and the Space Squids did to their navy, but they haven't seen what *we* can do yet. There was a book I read a long time ago—yes, I know Space Marines aren't supposed to admit we can read. *Mea culpa.*"

A wave of chuckles rumbled around the compartment.

"In fairness, I read it back in the distant days of my youth, before I was ever a Marine, even the first time," he continued. "I'd *never* do something like that these days!"

The chuckles became a welcome, rolling laugh, and he smiled. Then his expression sobered again.

"Truth is, that book is a major reason why I became a Marine in the first place, and it was by the same guy our armor's named for. In fact, it's the *reason* our armor's named for him. And there was a passage in it that stuck with me. He basically said that sometimes you don't want to spank a baby with an ax, and that's what Can Opener is supposed to be. A way to 'spank' the Puppies without using an ax—or a chainsaw—to do it. We're not here just to punish them for what Thikair did to us, did to Earth. We're here to convince *them* to submit, to surrender, to *us*. If President Howell and Ambassador Dvorak are right, once they do submit, they'll become our allies against the rest of the Hegemony. And that, people, is more important than any amount of 'revenge' could be."

He paused, then shrugged.

"From what we know about the Puppies' psychology, in our place, they would've submitted to Thikair as soon as he issued his surrender demand, before the K-strikes' dust had even started settling. But triggering that kind of instant submission here would have required us to do a Thikair of our own on them. And the truth is, even as pissed off as the human race is with the Shongairi—and as big a *right* as we have to be pissed off with them—I hope to hell there's not a single person in this briefing room who wants to go home to his or her family as a mass murderer on a planetary scale."

He paused once, those blue eyes sweeping the faces looking back at him, and this time the enormous compartment was filled with silence.

"I didn't think so," he said simply.

"But the problem is that it looks like we'd misinterpreted some aspects of how their honor code works. We knew Jukaris requires the alpha to demonstrate superiority and the beta to submit once he does. We even knew that the beta is required to *make* the alpha demonstrate his superiority. That he *can't* submit—not honorably—until he has. The kind of mass K-strikes Thikair unleashed on us would have obviated that requirement in our case, because the truth is that without Vlad, ultimately, we *couldn't* have resisted in the end. Not effectively. In fact, one reason the Shongairi on Earth were so pissed with us was that we didn't understand that we were honor bound to submit after Thikair had proved we couldn't win. Under Jukaris, that made all of us urmakhi, as far as they were concerned, and that meant we were beneath contempt.

"Obviously, we'd all hoped the Shongairi here would figure their 'betas' had fought hard enough to make us prove our superiority when we killed their entire navy. Unfortunately, however, we appear to have been . . . overly optimistic about that. So we've gotta find another way to make our point.

"For the record, now that their navy's out of the way, I'd like nothing more than to be able to convince them to roll over with a few demonstration K-strikes on empty planetary real estate somewhere out in the middle of Shongaru's Bumfuckistan. Sort of a way of saying 'Look, we could do a Thikair on you if we really wanted to. Don't make us do it for real.' But it looks like we can't do it that way, after all."

He shrugged.

"What the brainiacs are telling us now is that our Squids have clearly proven they can kick the Puppy Squids' asses, but that's not enough. They actually have to 'feel the pain'—they need to see us breaking things and killing people; their soldiers, not their civilians, if we can help it—before they can honorably acknowledge defeat. So unless we want Admiral Mallard to unlimber those K-strikes and fire for effect, we—specifically, you, me, and the rest of our people—still need to face the Puppy grunts directly, what you might call *mano a mano*, and prove to *both* of us that they couldn't keep us from killing their civilians in job lots *if that's what we choose to do*. If we don't show them that, as conclusively as possible, then they haven't made us prove that we could. And until they make us prove that, they can't surrender."

He shook his head, his eyes grim.

"That means that to get them to surrender, we have to break into their habitat, fight our way through their infantry, and *endanger* the civilians behind them. All right, I accept that. But I don't want to actually *hurt* any more of them than we can avoid, and you're right, Alexandre. In an operation like this, especially given how we're amending your ops plan, some of them *are* going to get hurt. Only certifiable idiots—not all of them civilians, unfortunately—would think we could execute this sort of 'surgical' strike and guarantee no civilian bystanders get caught in the gears. We all know that. But we need to hold those civilian casualties to an absolute minimum while demonstrating that we could kill *all* of them if we really wanted to. If that was what our mission orders called for.

"That's what General Cantrell, Brigadier Ascaso, and I are looking for here," he continued. "We've got a day or two to tweak our existing ops plan, and while you do that, remember Can Opener is a test case. We're still trying to get a really solid grip on the Puppies' psychology on this point. We hope we've got it now; we can't be *sure* we do till we test it, and we need to be *positive* we understand it before we go after the planets. The habitats offer us our best laboratory for that, so First Brigade will conduct the aforesaid 'surgical strike.'" He looked at Colonel Dvorak, whose battalion had been tasked to lead the attack. "You'll whip out your chainsaws and break through their defenses with an old-school 'shock and awe' attack designed to penetrate to the habitat rings where their civilians are sheltering. While executing this attack, I expect you to max-imize the shock factor you apply to the defenders—we want to scare the *shit* out of them when they realize what we *could* do to their civilians—but at the same time, you have to pull up short of actually inflicting any humanly avoidable civilian casualties. No one expects that to be easy, but you're Space Marines—*my* Space Marines—which means I know you can do it, anyway." He cocked his head. "Is that clear?"

"Well, Colonel?" It was Ascaso's turn to look at Dvorak. "Your people are carrying the spear on this, so do you want to take that one?"

"Aye, aye, Ma'am." Dvorak stood and faced Wilson.

"I believe the correct response is *crystal* clear, Sir," he said, then turned to the audience.

"You heard the General, people," he said. "We will overwhelm the Puppy defenders with a massive offensive strike that penetrates *to* the civilian enclave but does not actually *breach* it and kill anyone inside it. We will *hammer* them on the way through, so there's no question in their minds about our capabilities. No question that they've 'made' us prove we can kill them anytime we want and they can surrender *honorably* under their Jukaris code." He gazed penetratingly at his company commanders and senior enlisted. "That means we need your people to be as violent as possible, but *under control at all times,* so that when you get to the civilians, you can turn it off again."

Dvorak looked back to his uncle. "Does that sound about right, Sir?"

"It does," Wilson replied, and Dvorak nodded and sat back down.

"You heard the Colonel," Ascaso said with a crooked smile. "We'll spend the next couple of hours tearing the existing plan apart, looking for ways to punch up those aspects. I want the General's 'tweaks' integrated by the end of the day. Tomorrow, we'll run through it in the simulators. I don't expect we'll need to make any enormous changes. It's going to be more a matter of emphasis than anything else, I suspect, but let's make sure of that. And then let's make sure everyone in your units understands the revised plan and the rules of engagement we'll be operating under. Dismissed!"

T he brief really doesn't prepare you for the actuality of the thing," Major Robert Read said from his station at the back of the *Starfire* assault shuttle's cockpit. "I mean, sure, the *Relentless* is bigger, but as a target to assault . . . it makes me glad I'm not a Space Marine."

"You should see it out the front canopy," the lead pilot, Colonel Jeff Payton, replied. "It looks even bigger in real life."

Read switched to the view from one of the drones. The station was immense. A spindle and ring construction, it had a fifteen-kilometer-long central "spindle" portion with twelve spars, each about three hundred meters in diameter, that extended out to the two habitat rings. The inner edges of those rings were five and a half kilometers and seven kilometers, respectively, from the spindle. Each of them was half a kilometer across, and the pressurized spars extended through them, coupling them together so they rotated at the same rate. The rings completed about a third of a revolution a minute; the Puppies in the outermost ring experienced a homeworld-normal 1.0 g, while those in the inner ring experienced only about 0.79 g.

The spindle itself—aside from the band to which the spars mounted—didn't rotate. It was also three kilometers in diameter and held all the habitat's zero-g and microgravity industrial processes. The power generation and repair shops for the rest of the habitat were also located there, but recycling, hydroponics, and water purification were dispersed throughout the habitat rings. No one wanted the critical life systems concentrated in one spot where a single accident could have unfortunate consequences.

The spindle also held the habitat's hangar/shuttle bays, one of which was the *Starfires'* target. Permanently depressurized, the bays were fitted with "boarding tubes" that mated the incoming transports to the station's entrance galleries, the same way human airports of the previous century had used motorized walkways that extended to the aircraft once they'd parked, although these boarding tubes could be pressurized. The station also had larger, pressurizeable hangars designed to allow "shirt-sleeve" maintenance work, but the assault hadn't targeted them, since explosively decompressing them would have caused unnecessary damage and wastage of equipment.

"Of course," the copilot, Major Stan Jacobsen, noted, "if you look out the side windows, we have an awful lot of combat power headed toward it. I don't think I've ever seen this many *Starhawks* in formation before."

"Or this many *Starfires*, for that matter," Payton added.

Read nodded to himself. Each of the Expeditionary Force's five infantry brigades had been permanently assigned five of the massive assault craft—three to carry each of its three infantry battalions into combat, one to transport its attached drone battalion, and a spare. *Because even the PAF's equipment still breaks sometimes, especially once the troops get hold of it,* he thought. *Of course, our stuff doesn't break very often, anymore, but it does happen. And even if it doesn't, there's always enemy action to worry about. . . .*

This was the closest he'd ever seen to having all twenty-five of Brigadier Ascaso's First Brigade's birds deployed at the same time, though. Twenty-two of the craft were currently in space: fifteen loaded with infantry, five loaded with the specialized drones designed for combat inside spacecraft and habitats, plus two spares. According to plans, only two of 1st Brigades' battalions would be committed to the initial attack; the others were there for support, to reinforce if they turned out to be needed, and to execute what General Wilson had dubbed Operation Woodpecker if and when it was needed. If it turned out Woodpecker wasn't needed to support 1st and 2nd Battalion, the other battalions could be released for additional pre-planned attacks, if they were required.

At the moment, all of them held station, well beyond the habitat's limited defensive envelope, waiting for orders from Hawk One, the *Oracle*-class *Starlander* conversion configured to serve the old AWACS function for the Planetary Union Armed Forces.

"All units, Hawk One." Major Branson Gillespie's "voice" came over the circuit, transmitted direct to the flight crews' minds with the preposterous clarity possible only with neural links. "We are go for Can Opener. All Hawks, execute Iron Hand."

"Iron Hand Leader copies."

The response came back with the same crystalline clarity and the massed *Starhawks* headed toward the target, opening a gap between them and the assault force.

Read watched the link as the fighters neared the massive habitat. Although no one really expected the Puppies to send their assault shuttles out to play with the Terrans—especially after the pasting the defensive platforms had taken from Admiral Mallard's attack—that hadn't stopped the fighter pilots from hoping they would.

But the *Starhawks*—to their pilots' presumed annoyance—made it almost the entire way to the habitat without encountering a single Puppy shuttle. Which wasn't to say there was *no* resistance, however. Unlike the system defense platforms, Habitat One mounted no offensive weapons, but it did have a variety of short-range "sprint mode" point-defense missiles, autocannon, and lasers to protect it from meteorites, space debris, and any stray ordnance that made it past the defense platforms.

That was why *Starhawks*—like *Starfires*—carried drones, though. They were waiting, and as the facility's defensive stations illuminated the incoming fighters, the drones detected the emitters, localized them, and then destroyed them—and the weapons they controlled—with a combination of railgun, laser, and missile fire. The defensive systems had never really been hardened against attack, since they were purely secondary "insurance" for the *real* defenses aboard the defense platforms, and the entire "Iron Hand" flak suppression mission took barely ten minutes from the moment the first system spun up. Then, their mission complete, the *Starhawks* retreated to a safe distance to provide overwatch for the incoming *Starfires*.

"Hawk One, Iron Hand," the strike leader announced. "The road is clear."

"Hawk One copies," Gillespie acknowledged. "Break. Can Opener One, you are cleared to begin your run."

"Can Opener One copies, clear to begin our run," Payton replied, then looked over his shoulder with a tight grin. "Well, Rob, looks like it's our turn," he said. "You ready?"

Ready? I haven't been this scared since my first flight in the simulator doing emergency procedures training, Read thought.

One of the "goods" of being the shuttlewing commander's favorite weapons system operator was getting to go cool places with him. One of the "bads" was that it also meant being the lead *Starfire* in any assault, as Payton was very much a "lead from the front" kind of officer.

"Uh, yes, Sir," he said. Then he added, his voice a little stronger, "I'm all set; let's do it!"

"Here we go then," Payton said, and keyed his link to the *Oracle*. "Can Opener One is rolling," he announced, and pushed the throttles forward to their maximum.

"Hang on," he said over the intercom to the troops in the back. "We're making our run."

The lead *Starfires* surged forward, and Read steered one of his drones to take a peek at the target hangar bay as the last *Starhawk* moved out of the way. Not surprisingly, it was empty; they'd already known the station had sent the majority of its shuttles to the planet to keep them out of the inevitable human assault's path. The ones that remained—due to either maintenance issues or simply running out of time—had been pulled to the back of the hangar to give the defense teams clear fields of fire.

One of the Puppies manning a crew-served weapon pointed at the drone, and his team tried to take it under fire, but Read jerked it out of the way and then locked it to the skin of the station out of the defenders' sights for the moment. He'd gotten what he needed: high-quality imagery of the interior of the hangar bay.

"Looks like four—no, make that six—defensive stations inside the back of the hangar bay," he said, eyes closed as he digested sensor data over his neural link and his computers updated the wire diagram of the bay with threat icons. "I make that as four infantry autocannon and two heavy machine guns. Two of the cannon are mounted on what would be the 'ceiling' as we approach."

The concepts of floor and ceiling were tactically meaningless in micro gravity, but they still offered a useful means of orientation.

"I don't think the machine guns can crack our armor," Payton said. "The autocannon, though. . . ."

"Yeah, they have to go," Read agreed. "I'll get them first." He sent the targeting commands. "Drones are out, positioned, and targeted. Ready, sir!"

Read glanced at the link again. Any sense of apprehension was gone. He was too busy to be scared as the assault shuttles surged toward their target. They continued to maintain good positioning on the approach, although twelve of the shuttles would halt just outside the inner zone, waiting to see how 1st and 2nd Battalions' attacks went. His attention rotated back to his mental display of his target—the closest hangar, which was slowly coming into view as they rounded the spindle. The computer models assured him he had it timed right and would get there exactly on schedule.

"Coming up on braking maneuver . . . now!" Payton called.

"Beginning the assault," Read replied, even as *Starfires* flipped end-over-end, facing *away* from their destination, and decelerated at almost two hundred gravities. A perceived three gravities got through even human-tweaked inertial compensator fields, and Read grunted as it hit. But his concentration, totally focused through his neural link on controlling the drones, never wavered.

He sent the attack signal, and three of his prepositioned drones lifted off the skin of the facility and threw themselves into the hangar bay.

"Firing!"

The first two drones launched missiles at the autocannon hanging from the "ceiling" while the third dashed in to assault the concentration of defenders on the "floor." It launched one of its missiles then the picture from it went blank as one of the autocannon pounded it to scrap. The other two drones died almost as quickly, but both of them got their second missiles launched before they were destroyed.

He got his first direct look into the hangar as Payton flipped the *Starfire* once more and hit the bow thrusters hard to kill the last of their velocity and spin them toward the entrance. The assault shuttle's chin railgun was already tracking to starboard as they actually entered the hangar bay, and the shuttle quivered as Read triggered a five-round burst of 20mm high-explosive rounds. His flight computers automatically used the *Starfire*'s normal-space drive to compensate for the cannon's recoil, and his fire pulped the Puppies manning the last machine gun.

Their pieces floated away from the remains of their weapon, and he swept the targeting scope around all five sides of the hangar bay.

"Clear!" he announced. "Move 'em out!"

"Yes, Sir!" Payton said and called to the troops in the back, "Ten seconds! Ramp's in motion!"

Pink! Pink! Pink! Pink!

What sounded like hail on a tin roof echoed through the *Starfire* as it touched down, and Payton locked the struts to the deck of the hangar bay.

"All ashore who's going ashore," he called. "Watch out for several shooters with small arms scattered throughout the bay."

There wasn't much Read could do with the *Starfire* attached to the deck, but he swung the craft's railgun back and forth, looking for targets as the troops in the back—the battalion's infantry weapons company—engaged their boots' magnetic soles and pounded down the ramp in their M4 "Bangalore" suits. Configured for close assault—typically, breaching operations like this one—the Bangalores' armor was much heavier and more difficult to penetrate than a standard Heinlein. They were equipped with heavier weapons, as well, which, combined with the Bangalore's greater weight and more robust built-in jets, drove up the suit's power requirements. That resulted in a significantly shorter time between power cell replacements—less than eight hours in combat like that in which they were engaged—but for all intents and purposes, Bangalores were the next best thing to vampires for invulnerability.

Motion caught Read's eye as a door opened and a space-suited Puppy popped out of it with a shoulder-fired rocket launcher. Read swung the gun around, already firing, and walked it across the defender. When he released the trigger, he winced; there was nothing left but mist.

"Empty!" Jacobsen called. "Ramp's coming up!"

"We're out of here," Payton said. The *Starfire* lifted and surged backward toward the hangar bay exit on a heavy burst from the bow thrusters.

Below them, a rocket zipped out from one of the passageways to slam into one of the advancing M4s. The rocket hit the trooper in the chest and blew him backward to bounce off the wall. Read shook his head, sure that he'd just seen the first casualty of the assault, but then the suit's jets came on. The trooper stabilized, latched his boots back onto the deck, and fired his 25mm Naja railgun. The rocketeer was torn to shreds.

Read shook his head as the *Starfire* raced out into space. The Puppies were lucky the station was so big; it might give them places to hide from the Terran troopers. Otherwise, they were going to find themselves very dead, very quickly.

. . . . .

"ARE YOU OKAY, Avila?" Malachi Dvorak asked as the trooper—designated as PFC Santos Avila in his neural link-driven "HUD"—destroyed the Puppies who'd had the temerity to fire a rocket at an M4 "Bangalore" suit. The modified Heinlein suit lacked the standard armor's "Snapshot" railgun in its powered shoulder mount, but it was far more heavily armored. Its design was uncompromisingly optimized for the assault role, and Dvorak had known the Bangalores were tough—they'd been designed to be as close to impervious as possible to the best infantry-portable antitank weapons in the captured Shongair data files—but they'd never before been tested in actual combat, and shrugging off a direct rocket strike was still pretty damned impressive. Even more impressive than the return fire of a Naja, which had almost completely evaporated the team of defenders.

"Yes, Sir," the weapons company trooper replied. "Might have cracked a rib and I've got an amber alert on my chest plate, but I'm good to go. These Bangalores are tough."

"No kidding," Dvorak said as the last of the *Starfires* cleared the bay. Red smears on the rear bulkhead and the occasional drifting droplet of Shongair blood were all that remained of the defenders. While particularly effective at breaching defenses, neither the big railguns on the shuttles nor the M4s left much to interrogate, which was unfortunate. The Puppies—not surprisingly—had evacuated as many of their civilians as they could in the time they'd had. There were still a *lot* of them aboard the platform, and the Space Marines expected them to be in the outer ring. He hoped to hell the Puppies had been smart enough to do that, anyway, but actually knowing where they were hiding would both have made his job easier and helped to keep those civilians safer.

Of course, there were a *lot* of things that would have made his job easier.

Colonel Mihail's Intelligence people had put together the best information they could on the habitat's internal geography, but it was . . . limited, to say the least. Not even human-tweaked Hegemony tech could see through solid hulls. Especially not when those hulls were specifically designed to protect their interiors from extra-atmospheric radiation hazards. They'd carefully analyzed every scrap of data they *did* have, though, and that analysis suggested the next phase of the assault was about to turn difficult. The only paths to the spars connecting the central spindle to the habitat rings lay through heavily concentrated industrial zones, where ranges and firing lines would both be short. Probably *very* short. The specialized drones with which the assault force had been provided would help—a lot—with some of that, but they had to be gotten into position the hard way, first. And that meant doing way too much of 1st Battalion's entire job "the hard way."

Speaking of which. . . .

"Gold One, Silver One," he said, shifting his neural link to the Brigade net.

"Gold One," Brigadier Ascaso responded. "What do you have, Malachi?"

"We're inside. First objective secured. No casualties so far. Heading for the Phase One objectives now."

"Sounds good, Silver One. Go get 'em."

"We'll do that little thing, Ma'am. Silver One, clear."

Dvorak switched back to the tactical net.

"Master Sergeant Kim!" he said to the weapons company's senior enlisted.

"Yes, Sir!"

Dvorak pointed down the passageway to the closest spoke, trying hard not to look at the remains of the Puppies drifting behind the smashed barricade in front of it. "We've still got about seven kilometers to go today, and we're not getting any closer to our target. Lead us out."

"Right away, Sir!"

· · · · ·

"THEY'RE INSIDE, DIVISION Commander," Thyrack-ir-Gowan's tactical officer reported grimly.

Thyrack flicked his ears in acknowledgment. He hadn't really needed the report. He'd watched the "humans'" initial assault live on the visual feed and his own display showed a wire diagram of the portion of the enormous habitat surrounding the boat bays through which that assault had come as the scarlet icons of hostile infantry moved steadily deeper into it.

The enemy was clearly taking out active sensor nodes as he came, but Habitat One was liberally provided with traffic cameras, police data points, and even the security cameras of civilian commercial and industrial facilities. They were tied together by hardwired data conduits in the habitat's smart walls, so there was no broadcast for the humans to jam—or detect, for that matter. And taking that datanet down would require the physical destruction of the bulkheads through which it ran. So Thyrack felt confident he'd be able to see far more of what was going on behind the invaders' point formations than the enemy commander would like.

Not that he expected it to do him a great deal of good.

He turned to the com display at his right elbow, touched the screen, and looked down as System Commander Brath appeared on it.

"Division Commander," Brath acknowledged. "I assume the humans have landed on the habitat?"

"They have." Thyrack's ears nodded. "And this is going to be even worse than we expected, System Commander," he continued with grim, unflinching honesty. "I know we all expected it to be bad, given what their ships did to the Navy, but I'm afraid our most pessimistic assumptions were actually overly *optimistic*."

Brath's ears folded closer to his skull and Thyrack inhaled deeply.

"They've effected two hull breaches. The good news is that they went for two of our boat bays rather than just blasting holes in the skin, so it *looks* like they're trying to avoid explosive decompression. Whether that's for their own tactical purposes or to limit civilian casualties is unknown, but at this stage I'm prepared to settle for whatever blessings come our way.

"The *bad* news is that we didn't even slow their initial assault teams down. They have some sort of small armed shuttles or deep space fighters, and they used them to blow a path straight through our point defense stations for their actual troop transports. They suppressed all of our missile launchers and exterior autocannon, and then they used some sort of armed drones to clear the bays of defenders." His ears shrugged. "We always knew they could bring in enough firepower to sweep them, so I never expected to hold them, but I did expect the teams I had covering them to inflict at least some casualties. They didn't."

"None?" Brath's ears flicked in astonishment.

"None," Thyrack confirmed. "Let me show you something."

He tapped a screen, and Brath's eyes narrowed as the imagery captured by a boat bay camera appeared on his own display in Planetary Defense Headquarters in the mountains above the city of Chymarth. The bulkhead-mounted camera looked out across the bay's interior from behind a squad of infantry in armored vac suits. The troopers were dug in behind a parapet made of krystar plates from Habitat One's printers, covering one of the boat bay's access passages. Their parapet was pierced with firing ports and thick enough to stop anything short of a heavy antiarmor rocket, and the autocannon farther out into the bay were protected at least as well.

The troopers crouched behind the barricade, peering intently through their firing ports. Then they stiffened, and Brath watched over their heads as three drones—far smaller than the Shongairi's own Type Three Drone, but armed, which the Type Three wasn't—popped into the camera's field of view. They came from every angle, darting into the boat bay on widely separated vectors. They clearly knew where their targets were before they appeared, though, and their fire was deadly accurate. Thyrack's infantry, including the squad directly in front of the camera, was fast. They fired with desperate speed as the drones appeared, and despite the drones' evasive vectors, the waiting autocannon managed to destroy most of them.

But fast as the Shongairi had been, they hadn't been fast enough. Every one of those drones got off at least one shot of its own before it was destroyed, and the weight of that incoming fire simply blotted away the dug-in autocannon. Some of the rockets they launched punched straight through the gunners' krystar parapets with contemptuous ease. Others popped up and then dove sharply, exploding behind the barricades. And when they were done, the autocannon had vanished.

That was bad enough. What followed was worse.

A human shuttle swept into the bay. It was larger than the Shongairi's own *Deathwing*, but it was obviously an *assault* shuttle, because it was heavily armed. Its external ordnance racks were laden with still more of the drones, but it disdained to launch them. Instead, its chin-mounted autocannon tracked and fired with deadly precision as the rifle-armed infantry and machine gunners deployed to support the autocannon gunners tried to engage the enemy troopers spilling from the shuttle's hatches into the airless bay's microgravity.

Shongair rifle fire and machine gun bullets bounced and skipped from the shuttle's armor like so many raindrops. Brath wasn't surprised by that; he'd assumed it would be at least as heavily armored as a *Death-wing*. But—

"*Cainharn*," the System Commander muttered under his breath as the first human trooper touched down and its boots locked to the hangar bay deck. It was bigger than he'd expected from the imagery of the human Dvorak's message, bulkier, and his ears flattened even tighter to his skull as he realized that was because the humans' infantry armor was quite different from its Shongair equivalent. There appeared to be two different versions of it, one that looked heavier than the other and lacked what looked like some sort of powered shoulder weapon that its lighter companions mounted.

The humans spread out with smooth efficiency, obviously well trained in microgravity tactical movement, and they were massively armed, with weapons no Shongair could have carried. Indeed, some of them carried individual handheld weapons larger than any Shongair! They were in microgravity at the moment, of course, and Brath would have liked to believe that was the only reason they could manage such massive weapons. But he knew it wasn't. Unlike his own troopers, their armor obviously incorporated powered exoskeletons, and his blood chilled as he contemplated what that might mean for their individual lethality.

He saw some of that lethality in action as the human infantry returned fire on Thyrack's riflemen and machine gunners. The shoulder-mounted weapons of the lighter-looking armor snapped into firing position, swiveling like lightning, acquiring targets, and fired with deadly precision. The krystar armor stopped the humans' fire, but quite a few of the incoming rounds found firing ports, ripped through them, and wreaked havoc. There were too many of those freakishly accurate shots for them to be simple luck or coincidence, and Brath wondered numbly what sort of fire control system could pinpoint such tiny targets with such murderous accuracy in the midst of a savage firefight.

It got worse.

Even as their shoulder-mounted weapons fired, some of the more heavily armored humans raised rifles—"rifles" that were over a tarn long, for Dainthar's sake!—in a more conventional firing stance, stabilized their firing positions by locking their boots to the deck, and added their catastrophic weight to the fire, turning Thyrack's defenders into bloody pulp.

Brath bared his canines in a snarl of shock as half the squad directly in front of the camera disappeared in an explosive fountain of blood and shredded tissue. Those "rifle" rounds were bigger—and far more destructive—than those of the Shongair autocannon which had tried to oppose their arrival! Some of them actually drilled right through the krystar parapets and exploded behind them!

Yet the Shongair defenders stood fast against the murderous assault. Brath watched in mingled pride and heartsick despair as his troopers fired back, even as they watched their fire ricochet from the humans' armor. They must have known as well as Brath did that they stood no chance of stopping the assault, but they refused to yield, to withdraw.

And then a corner of the camera's field of view expanded, zooming in on a side passage as a single trooper popped out of it with a Type One rocket launcher. He must have been crouched there, hidden, waiting for his opening. Now he pushed into the open, sailing across the mouth of the passage on an arc which might—*might*—take him back into cover . . . if he lived long enough. His launcher was already aimed, though, and he fired before any of the humans could target him.

Brath's heart leapt as the rocket streaked across the bay. The Type One's shaped charge warhead was heavy enough to take out almost any armored vehicle in the Imperial Army's inventory! Surely—

It impacted squarely on its target's chest with perfect, flawless accuracy. It detonated in a blinding flash, and the armored human flew backward under the force of the explosion. It slammed into a bulkhead behind it . . . and then its feet hit the deck again, its enormous "rifle" snapped up into firing position, and the trooper who'd fired disintegrated as a vicious burst of explosive rounds reduced him to bloody gruel.

And the human's armor wasn't even scuffed.

The imagery disappeared, replaced by Division Commander Thyrack's face, and Brath waved his ears in slow, stunned disbelief.

"You see what I meant about our optimism, System Commander?" Thyrack asked with bitter humor. The sort of humor available only to someone facing his worst nightmare.

"I do," Brath acknowledged.

"Now that they've left the boat bays and crossed the hangar decks, our engagement ranges are a lot shorter," Thyrack continued. "So are theirs, though. From what I'm hearing so far, our fire's proving at least a little more effective, and we're compiling all the data from our camera systems and internal sensors. I'm forwarding it to you as it comes in. Hopefully, our analysts can at least identify the humans' most vulnerable firing aspects for us.

"In the meantime, I suspect their commanders are analyzing the situation just as fast and hard as we are. At the moment, they've restricted themselves to only two of the hangar bays. It looks like one force is advancing on Arm Seven while the other makes for Arm Eight. I'm deploying some of my reserves to bolster both Regiment Commander Ursahl and Regiment Commander Youna. But they've got enough shuttles, assuming all of them are comparably loaded, for at least another twelve of strikes just like this one. I'm afraid they're hoping to force me to commit my reserve—maybe even thin out the defenses on some of the other boat bays—before they launch a general assault. And they're probably watching the battle, updating their own tactical appreciations, while they wait."

"You may well be right. In fact, you probably are." Brath flicked his ears in unhappy agreement. "All you and your troopers can do is your best, Division Commander, and I know you will. Much as I would prefer to be able to offer you assurance of our people's ultimate victory, I can't. But this much I *can* promise: your names will never be forgotten, and the data and experience your warriors are dying to attain will be put to the best use possible when it's Shongaru's turn."

Their eyes locked, and the Division Commander's ears nodded.

"Then go with Dainthar, Thyrack," Brath said softly. "Fight your battle."

"We will, Sir," Thyrack promised grimly, and Brath's display blanked.

. . . . .

"ABOVE YOU!" CORPORAL Konstantin Volkov "shouted" over PFC Stan Johnson's neural link as they entered the industrial facility.

Johnson killed his boots' mag lock and threw himself to the side.

Zzzzzzt!

A stream of autocannon rounds slammed into the deck where he'd just been and ricocheted off like a cloud of angry bees.

Staff Sergeant Gabriel Dubois's shoulder-mounted "Snapshot" railgun followed the caret in her HUD as she searched for—and found—the weapon at the top of the industrial facility. She flexed her armor's knees forward against the recoil, automatically bracing against her own boots' locks, then fired, and the gunner's head exploded like an overripe watermelon struck by a sledgehammer. She panned the targeting indicator to the next Puppy as it tried to take the weapon's grips; its arm went spinning off to the side. A third Shongair soldier stepped up, but by then all the platoon was firing, and the Puppy team was obliterated.

The Space Marines stopped shooting—fire discipline was hammered into them from the first day of recruit training—and Dubois shook her head at both the senseless destruction of the Puppy heavy weapons team and the near loss of one of her troopers.

"Johnson, you stupid asshole! You just forget *everything* you ever learned about zero-gee?! Jesus!"

Johnson stood back up—cautiously. He locked his boots again and edged out from the shelter of the building corner behind which he'd found cover. It had protected him against the Puppies' fire. The staff sergeant's wrath was a bit harder to evade.

"In case you forgot—which you obviously *did*—up and down don't matter *squat* here! Even in a gravity well, you have to remember to check all over!" she continued. "But in zero-gee? The enemy can be fucking *anywhere!*" Dubois motioned to the facility—some sort of manufacturing plant where the Shongairi printed large structural pieces in more peaceful times. "If you don't keep your head on a swivel, you're gonna end up *dead* and then *I'm* gonna be stuck with the frigging paperwork and I'm gonna *really* be pissed!"

"The weapons company people said it was empty," Johnson muttered. He was careful not to reply over the neural net, but he'd forgotten that his backup com was up. And that the platoon's CO was monitoring it. Until—

"Oh, yeah?" First Lieutenant Absko Odhiambo asked. On the net, just to be sure everyone got to hear his response in all its sarcastic glory. "If they were *sure* it was empty, genius, then why do you think the Colonel asked us to check it out?"

"Uh . . ." the trooper temporized.

"Because they didn't see anyone in here, but it's not worth wasting their time and battery charge to make sure, when they can stay at the point of the sword and intercept all the incoming fire for *us*. There's a reason *we're* responsible for *their* flank security while they do that, Einstein. And unlike them, *you*—" Odhiambo pointed at the trooper "—have plenty of battery charge you can use to go up there and check it out. Which will also give you a look behind this building so you can make certain for us that this space is indeed 'empty.'"

"Keep a better eye on him this time, Volkov," Dubois put in, turning her glower on Volkov, Johnson's wingman, who looked even more disgusted than she did. The corporal was the more experienced half of the two-trooper "wing" that was the Space Marines' basic tactical unit and he was pretty sure he'd be hearing more about this from Dubois shortly.

"Show him how," Dubois continued. "And *try* to keep him on a shorter leash," she added.

"Come on, Johnson," Volkov growled. "And fer Christ's sake, keep yer eyes *open* this time!"

He gave the PFC a glower of his own, then blipped his jets to soar up to the top of the structure in the hub's microgravity. A chastened Johnson followed.

The facility—with the destruction of the autocannon team—truly was empty now, and the platoon hurried to catch up with the advance. Although the Puppies had evacuated the air from the spindle so the Space Marines couldn't hear the gunfire, the tactical nets were busy with contact reporting from a couple hundred meters down the passageway.

The platoon raced ahead but had to slow and look for an alternate way forward due to a heavy volume of fire coming down the thoroughfare.

"According to the intel," Odhiambo said as they worked their way forward toward where the firefight was continuing, "we're about a third of the way to the spoke. We don't have far to go."

. . . . .

"THEY'RE COMING DOWN Axial Three." The voice in Platoon Leader Ahzarl-ir-Nolar's earphones was preposterously calm. "Hasaar's blocking position slowed them down, but it didn't stop them."

"Third Platoon is only three shrekari out, Ferahl!" Company Commander Urkas's tone was far sharper than Platoon Leader Ferahl's. "They can—"

"Negative, Sir," Ferahl replied. "There's not time. Tell Third to fall back."

Silence hummed in Ahzarl's earphones for perhaps a tiskar. Then—

"Understood," Urkas said quietly. "Dainthar with you, Ferahl."

"And you, Sir."

Ahzarl closed his eyes and felt his ears trying to flatten in grief. His headphones might prevent that, but nothing could lessen the pain in his heart. He and Ferahl might be born of different clans, but they were brothers in blood, sworn companions since secondary school.

"Ahzarl." It was Ferahl. A glance at Ahzarl's visor HUD showed his friend was on their private channel, not the tactical net.

"Yes, Ferahl."

"They're coming even harder than they were," his fellow platoon leader said. "My people aren't going to stop them any more than Hasaar's did, but maybe we can slow them. Your troopers are all behind the yellow line?"

"We are." Ahzarl kept his voice level, though he knew Ferahl could hear the pain in it anyway.

"Their armor's even tougher than we thought it was," Ferahl continued. "Especially the heavy armor they're using to lead their assaults. We've taken down some of their more lightly armored troopers, but one of my fire teams hit one of the heavies head-on with a Type Two. It stopped him—his armor was obviously damaged badly—but he still got back out of our fire zone under his own power."

Ahzarl's skin tightened. The Type Two was the Imperial Army's long-ranged, heavy antitank missile. Using something with its range inside a habitat was the sort of insane tactic no rational Shongair would ever have contemplated . . . normally. But this wasn't a remotely "normal" battle, and Division Commander Thyrack had forward-deployed every weapon he had. There hadn't been a lot of Type Two's in his arsenal, but the ones he did have had been issued to his troopers. Ahzarl had thought that had to be a clear case of overkill—the Type Two had a kill probability of over ninety percent against even the heaviest Shongair armored vehicles at twenty myrtarni, for Dainthar's sake!

He'd seen the visual imagery of the advancing humans, and they'd looked even more alien—and far more terrifying—then they had in their initial message. As he'd watched the imagery of machine gun bullets and even autocannon rounds bouncing off their armor, he'd realized it had to be far tougher than his own troopers'. But not even that accounted for the cold chill he'd felt. They hadn't looked like flesh-and-blood enemies at all. Not as they'd advanced into that hurricane of fire. No, they'd looked far more like . . . like some kind of merciless, unstopping, unstopp*able* robots than like any merely mortal foe. But a direct hit with a Type Two hadn't stopped a single *infantry trooper*?

"Their armor's not as good from the flanks and rear, though." Ferahl was speaking more rapidly now, and the shifting icons on Ahzarl's handheld tactical display told him why. "We took down three of them, including one of their heavies, when one of my antitank squads got around behind them. I'm pretty sure at least one of them was a hard kill, and at least one of the soft kills was with a Type One, not a Type Two. So they *can* be killed."

"I'll remember that," Ahzarl promised.

"Good!" Ferahl said. Then his voice softened. "Tell Jarys I loved her."

"I will." Ahzarl's own voice cracked on the words, and in that moment, he was unspeakably grateful that unlike his friend, he'd never found the mate of his heart. *And I never will, now, either,* he thought. But he couldn't say it. Not any more than he could remind Ferahl how remote the chance that he'd ever have the opportunity to speak to Jarys for him truly was.

"Thank you. Now I have to go. Frygahr bless."

The com channel closed, and as Ahzarl looked down at the tactical display, he almost imagined he could feel the explosions and kinetic impacts raining down on his heart-brother's troopers vibrating through Habitat One's immense fabric.

Of course, it wouldn't be long before he wouldn't have to *imagine* anything.

He plugged into his platoon's com net.

"Therkak!"

"Yes, Platoon Leader!" Squad Leader Therkak-ur-Karys, Ahzarl's senior squad leader, responded instantly.

"Platoon Leader Ferahl says we can kill them from the flanks or behind. Pass the word."

"Yes, Sir!" Ahzarl heard the satisfaction in Therkak's voice, even though the grizzled veteran had to know how nearly impossible it would be to outflank someone in a confined battlefield barely two myrtarni in diameter. But at least there were plenty of hiding places, and if anyone could do it, Therkak could.

"They're coming down Axial Three," he continued. "They're obviously heading straight for the habitat arms and ignoring the inner axials and anything that heads in-hub. So far, at least. Things may not stay that way if we can slow them down on the axial, though. So keep an eye on our flank protection. I know we're supposed to limit damage as much as we can, but I'd sure as Cainharn rather blow the charges than have them coming up our asses."

"Got it, Sir," Therkak agreed. "I'll keep an eye on that. Personally."

"Good," Ahzarl said. "And tell the cubs they'll be here in a couple of myrtahli," he added more quietly, still watching that hateful display.

. . . . .

"THE 'TERRAIN' IS even worse than we'd expected, Sir," Brigadier Ascaso said. "And we're meeting heavier—well, more *effective*—resistance than we'd expected, too."

"I know. We're keeping an eye on it," Rob Wilson acknowledged. He didn't add how much harder he found that when his nephew's battalion was the lead formation. "Looks like our simulations were a little too optimistic."

"Not even a Bangalore can be made invulnerable to *everything,* Sir," Ascaso pointed out. "We knew that going in."

"I didn't say we were too optimistic about their weapons, Olivia. But you're right about the terrain, and it's pretty clear that even when we started rethinking Can Opener, we didn't allow for just how hard these 'betas' were going to fight. Christ, I wish they'd break! And not just because *we're* losing people."

Ascaso nodded. The Space Marines' losses were minuscule against the Shongairi's casualties. Every one of her sensors, every bit of tactical data, confirmed that. And the Puppies' body armor was just as useless against Terran weapons as they'd anticipated. But the habitat's design meant her battalions' lines of advance lay directly through one of its primary industrial sectors, between massive printers the size of five-story houses and their supporting—and freight moving—systems. That meant there were a lot of confined, narrow, straight-line passages that were natural fire traps.

And watching my niece's husband command our other assault isn't making me feel any better, Wilson thought. *I know they both damn well earned* their battalions, but how I wish Dave and I could have brought ourselves to exercise a little nepotism and keep at least one of them out of this shitfest!

"Second Battalion's terrain is even more cramped," he added to Ascaso. "All those damned storage bins might as well be armored bulkheads or fucking castle walls. At least they cut down on the cross passages and ambush sites, but Second's been basically frontal-assaulting from the get-go."

"We all are, really," Ascaso observed with a humorless smile. "I'm tempted to go ahead and clear Woodpecker."

"Not yet." Wilson shook his head. "I admit, it's tempting as hell. But bad as they hurt, our losses are nowhere near prohibitive yet."

He saw Ascaso's lips tighten on his display, and he couldn't blame her. For all of their tremendous hitting power, PUAF combat formations were extraordinarily small by pre-Hegemony standards. Malachi Dvorak's battalion had only five dead and eleven wounded, but that "only" sixteen represented just over five percent of his total personnel. Second Battalion had taken only nine casualties so far, but that was going to get worse as Raymond Lewis's people pushed deeper into the tight confines of the resource storage area.

"I'm not going to Woodpecker any sooner than we have to," he continued. "It's our psychological sledgehammer. We need to save it until the Puppies know their civilians are at risk."

Ascaso's nostrils flared, but she only nodded, and Wilson nodded back almost compassionately. And he knew why she'd brought it up in the first place. Olivia Ascaso was about as far from indecisive as an officer came, and she knew as well as he did why Woodpecker was off the table—so far, at least. Knew why it had to be saved, held in reserve. But the tactician in her, the officer who knew her casualty counts were only going to climb as her people continued hammering straight ahead, wished that it didn't. It wasn't at all surprising that she felt that way. And if bringing it up, letting Wilson be the one who told her she couldn't use it yet, let her focus her anger and regret on someone else, that was fine with him. It was one of the things that came with his stars.

"Understood, Sir," she said now, tightly. "I'll keep you advised."

"I know you will. Wilson, clear."

• • • • •

"KEEP YOUR HEAD *down,* goddamn it!" Staff Sergeant Eldridge Macadoo's mental "voice" sizzled across the neural link as the Puppy rocket ripped past Lieutenant Zakharovna's helmet. It missed her by perhaps four centimeters, then exploded against a bulkhead, silent in the vacuum, followed by Macadoo's belated "Ma'am" as Zakharovna flung herself to her left, flat on the deck behind one of the Puppy switching station's transformers.

It wasn't a whole hell of a lot of cover, but it was better than nothing.

"Stay there!" Macadoo sounded calmer, and she watched her mental HUD as 2nd Platoon's senior noncom—and Zakharovna's wing—sidled carefully to his own right. He paused for a moment, and then his shoulder-mounted Snapshot spat out a vicious, three-round burst.

"Clear," the staff sergeant said after a moment. "But *watch* that shit, LT! You scared the *hell* out of me."

"Sorry, Eldridge. I guess I was . . . distracted."

Macadoo didn't comment on her excuse, but he really didn't have to. Neural link communication was incredibly fast, incredibly accurate, and often carried "sideband" emotional overtones. That was especially true under stressful circumstances—like, oh, the ferocity of a firefight—and Macadoo's unspoken sniff came through quite clearly.

Intellectually, Zakharovna couldn't blame the staff sergeant. His job was one of the tougher ones in 2nd Platoon. Alyson Zakharovna might lead the platoon, but Eldridge Macadoo was the one who actually *ran* it, and in combat, he was also the one tasked with keeping her ass alive and un-shot so that she *could* lead it. Between the two of them, they represented the platoon's cohesion and direction, and ideally it was their job to stay far enough back they could provide it.

Sometimes, though. . . .

She checked her HUD again. Then—

"Collier!"

"Yo, Skipper?" Lance Corporal Andreas Collier replied instantly.

"Move left and up. There's an overhang at your ten o'clock high." She dropped an icon into the shared platoon tactical plot. "You and Casey take overwatch till we get Branigan and JayCee unstuck."

"On it," Collier acknowledged.

"Better move than that do-it-yourself crap, Skip," Macadoo sent her over their private side channel, and she was forced to agree. Which didn't make her feel any better as autocannon fire continued to rip away at the short wall—it looked like some sort of ornamental afterthought, which seemed even more alien than usual in the middle of an industrial site—behind which Corporal Takamasa Branigan and his wing, Jack "JayCee" Clements had taken cover. The cannon fire didn't really worry her; even their standard Heinlein raider armor could stand up to Puppy autocannon all day long. But Zakharovna had already lost Jannik Gregersen and Anastasia Beckman to rocket fire—although Anastasia was "only" WIA, thank God. That was twenty percent of 2nd Platoon's roster strength, and she didn't intend to lose any more Space Marines.

Which might explain why she'd almost gotten her own inattentive ass killed trying to reach a position from which *she* could cover them, although it sure as hell didn't *excuse* it.

"Okay," she continued on the platoon net as Collier and his wing, Casey Talmage, worked their way towards her icon. "Once Collier and Talmage are in position, I want Lennox and Macchione to move *right*. Those assholes with the rocket launchers are in that cross passage at our eight o'clock." She dropped another icon into the plot. "They're trying to pop us from the rear. So I want suppressive fire from the two of you."

Corporal Lennox, the senior member of Zakharovna's number four wing, flashed her icon on the plot in acknowledgment.

"Once Lennox and Macchione have them under fire, you pop a couple of Widows in there, Trevithick."

"Getting thin on the ground, Ma'am," Corporal Casper Trevithick replied.

He was the platoon's drone specialist, and Zakharovna grimaced at his (relatively) tactful reminder. Their supply of combat drones hadn't been unlimited to begin with, and they'd been expending them at a higher—*much* higher—rate than projected. Unlike her troopers, they were only very lightly armored, and the Puppies were faster learners than the intelligence pukes had predicted, based on their lack of adaptability during the invasion. They didn't have anything like the PUAF's armed drones, but they'd figured out what was happening, and they were damned good shots. They'd picked off a *lot* of Trevithick's drones and the corporal was down to his last half dozen or so. When they were gone, they were gone, unless the transport element could get a resupply forward. Which was . . . unlikely, to say the least. But she'd a hell of a lot rather use them up than expend her Space Marines.

"That's why Collier's laying down suppressive fire," she told Trevithick. "Hopefully, it'll keep the bastards' heads down till you get the Widows in on them." She twitched her head in the equivalent of a Heinlein-armored Space Marine's shrug. "Best shot we've got."

"Yes, Ma'am. Prepping them now."

"Strobe your icon when you're ready."

"You got it, LT."

Good thing it's a cross passage, not on our line of advance, Zakharovna thought.

"Lennox, as soon as the Widows go in, I want you and Macchione moving straight ahead," she continued over the neural link. "Kuba, I want you and Török—" they were her number three wing, now that Gregersen and Beckman were down "—holding position and watching their right flank. Any questions?"

No one's icon flashed, and she nodded to herself.

"All right, people!" she said. "Let's get this done."

· · · · ·

"THEY'RE COMING IN on us!" the wrong voice shouted in Therkak-ur-Karys's headset. It should have been Platoon Leader Ahzarl's; instead, it was Squad Leader Hirahk's.

And the only possible reason that it wasn't Ahzarl's was. . . .

"The Platoon Leader's dead!" Hirahk continued. "They're making for—"

The other squad leader chopped off into silence, and Therkak's ears flattened. He looked around the compartment at the surviving members of his own squad, saw the same recognition in their eyes, in *their* flattened ears.

"Squad Leader?" It was Chyrsak-dur-Hyra, Therkak's senior trooper, and Therkak looked up from his small, handheld display.

"We stay right here," he said grimly, twitching his helmeted head at the display. It was hardwired to the habitat's internal sensor net and he watched the invaders' advance formation slow as it broke through 1st Platoon's final positions . . . and ran into Platoon Leader Kairyl's forward autocannon twenty tarni farther along Axial Three. "Their point formation is Third Platoon's problem now, and this is where the Platoon Leader put us, watching Platoon Leader Kairyl's flank."

. . . . .

"WE'RE AT ALPHA Two," Lance Corporal Cruise announced over the neural link as he pushed another drifting Shongair body out of his path. "All clear so far—nothing but dead Puppies. We're approaching the side corridor now."

"Copy that," Staff Sergeant Takakuwa, the platoon's first sergeant, acknowledged. "Watch your ass."

"You got *that* right," Cruise acknowledged. He nodded to Private George Moore, his wing, then ducked into the cross passage the platoon had bypassed on its original advance. It was much narrower than the main passage—it appeared to be intended more for personnel than for heavy freight loads—which made it too cramped for the M4s leading the attack. The Space Marines hadn't exactly ignored it on their way through, though, especially after they took fire from it, and half a dozen more dead Puppies floated where railgun fire and grenades had left them.

Even if it had been broad enough for them, the support platoon of Bangalores assigned to Baker Company was otherwise occupied at the moment, tied down in a fresh, vicious firefight farther down the main passage through this warren of industrial printers and transport belts. The Puppies had clearly moved in reinforcements to support the prepared positions covering the passage, and they'd brought more of those frigging heavy rocket launchers with them, damn it. The PUAF had found out the hard way that not even an M4 Bangalore could stop multiple rocket hits. And even when the armor held, kinetic transfer energy could produce some nasty injuries.

Lieutenant McNamara, the support platoon's CO, had already lost one entire three-man "Naja" team—and a pair of WIA from two of his remaining five teams—as part of the process of discovering their Bangalores weren't invulnerable. Under the circumstances, he was less than enthusiastic about punching straight down a thirty-meter, straight-line passage into multiple Puppy autocannon and heavy rocket launchers. Which was why Lance Corporal Cruise and Private Moore had backtracked to probe ever so cautiously for an alternate route that might let Baker Company flank the damned Puppies for a change.

Cruise didn't much care for the potential surprises of the more constricted corridor, and its small, Puppy-scaled dimensions meant trying to use it for their main advance would have been a nightmare. But if they could sneak around and come in *behind* the hard blocking position the Puppies had put together to stop McNamara's people, he was all for it. Of course, he was even more in favor of not getting Martha Cruise's little boy Michael killed in the process.

Moore moved behind and a little above Cruise, walking along a side bulkhead at right angles to the "floor" and taking advantage of the microgravity to gain a firing angle past the lance corporal and up the passage. They passed another couple of dead Puppies in the first few meters, but after that the passage was clear. They made another thirty meters, and then Cruise paused with a grimace.

"Goddamn it," he muttered.

It wasn't the first barricade they'd encountered, but it *was* the first one that completely sealed a passage. Of course, this was a considerably smaller corridor, and at least this barricade didn't include a loophole for an autocannon or a rocket launcher. But it was still welded firmly in place, blocking the entire passage, and it looked damned solid. So much for flanking routes.

He poked at it in disgust, then frowned.

"What?" Moore asked.

"Lookee there." Cruise gestured at the weld that secured one edge of the circular barrier to the bulkhead. "Looks like some substandard work here, doesn't it?"

"Maybe." Moore leaned closer and brought up the magnification setting on his Heinlein's sensors. "You know, I think you could be right." He extended an armored hand and poked at the weld, then whistled soundlessly as all four of his gauntlet's fingers slipped into the gap. "Well, shit. Must've been in a hell of a hurry when they put this in. I could'a *soldered* a better weld than this."

"Then let's just see if we can't bust it loose," Cruise suggested with a grin, and pulled a stubby cylinder off his equipment harness. He prepped the demo charge through his neural link, configuring the shaped charge element carefully. Then he wedged it into the gap Moore's fingers had found and both Space Marines turned their helmet visors away.

"Fire in the hole!" Cruise announced, and sent the command.

There was no atmosphere to transmit blast, but they felt the detonation whiplash through the solid fabric of the habitat. They gave things a moment to settle, then turned back to the barricade.

"Damn," Moore said. The gap was wider, but the barricade was still there.

"Don't be hasty," Cruise replied. He drew his sidearm, aimed it into the gap, and studied the visual image its sighting camera projected onto his HUD. "Looks to me like we sorta shook things up a bit," he announced, reholstering the weapon. "Let's see how well."

Both Space Marines squatted, bracing their armored legs against the bulkhead while they leaned out perpendicular to the passageway and got a good grip. Then they heaved.

Their armor's servos whined. For a second or two, that was all that happened, but a Heinlein-armored Space Marine could have bench pressed a pre-Hegemony quarter-ton pickup truck. An amber warning blinked in the corner of Cruise's vision field as he pushed his exoskeleton's limits, and he grunted in disappointment. They couldn't afford to burn out their servos, so—

The blast-damaged weld sheared so suddenly and abruptly their combined efforts tossed the barricade away from them. If there'd been any atmosphere, the sound as it caromed down the passageway in the microgravity would undoubtedly have been deafening.

"Well, damn," Moore said. "Didn't know my own strength!"

"Yeah, sure!" Cruise shook his head, then opened a link to Lieutenant Ravelino, 1st Platoon's CO.

"LT, we got a little development here," he said, gazing along the dimly lit, empty bore on the other side of the barricade.

. . . . .

"LOOKS LIKE WE'VE hit a compartment boundary bulkhead, LT," Cruise said over the platoon link five minutes later. "We got us a manual hatch. Hinged, with a locking wheel, not a slider like the ones in the main axial. I'm thinking this here's a personnel hatch, not a cargo door. It's not real big, but I think it's doable. For Heinleins, at least."

"Open or closed?" Lieutenant Ravelino asked.

"Partially open," Cruise replied, and he and Moore grimaced at each other.

"We don't need any Trojan horses here, Mike," Ravelino said—rather unnecessarily in Cruise's opinion. "But we do need to find out what we've got. Can you sneak a Keyhole through it without anybody on the other side noticing?"

"Negative." Cruise shook his head, even though he knew Ravelino couldn't see him. "Hatch is maybe three centimeters open. Can't fit a Keyhole through without opening it a little wider, Sir. If they're there, they're bound to see it move."

"Shit," Ravelino growled.

"I can probably nudge it far enough to get the drone through, Sir."

"Go ahead," Ravelino said after a moment. "But be careful! Those drones cost money!"

"Yeah, I know, Sir."

Cruise rolled his eyes at Moore, and the private grinned. Ravelino thought he had a sense of humor, and no one in his platoon had the heart to tell him how wrong he was. And, Cruise conceded, it actually did help—some—at the moment.

"Taking the hatch," he said more seriously, and made a floating, palm-down gesture at Moore with his right hand.

"Sounds good," Moore agreed over their private link, and he and Cruise unlocked their mag boots and leaned forward.

Cruise goosed his boosters and he and Moore moved very cautiously forward, floating belly-down in the microgravity no more than twelve centimeters above the deck. Cruise left flank security to Moore—not a routine job after the way the Puppies' rockets had taken down PFC Willis and Corporal Young—and kept his head up, peering through the cracked hatch into the next compartment.

Cruise used the magnetic tabs on the tips of his armored fingers to brake his forward drift as he neared the hatch. As he'd told Takakuwa and Ravelino, it was a strictly utilitarian personnel hatch. It had never been intended for large objects, and given the Puppies' small size, it would be a tight fit for a Heinlein-armored Space Marine. In fact, the M4s couldn't have squeezed through it at all, but that could be a good thing, under the circumstances. The Puppies had clearly figured out the M4s were leading the human assaults. If they knew a Bangalore couldn't come at them this way, they might be paying less attention to it.

And they might not *be, too,* Cruise reminded himself as he prepped the Keyhole.

He and Moore had each started out with two of the little recon drones, but they were down to only one between them. Which was a pity. The Keyholes were less useful in microgravity than they would have been in a gravity well, because there was nothing for their tiny counter-grav unit to work against. That meant they had to be thrown, rolled, or launched, and that could be hazardous to the user's health if one got careless and there was a Puppy rocketeer in the vicinity. Despite which, they were still one hell of a lot better than sticking a Space Marine's head around a corner to see if anyone shot it off.

The drone was a little larger than a regulation softball—it had to be to incorporate the counter-grav that didn't work here—and they'd found out the hard way that Puppy rifles and autocannon could hit softball-sized targets. That was how Cruise and his wing had lost three-quarters of their drones on the way here, and Cruise kicked himself mentally for not stocking up before they headed out on this little venture.

All you had to do was ask. Worst thing that coulda happened was that no one had any to spare. But, no! You didn't think of it, did you, genius?

"Ready?" he asked over the neural link, and Moore nodded.

The question in Cruise's mind was how best to open that hatch wider.

Punch it hard and kick it all the way open, then fling the Keyhole straight through it and as far as he could? Or ease it gently, just wide enough, hoping any Puppy on the other side might not notice a sufficiently small movement, and then toss the drone through at an angle?

This is a time for subtle, he decided. The Keyhole's 360-degree coverage was pretty damned good. It should give him a clear look at whatever was on the other side. And opening the hatch no wider than he had to in order to fit the drone through would also leave the hatch itself as hard cover against any rifle or machine gun fire—*or frigging rockets,* he thought sourly—waiting in ambush.

He moved up close beside the hinge-side of the hatch, pressing the back of his armor against the bulkhead, and used one hand to ease the hatch gently, gently open *just* far enough. Then he flicked the Keyhole through the gap with his other hand and closed his eyes, concentrating on the imagery feeding from the drone over his neural link.

"Holy shit," he muttered.

⋅ ⋅ ⋅ ⋅ ⋅

"MOVEMENT!" SQUAD LEADER Therkak hissed as an icon blinked on his display. There was no need to whisper, but he couldn't help it.

"Cainharn!" one of his troopers whispered back.

⋅ ⋅ ⋅ ⋅ ⋅

"GOOD TELEMETRY, LT," Cruise announced to Ravelino, "and you ain't gonna believe this."

"Believe what?" Ravelino's mental tone was sharp over the link.

"This passage is a connector between two main axials, Sir. Must be a personnel shortcut. But it opens into another passage pretty much identical to the one we've been following. Except there's not a Puppy in sight."

Ravelino said nothing for a moment, and Cruise could almost feel the lieutenant's brain considering that unlikely report.

"You're saying the passage is completely clear?" he asked after a moment.

"I'm saying it *looks* that way, Sir," Cruise replied. "Take a look."

He shared the Keyhole's feed directly to Ravelino, and the lieutenant swore softly.

The broad passage on the other side of that hatch truly was identical to the one along which Baker Company had fought its bloody way for the last couple of hours. Except that it was totally undamaged, overhead light strips glowing, without a single corpse floating across it.

And without a single Puppy defensive position anywhere in reach of the Keyhole's exquisitely sensitive sensors.

"It's gotta be a trick," Staff Sergeant Takakuwa said.

"I'm inclined to agree," Ravelino said slowly. "But I don't see anything, Kinnojo. And all indications are we're pushing them hard. Cruise and Moore had to break through that barricade just to get there, too."

"You think they pulled anybody they had on this passage in to cover our main line of advance?" Takakuwa sounded skeptical.

"Look at this." Ravelino brought up the schematic the assault force had been building ever since it entered the habitat. It was only a narrow swatch "up" the spindle towards their objective, but it included everything they'd so far passed. Including several regularly spaced side passages like the one Cruise and Moore had just explored. The lieutenant entered a command over his neural link, and the much larger corridor into which the side passage led appeared on it. As much of it as Cruise's Keyhole could see, anyway.

"If this continues in the direction it seems to head," the lieutenant said, "the Puppies may not see it as a threat. It *looks* like it curves inside our line of advance, with no access to the spokes."

"In which case, it's headed the wrong way," Takakuwa pointed out.

"Sure. But so far we've passed four other side passages identical to the one Cruise and Moore just found, all on the 'inside' of our advance and spaced equidistantly. We didn't bother with them because no Puppies were coming out of them, they lead the wrong way, and the Bangalores couldn't squeeze through them. But what if they cross-connect with this other route—" the newly discovered corridor blinked on the schematic "—all the way along our assigned axial? And what if the Puppies know we can't come through that way because they welded all the cross passages shut the same way they did this one?"

Takakuwa's eyes narrowed, and then he nodded slowly.

Ravelino nodded back, then punched up his neural link.

"Captain Dabney, Ravelino."

"Go, Joel," Captain Mary Ellen Dabney, Baker Company's executive officer, replied.

"Ma'am, I don't want to get carried away, but we *may* have just found a side door."

. . . . .

"ALL RIGHT," RAVELINO said, fifteen minutes later. "You two—" he poked an armored index finger at Cruise and Moore "—have done good this far, and I'm not about to fuck around with something that's working. Lead out."

"You're so good to us, LT," Cruise said dryly, then twitched his helmet at his wing. "Come on, George."

The two Space Marines moved cautiously and alertly down the empty, brightly lit passageway. After the carnage of their original line of advance, there was something profoundly unnatural about its pristine, undamaged state. Not that any of 1st Platoon's personnel were about to complain about *that*!

They'd replenished their Keyholes when the rest of the platoon caught up with them, and they tossed the drones ahead of them as they went, closing cautiously up to each of them after it stopped moving, and then "leapfrogging" another farther along the corridor. Ridiculous as it seemed, there was absolutely no sign of the Puppies anywhere, and Cruise turned his head to grin at Moore.

. . . . .

"NOW!" SQUAD LEADER Therkak snarled, and punched the button.

. . . . .

"THE ENTIRE PLATOON'S a write-off, Ma'am," Malachi Dvorak said bitterly. "Lieutenant Ravelino's dead, and the medics don't know if Staff Sergeant Takakuwa's going to pull through. Even if he does, they've got three more dead, seven wounded, and only one wing that's still combat effective."

"What happened?" Olivia Ascaso asked.

"First Platoon walked into an ambush," Major Marconi, Baker Company's CO, grated. "Straight into it. And it's my fault for sending—"

"No, it's *not* your fault," Dvorak interrupted. "I agreed we needed to check it out. And they did everything right, Jamison. You know they did!"

"Then what happened?" Ascaso repeated.

"I don't know if it was a planned ambush or just a way to cover their flanks on the direct route, Ma'am," Dvorak said, "but it looks like the Puppies packed somewhere around three tons of explosives all the way around the perimeter of the passage Ravelino's people found. For what it's worth, I suspect it was a security measure, not a deliberate trap, but I've been back through the take from Ravelino's sensors. There wasn't a sign of it from *inside* the passage, so it had to be on the other side of the bulkheads and overhead. I don't know if it was wired to some passive sensor we didn't pick up, or if it was command detonated, but I'm inclined to think there was a finger on the trigger, because the timing was too damned good. It didn't go off when Ravelino's point team passed it. It detonated when the rest of his platoon moved up into the blast zone."

Malachi Dvorak's blue eyes were dark with the memory of another explosion on a planet called Sarth.

"It was like walking into the middle of a shaped-charge explosion, Ma'am," he said. "Most of the blast was focused inward, but it still blew a hole almost a quarter-kilometer 'deep' that opened an entire quadrant of the spindle to space. The Puppies had already dumped the pressure, and that helped—some. But without their Heinleins, none of them would've made it. Even with them—"

He shrugged bitterly, and Ascaso nodded.

"You may well be right that it was an access-denial move that just got really, really lucky from the Puppies' perspective," she said. "And at least we know to keep an eye out for any repeat performances." She bared her teeth in a humorless smile. "If it looks too good to be true, it probably is. Which doesn't mean you or Major Marconi were wrong to push it."

"Ma'am, we're getting bloodied worse than Can Opener ever visualized. My casualties are over ten percent now, and we're still half a klick from the spoke. I don't want to keep losing people this way. So—"

"I know you don't, Malachi," Ascaso interrupted him. "Neither do I. But we can't use Woodpecker yet. You'll just have to keep going. I'm sending Colonel Tigh's battalion to reinforce. He'll move up behind you, but this is still your show. Plug his people in wherever you need them."

"Yes, Ma'am," Dvorak replied after a moment. "We'll get it done."

"I know you will, Malachi. Ascaso, clear."

. . . . .

"IT'S REGIMENT COMMANDER Ursahl, Sir."

The communications tech's voice was taut. Which was scarcely a surprise, Division Commander Thyrack thought bitterly as he glared at the spreading cankers of crimson spreading like poison from the humans' entry points. The one punching steadily along Axial Three actually touched Arm Seven on the display.

"Put him through," he said, and a musical tone chimed in his earphones. It was almost obscenely bright and cheery under the circumstances.

"Yes, Ursahl?" he said.

"The humans are breaking through along Axial Three, Sir." Ursahl's voice was harsh, and Thyrack heard the urgent flow of combat chatter behind it. "I'm sorry. My troopers are fighting their hearts out, but the humans are into the transfer ring and they hold two of the main freight portals. We still have them pinned down, but we can't hold them much longer."

Thyrack closed his eyes in pain, but scarcely in surprise.

He opened them again, staring at his status boards, and swore with bitter, silent venom as he glared at the icons of human shuttles, still holding station off Habitat One. They weren't doing a single thing . . . except pinning his own forces helplessly in place. He'd already committed his entire reserve to support Ursahl and Regiment Commander Youna; the silent threat of those shuttles was the reason he couldn't commit more.

The offensive punching through Youna's 9th Regiment was making slower progress along Axial Four. That wasn't to say Youna had a prayer of *stopping* the humans, any more than Ursahl did, but at least they'd reach Arm Eight only after the humans had broken into Seven.

For all the good it would do.

"I know your troopers are fighting like heroes, Ursahl," the Division Commander said. "I wish to all the gods I could give you the support they've damn well earned. But—"

"But their shuttles are just waiting for you to strip one of the other docking bays," Ursahl interrupted. "I understand, Sir. All of us do."

Thyrack bared his canines in a challenge snarl directed at fate and

Cainharn Himself. Ursahl had spoken nothing but truth, and the regiment commander's understanding only made Thyrack feel even more helpless. But the humans had finished suppressing all of Habitat One's limited point defenses. They'd sent more of their infernal drones into six of the platform's other boat bays and used them to pick off the fortified defensive positions inside them. He had only a single battalion to cover each of those bays, and more of those reconnaissance drones floated in each of them. Watching him. *Spying* on him. The instant he pulled a single trooper back from any one of them, the humans would know. They'd know, and they'd pour yet more of their warriors aboard through the opening and completely swamp his defenders.

And we outnumber them by at least—at least!—*twelve to one,* he thought despairingly.

"Hold them, Ursahl," he said. "Hold them as long as you can. Make them pay for every tarn!"

"We have, Division Commander." Harsh pride echoed in Ursahl's voice while the combat chatter roiled behind it. "And we will. My promise on that."

"I knew that already," Thyrack said quietly. "Go now. Fight your battle. And save a seat for me at Dainthar's table."

"I will," Ursahl said, and Thyrack closed his eyes in pain as the link died.

There could be only one outcome, if the humans maintained their operational pace. He knew that as well as Ursahl did. But perhaps, just perhaps, they wouldn't. Perhaps, if the cost proved terrible enough. . . .

Stop reaching for the wind, he told himself wearily. *If the humans were going to back off, withdraw and rethink, they'd already have done it.*

The human formations were far smaller than he or any other Shongair had anticipated. They could not have committed more than three myri of their armored troopers, barely a twelfth part of his own strength, but the combat power of their individual troopers was terrifying. And the armed drones, the combat robots, they'd deployed were a fearsome force multiplier that made the odds even worse.

But the numbers still favor us. *Every warrior they lose hurts them twelve times as badly as it would have hurt us,* he reminded himself fiercely. *We've killed or wounded almost a fourth part of the troopers they've actually deployed, and they aren't fighting to protect their mates and young. Unlike us, they* can *pull back if the cost is too great. So maybe—maybe, please Dainthar!—if Ursahl can just bleed them enough more. . . .*

· · · · ·

"WHAT'S THE HOLDUP?"

Malachi Dvorak's voice was harsh. Not because he was angry with the lieutenant in front of him, but with the painful weight of too many dead and wounded Space Marines.

"Easier to show you than tell you, Sir," First Lieutenant Randall Willis, the Charlie Company scout platoon leader, replied. "If you'd come with me?"

"Sure."

He followed Willis as the scout led him forward, past the omnipresent, drifting Shongair dead toward the bleeding point of 1st Battalion's stalled advance.

"Watch your step, Sir," Willis said.

A bright orange-red line crossed the passage ahead of them, and despite his pain, Malachi smiled fiercely as he saw it. That line marked the transition from the main spindle's microgravity into the rotating "collar" section coupled directly to the habitat rings.

The deck on the outboard side of that line was moving, rotating steadily, and gravity lurked beyond it. Not much gravity. They were still a good hundred meters inside the spindle, and even at its outer limits, the apparent gravity would be barely 0.18 g, only about six percent higher than that of Luna. That was still enough to require a certain caution, however, and Malachi and Willis timed the rotation, then reached across the line and caught two of the looped straps. They looked for all the world like something Malachi might have seen in an old-fashioned subway on pre-invasion Earth, although they were rather awkwardly placed for someone of his height, since they were intended for the much shorter Shongairi. Unlike that subway's straps, however, these weren't static. Instead, they were mounted on individually powered tracks that plucked the two Space Marines out of microgravity and into the rotating section, and he grimaced as the sensation of up-and-down returned. It wasn't *much* of an up-and-down—not yet—but the strap he'd grabbed towed him briskly down to what had become an undeniable deck and not just one more side of a weightless passageway.

He released the strap, which zipped back up to its waiting position, and looked at Willis.

"Bit surprised they didn't shut that down," he remarked.

"Dunno if they *can*, Sir," Willis replied. "They can't shut down the rotation without throwing their habitat sections into zero-g. Seems like they *ought* to be able to turn off individual subsystems, but the more of their stuff I've seen, the screwier some of their design decisions seem."

"Tell me about it." Malachi rolled his eyes, and Willis chuckled sourly.

"This way, Sir," he said.

Malachi followed him, both of them moving through the apparent gravity with the low-trajectory, bounding strides of men who'd spent more than a few hours training on the surface of Earth's moon. Then a broad, open archway loomed ahead of them and Willis raised a cautionary hand, then pointed at the deck.

"Wanna get a little closer to the ground, Sir. Bastards aren't shy about trying to pop one of those damned rockets in anywhere they see movement. Basic geometry's on our side, but if they get lucky, they can generate a firing angle that works."

Malachi nodded, and the two of them eased up to the pair of Space Marines crouched on either side of the arch. Malachi stopped just behind one of them and leaned forward, looking over her shoulder.

His battalion's point had finally reached the union between the habitat rings' access spoke and the platform's central hub. Now he looked out across a circular, open, brilliantly lit void. That void was immensely deep, especially now that his inner ear had reacquired a reliable indicator of up and down. In fact, it was the next best thing to five *kilometers* deep, and its walls were lined with structures that seemed more . . . orderly, somehow, than the Escher-like warrens through which they'd fought their way to this point.

The center of the spoke was a cargo- and freight-handling bore just under a hundred and fifty meters across. The habitat rings' rotation gave counter-gravity something to work with, although it got inefficient as hell in the low grav at the top of the shaft. He knew the Puppies' usual procedure was to strap any freight they needed to move to a counter-grav pallet and let it find its own way down the bore, but they'd made rather more sophisticated provisions for moving personnel, and six transparent, equally spaced tubes ran down the shaft's walls. Actually, there were *twelve* tubes, not six, since each complex contained two side-by-side chains of elevator cars, both of them moving in endless loops from top to bottom and back again. The view from inside the elevator must be spectacular, a corner of his brain reflected, and he knew that each elevator shaft was fitted with regularly spaced emergency pressure doors that would seal in the event of a catastrophic hull rupture. Or in the event that the platform's defenders decided to dump atmosphere.

The elevator shafts passed through clusters of structures built out from the sides of the shaft, and unlike the industrial areas his people had fought their way through, they'd been designed with a clearly established up and down. He had no idea what most of those structures were for, although the majority of them still had a distinctly "industrial" look to them, but they'd been designed with plenty of windows—no doubt to allow the people inside them to enjoy the same spectacular view as the elevators' passengers. And—

"Shit!" he muttered.

It looked as if every single one of those windows had been turned into a firing position. They couldn't have been, really. There weren't enough Puppies on the platform to have put an autocannon into *every* window. But there were enough. As he watched, one of the Shongairi's heavy rockets came scorching across the shaft and exploded just below another access arch seventy-five meters to his right.

"Why I said it would be simpler to show you, Sir," Willis said. "They've turned almost all the buildings on both sides of the spoke into fortresses. I think they have every autocannon in their inventory in there, plus enough rocket launchers to bring down an entire air force."

"Sounds like you've got a fair handle on where they are, though."

"Yes and no, Sir."

The scout punched up a tactical display on his HUD and shunted it to Malachi. It showed dozens of the red, glaring icons that indicated hostiles, but at least half of them strobed in the blinking pattern that indicated uncertainty.

"I've used up a shitpot of Keyholes—and lost three Marines—figuring this much out." Willis's voice was much grimmer than it had been. "And the bastards keep moving from one position to another. We can nail them down to a specific group of windows, and they don't have the kinds of loopholes they built into their fixed positions between here and the boat bay. But they *have* done the equivalent of sandbagging their positions, and they're too frigging good at ducking back and forth between them. We're still picking them off, but it's taking too damned long, and they're getting too many chances to shoot back at us in the process. And unless we can clear them, ain't nobody moving down-spoke, Colonel. The autocannon—*pfffffft!*" He made a dismissive sound. "Standard Heinlein can stand up to that crap all day long. But those rocket launchers are bad medicine, and they've got sightlines—and firing lines—clear across the spoke. For that matter, they've got firing lines *up* the spoke. Found *that* out the hard way, too. Truth is, they've got a five-klick-deep fire zone against anyone who tries to go straight down-spoke."

"So it's still basically room-to-room."

"Sir, we could take them in a charge. Probably. Especially with the Bangalores out in front. But we'd lose a lot of people." Willis shrugged. "I don't know that the elevator tubes would be any better—too much like fish in a barrel for my taste, to be honest—but it looks to me it's either shinny down the outsides of the tubes, breach each roof as we come to it, and fight our way down through each building, or drop straight down the cargo shaft and try to blitz our way past 'em. And if they're still shooting at us when we try either of those, it's gonna really, really suck, Colonel."

"Agreed."

Malachi stood for a moment, gazing out across the spoke. Then he keyed his neural link.

"Gold One, Silver One."

"Yes, Malachi?" Brigadier Ascaso replied almost instantly.

"Ma'am, we've got the mouth of the spoke—sort of, at least—but it's looking kind of hairy. I've got an idea, but I'll need a little resupply, first."

· · · · ·

"**WHAT ARE THEY** *waiting* for?" Trooper Kurhal muttered fretfully.

"How the Cainharn do *I* know?" Squad Leader Lormak shot back.

"Sorry, Squad Leader," Kurhal replied. "It's just . . . just—"

"Waiting," Lormak said more gently.

"Yeah," Kurhal acknowledged. "The waiting."

Lormak's ears twitched in agreement, although Kurhal couldn't see it from his position. The truth was that the squad leader understood Kurhal's fear perfectly, and gods knew the trooper was entitled to it. The remnants of Lormak's squad had been driven back for over a myrtan, fighting hard for every tarn of that distance . . . and only four of its original twelve troopers were left. Kurhal had fought hard the entire way, but he'd also seen twelves of his fellow troopers, including two-thirds of his own squad, blotted away by the merciless human advance. Small wonder his belly had become a hollow, singing void as despair curdled his bowels. By now, everyone knew their backs were to the wall, and—like Kurhal—a part of the squad leader just wanted to get it *over* with.

"Well, look at the bright side," he said. "At least we're not—"

"Incoming!" someone screamed over the com.

.   .   .   .   .

MALACHI DVORAK'S SPACE Marines had made good use of the Planetary Union Armed Forces' specialized combat drones on their way in, but useful as those drones had been, deploying them effectively had been . . . challenging.

The CC-1 Gagamba—named for the Filipino word for "spider," and known to the troops as the "Black Widow"—was about the size of two shoeboxes, equipped with magnetized treads with "sticky" surfaces to help its tracks maintain contact with solid surfaces. It could be used almost anywhere, but it had been specifically designed for close-quarters combat in microgravity, where counter-grav wasn't available. It could scurry up bulkheads, cross overheads, and move evasively at a fairly high rate of speed along the floor, sides, or roof of a passageway. The Widows were designed to carry a variety of munitions, from incendiaries to antipersonnel to shaped charge explosives. In ideal circumstances, they deployed their payloads and then got the hell out of Dodge, leaving their explosive calling cards behind, but they were more often deployed in "kamikaze" mode. The industrial areas through which 1st Battalion had fought its way had offered opportunities for their use, but the Puppies had been too deeply dug in, with too much concentrated fire sweeping the approaches. The Widows had still been able to get through, but the loss rate had been severe.

The CC-2 Strider was substantially larger than the Gagamba. It had to be, because it was basically a machine gun on a crawler chassis. Known to the troops as the "Tunnel Rat," it was slower than the Black Widow, but it was also equipped with a sophisticated reactive camouflage smartskin, and its onboard AI was more capable. The Black Widow depended on reaching its target with an explosive payload, but the Tunnel Rat could engage hostile targets at much greater ranges. Or it could be deployed into a confined space to take hostiles under fire in the assault mode or programmed to "loiter" there as an area denial weapon.

The problem, up to this point, had been that both the Black Widow and the Tunnel Rat really needed either an open flank to sneak around or enough room to take meaningful evasive action, and both of those had been in short supply.

Until now.

. . . . .

"OH, *SHIT!*" SQUAD Leader Lormak snarled as the answer to Kurhal's question came racing down the walls of the cargo shaft.

It was the first time Lormak had actually seen them, but other troopers' encounters with the humans' infernal drones had been passed around the net. He knew what they were, but no one had reported anything like this! There weren't handfuls of them this time. There were Cainharn's own horde of them, pouring down the shaft like water through a pipe!

And instead of small firing ports, he and his troopers were bellied down behind these enormous damned *windows*.

"The drones!" he snapped. "Take out the drones! Don't let them get through the windows!"

. . . . .

MALACHI DVORAK'S SMILE was cold as the Widows and Tunnel Rats flowed down the cargo shaft's walls. The Rats were less nimble, but their camouflage made them harder to spot, much less target, and both drones were capable of short bursts of astonishing speed. The greater width of the shaft gave them the room to dodge they'd been denied in the earlier fighting, and the same width meant his Space Marines could deploy them not in ones and twos, but by the dozen. By the *score*.

The Puppies had amply demonstrated their marksmanship and fire discipline, but this time, that wasn't nearly enough. It wasn't—quite—like an elephant swarmed under by a tidal bore of army ants, but that was the only analogy he could think of. Dozens of drones were picked off by cannon and rifle fire, even by rockets, but nobody could have stopped them all.

Individual charging Tunnel Rats stopped abruptly as Puppies exposed themselves to fire at the Black Widows, and any Shongair trooper a Tunnel Rat targeted died. Quite often, the Tunnel Rat which had fired died moments later, as other Shongairi poured fire at it, but that was cold comfort for its victim. And while the Puppies were shooting at *it*, its fellows—and the tide of Black Widows—charged remorselessly forward.

Malachi bared his teeth as the first of the Widows reached a window, flung itself through it, and exploded with shattering violence. Other drones raced past it, hurled themselves into other windows, and a froth of explosions ran down the flanks of the Shongair strong points.

The defensive fire faltered as window after window blew outward into the shaft, and Tunnel Rats, following hard on the Black Widows' heels, took over the same windows, switching instantly to aerial denial mode, shooting anything without a Space Marine transponder that moved. A ring of fiery death went booming down the cargo shaft's flanks, receding into the depths, and Malachi's Space Marines kicked their boosters and stepped over the edge of that five-kilometer well. Only a handful of Shongairi lived long enough to fire at them with despairing courage as they plunged downward like railgun-armed meteors, and Malachi Dvorak realized they'd broken the final defensive crust at last.

"Gold One," he announced over the com net. "Silver One. Phase One complete. Spoke One is ours."

. . . . .

"STILL NOTHING FROM the humans?" System Commander Brath asked quietly from Division Commander Thyrack's display.

"Not since they punched out both arms with their damned drones, Sir," Thyrack replied bitterly. "I never imagined anything like that, even after everything they'd already done to us. I should have. I should've seen it coming, and I should've—"

"Peace, Thyrack," Brath interrupted. "There are a lot of things all of us 'should've seen coming,' at least once the humans announced their arrival. Cainharn! We *did* see it coming. There just wasn't anything we could do about it."

"You're probably right, Sir," Thyrack admitted after a moment. "That doesn't make it hurt any less, though."

"No," Brath agreed. "No, it doesn't."

Thyrack twitched his ears in acknowledgment. And he appreciated Brath's understanding, he truly did. But as he'd just told the System Commander, understanding couldn't ease the pain. Especially not after that final, totally one-sided tidal wave assault had swept down Arm Seven. It had utterly gutted what remained of 12th Regiment, and Regiment Commander Ursahl had died with his troopers as the drones rampaged through his position.

Regiment Commander Youna had at least known what to expect when the second human assault reached Arm Eight. Not that it had mattered, in the end. Youna had pulled more of his troopers out of their fighting positions along the cargo shaft, tried to make his stand where it debouched into the habitat ring. He'd managed to kill or wound a handful more of the attackers, but he—and all of his troopers—were just as dead as Ursahl.

Yet after taking the outboard ends of the arms, the humans had done nothing. The handful of Thyrack's surviving troopers on the far side of the inner habitat ring's sealed emergency pressure doors would have stood no chance against the combat power which had fought its way up the central hub and then down the arms to reach them. But so far, the humans had made no move to breach those doors. Youna's last message had come in almost three myrtahli ago, and Thyrack's nerves had twisted tighter and tighter as each tiskari ticked its way into eternity. When were they—?

"Division Commander, the human shuttles are moving!"

· · · · ·

"ALL UNITS, HAWK One," Major Gillespie announced from the *Oracle*'s command deck. "General Wilson confirms that we are go for Woodpecker. Execute on my mark."

He paused, watching the time display tick downward. The clock had started when Raymond Lewis's 2nd Battalion reached its Phase One objective, the better part of an hour behind 1st Battalion. Second's casualties had been marginally heavier than First's on its way through the central spindle, but Lewis had profited from Malachi Dvorak's tactics when he reached his assigned spoke. As nearly as the Space Marines could tell, most of the defenders in Lewis's path had pulled out of their positions lining the cargo shaft and forted up at its base, where they could concentrate their fire most effectively.

It hadn't helped. Not when the Black Widows and Tunnel Rats dropped straight into their faces with Lewis's Heinlein-armored troopers close on their heels.

Now it was time to finish this, assuming the Puppies had a single gram of common sense.

"All Hawks—execute!" he snapped.

· · · · ·

THIRTEEN *STARHAWK* ASSAULT shuttles darted suddenly toward Habitat One.

They didn't fire a shot. They only accelerated ferociously, then braked with equal power and thumped down on the outer skin of the inner habitat ring. Hatches opened, and company fire teams and engineers who'd waited impatiently, hating every minute of inactivity while 1st and 2nd Battalions fought their bitter way through the habitat, spilled out of them. They spread out, finding their precise positions, and the engineers positioned the assault locks carefully. Nanotech sealant welded the portable airlocks to the enormous platform's hull, their sides creaked as the engineers cracked the valves, filling them with a two-atmosphere overpressure while they watched eagle-eyed for leaks, and one by one the icons on Gillespie's master plot blinked green to indicate good seals.

"Fire in the hole!" he announced, and nodded to Lieutenant Christine Ortega, his ops officer.

Ortega punched the button. Actually, she tapped a touchscreen, but the result was the same. The circular breaching charges under the airlocks ignited, burning with a ferocity that dwarfed any pre-Hegemony thermite. They seared their way effortlessly through the meter-and-a-half-thick hull, and the overpressure in the locks blew the massive scabs of synthetic alloys into the habitat's interior.

Shouts of panic erupted through the sudden openings as the Shongair civilians, huddled behind the thin, bleeding line of their final defenders, realized the enemy was upon them.

But nothing followed the jagged-edged circles of broken hull.

Nothing but silence.

. . . . .

DIVISION COMMANDER THYRACK stared in horror at the imagery on his display.

The human breaching operation had been perfectly, flawlessly executed. There'd been no time for any of the defenders to react, and the breaches were spread widely enough to compromise almost a third of the inner habitat ring's compartmentalization. All the humans had to do was open their airlocks and the entire habitat ring's atmosphere would go screaming into space. Most of the civilians under Thyrack's protection had at least emergency vac suits, but they were *civilians,* without the relentless suit drills of his military personnel. And all too many of them were *children,* terrified and far too vulnerable to the sorts of accidents that had fatal consequences in death pressure. Or they could simply shovel grenades, or more of their infernal drones, through the openings to mow down everyone in their paths. If—

"Division Commander! You have an incoming message!"

Thyrack tore his gaze from the display, looked at the com officer.

"It . . . it's from the humans, Sir."

"Put it up," someone said in a rusty, broken voice Thyrack vaguely recognized as his own, and his display changed as a flat, muzzle-less human face appeared upon it. It wasn't the one who'd identified himself as Dvorak, a corner of the Division Commander's brain noted.

"Greetings, Division Commander Thyrack," the human said. "I am Lieutenant General Robert Wilson. In your parlance, that makes me Expeditionary Force Commander Wilson, the military commander of the Shong Expeditionary Force."

Thyrack's ears flattened slightly. He hated that betraying expression of tension, but he couldn't prevent it as the human's impossibly blue eyes bored into him. If the human claims of what Fleet Commander Thikair had done to their homeworld were true, killing every single Shongair aboard Habitat One would be less than a raindrop in a thunderstorm compared to their losses, and this human, this Robert Wilson, had just proven how easily he could do that.

But they could also have done that with a single missile strike, without putting a single warrior aboard the station, Thyrack, a voice said in the back of his brain. *They didn't need to pay the price in their own lives to reach this point. Do they truly understand us so well that—?*

"I greet you, Expeditionary Force Commander," he said out loud. "What do you wish to say?"

"Your men fought well, Division Commander, with all the courage and determination Jukaris could possibly demand of them. They've lost." It was impossible to read the alien's expression, but those blue eyes were colder than glacier ice. "Your civilians, your entire platform, are at our mercy. If it's necessary for us to prove that to you, we will. Is it?"

Thyrack looked back into those frozen eyes, and his ears went slowly flat against his skull. Then he bent his head, covering his eyes in the formal gesture of submission to a pack lord.

"It is not, Expeditionary Force Commander," he said. "I yield."

IMPERIAL PALACE,
CITY OF SHERIKAATH,
PLANET SHONGARU,
SHONG SYSTEM,
241.5 LY FROM EARTH,
MAY 2, YEAR 41 TE.

The silence in the council chamber could have been carved with a knife.

Shathyra Haymar looked around the council table at the senior ministers of his government . . . and at System Commander Brath, facing him from its far end, flanked by Army Commander Urdaar and Army Commander Therkaar. The three uniformed Shongairi were no strangers to council chambers and throne rooms, but today they clearly would rather have faced an enemy assault than their Shathyra.

And Haymar couldn't blame them.

"So that's your considered opinion, System Commander? You and the Army Commanders concur in it?"

"Your Majesty, every one of our warriors is prepared to fight and die. But the truth is that we can't defeat the humans." Brath met the Shathyra's gaze steadily, his ears unflinching. "Even in the confines of Habitat One, they inflicted hugely disproportionate losses on Division Commander Thyrack's troopers. The instances in which our own warriors were able to inflict any meaningful losses on the humans were virtually all close-range ambushes. In ranged combat, they were little more than targets, and the humans' individual battle armor is immensely more powerful—and harder to destroy—than anything we possess. Given that our heaviest antitank missiles were hard-pressed to destroy their armored *infantry*, we can only assume they'll be effectively useless against human armored *vehicles*. Their drones are far more capable than anything we possess, and they're armed, which most of ours are not. And given that we have no remaining orbital defenses, we have no way to prevent their starships and attack craft from taking position in low orbit and providing pinpoint KEW fire support to their ground forces."

The System Commander inhaled deeply.

"Your Majesty, the most we could hope for would be to inflict additional casualties upon them, and even that would be possible only under the most extraordinary of tactical circumstances. As the senior uniformed officer of your armed forces, it's my duty to tell you that your warriors have striven to the utmost, as Jukaris requires, and we've failed."

The silence returned, even more intense, and then it was Haymar's turn to draw breath.

"I thank you, System Commander," he said simply. "I know how difficult it was for you to tell me that, but I also know that, as always, you've given me nothing but truth. I thank you for that, and I thank all of your warriors, as well. They've given all, and more than all, any Shathyra could have asked of them. Give them my deep and profound gratitude. If the opportunity presents, it will be my greatest honor to tell them that in person."

"Your Majesty, you can't—"

Haymar's raised hand stilled Brath's protest.

"I am Shathyra of all Shongairi, System Commander. Your duty was to the Crown; my duty is to all of our people. I can—and will—do whatever that duty requires of me, just as you and your warriors have done all and more that your oaths required of you."

Brath posed his mouth. For a long moment, he looked back at his emperor. And then, slowly, he bowed his head.

"I think you should return to your commands now," Haymar said with a gesture that included both of the army commanders, as well. "Tell your warriors to stand down. I will have no more of them killed attempting to defeat a foe who can slay them with impunity."

"Of course, Your Majesty." Brath's voice was low, and as he stood, he bent his head deeply and covered his eyes in salute to his pack lord of pack lords.

The army commanders followed him, and Haymar sat back in his comfortable, throne-like chair as the carven chamber doors closed silently behind them.

"Your Majesty—" War Minister Timal began hesitantly, but Haymar stopped him with a single ear-flick.

"I said Brath spoke nothing but the truth, Timal, and that's precisely what he did. I've reviewed much of the imagery of that battle myself. And, truth to tell, calling it a 'battle' verges all too closely upon falsehood."

"Fairness, my son," Shathyrakym Yudar said. Haymar looked at his father, and Yudar returned his gaze levelly.

"A battle one cannot win is a battle still," Yudar continued. "And the humans shed blood enough of their own before it was over. Not as much as our own warriors, no. But given the number of their troopers who were actually engaged, their losses were high enough to satisfy any hyrsara's honor."

Someone inhaled sharply as the Shathyrakym used the term. In ancient Shongair, hyrsara meant literally "the superior one." In all of Shongair history, it had never been applied to any non-Shongair.

Until now.

"I can always trust you to speak the truth, as well, Sire," Haymar said. "And it's nothing I haven't already thought, already realized, for myself. But it's even harder than I thought it would be."

"You aren't the one who brought this upon our people," Yudar said. "If anyone in this chamber—anyone still living on Shongaru—can claim that 'honor,' that person is I. The fact that I would never have authorized Thikair's actions had I been there can't absolve me from the responsibility of *sending* him there. We thought we were being so clever, taking the weed-eaters' bait and turning it back upon them. But there were bigger, more deadly tyskari in those waters than we ever dreamed. And that rests upon my shoulders, not yours."

"I would've made the same decision, Sire. I know as surely as I'm sitting here that I *would* have made the same decision you made, given the information you had. But what matters now isn't the path that brought us here. What matters is what road leads forward from this point in our people's history."

"I fear it may be a dark one, Your Majesty," First Minister Urkal said somberly. "If what they say Thikair did to their homeworld is true—and, like you, I fear in my bones that it is—they would be more than mortal if they didn't seek to punish us severely for it. And in all honesty, I could never blame them for it if they did."

"That's true." Haymar's ears nodded agreement. "But I pray—and, indeed, I hope—that that's not the reason they've come to demand our submission."

"'Hope'?" Minister of Colonies Kiramar's ears quirked a question, and Haymar raised one hand before him.

"They waited," he said. "They waited until Division Commander Thyrack's troopers had fought their very hearts out. Until we *knew* we'd been more than simply 'defeated.' Until we knew we'd been *crushed*. And then they blew breach after breach through the skin of the habitat rings to *prove* how defenseless our civilians were, how completely unable we were to protect them in any way."

Kiramar's ears nodded, and Haymar's shrugged.

"And then they killed *no one*," he said softly. "Not a single civilian. They could have. At that point, even under Jukaris, they would have been justified in killing at least some of our civilians to drive home the completeness of their superiority. And they chose not to. They chose to show suukarma."

"But they aren't—" Timal began, then cut himself off.

"No, they aren't Shongair," Haymar said. "But I think they understand us far better than we've ever bothered to understand another species. So, yes, Timal, I think they understood precisely what they were doing, and that what they did was to choose the path of suukarma."

He let his eyes circle the table. Suukarma was yet another ancient Shongair word which had survived the millennia as a part of Jukaris. Once upon a time, it had meant only "mercy," but as its surviving companion words, its definition had grown and changed over those long and dusty years. Today, it meant not just mercy, but also compassion. And grace.

"I can't know that they did that deliberately," the Shathyra continued. "None of us can . . . yet. Perhaps it was only a coincidence they stopped at exactly that point. But perhaps it wasn't, too. And I fear we have only one way to find out."

H ave you lost your fucking goddamned *mind*?!"

"Rob!" Sharon Dvorak half-snapped.

Her brother looked at her, his expression almost incredulous, and matching blue eyes glared back at him. He closed his mouth and inhaled deeply.

"Better." She shook her head at him. "You know, after all these years, even a Marine—even a *Space* Marine—should be able to string together at least three consecutive sentences without an obscenity."

Wilson looked more than a bit apoplectic. Clearly the language he'd chosen to use was, in his considered opinion, totally beside the point.

Sharon looked at him levelly for another handful of seconds, then swiveled those blue eyes to her husband.

She, her brother, Dvorak, Vlad, Buchevsky, Merahl BryMerThor, and Alex Jackson had the briefing room to themselves. Arguably, she shouldn't have been there. Technically, Sharon Dvorak had no formally defined slot in the Shongair Expeditionary Force's command structure.

Technically.

"Despite Rob's language," she said now, to the man who commanded the entire Expeditionary Force, "his question stands. *Have* you lost your fucking goddamned mind? Not even *you* could possibly consider something like this!"

"I'm afraid I can," Dvorak told her, and there was something like a note of pleading in his voice. "I really can, Babe."

"Dave." Her voice was soft, her eyes dark, and he reached out to take her hand.

"It's the symbolism," he said. "The opportunity to nail this thing down, once and for all. The truth is, I can't *not* do this."

"The hell you can't." For the first time most of those present could recall, Rob Wilson spoke to his brother-in-law with more than a hint of genuine anger, and Dvorak's eyes moved to his face. "I frigging well nearly lost you in the goddamned woods in North Carolina. Then you got your *stupid* ass the next best thing to blown to bits on Sarth. And now you wanna do *this*?! Damn it, Dave, I am sick and tired of picking you up with a brush and a dustpan and hauling your ass home on a shutter!"

"Hasn't been a whole bunch of fun from my side, either," Dvorak said with a crooked smile. "And I didn't exactly plan on getting myself sent to the body shop those other times, you know. But you and Malachi lost too many of your people getting us to this point for me to not step up when it's my turn. You know that, Rob."

"Under their own damned code of honor *you* choose the place and the time. You can demand that Haymar come *here,* aboard *Relentless,* to make his submission, and it's his duty, his honor responsibility, to do exactly that. Jukaris is completely clear on that point." There was precious little give in Rob Wilson's eyes. "There'd be *plenty* of 'symbolism' in that, too, and it's exactly what his message just offered to do. It's how he's *assuming* it'll work!"

"It is." Dvorak nodded. "And that's why I'm not going to do it. This isn't just about Jukaris, Rob. Oh, it *is* about what we can demand from them under Shongair custom and law. Of course it is! But that's really my point, and you know it. Because it's even more about what happens after they submit, and it's about how we accept that submission. And, to be honest, it's more than time we injected a little human DNA into this submission mechanism of theirs."

"I don't—"

"Peace, Rob," another voice said, and Wilson's eyes snapped to the speaker.

Technically, that speaker had no more official place in the Shong Expedition's command structure than Sharon Dvorak, but he was also Vlad Drakulya, Prince of Transylvania, the being—the man—who had defeated the Shongair invasion of Earth.

"I understand your fears, Rob," he said gently. "And God knows I saw enough and more than enough treachery in my own life as a breather to understand the depths to which men—or, I suppose, aliens—can sink to stave off defeat. But I think Dave has read Shathyra Haymar correctly in this, and he is right that if we are not to deal with the Shongairi the way *I* would have chosen to deal with them, then anything that helps to bind the bleeding wound between us must be considered."

He looked at Merahl, one eyebrow raised, and the Sarthian's nasal flaps framed a deep, heartfelt sigh.

"I am . . . less than happy about this," Dvorak's sherhyna said. "And I can't speak for these Shongairi; they're no more my people than they are human. But if your xenologists have interpreted them correctly, then the Clan Ruler is right when he looks at the difference this could make. And if Shongairi were Sarthians—if they were Dvorakians—this would absolutely be the proper move to secure far more than their simple submission."

Rob Wilson looked around the compartment at all of the other faces, then at his sister. The one person he knew could change Dave Dvorak's mind. She looked back at him in silence for several seconds, and then her head bent. She looked down at the table, and Wilson's shoulders drooped.

"So you're really gonna do this?" he challenged his brother-in-law.

"I'm afraid I am." Dvorak quirked a smile at him. "I know it pisses you off, Rob, but I really think it's the way to go. The way we *have* to go."

"We don't *have* to do anything of the goddamned sort," Wilson shot back, although there was at least a hint of his usual tartness in it this time.

"Okay." Dvorak nodded. "Let me rephrase. This is the way we're *going* to go. And, as always, it'll be your job to scrape up the pieces as best you can if it turns out I've screwed up again. But the truth is, I really, truly don't think I have."

"No, and you didn't think you had on *Sarth,* as I recall," Wilson shot back.

"I remember something I read once," Buchevsky said thoughtfully. "It was a naval officer's fitness report, I think. And his superior said that the officer in question was 'possessed of a superabundance of that quality which in myself I should call tenacity and maintenance of purpose, but which in his case I can describe only as pure bloody-minded obstinacy.' I always thought that kinda suited you, Dave."

"You say the sweetest things," Dvorak replied, and even Wilson chuckled.

"I think perhaps we can set at least some of your concerns to rest,

Rob," Vlad said. "While I doubt from my review of the records of the expedition to Sarth that it would have made a great deal of difference to events in Dianzhyr, my reading of Jukaris suggests that there is no reason Dave should not be accompanied by his own retainers. Given his rank—and Haymar's—I believe we could easily send a half dozen or so of those retainers with him."

"Really?" Wilson looked more cheerful than he had in quite a while. "And just which half dozen would you happen to have in mind?"

"Actually, I was thinking of Stephen, Taki Bratianu, Longbow, Calvin, and Francisco."

"That's only five," Wilson pointed out.

"Is it, indeed?" Vlad shook his head. "Forgive me, I was ever a poor mathematician. Perhaps I should accompany him, as well, then. Simply to make up the numbers, you understand." Wilson snorted and Vlad smiled, but his eyes were serious.

"And while we could not prevent the Shongairi from blowing him up as the Qwernians did on Sarth," he continued, "I rather suspect that the six of us would be ample to demonstrate the error of the Shongairi's ways should they harbor any other last-minute designs of treachery."

His smile grew broader, and his canines lengthened ever so slightly.

HIGH TEMPLE OF DAINTHAR,
CITY OF SHERIKAATH,
PLANET SHONGARU,
SHONG SYSTEM,
241.5 LY FROM EARTH,
MAY 6, YEAR 41 TE.

The temple was enormous.

Like the medieval cathedrals of Earth, its construction had been the work of lifetimes. That construction had begun almost two Shongair centuries ago, and even today, the temple remained a work in progress, ever growing and changing as generations of worshipers completed their irshika, the ceremonial pilgrimage to Dainthar's Home on Shongaru. As part of the irshika, each pilgrim was required to leave the work of his own hands behind. That work could be large, or it could be small. It could be the work of one set of hands, or the combined work of many. But it had been ongoing for over two hundred and eighty Shongair years—almost seven hundred Earth Years—and so the temple was surrounded by landscaped gardens, ornamental trees, spectacular beds of flowers, statuary, and prayer shrines.

It was the highest and most holy spot on the surface of the planet. Indeed, in the hearts and minds of all Shongairi everywhere, and word that the aliens who had invaded their home star system had chosen this site, of all they might have selected, had spread across the planet like wildfire. Among their own people, they knew, it would have been a gesture of honor, a recognition of how valiantly their warriors had met the stern demands of Jukaris. But they were aliens, these humans. Who knew how *they* might view their demands?

It was also, Dave Dvorak thought, one of the most beautiful places he'd ever seen, and he pushed down a reflex surge of bitterness as he thought of the Vatican, the Temple Mount, the Dome of the Rock, the Taj Mahal, and a hundred other "beautiful places" a Shongair named Thikair had destroyed forever.

You've told everyone else it wasn't these *Shongairi,* he reminded himself. *Might be a good thing to remind* yourself *from time to time.*

The air car which had unloaded from his *Starlander* at the Sherikaath Spaceport was far more stylish than the modified Airaavatha APCs the expedition to Sarth had used, nor was it escorted by a single *Starhawk* or even an armed drone. It was almost as heavily armored as an Airaavatha, however, and equipped with an even better electronic warfare suite . . . and a point defense system no one had tried very hard to disguise. All that armor and all those defensive capabilities couldn't have prevented its destruction if the Shongair Empire had opted for treachery, of course, but that wasn't really the point. Besides, Jukaris or no Jukaris, the Shongair were just as capable of producing lone lunatics as any other species.

Now that air car descended smoothly, silently, to the waiting landing pad just outside the temple's precincts.

An enormous crowd—it looked like the entire population of Sherikaath, although it couldn't really have been more than a couple of hundred thousand Shongairi—filled the vast Temple Square to capacity and beyond. Shongair troopers formed a cordon, holding them well clear of the landing pad, but the deep susurration of at least forty or fifty thousand murmuring conversations flowed through the cool morning air like some invisible sea.

The air car hatch opened, and all of those conversations ceased in an instant as Stephen Buchevsky, in the uniform of a United States Marine Corps master sergeant, led the way out of it. By now, every living Shongair must have seen imagery of the vengeance-seeking aliens who'd come to their star system, but this was the first time anyone in that enormous crowd had ever seen a human being with his or her own eyes.

Buchevsky looked around, brown eyes hard, probing with all of the enhanced senses of the "vampire" he'd become. He'd led the way for several reasons, not least the fact that the Shongairi had demonstrated no weapons that could kill a vampire. But that wasn't the only consideration, by a long chalk, and he felt his dead wife and daughters at his back as he set foot on the soil of the world from which their murderers had come.

He stood a moment longer, then stepped to one side, and Calvin Meyers, also in the uniform of the U.S. Marines, Daniel Torino, in the uniform of the U.S. Air Force, and Francisco Lopez, in the uniform of the U.S. Army, joined him. There was a message in those uniforms, although Buchevsky doubted anyone in that crowd understood it.

Yet, at least.

They formed a short arc around the hatch as Dave Dvorak stepped through it in civilian dress. For this occasion, he was accompanied by two of his Sarthian sherhynas: Merahl and Brykira. They stood at his back, as fragile and killable as he himself, and he felt their calm presence behind him as Vlad Drakulya and Taki Bratianu joined them. Like Dvorak, Vlad and Bratianu wore civilian clothing, but the short sword at Bratianu's side was just as functional as and—in a vampire's hands—far more lethal than the Sarthians' holstered pistols.

A single horn sounded. Not a trumpet, not a brass of any sort, but the voice of an ancient, gem-encrusted kyrmath horn. The kyrmath was the fiercest, although far from the largest, herbivore of Shongaru, with a personality that would have been right at home in a Cape buffalo. Indeed, it rather resembled the "caffer," although it was about ten percent larger with a horn spread more reminiscent of a Texas Longhorn. For millennia, the taking of a kyrmath had been one of the traditional avenues by which a beta proved his right to challenge his pack lord for supremacy, and the kyrmath was a totem animal of Dainthar Himself.

The crowd parted, opening an avenue from the landing pad to the broad flight of shallow steps that led up to the temple portico. A priest of Dainthar, in elaborate ceremonial robes, stood on an outthrust balcony, holding the kyrmath horn (which was very nearly as long as he was tall), while another, even more elaborately garbed cleric, stood upon the temple steps themselves. He raised his hands in a gesture of blessing, and his amplified voice sounded clearly across the crowd.

"Let he who has proved himself hyrsara come forth to the house of the Great Hunter that all may know him."

Dvorak drew a deep, hopefully unobtrusive, breath and started forward along that opened avenue, flanked by his protectors. The walk was no more than fifty meters, but it seemed far longer, and the sound of his own heels on the ornamented pavement was clearly audible in the utter stillness and silence echoing about him.

They reached the temple steps at last, though, and the cleric—the high priest of Dainthar, which made him the senior prelate of the entire Shongair people—held up one hand as he reached them.

"Who comes to the house of the Great Hunter?" he asked.

"My name is David Dvorak, son of Radomir and Alicia Dvorak," Dvorak replied in a clear, strong voice, and his translator rendered it in flawless Shongair.

"And by what right do you come to this house, David Dvorak?" The high priest's attempt to pronounce the human name was not a success, although it was obvious he'd practiced hard ahead of time.

"By right of Jukaris," Dvorak said. "By pack lord right. By strength of arms."

"And these things you have proven?"

"I have."

The high priest looked at him for a moment, then lowered his raised hand and inclined his head.

"Then pass into the Great Hunter's house, David Dvorak, and there take up that which is yours."

A great sigh whispered its way across the crowded square as the cleric stepped aside and Dvorak—and his guardians—stepped past him into the vast, dimly lit beauty of the High Temple.

For all its size, it was very nearly empty. Only three Shongairi awaited them before the high altar. That altar was flanked by a life-sized, magnificently sculpted kyrmath, rearing in rampant challenge, faced by an equally magnificent sculpture of a lion-like urgaro. The urgaro—Shongaru's most fearsome hunter (after the Shongairi, themselves)—bore a very strong resemblance to a six-hundred-kilo sabretooth tiger. With the kyrmath, the urgaro enshrined the duality of Dainthar's nature as both Lord of the Hunt and Protector of the Prey, and Shathyra Haymar-dur-Tyru-zik-Shayma stood in the temple's sanctuary, between those exquisitely rendered statues, flanked only by his father, Yudar-zik-Shayma, and System Commander Brath-dur-Jyrak-ir-Horal.

They watched as Dvorak followed the high priest down the long nave toward them. They stood with their heads and ears high, waiting, and Dvorak watched Haymar's steady eyes.

The high priest halted just outside the sanctuary and looked at his Shathyra.

"One comes who claims right of hyrsara," he said.

"I behold him." Haymar's tone was level, his eyes unflinching.

"Does one come who testifies that he has proved right of hyrsara?" the priest asked.

"I do," Haymar replied. "I have seen that proof, written in blood and honor. As the Law requires, I bring with me witnesses who have beheld that proof at my side."

"And do they testify to that proof, as well?"

"I do," Yudar said.

"I do," Brath echoed.

"And have you seen proof that honor has been met by these, who recognize your right of hyrsara, David Dvorak?" the high priest asked, turning to the human.

"I have seen that proof," Dvorak said. That was all he was required to say, but he looked past the priest, holding Haymar's gaze with his own, and continued steadily. "I have seen that proof . . . and more. I have seen the valor with which my people's challenge was met. I have seen the blood of those who died, striving even in death to uphold the honor of *their* people. And I have seen the honor their courage, and their sacrifice, and the deaths of so many worthy foes, have paid to my people. I declare, before you and before Dainthar and before my own God, that no one could have more valiantly and gallantly contested the right as Jukaris demands. The fashion in which their champions upheld the honor of all the people of Shongaru upon the field of combat will be sung in the hymns of the Shongairi so long as the Shongair people exist."

The high priest's eyes widened, and despite his high office, despite his decades of service, his ears twitched ever so slightly. Yet that was the only betrayal he allowed of his astonishment, and he recovered himself quickly.

"And will you accept the submission of your tukarasi, David Dvorak?"

"I will."

Haymar moved then, stepping to his left, taking a position under the kyrmath's raised, rearing hoofs. He stood under the shadow of those hoofs, waiting, and Dvorak stepped into the sanctuary. He moved to his own left, until *he* stood before the urgaro. He was taller than any Shongair had ever dreamed of being, and the urgaro's curved, dagger claws were level with his own ears as he faced Haymar.

And then the Shathyra of all Shongairi bent his head deeply, covering his eyes with his hands.

"I yield before the proof of your power, of your strength, of your right," he said. "And with me, I yield my people into your hand as your tukarasi, to govern and command as you will."

"I accept and honor your submission, and with it the submission of all your people, as your hyrsara," Dvorak replied.

Silence held for a long, shivering moment, and then Haymar lowered his hands and raised his head once more. He looked across at the alien to whom he had just surrendered his empire and his entire species, and brown, human eyes looked back at him.

"I thank you for your mercy, hyrsara," he said then.

"I won't pretend it was easy," Dvorak replied levelly. "Not when I remember how many dead we never had even the chance to bury. Not when we were never even honorably challenged."

"Not when your people were murdered in their millions by our hand," Haymar said softly.

"Had it been by *your* hand, we wouldn't be having this conversation." For just an instant, Dvorak's voice was flat, hard as iron. Then his nostrils flared. "But it wasn't by your hand, or even—" he looked past Haymar to Yudar "—by your father's hand. It was by Thikair's. Retribution, yes. That, at the least, we owed to our dead. But revenge upon all your people for the actions of Shongairi who are all dead, who've already paid with their own lives for their actions? No." He shook his head. "That would be simple vengeance, not justice."

"I hope that in your people's place, my own could have been so generous of spirit," Haymar said. "I do not think we could have."

"I don't know about that. From what I've read of your people's history, of your beliefs, I think perhaps—just perhaps—you might have surprised yourself in that regard. And what matters now is that from our perspective, as well as from yours, justice has been served. The debt between us is resolved, and we'll face whatever happens from this day forward together."

"Whatever happens from this day forward?" Haymar repeated, and Dvorak nodded.

"We have a great deal to discuss, you and I," the human said. "A great deal of history to explore. I think that along the way, we'll discover just how much we truly have in common. And—" he showed his teeth in a challenge smile any Shongair might have envied "—just how many bones we both have to pick with the Hegemony."

The human starship was even vaster than Shathyra Haymar had expected.

It shouldn't have been. He'd seen more than enough imagery of it, seen three-dimensional holograms of it that incorporated same-scale Shongair starships to provide a sense of its size. But that hadn't actually helped him visualize just how immense this ship called *Relentless* truly was. A Shongair-built dreadnought like the ones the humans had destroyed was already too enormous for anyone to really visualize one of them in relationship to the mere speck of his own size, and so his brain had simply filed the human ships away as "even bigger than inconceivably big." It wasn't until now, as he beheld the reality through the viewport beside him, that he could truly grasp the fact that this ship's length would have spanned the width of his capital city. He'd never even dreamed of a mobile structure that huge.

He was the only Shongair aboard the shuttle approaching the ship. He knew his sire and his ministers had been unhappy about that, although they could never—would never—have said so. It was the first time in his entire life that he'd ever gone *anywhere* without his own security personnel, which explained his ministers' concern, but adding even one of them to the passenger list would have been an unforgivable insult to his hyrsara. He'd sworn his submission to David Dvorak, and as his hyrsara, the human was now responsible for his newly won tukaras's safety. Suggesting that he might fail in that responsibility would have verged perilously closely to an act of urmakhis.

Now the shuttle braked, decelerating smoothly toward a yawning boat bay that looked like a mere pinprick against the starship's gleaming flank. It was a human shuttle, though its *Starlander* ancestry showed clearly in its lines. As seemed to be the case with every other bit of Shongair and Hegemony technology they'd acquired, however, the base model had been refined into something far more capable. He'd already learned that their version was capable of sustained Mach 3 *level* flight, with its wings swept, whereas the original *Starlander* had been subsonic in atmosphere, and that its counter-gravity had been tweaked to permit vertical takeoff and landing even at maximum overload cargo weights, which had never been the case before. The original from which they'd begun had been the Hegemony standard for at least four hundred years, and it had served admirably over that length of time. Despite which, it appeared the humans had been unable to resist the temptation to improve radically upon it.

He thought about that, and about the report on humans' inventiveness Base Commander Shairez had produced for Fleet Commander Thikair before Thikair unleashed his kinetic devastation upon their homeworld. He'd suspected at the time that there'd been a reason the humans had included that report among the other captured memos and records they'd provided as their damning indictment of Thikair's decisions and actions. Now he was sure of it, and he turned his head, looking at the being who had become his hyrsara, and through him, the hyrsara of all Shongairi.

"I don't doubt your word about the level of technology your people had attained before Thikair's arrival, Pack Lord," he said. "Yet at the same time, I can't conceive—literally, *can't* conceive—of how you could have gone from that to . . . this—" he waved at the viewport and the gigantic vessel awaiting them "—in less than forty of our years."

"No, I don't suppose you can," Dave Dvorak replied, gazing out the same viewport at *Relentless,* looking at the starship which had brought him so far from home with fresh appreciation as Haymar saw it for the first time. "Frankly, before it happened, we couldn't have imagined it either. But there's an old saying among humans. Roughly translated, it would be 'When a man knows he's going to be executed in a six-day, it concentrates his mind wonderfully.'" He shrugged. "I'm certain we'd have made a lot of advances, taken a lot of very long strides, after we got our hands on the Hegemony's basic tech platform, under any circumstances. It's obvious to us that Base Commander Shairez was correct when she theorized that something about us, about our psychology or our mindset or whatever, makes us far more innovative than most of the species the Hegemony has encountered, including yours. But the circumstances that actually apply 'concentrated our minds wonderfully.'"

"But, forgive me for pointing this out, you'd already defeated and disposed of your 'executioners,' Pack Lord."

"No, we'd defeated Thikair's invasion. And now, we've defeated the rest of your people—*my* people, really, I suppose, according to Jukaris—as well. But the truth is, Haymar, the Shongairi were never our true enemy."

Haymar quirked his ears at the human, and Dvorak made the snorting sound the shathyra had already realized was one of the ways humans laughed.

"Don't worry. I'm not trying to be deliberately mysterious. Once we've gotten aboard ship and had a chance to lay out some groundwork, I think you'll understand exactly what I mean."

· · · · ·

ONE DIFFERENCE—AMONG many—between humans and Shongairi, Haymar decided, was the integration of their females into positions of authority. That wasn't something the Shongairi were very good at. Indeed, to be fair, it wasn't something they'd even worried about until fairly recently in their history, which was what had made Base Commander Shairez's status in Thikair's ill-fated expedition so unusual. His father, before his age-mandated transition from shathyra to shathyrakym, had inaugurated a deliberate policy of opening doors for promotion in traditionally male positions to females, but the age-old mechanisms by which challenges for position were resolved had worked against it.

It was clear the humans managed much better in that regard, given that at least a third and more probably half of the humans they'd passed aboard ship were females. Their societal imperatives were obviously very different, and he found himself wondering how that had played into the process.

At the moment, he found himself confronting one of those females, this one in a spotless white overgarment of some sort. She was only a very little taller than Haymar himself, which was rather a relief, given the giants all about him, and her long, braided hair was dark as night.

"Shathyra Haymar, meet my daughter, Maighread Lewis," Dvorak said, and Haymar bent his head in the profound respect due to the off-spring of his hyrsara.

"I greet you, Pack Lady," he said.

"Shathyra," she replied with a rather more shallow bow of her own.

"Maighread is one of our expedition's senior physicians," Dvorak continued. "Along with her sister Morgana—who, unfortunately, isn't with us here—she's worked closely with Marcos Ramos. You'll be meeting him, too, in the next few days. He's a very senior psychologist who's made the study of other species one of his specialties. His work was fundamental to our ability to grasp the tenets of Jukaris and the way in which they're interwoven into every aspect of your people's society."

"Then I'm impressed by his perspicacity, Pack Lord." Haymar's ears twitched a small laugh of his own, but his tone was serious. "I suspected from the outset that you understood our people far better than the weed-eaters ever have. But it wasn't until your demonstration of suukarma aboard Habitat One that I realized how deep that understanding truly went. It's obvious you've studied us far more deeply, and with much greater insight, than any of the Hegemony's weed-eaters have ever even bothered to try."

"If I may, Shathyra," Maighread said, "that's mostly because the Hegemony's psychiatrists have been too comfortable for far too long with psychological templates based on whether a species is carnivorous, omnivorous, or herbivorous." Haymar cocked his ears at her, and she gave a human shrug. "It's obvious—to us—why they've done it, and it's actually a very useful . . . sorting tool at what you might think of as the macro level. There truly are a great many psychological and societal traits which appear to be both close to universal and intimately bound up with whether a species evolved as predator or prey, so it has a certain obvious applicability. But it's also lazy."

"Lazy?" Haymar repeated.

"So far, yours is only the second nonhuman toolmaking species with which we've had the opportunity to interact." Her translating software's tone was very serious, Haymar realized. "That's a very small sample size, compared to the scores of intelligent species scattered throughout the Hegemony. But we've already realized that the Hegemony's comfortable systems of classification ignore what's truly important about both you and the Sarthians—and about us. Because what's *really* important is the ways in which each of our peoples *depart* from those templates, those classifications. The Hegemony files species away into different, isolated categories with sharply defined limits and boundaries, but the truth is that those categories . . . bleed over into one another. They don't seem to see that, or to be willing to admit it, if they do. Probably because it would destabilize their system. But it's something humans can't *avoid* seeing, if only because we've had to deal with it—or something very like it—for as long as we've been building civilizations. I couldn't begin to tell you how many different cultures, how many different societal matrices, humans have evolved. In that respect, it would appear we truly are rather different from the galactic norm. There are certain core psychological values which permeate all of our cultures and matrices, but most of the other species in the Hegemony—including your own—weave enormously fewer variations around those core values. Those variations exist, however, and the fact that the Hegemony doesn't understand how they arise—or the ways they can be made to work together—creates an enormous blind spot in their own thinking. One we fully intend to exploit."

"I don't understand, Pack Lady," Haymar said, ears frowning in concentration.

"You don't understand *yet*," Dvorak said, and Haymar's eyes moved back to him. "I think you will, though." He looked over his shoulder at the two nonhuman aliens who apparently accompanied him everywhere and one of his eyebrows quirked.

"Merahl?" he invited.

"Shathyra," the being he'd addressed said, "you've probably noticed that I and my mate here are also no more human than you are." Prominent nasal flaps shifted in what Haymar suspected was a chuckle. "I expect the fact we're not as tall as they are, either, might tend to give it away."

The nasal flaps moved more energetically in what Haymar was now certain was a laugh. But then they stilled.

"In the very earliest days of our civilization on Sarth, our societal models were almost as monolithic as yours are now," the Sarthian continued in a much more serious tone. "The same sorts of societies evolved virtually everywhere, although their physical environments tended to shape them in certain directions. My own ancestors' society evolved from nomadic origins on vast plains, and we eventually built a powerful empire that dominated half the world. The customs and laws of our rivals for domination, the Diantians, grew from a much more sedentary society of farmers that evolved among mountains and rivers. So far as I can tell, we Dvorakians—although we were *Qwernians* at the time—" he shot what was clearly a humorous glance at Dvorak "—were far more akin to your people than the Diantians ever were. Yet even though our society was governed primarily on the basis of custom rather than law codes and the Diantians were insufferable law mongers, our fundamental institutions were very, very similar. I suspect that in time our Empire would have evolved along the same lines as the Republic of Dianto, although it would have taken a long time if not for the humans' meddling.

"But what the Clan Ruler is getting at is that all of Sarth has been forced to make—is still *being* forced to make—enormous changes since the humans appeared on our doorstep. And as we make them, we're discovering that we're even closer akin to them, that the differences between us are much smaller, than any of the Hegemony's senior races would ever acknowledge. That's the reason we've been able to understand one another as well as we have."

"And that's not something the Hegemony has ever really been interested in," Dvorak said. "They've given lip service to it, but the entire Hegemony is really just a construct designed to safeguard and promote the Founders' position and security. Don't misunderstand me. When species have planet-killer-level technology, it's only simple sanity to worry about that tech getting out of control, wreaking havoc throughout the galaxy. We understand that. But the Hegemony's solution has been to impose its own structure, its own inflexible and inviolable bureaucratic control, to accomplish that. And there's another human saying: 'When the only tool you have is a hammer, every problem looks like a nail.'"

He paused, head cocked, and Haymar's ears nodded. That particular metaphor would never have occurred to him, but it was actually a very good one, and he filed it away for later reuse.

"That's the Hegemony." Dvorak gave one of those human-style shrugs. "To the Hegemony, every species—especially the 'junior species'—are nails, and the Hegemony is designed to hammer the hell out of them until they fall into line as part of the system that controls the dangers of technology. And along the way, they've become the perfect example of yet another human cliché: 'doing well by doing good.' The Founders' selfless devotion to the galaxy's well-being—" the bitter sarcasm in his translated Shongair was devastating "—just *happens* to make them the absolute overlords of all they survey. And they aren't about to let anything upset that state of affairs. Ultimately, your people's desire to create your own empire—one in which *you* would control what you did and the decisions governing your fate—would have led the Hegemony to crush you, because it would have threatened the absolute control the status quo's placed in the Founders' hands."

Haymar's ears nodded soberly. The Shongairi had always been aware of that. It was one of the primary reasons their efforts in that direction had been so . . . circumspect.

"Well, if they would have been unhappy with what your people had in mind, they'd have been *terrified* at where we humans will inevitably go . . . unless they stop us." Dvorak showed his teeth. "In a whole lot of ways, we represent the Hegemony's worst nightmare, and we realized that as soon as we got access to its knowledge base. The Founders saw the Shongairi as a hammer to beat our particular nail into place before we got around to disturbing their peace of mind. Since that didn't work—and especially since it failed so spectacularly—there's no doubt in our minds that the human race is ultimately under sentence of death in the Hegemony's eyes. The Founders can't allow us to survive and reach the stars, so as soon as they figure out what happened to Thikair, they'll start looking for an even bigger hammer, and eventually, they'll find one.

"If we let them."

Haymar's hyrsara's smile grew much broader, much . . . hungrier, and Haymar felt the tips of his own canines creeping into sight.

"That's one of the things that's pushed our R&D so hard, one of the reasons we've become even more innovative than we ever were before," Dvorak continued. "We've been in what amounts to a permanent cycle of emergency wartime research and development for almost fifty of our years now, and even our normal peacetime rate of advancement is several times that of the galactic norm. It's our intention to get big enough and dangerous enough the Hegemony will think two or three times before it tries to bring that hammer down again in our case. But that's going to take more than just hardware, which is the real reason we're here."

"I suspected from your actions that you had rather more than simple retribution in mind, Pack Lord."

"We do, indeed." Dvorak's lips twitched in a smaller smile that showed no teeth. "And I intend to explain what else we have in mind, but before we do, you need to be brought up to speed on some of the things we've dug out of the Hegemony database and get a more complete idea of where our hardware stands at this point. Which is why we're talking to Maighread."

"I beg your pardon, Pack Lord?"

"I said she and Morgana have both worked closely with Doctor Ramos, but they have rather different specialties and understanding alien psychology is only one of his areas of interest. Morgana is a psychologist, and that's the side of his shop she works on. But Maighread is a medical doctor, and she's been deeply involved in the hardware side of one of his other interest areas."

Haymar's ears nodded his understanding, then looked back at Maighread.

"Among other things, Shathyra, we've perfected fully functional, two-way neural computer links," she said, and Haymar's ears lifted in astonishment. "We developed them first for humans, but we were able to adapt them to Sarthians with very little difficulty. And as you know, we have a complete database of Shongair physiology. So before we departed for the Shong System, we created a neural link which ought to be fully compatible with your people."

"That's . . . remarkable," Haymar said.

"We haven't yet been able to test it, you understand," Maighread continued, "and we have no intention of actually implanting it in any Shongair until we've been able to conduct better simulations, clinical trials, and external hardware tests in cooperation with your own physicians. But I don't expect there to be any problems, and while the required net of neural feeds and sub-processors is complex, implanting the actual hardware is a fairly simple nanotech application that takes less than a day to complete.

"In the meantime, however, we've also made some modifications to the Hegemony's neural educators. In effect, we've established a neural linkage—we have an external version of it which won't require any implants in a Shongair—that allows two-way, conscious communication between the recipient's brain and the educator. We've discovered along the way that it helps enormously with integrating the new knowledge, the new data, with existing knowledge. It lets us steer the new information into the proper 'filing cabinets,' as it were, and attach it to knowledge we already possess on arrival. One of the most frustrating things when we first began using the neural educators was that the information and knowledge we received wasn't really 'ours' until we could dredge it up and consciously integrate it into our mental toolboxes by actually using it. Quite often, we didn't even realize we'd 'learned' something because it was buried too deeply, without any association to the things we already knew, no cognitive 'handle' to bring it up when we needed it. The modifications we've made obviate almost all of that difficulty."

Haymar's ears were fully erect now. In its own way, this new, smaller technological magic was even more impressive than the vast size of the humans' starships.

"What we propose to do," Dvorak said, recapturing his attention, "is to use the educator to provide the knowledge base that will help you understand our purpose here without days or six-days of discussion which might still—almost certainly would, for that matter—leave holes in our mutual understanding of one another. And Maighread is here to ensure that the modifications we've made to the educator work as well—and as safely—with a Shongair brain as they do with a human or Sarthian brain. You're my tukaras, Haymar, and I take my responsibilities as your hyrsara seriously."

Haymar looked at him for a moment, then bent his head once more.

"I believe you, Pack Lord," he said simply, and looked back at Maighread. "Whenever you're prepared to begin, Pack Lady."

. . . . .

"THAT WAS . . . A remarkable experience," Haymar said some time later.

"I know." Dvorak grinned, and Haymar's ears smiled back. Included with the vast amount of new knowledge and new information he'd acquired was a complete guide to both human and Sarthian physical and tonal modes of expression, and Doctor Maighread had been correct about how quickly accessible that knowledge would become.

"I remember when we first dove into the educators we'd captured from Thikair," Dvorak continued. "It was like magic! The speed with which we could learn new stuff was absolutely astonishing to people who'd grown up without it. It took us a while to realize we hadn't really 'learned' anything until we'd actually *used* the new knowledge, the new skills. And I think it was probably even more frustrating for us because we were adding such an enormous knowledge platform to the one we already had. We knew how to get around the old knowledge with—you should pardon the expression—the speed of thought. Finding the connections between that and the new knowledge was an unmitigated pain in the ass. One that was more than a little . . . frustrating upon occasion."

"Oh my God." The red-haired human Haymar now recognized as Lieutenant General Wilson, the brother of Pack Lord Dvorak's mate, rolled his eyes. "Do you remember Karahalios? He was the damn poster boy for that kind of 'frustration.' That's what made him such a pain in everybody else's ass!"

"Fair's fair, Rob. All of us were feeling our way into it. In fact, I seem to recall a certain Space Marine who set up a series of exercises to illustrate just how risky it was to rely on neural education where military skills were concerned."

"Yes, I *was* pretty clever that way, wasn't I?" General Wilson replied.

His tone was rather complacent, and Haymar's ears laughed. But at the same time, he understood exactly what the humans were saying. And the fact that he could now recognize such finely nuanced human humor just as easily as he would have recognized it in another Shongair was another indication of just how much they had improved the neural education process.

But his ears flattened slightly as he thought about the other new knowledge he'd filed away.

He looked around the compartment. Dave Dvorak had been joined by his mate, two more of his sherhynas, General Wilson, Admiral Mallard, and almost a twelve more of his senior advisors and subordinates. And—Haymar's eyes cut sideways for a moment—by the leader of the . . .

beings, the "vampires," who'd truly broken Thikair's invasion force. And who, if Dvorak's suspicions were correct, were the product of. . . .

"I see, now, I think, what you have in mind, Pack Lord," he said soberly. "You are clearly a human who relishes monumental challenges."

"First, you do understand that although I may be your hyrsara, I'm definitely not the ruler of my own people and that you, as my tukaras, are subject to the same laws that I am? And that our desire is to include the Shongairi as full partners in the alliance we're in the process of building?"

"Of course I understand that, Pack Lord," Haymar said, and watched Dvorak wince ever so slightly.

Obviously, the human understood his use of that particular title. It expressed Haymar's personal submission to Dvorak. A submission—although he suspected, now that the educator had given him command of his hyrsara's language, as well as his own, that "fealty" might be a better human word for all it entailed—which superseded any mere obligations of written law. For his part, Haymar understood that Dvorak saw himself only as a representative of the Planetary Union and Haymar's submission to him as submission to the government of that Planetary Union. Unfortunately, for all of the time and conscientious effort Dvorak had invested in understanding the Shongairi, he was going to be disappointed in that regard. Which, when Haymar thought about it, had a certain ironic resonance with what he now knew had happened when the humans first contacted Sarth.

"Then I think you can understand what we were talking about earlier," Dvorak continued resolutely.

"I believe I do," Haymar said. "Even with the marvelous modifications you've made to the neural educator, I still have much to digest before I can say that with absolute certainty, however."

"But on the basis of your current understanding, do you think it's workable from the Shongair perspective?" Dvorak asked very seriously.

"I'm confident that it's absolutely workable, Pack Lord." Haymar's ears shrugged. "As with your Dvorakians, you have only to give the order, and your tukarasi will obey. All of us."

"That's . . . not exactly what we had in mind," Dvorak said.

"Oh, I'm aware of that, Pack Lord. And I understand now what Doctor Maighread—" he nodded courteously to Maighread Lewis across the human-style conference table "—meant when she spoke of the 'variations on a theme' in human social evolution. As with the Sarthians, our Shongair 'variations' are much less fundamentally different from one another than the ones you humans have managed to somehow survive." His ears twitched again. "It seems to me that whether it's inherent in your psychology or simply a quirk of history, your people have demonstrated a much greater capacity for . . . harmonizing those variations."

"Speaking as another nonhuman, I wouldn't phrase it quite that way," Brykira BryMerThor said, and glanced at Dvorak. "With your permission, Clan Ruler?"

"Go ahead."

It was obvious to Haymar that Dvorak would have much preferred to dispense with any formal titles of respect. It was equally obvious that his Sarthian sherhynas were no more likely to allow that than Haymar himself was.

"As one looking in from the outside," Brykira continued, "while you humans have, indeed, acquired a much greater degree of 'harmony' than my own reading of your history would indicate you had ever achieved before Thikair's attack, harmonization is not your true strength. Your *true* strength is the ability to bring *dis*harmonious elements together in a forum and in a format that permits cohesion without requiring some 'one-size-fits-all,' to use the human idiom, conformity. It's a cohesion of disparate elements which nonetheless find a way to work together in a fashion not even the Diantians have accomplished back home on Sarth. Mind you, they were far closer to it than the Qwernian Empire ever came, but there's a reason we had so many 'proxy wars' on Sarth before your arrival."

"Don't think humans haven't had exactly those same problems," Dvorak said soberly. "We've done a hell of a lot better since the invasion and in the face of the danger the Hegemony poses, but before that outside, overarching threat turned up, we spent millennia killing each other over those 'variations.' We're as much or more liable to tribalism and distrust of 'the other' as any other species."

"You are," Brykira acknowledged with a Sarthian headshake of agreement. "It was never my intent to suggest you always produce that sort of cohesion. But you've demonstrated that you're vastly better at accomplishing it than Sarthians or Shongairi. On the basis of my own study of the Hegemony database, I'd venture to say you're better at it than almost any other species the Galactics have yet encountered. And it's an ability, a skill, in which none of the Founders appear to be interested. Indeed, I believe it would be fair to say that it's one they wouldn't even *recognize.*"

Brykira and the other Sarthians were more than simple bodyguards, Haymar realized. They were more even than members of Dvorak's clan, his family. They were also *advisors,* and with the advantage of his newly implanted knowledge, it was obvious from Dvorak's expression that he took their advice, their insights, very seriously, indeed.

"Captain Brykira's had far longer to think about this than I have, Pack Lord," the Shathyra said, "but from what I've so far seen, I think ou is almost certainly correct. Speaking as both your tukaras and as one who's ruled a seven-star-system empire in his own right, I believe you humans have two unique strengths."

Dvorak gazed at him for a moment, then nodded for him to continue.

"First, and most obvious, is your ability to innovate, to continually upset the technological stasis the Hegemony holds so dear. I believe the Shongairi have more of that ability than most of the other Galactics, but I very much doubt we could come even close to matching you in that regard. I agree with your xenologists' hypothesis that we've internalized much of the Founders' antipathy towards 'unbridled technology' without even recognizing that we had, but looking at our pre-Hegemony history, we still never equaled your people's rate of progress. It's that strength, that ability, which will terrify the Founders, but that represents their own overriding blind spot. Because slow though they may be to recognize it, that isn't the greatest threat you pose to the Hegemony. Not by a wide margin."

"No?" Dvorak watched him speculatively, although Haymar strongly suspected the human already had a shrewd notion of at least some of what he was about to say.

"No, Pack Lord. It's true your technological capabilities will make you dangerous to the Founders. But if your suspicion that there was once a *fifth* Founder, one who may have been more technologically capable than the others," he nodded at Vlad Drakulya, who sat to Dvorak's left, "is correct, I think it's entirely probable that the other four found an answer in sheer numbers. It's impossible for any of us to know if the gap between the fifth Founder and the others was as great as the one your own people have been opening between the current Founders and yourselves, but the historical record suggests it would be folly to rely solely upon the superiority of your hardware when you inevitably confront the Hegemony.

"Which brings me to your second, far more dangerous strength. One the Hegemony may be much slower to recognize. And that's the one Captain Brykira just summarized. Neither Sarthians nor Shongairi could possibly build the sort of alliance your President Howell contemplates. We simply couldn't do it. We lack the . . . modalities to give it the cohesion, the unity of direction, it will absolutely require to stand in the face of the Hegemony's power. Believe me, I say this from the perspective of a shathyra who's ruled the Shongair Empire for almost twenty-seven of your years. I've invested an enormous amount of energy in adjudicating differences between packs, all of whom spring from the same species-wide, universal societal matrix. Differences far less major than many of those your own people have faced. I couldn't even begin to adjudicate differences between multiple *species*."

"You seem to be doing a pretty fair job of analyzing the task," Dvorak pointed out.

"It's one thing to analyze the task, Pack Lord; it's quite another to perform it. I am Shongair, and I'm proud of my people's heritage, our accomplishments, our culture. Yet it never once occurred to us, when we sought to create our own empire as protection against the Hegemony's 'hammer,' to do it in any fashion other than by conquest. Other than by forcing other species to submit to us. In fact, by becoming our own version of the Hegemony, hammering one nail after another into our empire. That's the way our customs, our social mechanisms, our basic psychology work.

"And that, Pack Lord, is very different from what your President Howell believes—rightly, I think—is essential for any possible hope of resisting the Hegemony. This 'alliance' of his is something neither Sarth nor Shongaru is equipped to create and sustain. It's possible that—in time—we could *learn* to do that, but not even your marvelous modifications to the neural educator will make that easy. *Knowledge* is one thing;

customs and habits of thought are quite another, especially when they run thousands of years deep."

"I agree, Clan Ruler," Brykira said quietly, and Dvorak looked at oum. "I will say that despite Shathyra Haymar's reservations, I'm confident we could eventually learn to do that, if only from the human example. Indeed, Grandbearer Yairka is working hard on those lessons at home. The problem is that the Shathyra is right that it will take time. Probably a *lot* of time, and time is a resource of which we have only a finite supply."

"No," Dvorak said firmly.

"Clan Ruler, you know my thinking on this. And you know—Grandbearer has told you so, often enough—that I'm far from alone in that thinking among your Dvorakians. For that matter, among the people of Sarth in general."

"It isn't going to happen," Dvorak said even more firmly.

"Clan Ruler—"

Dvorak's raised hand cut the neutro off. But then he looked around at the table and saw several sets of human eyes regarding him with intense speculation.

"Would it happen that there's something you haven't gotten around to mentioning to the rest of us?" Rob Wilson asked after a moment.

"That's actually a pretty good question," Alex Jackson said. He bent a particularly speculative look upon Dvorak. "I know there are tons of good reasons Clan Ruler Dave should be getting confidential messages from Chancellor Yairka, but it's interesting that there's been a whole clutch of them you've never gotten around to mentioning to me at all. For that matter, I've had the feeling for a while now that there's been something cooking away under that utterly discreet Sarthian surface of Brykira's. And I've wondered why ou never discussed whatever it was with me. Why do I suspect the reason is that you told oum not to, Boss?"

"Because—" Dvorak began, then cut himself off.

"Forgive me, Dave," Vlad said, "but I, for one, would very much like to hear whatever Herdsman Belsorak—" he stressed the title of nobility ever so slightly "—might have to suggest. And—" he continued calmly when Dvorak opened his mouth again "—I think I may already have a fair idea of what that suggestion is."

He held Dvorak's eyes for several seconds, and then Dvorak shrugged and waved both hands in the air.

"Go ahead, Brykira—go ahead!"

"Thank you, Clan Ruler." Brykira shook ous head respectfully, then looked at Vlad.

"The truth is simple," ou said. "Shathyra Haymar is absolutely correct about the inability of his people or my own to . . . orchestrate something like President Howell's alliance. For that matter, the very notion of an 'alliance' isn't something with which we Sarthians or, I suspect, the Shathyra's people would be truly comfortable. In our historical experience on Sarth, alliances have come and gone far too often, and for what in retrospect often turned out to be trivial reasons. Friction between 'allied' heads of state, factionalism, personal power-seeking, jealousy of individual sovereignty and national 'freedom of action.'" The neutro nodded ous head sadly. "The history of Sarth is littered with alliances which have failed, and *this* alliance simply cannot be allowed to do that, especially if the Clan Ruler's theory about what happened to the fifth Founder is accurate. If any of our species are prepared to challenge the Hegemony, then it must be in the knowledge that the only possible outcomes are victory or death, because that certainly appears to be precisely what the surviving Founders did to their vanished fellow Founder."

Human heads nodded somberly all around the compartment. Only Dave and Sharon Dvorak's didn't. He sat stonily silent; she sat looking at him in more than half-horrified speculation.

"Understand, Prince Vlad," Brykira continued, "my spouses and I agree—I think virtually all of *Sarth* agrees—that President Howell is right that the Hegemony must be resisted. But even though we've joined his 'Terran Alliance,' the truth is that something stronger, with deeper foundations than the simple alliance President Howell's envisioned, is necessary if his overall strategy is to succeed. I find it somewhat ironic that the President saw that so clearly in the case of your own homeworld but not in the case of his Terran Alliance."

"You are thinking not about an alliance, but about a nation," Vlad said softly, and the breathing humans in the compartment stiffened.

"I am," Brykira acknowledged with a firm shake of ous head. "And it must be a star nation which can orchestrate all of its disparate elements, create that cohesion and unity of purpose."

"I realize I've had far less time to think about any of this," Haymar said, "but that's very much what had occurred to me. And at this moment, Pack Lord, I can think of only one basis for an interstellar government that would work for my own people and what I so far understand about the people of Sarth."

"*That's* what you've been sitting on from Brykira and the others," Sharon Dvorak said quietly. "I knew you were shutting them down about something!"

"Because I can't—*won't*—do it!" Dvorak slammed the palm of one hand on the tabletop and half glared at the others. "What happened on Sarth was a damned *accident*. It wasn't planned, it wasn't anything I wanted, it just frigging *happened*. And Alex and Fikriyah are absolutely right—I had no choice but to accept it if I didn't want to destabilize half the goddamned planet! So I took the job, and I've done my best to do it. Or at least find a way to accommodate to it. And now," he looked at Haymar, "I'm hyrsara to the entire Shongair species, because that was the only way to get them sat down at the table. But I'm not about to become some sort of interstellar 'emperor' because of a couple of accidents. I'm not suited for the job, just for starters, and there's no way in hell I'm going to abuse my position as ambassador to take it. No way. It is *not* going to happen!"

He closed his mouth with an almost audible snap, and silence enveloped the compartment. It lasted for seemingly endless seconds, and then Haymar raised one hand.

"It will take me some time to actually internalize the differences between human and Shongair honor codes, Pack Lord. Despite that, I believe I understand your position. At least I understand that assuming that sort of position would be impossible for you under your own code of honor. I respect that, deeply. And it's possible Captain Brykira is too pessimistic about the long-term sustainability of an alliance, as opposed to an actual government. *Possible*, but I doubt it. I think ous idea needs to be carefully considered, however, and not least because among my own people, the direct personal rule of an emperor—or a pack lord—is our 'hardwired' default position. The long-term stability of any other form of governance would be . . . questionable."

"Haymar, I *won't* do it." Dvorak's voice was hammered iron, and Haymar's ears nodded.

"I understand that, Pack Lord. And I accept it. But by the same token, you must accept that Brykira has raised a very good, very telling point. One I fear we have little choice but to address. Understand that from the moment I submitted to you in the High Temple, the people of Shongaru became *your* people. That's how they see you and how they will always see you, and there is unfortunately no way to change that.

"But," he continued as Dvorak's eyes grew almost desperate, "as you yourself said to me, you are subject to the rules and the laws of the government—of the Planetary Union—to which you swore your oaths as I swore mine to you. And because you are, *we* are. You need not become Shathyra if by the oath you swear someone—or some entity—else assumes that role. In that instance, you would become the channel, the conduit, through which *that* shathyra's authority flows to us. I suppose the human equivalent, if I have this correct, would be that you would become our 'grand duke,' rather than our emperor, and that as you owe fealty to your government, we would, as well, because of our fealty to *you*."

"But the Planetary Union doesn't *have* an emperor," Dvorak protested. "It's a republic!"

"You know," Jackson said thoughtfully, "that's true. But look at it this way, Boss. Under President Howell's proposal, the Sarth System, the Shongair Empire, and the Planetary Union would all have become sovereign members of the 'Terran Alliance,' right?"

"Of course." Dvorak nodded a bit impatiently.

"Well, suppose that instead of a simple alliance, we created this interstellar government Brykira's talking about. And suppose it had a federal structure, like the Planetary Union, and that Sarth, the Shongair Empire, and the Planetary Union all became member states within it."

"I don't—" Dvorak began, then stopped and sat staring at something only he could see.

"You know," he said at last, slowly, "that . . . *that* might actually work. Figuring out how to structure something like that would probably be an enormous pain in the ass, but making Judson's 'alliance' work was going to be a major pain, anyway. Nothing along those lines had occurred to anyone on Earth when we headed out, though! I expect that if we come home and cheerfully propose the creation of some sort of interstellar union it's going to cause just a few hissy fits."

"'Hissy fits'?" Vlad repeated quizzically. "And what, pray tell, is a 'hissy fit'?"

"It's a sissy name for what we more manly Space Marines call a shit fit," Rob Wilson replied for his brother-in-law. "And it's probably an understatement, too. But does that mean it won't work? I mean, I can't even begin to count the things we've done since the invasion that nobody *before* the invasion would have thought could possibly work. Since then, I think we've all turned into the White Queen!"

"And what kind of Space Marine reads Lewis Carroll?" Dvorak demanded with a grin. "Still, you've got a point. We *have* had a lot more experience believing 'impossible things before breakfast' since we got hammered, haven't we?"

"Damn straight, Skippy," his brother-in-law said, earning a chuckle from his sister.

"Geez, if I'd guessed for a minute where it was going to lead, I never would have accepted Judson's invitation to Greensboro," Dvorak muttered.

"Oh, don't go there!" his wife said scornfully. "Of course you would have! For exactly the same reasons you got yourself shot in the woods and blown up on Sarth!"

"And what would those be?" Dvorak asked suspiciously.

"Well, the first one is *stupidity*," she replied in withering tones. "And the second is even worse—responsibility! All they have to do is say to you—to either of you," she added, glaring at her brother "—is that they *need* you. It's like you've both got some kind of Pavlovian switch in your heads!"

"I do not—" Dvorak began, then paused as he met his brother-in-law's eyes across the table. They looked at each other for a long moment.

"*Anyway*," Dvorak said, moving his eyes elsewhere, "like I say, Alex may be onto something here. It's going to take a lot of thought, though."

"Well, at the very least you've got the voyage time back to Earth," Wilson pointed out. "Might be a good idea to get the basic proposals nailed down before you head out, though. I suspect that the Shongair perspective—" he glanced at Haymar "—will have to weigh pretty heavily. I mean, I know they're your tukarasi and all now, Dave, but they *have* colonized seven star systems while we only have one."

"You know, for a Space Marine, you actually have a good idea every once in a while, don't you?" Dvorak said.

"Please!" Wilson rolled horrified eyes. "Whatever you do, don't let *that* get out!"

II

Fire in the Stars

MANTOURA RESORT,
CITY OF ITHYRA,
PLANET TAIRYS,
TAIRYON SYSTEM,
419.9 LY FROM EARTH,
NOVEMBER 9, YEAR 42 TE.

First Minister Sherak, Second Hatched of Her Brood, Daughter of Ursahl, of the Line of Sercom, allowed her breathing slits to sag open as she relaxed in the mud bath. *Pure bliss*. Every third day, she gathered with her friends at the exclusive spa for a little girl time. It also let her keep her digit on the pulse of how things were going in the community at large, and that had allowed her to surprise her aides on a number of occasions by turning up with information they'd been trying to keep from her, for one reason or another. Which usually had something to do with lucrative transfers of credit. *Kairsiak* was a noble ideal, and Sherak was prepared to allow her subordinates a reasonably free hand in achieving all that they could, but there was reason in all things. That was why those aides were no longer in her service.

In fact, one of them was no longer even alive, having been dropped in the middle of a desert to bake.

Her eye turrets swiveled slowly in opposite directions, but her panoramic scan wasn't taking in the amenities of the Mantoura Resort or the glories of the Ithyra Bay over which it looked. She was, in fact, watching the male attendants who strutted around the facility, and her bioluminescent hide was a contented shade of blue.

"I think I'll take that one," she said finally, her left eye settling on one of the males while her right eye ensured her fellow mud bathers had marked her selection.

"You always take the largest one," Korash, Third Hatched of Her Brood, Daughter of Teeros, of the Line of Maljona, complained. "Coming here with you, my chances of ever getting Barsulo are zero."

"He's not here today, anyway," Histaro, Second Hatched of Her Brood, Daughter of Kosikal, of the Line of Pornahk, noted, her hide coral in amusement. "I was here yesterday, and he wore me out. The trick is not coming on a day when First Minister Sherak is here."

"Besides," Sherak noted, "Barsulo, First Hatched of His Brood, Son of Intorsul, of the Line of Shelmak, is far too hetero for you. You wouldn't walk right for a week."

"Truth," Histaro said. "I know I won't be ready for more for at least another couple of days."

"I can't afford to come here more often than I do right now, anyway," Korash muttered with a sigh, her hide turning a jealous chartreuse.

"Why is that?" Sherak asked. "I know this is the best resort on this side of the continent, and its prices are exorbitant, but that only serves to keep out the riffraff. You're one of the richest matriarchs on the planet, and you've never had an issue with the fees here before. What's changed?"

In fact, she knew, Korash was an inveterate credit-clutcher, the worst miser on the face of Tairys. Despite her enormous personal wealth, she was the sort who never had—*could* never have—enough of it. That had quite a lot to do with why she and Sherak were such close companions, friends . . . and mutual back-scratchers. There was almost always something the First Minister could do to help along her friend's interests. And vice versa, of course.

Now Korash sagged into the mud a moment, then shook herself to clear her breathing slits.

"It's the nuisance animals again," she said. "They're interfering with my Surak Lakes plans. There are so many of them in the area that the completion of my mansion is almost two weeks behind schedule, and the costs are soaring well over budget."

"I don't understand your fascination with the Surak Lakes in the first place," Histaro said, her hide turning a light, confused maroon. "The Kurian Highlands are way too far inland to be of any interest."

"True, but the lakes are beautiful and deep." Korash bobbed a seated shrug. "Besides, it's about halfway between here and the Kryirus Inlet. In addition to being a *major* resort area, with half a dozen spas almost as good as this one and for *half* the price, I also have a number of ongoing . . . operations on the inlet that I like to keep an eye on."

"But the Highlands are so *dry*. I'll bet your hide turns rough and pasty in less than a stohmahl," Histaro noted.

"Not with the water walls I'm having built into the mansion." Korash's hide turned a proud khaki color. "There's one in every room to keep the humidity up. It also provides a soothing, splashing sound as the waters tumble into their pools and mud wallows."

"That sounds very relaxing," Histaro said, bobbing slightly in agreement.

"It is . . ." Korash replied. Her chewing surfaces grated as her hide turned amber. "Or it *would be* if the stupid nuisance animals weren't upstream of the site, polluting the water with their filth."

"This is the project you told me about last month?" Sherak asked. "The one you're supposed to have finished next month?"

"It is." Korash sighed. "We're going to have to push back the wallow-warming party, though, if something isn't done about the nuisance animals. My construction manager is complaining about his people drying out up there. They go into the bush to chase off the nuisance animals and it seems they've succeeded, but then the accursed creatures come right back again the next day, as if they were too dumb to understand it's not their land anymore!"

"Hmmm . . ." Sherak lost her blue coloration as she thought. "There were a few credits in the budget—" her hide turned coral "—well, they weren't *in* the budget, so much as manufactured *by* the budget, if you take my meaning. . . ."

Korash and Histaro bobbed knowingly.

In many ways, there was no such thing as a Tairyonian "budget" in the sense a more primitive species might have used the term. The star system's massive industrial infrastructure was capable of producing everything that a far greater number of Liatus might have required. All of that capacity belonged collectively to the system's population as a whole, but some means of administration had to be found to manage its allocation, and Tairyon relied on the same system which had evolved long, long ago on the Liatu homeworld.

The system government administered that industry, and each of the Tairyonian ghyrhyrmas, the great herds of the system, was allocated its own share of the total capacity. For ease of calculation, that share was quantified as credits, something a lesser species might have called "money." Each ghyrhyrma was responsible for administering its own share of capacity, but individual Liatu were free to determine how their personal portion of their ghyrhyrma's share was utilized. Most of them used enough of it to provide basic housing, food, and other necessities, then "banked" the rest of it—as credits—for discretionary use, purchasing things like this visit to the Mantoura Resort, or for a new model air car, a coveted piece of art, or to reimburse another Liatu for the performance of a personal service. Korash's construction crews were a prime example of just how those credits might be used to procure the service of skilled professionals, for instance. It was a flexible, fungible system which also provided incentives for Liatus to participate in activities which permitted them to amass greater individual credit accounts. Incentives which some of them—like Korash—took to extremes.

In *theory* the government itself needed no credits. All it needed to do was to allocate resources from the portion of the capacity reserved to its use. In fact, it was much more convenient for bookkeeping purposes to use the credit system to manage its own resources. And if that just happened to create a situation in which portions of the far more liquid stream of credits could be diverted to other ends—or Liatus—well. . . .

Both of Sherak's companions were well aware of her ability to "cook the books" of the star system's budget in order to hide—or find—credits whenever she needed to.

"In any event," she continued now, "I think there are some credits available for Prosesecha training that haven't been allocated yet. In fact, I think System Prosesecha Commander Frelika has let his forces slack off recently, and he probably needs a little motivation to keep them in shape. Perhaps clearing some of the stupid animals from your property might be just the thing for him to keep his forces at peak efficiency."

"You think so?" Korash asked.

"I know so." Both of Sherak's eyes swiveled to focus on Korash. "And while we're chatting, I heard from Delegate Tumarky just day before yesterday."

Korash nodded. Tumarky, Seventh Hatched of her Brood, Daughter of Kyrmar, of the Line of Harn, the senior System Gyrtoma delegate from Pryhika and one of Sherak's closest allies, was up for reelection. The elections themselves were little more than a month away, and she was lagging in the polls behind an upstart but ambitious and well-organized challenger.

And it just *happened* that Korash did a great deal of business—and had a commensurate degree of political influence—in Pryhika.

"How *is* Delegate Tumarky?" Korash asked. "I haven't spoken to her in *forever*. I should probably pop over to Pryhika and throw a little soiree for her. Remind everyone what a good friend of mine she is, how much I appreciate their supporting her. And perhaps I should make sure she gets an invitation to the wallow-warming, as well."

"I'm sure she'd appreciate both of those things," Sherak agreed with another flash of coral amusement. "However, speaking of wallow-warmings, I'll expect this one to be something of a legend."

"It will be, of course," Korash said, bobbing.

"And I'll expect a private wallow, with Barsulo to take care of my . . . needs."

Korash's hide took on a gray tone.

"But he works here—"

"I'm sure you'll find a way to get the management to allow him to . . . work offsite, shall we say?" Sherak asked. "Credits talk, after all." Her hide took back on the blue tint she'd had earlier. "You can even have him when I'm done with him."

"Just make sure you don't have anything to do but recover the next day," Histaro said with a chuckle, her own hide a much deeper shade of coral.

"So we are in agreement?" Sherak asked.

Korash took a deep breath, and her breathing slits opened to sigh heavily.

"Yes, Sherak. We have a deal."

Sherak bobbed slightly.

"Good," she said, her eyes swiveling again to track two of the male attendants. "And speaking of the elections, that wretch Kilmartu is actually planning to challenge me for *my* Gyrtoma seat again. I would have expected even her to have learned better by now, but she *is* persistent. Have either of you heard anything interesting about her or her businesses I can use against her?"

How long . . . how long is this going to take?" Korash asked.

She waved an arm toward the half-completed mansion on the far side of the lawn on which the Prosesechas had parked their air cars when they'd arrived. Those didn't seem to be damaging the landscaping—not too much, anyway, although the troop transport was making a number of large divots the construction crew would have to fill in.

More costs! She turned an orange-red in anger. *One more thing to blame the nuisance animals for!*

"Shouldn't take more than a few stohmahls," System Prosesecha Commander Frelika, Second Hatched of His Brood, Son of Cormad, of the Line of Hylis, replied. As the System Prosesecha commanding officer, he was both the highest law enforcement officer for the star system and—for all practical purposes—the chief game warden for the nuisance animals, responsible for "managing" their herd size and ensuring they stayed in their specified preserves. "The key to doing this successfully is ensuring they don't come back, which means displacing them significantly from your lands."

"Absolutely!" Korash said, her hide yellow in disgust. "We've chased them away a number of times, but they always seem to come back again. I gave my crew the rest of the day off. Take all the time you need to make sure the vermin go far, far away."

"We will, Domynas," Frelika said with a small bob, his hide brown in determination. "We saw several herds of them on the way in, though, and we'll want to make sure we drive *all* of them out of the local area. Where there are some, others will gather."

"Please make sure all the vermin are gone! If there's anything I can do to assist, please let me know."

"I'll be in my command vehicle if you're looking for me," Frelika said. "It *is* a bit dry here, after all."

"I totally understand," Korash said. "I look forward to being rid of these pests so the crew can get the wallows installed. My life—and my temperament—will be greatly improved!"

"If you'll excuse me then, Domynas, I'll get to work."

The female bobbed and loped off, and Frelika watched her go with one admiring eye, his hide puce in appreciation. Hopefully, they could get this done quickly; if so, he might be able to wrangle an invitation to the exclusive wallow-warming he'd heard was going to be held once the mansion was complete. The party was normally a little over his social status—it was a gathering of elite industrialists and their political cronies who seldom wanted a law enforcement official's potentially inhibiting presence while they spoke of their dealings—but if his job was done well, and it allowed the construction to conclude satisfactorily. . . .

He bobbed once to himself and loped back to his command vehicle. Clambering aboard, he closed the door as quickly as he could and his hide purpled at the increased humidity.

Why would any reasonable person want to live here? he wondered yet again. And, yet again, he had no answer for the question.

His people were amphibians, and they *could* go for as much as two or three days without immersing themselves in water. That wasn't to say that sort of abstinence was good for them, however, and the truth was that he enjoyed it even less than most. His hide had begun tightening painfully in the arid climate outside, and he didn't envy 3rd Platoon, the troopers who'd be on the ground. Given the amount of exertion they were looking at, the enviro suits which would keep them hydrated while they lumbered around the countryside would be a necessity, not a luxury, by the time they were done. Of course, one of the perks of superior rank was a comfortable perch in a humidity-controlled air car. He allowed himself a coral flash of amusement, then shrugged, climbed onto his couch, and began adjusting his equipment in preparation for the operation's commencement.

The panels in front of him included three monitors, as well as radio equipment that allowed him to transmit and receive on three frequencies simultaneously. Each of the monitors and radios was linked to one of the platoons he'd assigned to today's task, and the monitors could display the body camera view from a single Prosesecha or the entire platoon, as well as the gun camera footage from any of the air cars.

"Are we ready?" he asked, one eye swiveling to look down the line.

"First Platoon is ready," Lieutenant Kerbal said. "All cars indicate green."

"Second Platoon is set," Lieutenant Salgar reported. "All cars indicate green."

"Third Platoon is . . . stand by."

Lieutenant Garnach muttered something into his radio, but Frelika's aural implants didn't pick up what the officer said.

"Third Platoon is ready," Garnach said after a moment. "One of my troopers had a problem getting into his suit. Too much living the good life in the barracks, I guess. Don't worry, Domynar; we'll run him back into shape when we're done with this."

"Very well," Frelika said. "Stand by to execute."

"We get to execute them?" Garnach, who was new, asked. "I thought—"

"No," Frelika said, cutting him off, "we're not supposed to use lethal force." He flashed a coral chuckle. "That said, if it should happen that some of them get trampled under by their own kind, well, they're just animals, and the herds around here are too big, anyway. The truth is, we really should have culled some of them out years ago. There are probably too many for the range to support, even if they weren't being so destructive to Industrialist Korash's property. So a little breakage is probably okay . . . assuming it happens accidentally."

The three lieutenants bobbed their torsos respectfully.

"Move out," Frelika said.

The lieutenants began issuing orders, and the scenes displayed on his monitors went into motion. Third Platoon split up, with its first squad heading north to function as beaters for First Platoon's air cars and its second squad heading east to do the same for Second Platoon's air cars. The mansion was located on the north shore of the westernmost Surak Lake, in the steep foothills of the mountain chain that ran down to the lake's shoreline.

It didn't take long for the air cars to begin calling in movement on the ground below them, and the lieutenants vectored their troops and air cars to intercept the creatures.

"Got one band to the north," Kerbal said. "Air Car Two is on station."

Frelika switched the 1st Platoon monitor to the appropriate car's feed and looked out onto the foliage of a Kurian Highland hillside. The view zoomed in on some darker motion, and a herd of the nuisance animals came into view.

"That's them," Frelika noted. He'd been System Prosesecha Commander for over thirty local years, and he'd seen more of the destructive, filthy nuisance animals than he could have counted. Certainly Entropy's own lot more of them than he *wished* he had!

They moved slowly across the hillside, obviously not having heard the air cars yet. Although they had the ability to walk on two legs, the nuisance animals usually moved in a more natural quadrupedal stance, leaning over to walk on their too-long arms. The animals stopped periodically to grab an ilar fruit while their young cavorted around them, climbing the small trees and wrestling with each other.

"They don't even wash the stuff they're eating before they cram it down their throats?" Garnach—who'd just joined the company and was on his first animal control operation—asked, yellow in disgust.

"They're just animals," Kerbal said. "What do you expect?" He paused, issuing orders, then chuckled. "Watch this."

On the screen, one of the air cars flashed past the group from west to east, its autocannon firing, and a row of divots opened up to the south of the creatures. The image was silent, but Frelika could see the light flashing on top of the air car and knew its siren was also screaming to help panic the creatures and get them moving.

It worked. The nuisance animals reacted in immediate, stark terror. The whelps who'd been rolling around in the dirt and leaves came to their feet, squalling in frightened distress, and dashed madly toward the adults. The females to whom they'd run scooped them up, slinging them onto their backs, where they clung desperately while the adults dropped to all fours and raced away to the north in headlong terrified flight.

"My squad isn't going to be able to keep up with that!" Garnach complained.

"Don't worry about it," Kerbal replied. "We've done this a bunch, and we know what we're doing. Just keep your troops headed north in case the air cars missed any of them or the stupid animals run the wrong way."

Frelika watched the monitor and silently agreed with Kerbal as he listened to the communications through his aural implant. The 1st Platoon troopers knew what they were doing. They set up a holding pattern above the herd and took turns diving down on the animals to fire alongside or behind them, driving the creatures in the direction he'd pre-briefed. Every third or fourth run, they dropped a half dozen flash-bang grenades into the midst of them. The grenades detonated with brilliant thunderclaps of sound guaranteed to get any nuisance animal moving and keep it that way.

Second Platoon hadn't found any of the creatures yet, so Frelika continued watching 1st Platoon work. After a few siltahls, the herd's flight slowed as the younger ones—and the older ones, for that matter—tired. The 1st Platoon troopers responded by firing closer to the animals, and their pace sped up again as adrenaline gave the terrified animals a second wind.

"What's that?" Garnach asked. He pointed to his monitor. "Just northeast of the herd?"

"Looks like rough ground," Kerbal said. "Maybe a set of ravines? Hmmm . . . that's not good."

"Because the nuisance animals might fall in and get hurt?"

"No. Because it's going to slow them down." He issued an order to drive the herd back to the west, and another car ripped past, but at least one of the smaller ones fell headlong into one of the ravines. It smashed into the ground and lay still.

"Oh, for Entropy's sake," Kerbal muttered as a second, larger animal jumped into the ravine. It came back out again, carrying the first, which wasn't moving.

"Looks dead," Salgar said, swiveling an eye to his left.

"Yeah."

"That's going to slow them down."

"I know," Kerbal said, tinting an angry orange-red, and Salgar chuckled.

"I thought you said your guys knew what they were doing," he jabbed.

"Shut up and mind your own platoon."

Kerbal issued several orders, and another air car flashed across the screen. The rounds intersected the running animal and put it down.

"There," Kerbal said, his hide turning a happier shade of violet. "Problem solved."

"That works, too," Frelika said.

"Animals!" Garnach shouted suddenly.

Frelika swiveled an eye to see the camera number Garnach was looking at and brought the feed up on his monitor. Some of the ground troopers had come up on another herd of the nuisance animals, hiding under a copse of trees, and had nearly stepped on them before seeing them. Several of the males yelled and brandished their flint-tipped spears, while the females and young fled.

Before Garnach could say another word, his troopers shot the males down.

"Help them!" Garnach said to Salgar.

"Love to," Salgar replied, "but your troops are too close. I need separation, or I'm just as likely to drive the animals *into* your troops."

Garnach turned maroon, not sure of what to do, while his troops threw several flash-bang grenades.

"Dumbass cherjuks," Salgar growled as the grenades detonated and—blinded by the grenades—several of the animals walked *toward* the 3rd Platoon troopers. The rest fled, running hard, as the troopers shot down the approaching flash-blinded creatures. "Bunch of rookies."

Frelika bobbed slightly in agreement. The engagement was sloppy and had resulted in a number of nuisance animals' deaths, but it *had* gotten the rest of the group to flee. Within a maunihirth, the nuisance animals had opened up enough separation for Salgar to call in his air cars, and the rout was on. With the situation in hand, Frelika flipped back to 1st Platoon's animal drive. The herd they were chasing was already several shrevjesh away from the mansion, although the group had slowed considerably again. Even though rounds were landing nearby, the animals didn't speed up again.

"That group is spent," Frelika said. "We'll come back to them in a bit. In the interim, have your air cars set up a search pattern in conjunction with the ground troops, and let's make sure we didn't miss any."

Frelika rose from his couch a satisfied shade of violet. The group 2nd Platoon was harrying was now in full flight—those who weren't dead, anyway—and some of the air cars were breaking off to search for additional groups. Everything was going according to plan, and they should be finished up right on schedule. The rest of the operation should be easy; they were only dealing with animals, after all.

The Liatu word for them was guharnak. Literally translated, it meant "nuisance animal," and that was precisely how Liatus thought about them. It was the only thing they *ever* called them, and what that resulted in was plain to see. But at least the recorded imagery in the holo display above the conference table was silent. That was something.

At least he didn't have to listen to the screams.

Instead, he watched in the silence, with eyes of brown flint, as the terrified Tairyonians fled the "harmless" flash-bangs and the "only firing over their heads" machine gun fire that ripped up the terrain all about them.

He and Sarah had visited Africa with Jolasun Olatunji often over the last several decades, and they'd made it a point to make a stop in Bwindi Impenetrable National Park in the mountains of Uganda, above Lake Mutanda, on most of those occasions. It was three thousand kilometers from Jolasun's Nigerian hometown, but that was less than an hour by air car, and it was always worth the trip. And the reason it was—for him, at least—were the silverback gorillas. He'd watched them for hours, admiring their demeanor, their lordly movement, the openly displayed affection of their family groups. Indeed, their majestic presence as they stalked through the lush greenery was what he associated most strongly with the park's misty mountainsides and gorgeous vistas.

Which made this even worse, even harder to watch.

The Tairyonians' resemblance to gorillas had become even more pronounced as their intelligence receded under the impact of the Liatu genetic bomb and they dropped back into the four-footed stance of their most primitive ancestors. As they'd evolved into toolmakers and users, they'd almost entirely abandoned that stance in favor of an undeniably more awkward, almost waddling (by human standards) bipedal stance on their short, powerful rear legs. But a species which could barely re-member how to knap flint had less use for an upright posture that freed their hands for use, while a species whose only defense from its planet's apex predators had become flight needed all the speed and agility its members could muster as they fled madly across the wilderness of which they had once been masters.

Even before that, Tairyonian babies, like infant gorillas, had habitu-ally ridden their mothers' shoulders. That, too, had become even more pronounced as the species devolved mentally. But it was a more pre-carious perch for a young Tairyonian, because, for all of the apparent similarities between them, Tairyonian females lacked the dense hairs to which gorilla babies clung.

Now he watched a Tairyonian mother fleeing desperately from the pursuing Liatu Prosesechas, tearing a path through the scattered scrub while her baby clung frantically, arms wrapped around her massive neck. He couldn't see the mother's face, and even if he could have, the translating software which would have read a *Liatu* expression wasn't up to the task of reading Tairyonian facial expressions. None of the He-gemony's xenologists had cared enough to record sufficient data about the "nuisance animals" whose world this had once been for even human cyberneticists to program the software for that. But he didn't need to read expressions to recognize a mother's terror for more than just her own life when he saw it.

The entire, panicked band fled with her. The males tried to stay between the females and young and the pursuing Prosesechas goading their terri-fied flight, waving their crude, flint-tipped spears in futile defiance of the wheeling, diving, terrifying air cars. One of the not quite adolescent chil-dren went down, catapulting into a narrow, sheer-sided ravine, cartwheel-ing as he—or she—flew through the air . . . then smashed headlong into the unforgiving stone of the ravine's far wall with shattering force. A female stopped, hurled herself down into the ravine, scooped up that broken, un-moving body, and ran onward, clutching the child—*her* child, he knew—to her chest with one arm while she fled on her other three limbs. She ran madly . . . until a single bust of gunfire wasn't fired "over their heads."

The heavy machine gun rounds ripped through her *and* that shattered child in an explosion of blood and ruptured tissue. She went down, still trying feebly to claw her way across the terrain after the rest of her band, clinging to her child. Her struggles grew weaker yet.

Then her head drooped, and her struggle ended in stillness.

Another mother crashed into a barrier that didn't yield. She went down, rolling, and her infant lost his grip and flew through the air as the older child had done. But this time, miraculously, one of the adult males managed to throw away his spear, reach out, snatch that small, frail body from the air. And then he was running, holding the baby, his body arched over it to protect it from the diving, wheeling, shooting, siren-wailing Prosesecha air cars.

An older member of the band, probably one of its elders, stiffer and slower with age, fell behind. A younger adult raced back, seized the older Tairyonian's arm, tried to help him flee. The air cars singled them out for special treatment, harrying them mercilessly, and he could almost physically *taste* their panic and helpless, hopeless terror.

He closed his eyes, then inhaled deeply.

"That's enough," he said quietly. "I think we've all seen enough."

"Of course, Mister President." Assistant Ambassador Arthur McCabe's voice was soft. He sent a command over his neural link, and the hologram vanished.

Judson Howell nodded his thanks, although he also made a mental note to remind McCabe—again—that he was no longer President of the Planetary Union. Not that he expected it to do any good. He knew he'd never be allowed to shake free of the title, but he rather wished he could.

He opened his eyes and looked around the conference table. None of the faces looking back at him were any happier than he felt.

"It's about time we made our presence known to these . . . people." His voice was as flinty as his eyes. "I know we all hated watching that, but I think it's good we did. I think the way it puts things into perspective will be valuable going forward."

One or two of the others looked as if his words made them a little uncomfortable. Or worried, perhaps. As if they were afraid he'd allow his fury to drive his policy into extreme measures. It was interesting that McCabe didn't, though.

Howell made himself sit back, consider whether or not the people behind those uncomfortable expressions might have a valid cause for worry.

And whether or not he much cared, if it turned out they did.

The Tairyon Mission had left the Sol System four years after the Shong Expeditionary Force. Yet despite the fact that the Tairyon System was almost a hundred and eighty light-years farther from Earth than the Shong System, here the Mission was, little more than a year after Dave Dvorak and his expedition must have reached Shongaru. They'd known well before Dvorak left that Charles Gannon and his crew were likely to improve the Gannon Drive's efficiency even further, but it had been impossible to predict how long the drive tweaks might take, or precisely how effective they'd be once they happened. And because it had been essential for Dvorak to overtake *Târgoviște* before Vlad Drakulya carried out his mission to bombard the Shongairi back into the stone age, they'd been unable to wait for that to happen. He and his expedition had left at the very last moment they could be confident of arriving in time with the *current* iteration of the drive.

Those tweaks had happened since, however, and PUNS *Inexorable,* Howell's flagship, was eighty percent faster in phase-space than Dvorak's *Relentless.* She also had a substantially higher energy budget, because her "energy siphon" reached even higher into p-space to drink still more deeply of its endless fountain. As a result, her energy weapons were about ten percent more powerful, but aside from that, the two superdreadnoughts were essentially identical . . . as were the other seven *Relentless-Alpha*-class ships which accompanied *Inexorable.* In fact, Second Fleet, the military component of Howell's expedition—although it was technically a "mission," not an "expeditionary force;" Jolasun and the State Department had been firm about that before they left—was twice as strong as the task force that had accompanied Dvorak.

Partly, that was because they'd had four more years to prepare it. Even more than that, however, it was because the Liatu had no equivalent of the Shongair Jukaris code.

Submission and dominance they understood, yes, but for all their contempt for the "brutality" of the carnivorous Shongairi, it had never been codified into their honor code. For that matter, despite their self-recognized status as one of the galaxy's most enlightened species, it would have been impossible—not difficult; literally *impossible*—for them to visualize any circumstances under which an honor obligation to a non-Liatu could take precedence over the interest of their ghyrhyrma. Over *any* interest of their ghyrhyrma. Anything that contributed to their ghyrhyrma's horkaraha—their herd's "potency" and strength—was automatically honorable. Anything that detracted from that power and strength in any way whatsoever was dishonorable. The strength of the contribution might make an act more honorable, and the cost of the detraction might make an act less *dis*honorable, but that was the basis for almost all their herd morality and honor constraints, to one degree or another.

That was true even among competing Liatu ghyrhyrmas, but they'd evolved social constructs, portals, through which ghyrhyrmas had learned over the millennia how to resolve most—well, *many*—of their intra-species conflicts. They'd even evolved the notion of a species-wide ghyrhyrma that encompassed all Liatus, although that concept still took second place to their loyalty and their obligations to their individual ghyrhyrmas. In fact, they regarded their membership in the Hegemony as an *inter*-species modality dedicated to much the same purpose. In their view, it was a defensive association of species who had banded together to prevent any of their fellows—and, especially, any species from outside that association—from encroaching upon their horkaraha. They followed the Hegemony's inter-species legal agreements scrupulously, with painstaking attention to detail, because that was how they protected their own ghyrhyrma from those inherently competitive "herds." But the possibility that their membership in the Hegemony might imply any moral or honor obligation to any other species—or that they might be expected to honor even the Hegemony's dictates for any reason other than pure pragmatism and self-interest . . . or fear—was simply beyond their mental horizons. As a consequence, the notion of negotiating in good faith on the basis of anything beyond raw power was equally beyond them, despite their disdain for the Shongairi.

Under the circumstances, that had suggested this was a time, as one of Howell's presidential predecessors had suggested, to "carry a big stick."

And, further buttressing that suggestion, this was the expedition most likely to be reported to the Hegemony Council, eventually, at least. That, too, made this a time to project strength as emphatically as possible.

Judson Fitzsimmons Howell intended to be very emphatic, indeed.

The one thing humanity simply could *not* do was project weakness, offer the Hegemony *any* reason to think Dvorak's "monkey boys and girls" might be bluffing. There were those back on Earth who'd been only too obviously worried that Judson Howell would channel his inner avenging angel once he reached Tairyon. And he was honest enough to acknowledge that they might have been right to worry about that. On the other hand, as "Jackie" Fisher had said in 1899, "If you rub it in both at home and abroad that you are ready for instant war . . . and intend to be in first and hit your enemy in the belly and kick him when he is down and boil your prisoners in oil (if you take any), and torture his women and children, then people will keep clear of you."

Howell had never heard of Fisher until Dave Dvorak introduced him to the British admiral's biography, and Fisher, who'd never done anything in his life in half measures, had been deeply in love with hyperbole. As one of his contemporaries had said, crossing Fisher had been rather like being run over by a bus without suffering physical injury. Which didn't mean that there wasn't a certain degree of truth buried in that particular flight of hyperbole, because Fisher had also been right when he said, "The essence of war is violence."

Howell didn't want a war with the Hegemony. He simply didn't see any way to avoid one, except—possibly—for the threadbare hope that the ultra-cautious Galactics could be convinced that the Terran Alliance was too dangerous, too far outside their neat power structure, for them to risk what it might do if they attacked. Or, as Rob Wilson had boiled down Fisher's injunction, a Hegemony that believed the entire Terran Alliance was "bug-fuck crazy" might just decide to "keep clear" of it.

He didn't know about convincing the Hegemony Council of that, but he did know that humanity's only long-term hope of survival was to draw a line and then hold it, no matter what the Galactics might bring to bear. And that was the real reason he was here.

To start drawing that line, right here and right now.

He'd assembled a seasoned team to help him do that. Dvorak was obviously the most experienced human ambassador when it came to dealing with aliens, since he was the only one who'd ever done it, and Rob Wilson had commanded the planetary combat component of the mission to Sarth. But Howell's senior military commander was Admiral Francisca Swenson, who'd commanded the naval component of the Sarth mission, and his senior Space Marine was Lieutenant General Aleandro Palazzola, who'd been Wilson's chief of staff on Sarth. And on the xenology side, Dvorak might have taken Marcos Ramos with him, but Howell had Doctor Evelyn Shumate, Ramos's research partner, who'd focused her own specialization on the Founders in general . . . and the Liatu in particular.

And then there was Assistant Ambassador McCabe, a man who'd learned a great deal on Sarth and even more since his return from that system. Once upon a time, Arthur McCabe had been numbered amongst the humans who believed Howell and his allies' assumption of the Hegemony's automatic, implacable hostility to humanity, when it finally learned the "monkey boys and girls" were loose among the stars, was unnecessarily pessimistic. Now, after his experiences on Sarth—and three more years as one of Dave Dvorak's deputies (and the senior analyst assigned to the Tairyon System) before Dvorak's departure—Howell suspected he was prepared to make humanity's point to the Liatu even more emphatically than Howell himself.

But McCabe was only an *assistant* ambassador, number three in the diplomatic chain of command. Howell's senior diplomatic deputy was Ambassador Fernando Garção, onetime President of Brazil, onetime Planetary Union Senator for Brazil, and one of Judson Howell's closest friends.

"All right," he said now, looking at the military side of the conference table. "Can you recap what we know about the Liatu's capabilities, Francisca?"

"A lot of what we think we know is actually inference, Mister President," Admiral Swenson replied. "We do have quite a bit of hard observational intel, but even that observational data has to be treated with a great deal of caution until we actually see their hardware in action."

Howell nodded.

Everyone in that spacious compartment was confident that humanity's current technology was superior to that of the Hegemony. They had the Hegemony's own database to confirm that. But they had a less than complete—as in virtually nonexistent—window into how the Hegemony's various species might have applied their own technology to their military needs. Well, that wasn't quite accurate. They did have complete information on the *Shongairi's* military hardware, courtesy of Fleet Commander Thikair's captured ships, but they had none at all on the Liatu. Each Hegemony member species' navy—for those who maintained a navy, at least; not all of them, especially among its junior members, did—was its own business, officially at least. No doubt some office in the Hegemony's labyrinthine bureaucracy kept tabs on what each species was building, but there was no requirement for that information to be shared with other species. And especially not with someone as juvenile, bloodthirsty, and carnivorous as the Shongairi. Which meant that although there'd been some information on the Liatu's naval capabilities in Thikair's files, all of it had been speculative, and none of it had been confirmed.

Because of that, Swenson's watchword, with Howell's firm approval, had been circumspection. She was as confident as he was that she had a big enough hammer, if she needed it, but until she found out just how resistant this particular nail might prove, she had no intention of making her own presence known.

Now the admiral turned her head to look at the uniformed PUN captain sitting to her right and smiled slightly.

"You want to take the President's question, Tifton?"

"Of course, Ma'am," her chief of staff replied, and looked across the table at Ambassador Howell . . . who happened to be his father.

"Essentially, Sir," he said—Tifton Howell was the only member of the mission's command staff who never addressed his father as "Mister President," possibly because he suspected the father in question would strangle him if he did—"we've demonstrated to our satisfaction that the Liatu are even more . . . myopic than we'd expected. This is really more Hector's bailiwick than mine," he nodded at Commander Hector Lopez, Swenson's staff intelligence officer, "but it's pretty clear they don't have a clue we're here. We've been in Tairyon space for over two months now, and we're less than twenty light-minutes from their inhabited world."

As he spoke, his neural link flicked his listeners a mental display of the star system, showing the mission's location on the fringe of the local asteroid belt, a third of the way between Tairys and Sembach, the inner of the system's two gas giants. They were just far enough above the system's ecliptic to keep them off the same plane as the Liatus' system infrastructure.

"Despite how long we've been here, there's no indication they've picked up even a trace of our ships," he continued. "Their system traffic control certainly hasn't issued any challenges or attempted to contact us, at any rate, and we haven't seen any indication they've even gone to a higher readiness state. We can feel pretty confident at least one of those things would have happened if they'd noticed us. And anybody with a particle of situational awareness should have. Hector?"

He glanced at Lopez, and the black-haired commander nodded.

"Tifton is correct, Mister President." Lopez was Guatemalan, and while his English grammar and vocabulary were impeccable, the accent of his birth language clung almost aggressively to his pronunciation. "In fairness, their outer surveillance systems are tasked to look for phase-drive signatures from arriving FTL ships, and we don't have a phase-drive. Or not in the sense the Hegemony does, at any rate. The Gannon Drive's signature when we go sublight is quite different and rather 'quieter,' for want of a better word. It's primarily the sudden appearance of an intense gravitic point source, not the energy-shedding effect of the Hegemony's drive—you might say it sucks energy *in* instead of radiating outward—which means it's not anything their platforms would be specifically looking for. And the grav-spike lasts less than ninety seconds, so even if they were looking for it, their detection window would be far briefer than for a conventional p-drive. For that matter, our cloaking technology is much better than anything we found in the captured Hegemony database. Even if they'd been looking, very little of our Gannon signature would have leaked out.

"But as Tifton's also pointed out, we've been here for quite a while. We can't help occluding the occasional star if anyone glances our way, and ships this size can't avoid some EM signature. For that matter, we radiate a *lot* of waste heat. Our cloaking fields let us trap and divert both those signatures—radiate them in a direction of our choice—but they still have to go somewhere. We're directing them away from the inner system, where most of their infrastructure and all their military installations are located. In fact, we're radiating most of it straight 'up,' perpendicular to the plane of the ecliptic. But even so, there are enough outer-system platforms, associated with their asteroid extraction and the orbital gas mining operations around Sembach—and, especially, enough intra-system traffic moving back and forth between Tairys and Sembach—that any remotely alert passive system should have seen *something* by now."

"Which is what leads us to conclude they're probably even more complacent than we'd expected," Captain Howell said. "The fact that we've been able to insert drones clear into the *planetary atmosphere* to record things like . . . that—" he gestured at the space the horrific hologram had occupied "—without anyone's noticing only suggests that even more strongly.

"At the same time, it's important to avoid equating complacency with lack of capacity or capability. As the Admiral said, we've amassed quite a bit of data, both from direct shipboard observation and, even more, from the remote platforms we've inserted into the inner system. We know, for example, that there are fewer Liatu naval units in Tairyon than we'd originally anticipated. On the other hand, their orbital defenses seem to be at least fifty or sixty percent heavier than we'd projected." He shrugged. "Obviously, we'd be happier if they weren't, but I don't think anyone should be surprised our initial estimate was off, since in all honesty, what it really was was a *guess*timate.

"Some of the additional fixed defense may be because they also seem to have more and larger orbital habitats to protect than we'd anticipated, given our analysis of their patterns of colonization. Everything in the captured database emphasizes how much most Liatu hate artificial habitats. They build a lot of their infrastructure on dry land, primarily because building constraints make that simpler and more convenient, but they *are* amphibians. They're clearly biased in favor of the watery side of their environment when it comes to living quarters, and at least two-thirds of their recreational activities seem to center around large, open bodies of water. They're not unique in loving water, of course, but they do take it to an extreme most toolmaking species don't. Back on Earth, even today, somewhere around sixty percent of the human race lives within a couple of hundred kilometers of the coast; for the Liatu, it's more like ninety-five percent living within *one* hundred kilometers of the coast. Or of a major river or a lake, at least. I suppose there's no reason these orbital habitats couldn't incorporate a lot of water area, but it would present some significant engineering challenges, especially for a species that can't generate gravity to order.

"As far as their defensive installations are concerned, they carried out a live fire exercise for one of their orbital weapons platforms while we were watching, and we got a lot of data from that. It doesn't look like they have anything the Puppies didn't have, although their energy weapons seem to be rather more powerful and longer ranged. One thing we weren't able to get was any hard data on their shipkiller missiles' capabilities. Overall, the way they polished off the 'opposition forces' looked pretty competent. In fact, it may have looked *too* competent. To be honest, I think the Admiral would have been pretty unhappy with me if *I'd* arranged that exercise." He grimaced. "We can't be sure without a better read on their weapons' capabilities and with no idea at all how they briefed in the participants ahead of time, but that looked an awful lot more like a 'gimme' than a serious exercise designed as a challenge."

"I realize we don't want to underestimate these people, Mister President," Admiral Swenson put in, "but I think Tifton has a point about that, and it actually makes a certain kind of sense, when you think about it."

Howell raised an eyebrow at her, and she shrugged.

"Let me preface this by saying that, having been exposed to Ambassador Dvorak, I've developed an interest in history as a sort of self-defense mechanism." Howell's lips twitched at her dry tone. "And if the Ambassador were here, I suspect he'd point out the historical parallel between, say, the British Royal Navy of 1890 or so and the current Hegemony."

Howell hid a smile at both her tone and the way in which her prefatory comment echoed his own thoughts—courtesy of Dvorak—from a few moments before. On the other hand, he was pretty sure he knew where she was going—he'd read Fisher's biography, so he knew the Sisyphean task the long-dead admiral had faced in dragging the Royal British Navy kicking and screaming into the twentieth century. But if he was right about where she was headed, it was a remarkably valid point, and one eminently worth making for all present. So—

"In what way?" he asked.

"In the wake of the Napoleonic Wars, the Brits were *the* naval superpower," Swenson replied. "By the end of the nineteenth century, the British Empire covered a quarter of the Earth's surface and ruled twenty-three percent of its population. For obvious reasons, they had the world's biggest merchant marine, and that meant their navy was the largest on the planet, as well. They built to a 'two-power' standard, which assumed their fleet had to be at least equal in power to the next two largest navies combined, and they'd been—literally, not just figuratively—the world's oceanic 'policeman' for almost a century. Quite a few other nations resented that, but most of them were perfectly content to let someone else shoulder the responsibility and pay the price tag to protect *everyone*'s commerce. And resentment or not, no one—at least until Kaiser Wilhelm came along and stepped on his sword with both feet—was stupid enough to think they could challenge the British Empire's naval supremacy. And the officers and men of the Royal Navy knew all of that. So since there was no *military* threat on their mental event horizons, at least until the Kaiser got antsy, they concentrated on things like seamanship, smartness of drill, and showing the flag instead of actual preparation for battle with anything like a peer competitor. Of course, eventually Wilhelm and Tirpitz did come along and decide to build their 'risk fleet,' which dragged the Brits into an enormous upgrade of their own to maintain their superiority."

She gave Howell a respectful but rather pointed look, and he nodded back ever so slightly in acknowledgment. He had no desire to reprise Alfred von Tirpitz's role and evoke a Galactic Fisher and a Hegemony "dreadnought revolution." Unfortunately, he strongly suspected it would be better to do that than to rely on the Hegemony's nonexistent restraint and benevolence.

"So what you're saying," he said out loud, "is that it looks like the analysts back home who predicted that the Liatu—the Hegemony in general—would have allowed their military preparedness to atrophy because they'd gone so long without facing any meaningful threat may have been right?"

"Mostly." Swenson nodded. "That would certainly seem to be a fair description of their present mindset, at least, based on what we've seen so far. And given the fact that any halfway capable system sensor net should have seen *something* to suggest we're here. But at the same time, given what we know about their basic technological capabilities, those weapons platforms of theirs appear to be *very* heavily armed by their own standards. They may be so invested in a 'peacetime' mentality that they're basically blind as bats, but that doesn't mean they've skimped on firepower. I'd hate to go up against what we've seen so far with Hegemony-level technology, to be honest."

"What we've been able to infer about Liatu psychology makes it abundantly clear that benevolent altruism or anything remotely like trust for anyone outside their own 'herd' aren't part of their psychology," Doctor Shumate reminded them. "Admittedly, those qualities don't seem to be much of a factor for *any* of the Founders, at least on an inter-species basis, but the Liatu take that to a level all their own. The fact is that, as far as we can tell, they have the next best thing to zero empathy for any other species. Their record here in Tairyon is only one instance of what the 'peaceful herbivores' have done when a less-advanced species . . . inconvenienced them. For that matter, let's not forget that the first contact between any of the Galactics, long before the Hegemony was created, was when the Kreptu ran into the Liatu in the Kanzhyquo System after the Liatu had already claimed it." She shook her head. "That led to an actual shooting war. They managed to turn it off pretty quickly, by Galactic standards, but the Liatu have that tucked away in their memory banks, and their basic attitudes towards other species really haven't changed a lot.

"So it probably shouldn't be a surprise that they'd build defenses based on what someone with that mindset would expect—or fear, at least—out of those other species. And we know from the Hegemony database that the Liatu are one of the species who were most opposed to the expansion of the Shongair Empire. They protested every single decision by the Hegemony Council to allow the Shongairi to claim new star systems. Well, except for the decision to hand over Earth, anyway." She shrugged. "I suspect they had an even better appreciation than most of the long-term threat the Shongairi posed to the Hegemony's neat little mafia because it was more or less what they would have expected out of *themselves*, vegetarians or no, had the positions been reversed."

Howell nodded slowly. That tracked with his own pre-mission analysis. Which, he reminded himself, was the best reason not to wed himself too firmly to it. Preconceptions were one of the best ways ever invented to shoot oneself in the foot.

"That's understood, Evelyn," he said out loud, and looked at Garção. "What's your take, Fernando?"

"The same as yours, I'm quite sure," Garção replied with a slight smile.

"I believe the consensus of our military experts is that we've learned all we can from passive, covert observation." He quirked an eyebrow at Swenson and her uniformed subordinates. They nodded firmly, and he shrugged. "Given that, and given what we've actually seen of their . . . behavior since our arrival," it was his turn to gesture at the space the hologram had occupied, and there was no trace of a smile on his face when he did, "I believe it's time to move to Phase Two."

"You're right, that *is* what I was thinking. And since we happen to be two of the smartest people I know," he bared his teeth at Garção in a fierce grin, "I agree with your estimate."

His grin vanished, and his expression was much more serious as he looked around the table one last time.

"Let's do this," he said.

PALACE OF GOVERNMENT,
CITY OF ITHYRA,
PLANET TAIRYS,
TAIRYON SYSTEM,
419.9 LY FROM EARTH,
NOVEMBER 18, YEAR 42 TE.

First Minister. Forgive me, First Minister, but you need to wake up."
First Minister Sherak opened her eyes unwillingly, then blinked
up at the aide standing beside her bedchamber wallow. She rolled
one eye to check the time display without taking the other from the obviously nervous male and scowled as she discovered that it was almost
exactly midnight.

"Why?" she snapped.

"I apologize profusely, First Minister." The aide ducked his head, covering his eyes in abasement. "I would never have interrupted your sleep
period if it wasn't an emergency!"

"Emergency?"

Sherak's eyes narrowed. She thrust herself up out of her wallow and
felt the bedchamber's warmer air circulate about her. She kept her own
wallow set to an even lower temperature than most Liatus. At her age, she
needed the chill to help her settle into sleep, but there were disadvantages
to that. Like the fact that it took longer for her wits to come fully online
when she was dragged from her slumber unexpectedly.

She draped a smartfabric wrap about herself, turning up its temperature to help the warming process, and glared at her hapless aide. From
his body language, it seemed likely he realized her thoughts were not at
their best and knew better than to admit he did.

Which irritated her even more deeply.

"What sort of emergency?" she demanded.

"It's a com message, Domynas."

"You woke me from a sound sleep for a *com message*?"

Her tone promised dire consequences, and the aide covered his eyes
once more, his hide tinged with the gray of worry and just a touch of

ocher fear. Her fulminating gaze should have ignited him on the spot, but she made herself draw a deep, whistling breath through her breathing slits.

"And just who is this 'emergency' message from?"

"We . . . we don't know, Domynas."

"What?" Sherak blinked both eyes, certain she must have misunderstood.

"It came in addressed specifically to you, First Minister. It had the proper access protocols for the Palace communication center, but it was voice only, with no visual. And there was no return address, no originating data stamp."

"That's impossible."

"It should be, Domynas." The aide bobbed his torso in acknowledgment. "But it happened. And if the . . . person who sent it is telling the truth. . . ."

His voice trailed off, and Sherak glowered at him, her hide touched with the orange-red of anger, although that anger was directed less at him than at the obvious absurdity of what he'd just said. The system datanet logged the origin and destination of every com call. That was hardwired into the computers, damn it!

She started to tell the aide exactly that, in no uncertain terms, but her brain was beginning to function with more of its wonted efficiency as her blood temperature rose.

"And what did this 'person' have to say?" she asked instead, in something closer to a normal tone.

"I think it would be best if you heard it for yourself, First Minister. With your permission?"

The aide gestured at the wallowside data terminal. Sherak bobbed curt permission, and he tapped the touchscreen, bringing it online.

"Greetings, First Minister Sherak," a voice said from the terminal. It spoke perfect Liatu, which was no surprise . . . until it continued. "My name is Judson Howell, and I am speaking to you on behalf of the human race."

Human race? Sherak blinked. What in the name of Entropy was a "human," and what was one of it doing in *her* star system?

"We've come," the alien voice continued as if it had read her mind, "because one of your Hegemony's member species recently attacked our homeworld without provocation or challenge. The attack took us by surprise, and the initial kinetic bombardments inflicted heavy casualties upon my people." The voice hardened. "We were . . . displeased by that. Which is why our defenders killed every single one of our attackers and captured their entire fleet intact."

Sherak's breathing slits closed. Killed them all? Captured their *entire fleet*? No lesser species in recorded history had ever so much as driven off a Hegemony capital ship, far less defeated and captured one of its *fleets*!

"What happened to the individuals foolish enough to attack us, and the fact that I'm here, in your star system—not to mention the fact that you haven't so much as noticed my starships' arrival—should indicate to you that we possess a high level of technological capability. I advise you to bear that very carefully in mind during the course of our visit here."

Sherak forced her breathing slits to open. Whatever else might be true, the "human's" translating software was clearly superior to that of her own species. The soft menace in that last sentence came through perfectly.

"I've been sent, with a suitable escort, to make contact with the Hegemony. My mission here is to determine if peaceful intercourse with any of the Hegemony's member species is possible . . . or worth the bother."

The alien's coolly dismissive tone was as infuriating as it was frightening. And it hadn't mentioned how powerful its "suitable escort" might be, Sherak noted. Somehow she doubted that had been a simple oversight.

"As part of that determining process, our purpose is to . . . evaluate the Hegemony. A significant part of that evaluation will include your species'—and the Hegemony in general's—mode of interacting with other intelligent species. Frankly, our initial contact with you 'Galactics' was less than promising in that respect. Killing half our homeworld's population was an . . . infelicitous way to introduce yourselves to us.

"In the event that we decide the Hegemony isn't worth joining, or that it poses an ongoing threat—bearing in mind that one of its members has already attacked us—then this visit will be the first step in neutralizing any such threat, instead. And we will neutralize it in what I can assure you will be an effective manner."

The alien's tone cut like a knife, now, and orange-red fury—fueled in no small part by something far too much like panic—flooded through Sherak like a tide of acid.

"I will be back in touch with you shortly, First Minister," the "human" said. "For now, I'll leave you to consider what I've already said. And I'll also add for your consideration that it would be . . . unwise to react belligerently when our warships allow themselves to be detected."

The com went silent, and Sherak, Second Hatched of Her Brood, Daughter of Ursahl, of the Line of Sercom, stared at the blank display while icicles of fear fluttered up and down her spine.

COUNCIL CHAMBER,
PALACE OF GOVERNMENT,
CITY OF ITHYRA,
PLANET TAIRYS,
TAIRYON SYSTEM,
419.9 LY FROM EARTH,
NOVEMBER 18, YEAR 42 TE.

U nacceptable," First Minister Sherak said half a stohmahl later as she addressed the council, her hide a bright orange-red. *"Unacceptable!"*

Her eyes swiveled to encompass the entire council—the other four ministers, High Ghyrcolar Ithral, Ghyrcolar Urtal, and Navy Commander Segmar—and she was encouraged to see their hides were similarly colored.

"What part is unacceptable to you?" Second Minister Hyrak, Fifth Hatched of Her Brood, Daughter of Yorach, of the Line of Sercom, asked.

"All of it!" Sherak exclaimed. "The temerity of this—this, *human!* To talk to one of the Founding races in such terms is unacceptable! He will be taught his place. What is even more unacceptable, though—" she turned to look at Navy Commander Segmar *"—is how they were able to sneak up on us in the first place."* If anything, her color brightened, although it stayed orange-red. "And also, *where in Entropy's sake are they?*"

"I have people looking into it," Navy Commander Segmar, Second Hatched of His Brood, Son of Kalisar, of the Line of Jorik, said. "We'll find out what happened and rectify it."

"I don't want to know later, once you've had time to think up excuses, and I don't care about rectifying it for later; I want to know *right now* what went wrong, and I want to know where they are!" She emphasized each of the last three words. "How did they sneak up on us?"

Segmar looked down and covered his eyes, but when he looked up again, he met her gaze.

"I do not—at this moment—know where these 'humans' are," he admitted, "but I do have some idea about how they were able to approach us undetected." He turned a light shade of green in embarrassment. "I fear, however, that you won't like it."

"I already don't like it!" Sherak screamed. "What is it that I'll like even less?"

"I fear that all of our systems were not online or scanning," Segmar replied. One eye twitched toward Lyralk then came back to Sherak. "That may be how it was possible."

Sherak turned to Third Minister Lyralk, who a more belligerent species might have called the Tairyon System's Minister of War.

"Can you tell me why in Entropy's sake our systems *weren't* online and scanning?"

"Because, up until now, there was no need," Third Minister Lyralk, Third Hatched of Her Brood, Daughter of Yortha, of the Line of Symalk, said. "Operating the defense forces, warships, and orbital platforms increases wear and tear on the systems. It degrades their lifetimes, requires additional maintenance and replacement. It is—or it was, anyway—more efficient to have most of them in a state of readiness, rather than actually operating. It maximizes the ghyrhyrma's horkaraha."

"I am having difficulty seeing your reasoning. How exactly does allowing someone to sneak up on us maximize the herd's potency?"

"Equipment that's operating wears out and has to be replaced. That's a net drain on resources. By not operating all the equipment, we save those resources, or find ourselves in a position to divert them to other beneficial ends, which maximizes our horkaraha." She bobbed a shrug. "In the past, we always knew when someone had arrived because our outer surveillance systems detected the arriving ships' phase-drive signatures. The phase-signature detectors couldn't tell us anything about the ships which had made them, but it did warn us that someone was out there. When we received that notification, we had plenty of time to bring up our other, more sensitive systems to locate and, if necessary, deal with the intruders."

"So what happened this time? Why didn't we get the notification? Is the system broken?" Sherak's coloration cooled from anger to the amber of frustration.

Lyralk swiveled an eye toward Segmar, who answered.

"No, First Minister, it isn't broken; I checked." His shading went to the maroon of confusion. "Nor do I know why we didn't detect their arrival, since our phase-space sensors most definitely were up and online. I can only hypothesize that they've found some way to mask the energy-shedding effect of re-emergence into normal space."

"And how is *that* possible?" the First Minister demanded.

"In that respect, Domynas, neither I nor any of my technicians can even begin to speculate." Segmar's hide was an odd mixture of maroon confusion, gray uneasiness, and embarrassed green. "Frankly, I find the ability to do that extraordinarily difficult to accept even as a purely intellectual possibility. Unfortunately, any conventional phase-drive signature *would* have been detected. Unless, of course, they dropped sublight at least half a standard light-year out. But then, at eighty percent of light-speed, it would have taken them *months* to reach us. And—" he acknowledged less than happily "—we certainly should have detected the energy signatures their particle shields would have generated at that velocity." He bobbed his torso in a gesture of perplexity. "Neither of those possibilities is anything I'd call remotely *likely,* First Minister. It's just that my analysts can't come up with any other workable hypotheses. Which means that however *un*likely those explanations may be, one of them must be accurate."

Sherak regarded him a bit balefully. And, little though she cared to admit it, a worm of worry gnawed deeper into the pit of her second belly as she contemplated what he'd just said. In the end, she decided, the second possibility—that the humans had simply made their phase-space translation beyond detection range and then crept in on Tairyon sublight—was by far the more likely. The phase-drive predated even the Hegemony. It had been a mature technology for almost 75,000 Standard Years! And these . . . "humans" were supposed to have come up with an entirely new version of it that no one else could even *detect*?

Ridiculous!

"That may explain how they got here," she said out loud, "but it does nothing to explain how they've snuck up on us!"

"That also is something I have no answer for, but one thing I am sure of is that there are ways to get around whatever cloaking effect they're using to hide their ship. Now that we're aware of their presence, we can look for stars that are suddenly occluded, for example. No matter how good the cloaking, if they come between our sensors and another star—even another planet, here in Tairyon—it has to interrupt our observation of that star or planet. We'd see that if we were looking. Also, they must have some sort of electromagnetic and waste heat signatures that we can look for."

"If we haven't already seen it, what makes you think you can find it now?"

"Perhaps they're directing it somewhere else," Segmar said.

"How? And where?"

"Again, we don't know the 'how.'" Segmar obviously hated admitting that, but he did so without flinching. "It's not something we've ever explored. And I think we have to bear in mind that we know nothing about this species. It's entirely possible that they've managed to come up with a few tricks that simply haven't occurred to us. In the end, though, the laws of physics are the laws of physics, Domynas. Whatever Kreptu fairy tales may say, there isn't really any such thing as 'magic.' So I'm confident that, eventually, we *will* know how they've done it. In the meantime, my analysts and System Surveillance Commander Urdia's technicians have been focused on the 'where' portion of your question."

"And?" Sherak demanded.

"The greatest likelihood, at the moment, would appear to be that they're somehow directing their emissions away from all of our near-space sensor platforms into the outer system. Our inner-system arrays face outward, and there was never any reason to build *outer*-system arrays that looked inward. Aside from active navigation and traffic control systems, all of our outer-system platforms are designed solely to detect phase-drive signatures from beyond the system periphery. Perhaps if we were to turn them toward the inner system, rework their software, we *might* catch a glimpse of the intruders. . . ."

"Perhaps?" Sherak asked. "That's the best you can do? There must be something else we can do to increase our chances of finding them." She swiveled one eye each toward Segmar and Third Minister Lyralk.

Segmar and Lyralk looked at one another for a moment, then Segmar said, "Well, as I've said, Domynas, the arrays out there aren't designed for this. Their design function is to detect the intense, concentrated energy signatures of a phase-drive emergence. Waste heat and electron leakage can be very powerful, especially in something the size of, say, one of our dreadnoughts, but compared to a phase-drive signature, they're very weak. Probably too weak for the platforms we already have in place to resolve reliably. But if we could get some additional passive arrays out there—arrays that *are* designed to look for thermal signatures and neutrinos—"

"Yes." Sherak bobbed her torso emphatically. "Augment the detection gear. There are a lot of places we can hide them in the out-system industrial platforms, especially the gas-mining platforms around Sembach and Corsalt. But do it *quietly*—I don't want the humans to know what we're up to. There are routine cargo shuttles that go to the outer system; use them."

"Yes, Domynas." Segmar covered his eyes. "It will be done. We will find the humans."

"Is there anything else can we do, Navy Commander?" Third Minister Lyralk asked.

"I've already authorized the launch of a number of reconnaissance drones. We were able to fix a rough position from which the transmission you received must have originated through cross-plotting several lines of bearing. If we send up enough platforms, we should be able to find them in that volume."

Sherak bobbed slightly.

"Whatever you were going to send, double it," she said. "I want these humans found, and I want them found now!"

W e're ready when you are, Mister President," Francisca Swenson said from Judson Howell's display.

Inexorable was more than large enough for as many command and control centers as anyone could have wanted. At the moment, Swenson sat in her command chair, surrounded by her staff, while Howell was in Mission Control Central, also tucked away in the ship's heavily armored core hull and a mere two kilometers aft of Flag Deck.

Three of the planet Tairys's 25.4-hour days had passed since he'd transmitted his message to First Minister Sherak. And, he reflected with a nasty smile, made sure she received it in the middle of the night. Nothing like being awakened from a sound sleep to face a nightmare, he thought, and his smile vanished as he remembered the morning a governor of North Carolina had experienced just that.

But that had been then. This was now, and he'd let Sherak and her advisors stew in their own juices long enough. And given his own analysts time to observe the Liatus' response to the way he'd just kicked over their amphibious little anthill. And kicked over their complacent confidence that they were masters of all they surveyed, right along with it. They might not have admitted that even to themselves yet, but deep inside, Sherak, at least, had to suspect it was coming.

Swenson's highly stealthy remote platforms had kept the space around Tairys under close observation. They'd watched as the system's defense forces, warships and orbital platforms alike, moved to a far higher state of readiness. Eventually, at least. It was informative that it had taken them over six hours just to bring their active sensor net completely online. If he'd chosen to announce his mission's arrival with a missile salvo, none of those defenses would even have seen it coming before they died.

Although he'd been badly tempted to have Swenson insert still more drones into the planet's atmosphere for his intelligence staff, he'd resisted the urge. He wasn't sure how much of his temptation had stemmed from an actual desire for more information and how much of it had been the desire to underscore the PUN's ability to do that at will, even if only to himself. Nor was he remotely certain they could do it without being *detected*, now that the Liatu knew the mission was here. Even though they obviously still hadn't figured out exactly where "here" was, they were clearly watching near-planet space with every system they had, and it was probable they *would* spot any additional inbound platforms. Of course, there were some psywar arguments in favor of letting them see the humans spying on them, letting them know just how closely they were being observed. But it wasn't as if Howell really needed any more air-breathing reconnaissance, and there were plenty of countervailing psychological reasons to avoid letting the Liatus spot any of the humans' platforms or—especially—warships until he was good and ready to reveal them.

Swenson's sensor teams, on the other hand, had detected and tracked scores of Liatu recon drones spreading out, searching for the human ships they knew had to be there somewhere. For the most part, they'd concentrated their search within no more than four or five light-minutes of the planet. Apparently, they'd managed to at least roughly backtrack his initial com transmission's point of origin. Unfortunately, they had no way to know that Admiral Swenson had dispatched a stealthed communication relay to send it from relatively close proximity to the planet, which was why they were smothering the volume closer to the planet. Still, they had sent at least a handful of drones farther out-system. None of them had come within detection range—not even detection range for *human* remote platforms, let alone those of the Hegemony—of the cloaked starships lurking just above the asteroid belt, however.

Watching all that activity had been highly informative, both in terms of technical capabilities and the responses the Liatu had used those capabilities to generate. But now it was time, and Swenson had moved thirteen stealthy light-minutes farther in-system, to a point barely six light-minutes from Tairys.

"All right, Francisca," he said now. "You can make your bow to the sensors whenever you like."

"Executing Reveal now, Mister President."

COUNCIL CHAMBER,
PALACE OF GOVERNMENT,
CITY OF ITHYRA,
PLANET TAIRYS,
TAIRYON SYSTEM,
419.9 LY FROM EARTH,
NOVEMBER 22, YEAR 42 TE.

Well, *that's* as useful as lye in a sleep wallow!" Fourth Minister Gortuni said, glaring across the low conference table at Third Minister Lyralk.

Gortuni was the minister responsible for managing the Tairyon System's industrial base, and at a mere thirty-seven Standard Years, she was the next to youngest of First Minister Sherak's ministers. She was also intelligent, hard-working, and an excellent administrator . . . who happened to be on mutually lucrative burrow-sharing terms with her good friend Korash. At the moment, both her eyes were trained on Lyralk. There was precious little approval in them, and her hide was an unpromising shade of yellow-tinged red.

"Would you prefer that my people make up fancy stories or lie to you?" Lyralk demanded.

"I'd prefer for them to do their *jobs* and find these . . . these creatures!" Gortuni shot back, her tone as disgusted as the color of her hide. "You've had *three days* to figure out where they are!"

"And we've searched for them with every resource we have!" Lyralk's tone was as angry as Gortuni's, and her hide was an even darker, oranger red.

"I don't really give a cherjuk's ass how hard you've *looked*," Gortuni shot back. "I want to know what you've *found*, and the answer to that question seems to be not a damned thing!"

"Well, one thing I *can* tell you is that they aren't within two lightsilthals of Tairys!" Lyralk snapped. "If they were inside that zone, Segmar's sensors and drones would have found them!"

The Navy Commander bobbed his torso in emphatic agreement with the Third Minister, but Gortuni swiveled one eye to each of them, her color skeptical.

"It would be nice if you could be remotely as positive about where they are as about where they *aren't*," she said tartly.

"Eliminating volumes in which they could be but aren't narrows down the volumes in which they actually are, Minister," Segmar pointed out. "At the same time, a star system is an enormous volume, and it's obvious that they must have even better cloaking technology than System Surveillance Command initially assumed. It will probably take us a while to determine where they're hiding. Once we have, my warriors will know how to deal with them!"

"Indeed? If that's the case, then—"

The sudden clamor of an alarm chopped Gortuni off in midflight. A lurid light flashed across the smart surface of the conference table, and Segmar swallowed an oath of disbelief as the flashing light segued abruptly into a tactical display.

Four icons blinked the yellow of unidentified ships, and they were nowhere near two light-silthals from Tairys. In fact, they were barely more than *one* light-silthal from the planet!

"It must be a mistake!" he blurted, shoving his torso half up and off of his chair. "Or a trick of some sort! No one could get that close without—"

He broke off, listening to a voice over his aural implant, then sagged back down on the chair, and the other Liatus watched his hide turn the pasty white of shocked disbelief.

"What is it?" First Minister Sherak demanded.

"According—" Segmar had to pause, clear his throat. "According to System Surveillance Commander Urdia, those ships—" he jabbed a digit at the icons strobing from the table's surface "—are over ten shrevjeshes long."

"That's ridiculous!" Gortuni snapped with the assurance of the minister responsible for every starship built in Tairyon. "No one could get something that size into phase-space!"

"Tell me something I don't know!" Segmar shot back. "That's five *times* the size of my biggest dreadnought!"

"Is it some sort of trick?" Fifth Minister Sordal asked. Sordal was a rarity, the sole male on Sherak's council. He held that position because he was also its most astute political calculator and one of its more intelligent members. But at that moment, he sounded more like a child seeking reassurance than a senior minister and powerbroker, and his hide was tinged with ocher. It wasn't a dark enough hue to be called panic, but it was headed that direction.

"That must be it!" Segmar bobbed his torso in enthusiastic endorsement. "We know they have excellent cloaking technology. If they can convince Urdia's tactical crews their ships are so enormous, they obviously have equally good *offensive* electronic warfare capabilities!"

"I don't—" Sherak began, then broke off as her own aural implant spoke to her. Her hide flushed amber with frustration and her breathing slits closed for a moment. Then they opened, and her eyes swiveled out and around the circle of her subordinates.

"We have another message from the humans," she said. "It originated exactly where System Surveillance Commander Urdia detected those ships. And to get here now, it had to be transmitted well before her systems detected them." She snapped her mouth in bitter amusement. "Apparently the humans timed the moment when they allowed us to see them with care."

"*Allowed* us?" Segmar sounded profoundly offended, and Sherak glared at him.

"With all due respect, Navy Commander," her tone didn't *sound* especially respectful, "that's clearly what just happened. Those ships—" it was her turn to indicate the icons on the tabletop "—aren't moving. They aren't decelerating; they're *parked*. They're motionless relative to this planet. Which means they didn't just magically move into the range of System Surveillance Commander Urdia's systems. They've been there, waiting for at least a silthal while their message was in transit, and Urdia's sensor techs didn't see fish shit."

Segmar wilted under her fiery gaze.

"May we view their message, First Minister?" Second Minister Hyrak asked in a painfully neutral voice, and Sherak transferred her glare to her closest political ally. But only for a moment. Then its anger faded, and she bobbed in agreement.

"Display message," she said to her senior aide, and the tactical display vanished from the tabletop.

A stir of uneasiness ran around the table as they saw the frozen image of one of the "humans" at last.

The biped before them had a flat face, with a pronounced nose (but nothing remotely like the muzzle of something like a Shongair), and the ridiculously long and skinny neck of a true biped. Its head was covered with a dark brown growth, almost like one of the nuisance animals' pelts, although it was cut much shorter. Its small, repulsively deep-set eyes—as brown as its head growth—clearly lacked any decent range of motion, and when its narrow mouth moved, it showed the small white teeth of an omnivore.

Sherak waved an impatient hand at her aide, finger webs spread, and the image unfroze.

"Greetings, First Minister Sherak," the alien said, and Sherak recognized the voice from the humans' first message. That was no proof this was who'd spoken to her then, of course. The flawless Liatu had to be the product of a sophisticated translation package, and anyone could have used the same computer-generated voice.

"I told you I'd be back in touch with you," the human continued, "and here I am. I trust you've spent the intervening time considering what I said to you in my first communication. *We've* spent it continuing our observations of your presence here in Tairyon. In fact, we've had over one and a half of your months to evaluate your operations here, and I must say that our analysis is less than completely favorable to you and your people. I've discussed that with my advisors and subordinates, and I feel the time's come for us to have a face-to-face conversation, without lightspeed transmission delays and without ambiguity. I'm afraid, given our experience with your fellow Galactics, that I'm disinclined to come down to your planet and trust my safety to your good intentions. So, instead, I invite you to come aboard my command ship. I would strongly urge you to accept my invitation as a means to avoid significant . . . unpleasantness. You may transmit your acceptance to me, and I'll arrange clearance for your shuttle."

More than one of the ministers around that conference table took on the orangey tint of anger at the human's tone, but it continued unhurriedly.

"I'm sure some of your advisors will urge you to reject my invitation.

They may even categorize it as an 'arrogant demand.' Our observation of your species indicates a certain belligerently arrogant chauvinism, which would undoubtedly incline them in that direction. But whether you accept my invitation now, willingly, or only after that 'unpleasantness' convinces you to do so, I would strongly urge you to avoid anything my military commanders might construe as a threat. I'm equally sure some of those same advisors will tell you that a mere four starships, even the size of mine, are no match for your dreadnoughts and your orbital weapons platforms."

That narrow mouth moved again, curving more sharply and baring those pearly teeth.

"If I were you, I would point out to them that a species such as my own, which has already been attacked by another of the Hegemony's Galactics, wouldn't be here, and wouldn't have chosen to reveal itself to you, if we weren't confident we could defeat any attack you might launch upon us. It's always possible our confidence might be misplaced, but bear in mind that we have a complete database on the Hegemony's technological capabilities, whereas you know absolutely nothing about ours. Except, of course, for the fact that you never even suspected we'd entered this star system until we chose to tell you we had. Which ought to suggest to you, among other things, that we may not have revealed our full strength to you even now."

The alien paused to let that sink in.

"I would also suggest," it said then, its voice soft, "that you remember that we've already killed every single member of the force which attacked our homeworld. If we find it necessary to kill still more Galactics, we're quite prepared to do that, too.

"I'll expect a response to my invitation, one way or the other, within one local day from now. Please don't disappoint me."

Those brown eyes gazed out of the tabletop for another long, still moment. Then the image disappeared as the message ended, and Sherak and her ministers stared at one another in silent, stunned shock.

The "human" starship really was over ten shrevjeshes long.

First Minister Sherak hadn't truly believed it. Or perhaps, she admitted to herself—grudgingly—she hadn't *wanted* to believe it. But it was, and she felt a fresh douche of anxiety while she gazed out the viewport of her palatial shuttle as it approached the alien flagship.

"First Minister."

The voice in her aural implants was her pilot's. Her tone sounded a bit odd, and Sherak looked down at the armrest viewscreen.

"Yes?"

"Domynas, System Surveillance reported four alien ships."

"Yes?" Sherak repeated more impatiently.

"Well, I have visual confirmation on *five* of them."

"What?" Sherak said blankly.

"Five, Domynas. I don't—Wait, *another* one just popped up visually, and—"

The pilot broke off. Then—

"First Minister," she said very, very carefully, "we have visual confirmation on two additional ships. Their EM and thermal signatures match the ones we've already seen . . . but neither of them is generating a radar or lidar return."

Sherak looked at Third Minister Lyralk, straddling the chair beside hers. The defense minister looked back at her with a gray flush of anxiety.

"How is that possible?" Sherak demanded.

"So far as I know, it *isn't* possible," Lyralk replied. "Maybe Sordal had a point. Maybe it *is* some kind of trick!"

"Both of the additional ships have disappeared again now, Domynas," the pilot said over Sherak's aural implants. "We can't see them at all. But . . . it appears something is occluding at least some of the background stars where we first sighted them."

"The unfertilized egg thieves are playing 'tricks,' all right," Sherak said grimly. "But those ships were there. I'm sure of it."

"But, First Minister—" Lyralk began.

"I don't know if they let us see those two ships by mistake or if they did it on purpose, but either way, they're telling us we can't be positive we've seen their entire force." Sherak's voice was grimmer than ever, and her hide mingled the amber of frustration with the orange-red of anger. "That's bad enough if it was an accident. If it was *deliberate*, it's even worse. In that case, they're making sure we *know* we haven't seen all of them. *And* they're showing us they can appear and disappear at will, like something out of one of the Kreptu fairy tales about demons and devils."

"But how is that even possible?" Lyralk said, as if unaware she was repeating Sherak's question of only maunihirths before. Sherak wanted to snap at her, but she didn't.

"I don't know that any more than you do," she said instead. "But the evidence says it *is* possible . . . for them."

Lyralk looked at her, both eyes wide, and Sherak bobbed a seated shrug.

"We knew it was possible they had more ships hiding from us," she reminded the Third Minister. "That's why I authorized you and Segmar to augment the out-system passive arrays." She scowled the yellow of disgust—self-disgust, in this case. "We should have done that years ago. But you and Segmar were right. They can't *prevent* electronic and thermal radiation. It still has to go *somewhere,* and if we haven't yet detected it, they *must* be able to somehow control the direction in which it's radiated. So if Segmar and Urdia can get enough platforms out there, look at them from enough different angles. . . ."

She let her voice trail off, then bobbed a shrug and turned back to the viewport as the shuttle drifted slowly and delicately into the huge, brilliantly lit cavern of the stupendous alien starship's boat bay.

It kissed the docking buffers and a boarding tube ran out to its hatch. It configured itself to mate with the hatch's collar, and she saw a party of obviously armed humans waiting in the boat bay gallery at the tube's shipboard end.

"Good seal, Domynas," her pilot announced, and she shoved up off her chair. The commander of her Prosesecha security detachment started to stand as well, but Sherak waved her back.

"Stay here."

"But, Domynas—!"

"Entropy only knows how many of these . . . creatures there are aboard this ship," Sherak interrupted. "The one thing we can be certain of is that there are hordes of them, certainly more than enough to overwhelm you and your detachment. And another thing we can be certain of is that they won't let you aboard with your weapons."

"But we can still—"

"I won't give them the satisfaction of telling us that," Sherak said flatly.

The Prosesecha looked at her for a long, still moment, then dipped her head in acknowledgment.

Sherak inhaled deeply through her breathing slits, then bobbed to Lyralk and Adjunct Yursak, her private secretary and chief aide.

"Let's go," she said.

· · · · ·

THE MEMBERS OF the armed human "greeting party" were smaller than Sherak had expected. Or, at least, their body lengths were considerably shorter than those of a Liatu male, like Yursak. On the other hand, they were aggressively bipedal, standing fully erect on their flat feet and columnar legs, which put their heads farther off the deck than any Liatu's.

It was impossible to read any expression in their flat faces or body language. Like the Kreptu, their disturbingly smooth hides apparently came in a wide variety of colorations which, presumably, had nothing at all to do with their emotions. It was hard to be certain of that, given the quantity of clothing they wore. From the colors and styling of that clothing, she suspected it was a military uniform of some sort.

One of them stepped forward as she and her companions exited the tube.

"First Minister Sherak," the human said. Or, rather, its translating software said the words in perfect Liatu. It touched the front of its headgear with the edge of a five-fingered hand. "Ambassador Howell extends his compliments and asks you to join him in his conference room."

"That's very kind of Ambassador Howell." Sherak managed to keep her tone civil, although given the capabilities of the humans' translating program and the knowledge about the Liatu they'd already displayed, she was confident this human understood the faint orange-red tinge of her own hide indicated suppressed anger.

It would have been nice if she'd had any means of evaluating the *human's* emotional state, in return.

"If you'll come this way, Domynas," it said, and its fellows fell in around the three Liatus as it led the way out of the boat bay.

"They can generate gravity!" Lyralk subvocalized to Sherak's aural implants over their secure channel. The First Minister swiveled one eye to look at her, and the Third Minister showed the white cast of surprise. "They don't need a spin section!"

At least Lyralk had managed not to blurt it out loud. That was Sherak's first thought. And then the implication hit. No Galactic had ever been able to generate artificial gravity. Counter-gravity, yes, but never gravity itself. The new evidence of these creatures' technological prowess filled her with fresh dread, and not simply because of what it implied for the present balance of military power here in Tairyon. The thought of what a species with technology like this could do to the Hegemony's carefully managed technological balance was terrifying.

Their escorts—or perhaps, more accurately, their *captors*—ushered them down a long, straight passage that was generously large for a human and comfortably cramped for a Liatu, and into an intra-ship car that was large enough for their entire party. Sherak had spent enough time aboard starships and spacecraft in general to know that even aboard a Liatu dreadnought, space was always at a premium. The size of that intra-ship car drove home, yet again, just how vast this human starship was.

So did the duration of their trip once they'd boarded it. The journey lasted a good two siltahls before it finally ended and the doors slid open on another long passage. Sherak and her companions loped down the hall with frigid, formal dignity, surrounded by their human escort, and a bulkhead door slid open at their approach.

"First Minister," the commander of their guards murmured, coming to a halt and extending one hand in a curiously graceful gesture that obviously invited—or commanded—Sherak to step through that door.

She bobbed her torso in acknowledgment, then stalked past him.

The compartment was large, although not overwhelmingly so. A table sprouted from the deck at its center, and seven humans stood on its far side, in front of what were obviously chairs, despite their bizarre shape. Three far more sane-looking chairs configured for the Liatu body form faced them across the table. Sherak didn't much care for the thought of seating herself with her back to the door, but there seemed no other option. Besides, what difference did it make? If the humans were inclined toward murderous treachery, there was nothing she or her companions could do about it.

She loped forward and settled her torso onto the center of the three chairs, with Lyralk in the position of honor to her left and Yursak to her right. The humans waited until they'd taken their places, then settled back into those human-style chairs which couldn't possibly be as comfortable as they made them look.

"First Minister Sherak, I am Ambassador Judson Howell, the commander of this mission," the human in the center of the far side of the table said. Sherak had already recognized him, although as outré as these creatures looked, it was always good to have that confirmed.

"This is Ambassador Garção, my deputy," Howell continued, indicating the shorter, darker human seated to its right. "This—" it gestured to the human to his immediate left, "is Admiral Francisca Swenson, the commander of the mission's naval escort. Beyond her, is Lieutenant General Palazzola, who commands our planetary combat component. To Ambassador Garção's right is Assistant Ambassador McCabe, and sitting behind us here are Colonel Ushakov and Commander Sherman, my special advisors and aides."

Sherak bobbed a frosty acknowledgment of the introductions.

"I recognize Third Minister Lyralk, of course," Howell said then. "And this other gentlemale is—?"

Sherak's chewing surfaces grated at the fresh evidence of just how thoroughly the humans must have penetrated her star system's info systems. She couldn't quite suppress an amber flush of frustration, but she managed to keep her tone even as she replied.

"This is Adjunct Yursak, Third Hatched of His Brood, Son of Gurdahn, of the Line of Chairlys," she said. "He is my private secretary and my senior aide. He'll be recording our conversation."

She put just an edge of challenge into that last sentence, but the human only bobbed its head—the movement looked shockingly loose, as if it had somehow broken its slender, overly long neck.

"That will be acceptable," it said.

Then it leaned back in its chair, regarding her with those beady, barely mobile eyes, and said nothing else.

Maunihirths dragged past in silence, and Sherak felt a fresh, dull burn of anger. Obviously, the human was prepared to sit here until the energy death of the universe . . . or until Sherak broke down and ended the silence. She was tempted to match it silence for silence, however long it took. Who was this human to mock her this way?! She was First Minister of an entire star system! Her species had ruled Tairyon for over four hundred Standard Years! How *dared* it—

She chopped that thought off. The last thing she could afford was to allow this . . . this *creature* to goad her into an intemperate response it could use against her. And so she drew a deep breath and swiveled both eyes to Howell.

"Why are you here?" she asked bluntly. "Oh," she waved one hand, webbed fingers spread, "I know you told me some member of the Hegemony attacked your homeworld. I notice you haven't said *which* race, however, and I strongly suspect you would have if your attackers had been Liatu. Given that it's never been our way to attack other species, it—"

"Pardon me for pointing this out, First Minister," Howell interrupted in a tone of cool courtesy, "but I suspect the Farshu, Gyrdar, and Ichanti would probably dispute that."

Those beady little eyes bored into Sherak, and she inhaled sharply. How did this human know . . . ?

"I told you we'd captured the ships of our attackers," he said. "That included their databases. It would be wise of you to assume I already know a great deal about your species and its history."

Sherak's left eye tried to swivel to Lyralk, but she called it to order before it could. She also clamped her jaws tightly for a breath or two, then bobbed her torso in curt acknowledgment of Howell's interpolation.

"Very well," she said harshly. "But my point stands. I doubt very much that you were attacked by the Liatu. So why have you come *here*, to *our* star system, instead of to that of whoever *did* attack you? Or to the Erquoid System, to take this up directly with the Council? I don't think you would have come to Tairyon unless you had an agenda that extends beyond simply making contact with the Hegemony." Both of her own eyes stared at the alien. "What is it?"

"You're correct," Howell said after a moment. "As for our reason for being here, my people have a saying that 'a picture is worth a thousand words.' So let me show you a picture, First Minister."

It said nothing more, made no gesture Sherak could see, but a hologram appeared suddenly above the conference table.

For a moment, Sherak stared at the frozen image with no idea what she was seeing. Then she recognized the foliage, the hillsides of the Kurian Highlands . . . and the herd of nuisance animals Korash had asked her to move.

The hologram awoke, and the nuisance animals moved ponderously across the hillside with their customary slow, heavy gait, pausing occasionally to break off an ilar fruit or grub out a kumak root and chew on them. Some of their young rolled around through the grassy slopes, in and out of the denser foliage, wrestling with one another. She could almost hear the uncouth shrieking sounds the nuisance animals made at moments like that.

But then, suddenly, the hologram changed. A flash of brilliant light erupted savagely in the midst of the slowly moving herd. Then a second—a third!

The nuisance animals reacted in instant panic, turning, racing away from the flashes. And then she saw tracer rounds, streaking down from the heavens, shredding the foliage and undergrowth to either side of the herd, driving it across the rugged terrain like a lash of fire.

The nuisance animals fled, charging through the underbrush, no doubt bellowing their terror, and a pair of Prosesecha air cars flashed across the hologram. There was no audio, but she'd seen enough similar footage with sound to know the air cars had added the howling scream of their sirens to the bedlam driving the nuisance animals away from Korash's property.

Some of them fell as they fled, tumbling over unseen obstacles in their panic. At least two or three of their whelps went down, as well, but the Prosesechas kept the pressure on. From experience, Sherak knew that if they weren't sufficiently frightened, the nuisance animals would only return as soon as the air cars left. Clearly, the Prosesechas were taking no chance of that.

The hologram played for perhaps a siltahl, then one of the younger nuisance animals sprawled into a ravine and smashed itself into its stony wall. A female adult sprang down into the ravine, gathered up the fallen creature, and leapt up and over the ravine's lip. It fled, swerving to one side . . . and a burst of cannon fire found it, ripped through it, hurled it to the ground. It struggled for a few moments, then lay still.

And that was when the hologram froze once again, focused on that single dead nuisance animal and the whelp half under its body, still cradled in the crook of its arm.

"This, First Minister," the human said. "*This* is why we're here."

Sherak stared at it, her hide the dull maroon of deep confusion. The nuisance animals? This human was claiming they were here because of the *nuisance animals*? What in the name of Entropy could the nuisance animals have to do with another species? Surely these creatures weren't saying—?

The silence stretched out, and Sherak tried—she truly *tried*—to comprehend what the human could be getting at. She had no idea how to read human body language, but from the stillness on the other side of the table, they were clearly . . . tense. Even upset. But why?

"I'm trying to understand," she said finally, into the stillness, "but I don't. What you're showing us happened just a few days ago. It certainly hadn't happened when you set out from your star system to ours. So how could *that* have anything to do with your presence here?"

"You truly don't comprehend why we might find your treatment of the Tairyonians—" that word was apparently from the humans' own language, since it wasn't translated, but Sherak assumed that it applied to the nuisance animals "—objectionable?" Howell's translated voice was cold.

"They're *animals*," Sherak said as reasonably as she could. "I will agree that, in this particular instance, the Prosesechas may have been . . . overenthusiastic in the way they performed their duties. But it's not as if the nuisance animals were capable of actually utilizing the land they squatted on!"

"No?" Howell leaned back and cocked its head. "They are tool users, aren't they?"

He never looked away from Sherak, but the hologram shifted, zeroing in on one of the nuisance animal males as it waved its ridiculous spear at the air cars.

"You call *that* a 'tool'?" Sherak flushed the maroon-tinged white of disbelief.

"It looks like one to me," Howell replied, and its cold voice had taken on a harder edge.

"I can tell that this has . . . upset you," Sherak said, choosing her words carefully, "but the fact that they can chip flint and tie it to the end of a stick. . . . It's not as if they were an advanced, intelligent species! Why, even if we'd never arrived in the system, it would have been millennia before they mastered electricity!"

Howell gripped the arms of its chair and half rose, and for the first time one of the humans' hides showed a tide of color. But the hue touching its face was a deep red, and the one thing Sherak was certain the human *wasn't* feeling was exultation.

The human to its right—Garção, or whatever its name was—put a hand on Howell's arm, and after a moment, it sank back into its chair.

"Really?" it said then, and its tone might have been liquid helium. "You think that? It would have taken them 'millennia' just to discover electricity if you hadn't so benevolently found a better use for their planet than *they* could possibly have found? That's what you think?"

"Well—"

Howell never took its stony gaze from Sherak, but the hologram changed again, and this time there was sound. The wail of sirens filled the compartment, and both of Sherak's eyes darted back to the display and widened. It showed a street scene—an incredibly *primitive* street scene—with crude ground cars swerving out of the roadway, doors opening, humans piling out onto paved walkways and fleeing madly. The sirens howled louder, and she heard voices—human voices—screaming through the ear-piercing shriek. And then, suddenly, the image disappeared into an enormous flash of brilliance, an explosion too bright and terrible for the eye to endure.

The image changed abruptly, and then they were looking down on an entire planet Sherak had never before seen, a blue and green and brown jewel, floating in space, as the terrible pinpricks of a kinetic bombardment swept across its nightside in lethal blossoms of fire.

Another change, and she saw a flight of shuttles—from the markings, they were Shongair—sweeping through a planetary atmosphere. And then, without warning, they began to explode, to disintegrate, to plunge out of the air in fountains of flame as a shoal of what had to be primitive *air-breathing* aircraft swept through them, dealing death as they came. And then there were scenes of crude, lumbering armored vehicles of some sort—armored vehicles which, despite their antiquated clumsiness, effortlessly shattered GEVs and armored personnel carriers with the fury of their enormous, primitive cannon before they were destroyed in turn by precision KEW strikes.

The hologram changed to more aerial views, views of city after city, town after town. All of them were indescribably primitive, like something out of the dim, long-forgotten past, but they swarmed with humans. And, one after another, they were blotted away in the fiery mass-death of kinetic strikes.

"That was our homeworld, First Minister." Howell's voice was iron. "Those were our cities, our families. And *this*—" the hologram showed an image of one of those bumbling armored vehicles "—is what *our* technological capabilities were. Not 'millennia' ago, First Minister Sherak. Only fifty of our years—barely *twenty* of yours—ago."

Sherak stared at it, and her hide was the purple-gray of horror.

The holograms proved these humans were even more bloodthirsty and better at killing other sentient creatures than the Shongairi! That was terrible enough, but at least the Shongairi were contained. Eventually, the Hegemony would be forced to deal with them. That was the dirty little secret none of the Founders ever openly discussed. Yet it wasn't as if they would ever be allowed to pose any sort of genuine threat to the massed power of the rest of the Hegemony.

But these humans—!

Assuming Howell's visual records were telling her the truth, they'd springboarded from a pre-space technology to one that clearly surpassed that of the Hegemony, at least in some respects, in an obscenely short eyeblink of time.

"I don't understand," she said, and it was nothing but the simple truth. "From those images—" she waved a hand at the hologram "—it was the *Shongairi* who attacked you, not the Liatu! They're *carnivores,* for Entropy's sake! Surely you can't hold the other races of the Hegemony, like us, responsible for what those bloodthirsty, carnivorous monsters did to your world! The very idea is . . . It's *ridiculous!*"

"So you're telling me the Hegemony didn't authorize the Shongairi to conquer us?"

"The Hegemony's ability to control all of its member species' actions is limited, Ambassador Howell," Sherak said as reasonably as she could. "Its actions must be consensual, and its ability to compel adherence to its rules depends upon that consensus. But habitable worlds are rare, and more prim—*less advanced*—species seldom . . . make the fullest use of them. It would be impossible for the Hegemony to forbid more advanced races from spreading throughout the galaxy, competing for those same habitable worlds. So the best the Hegemony Council can do is try to . . . keep the process under control. To moderate it. And that's precisely what it does. Whatever the Council might have authorized the Shongairi to do in your people's case, I'm certain they never visualized anything like what actually happened to you! And I assure you that we Liatu would *never* do something like that!"

"No, you wouldn't," Howell said. "You prefer a more subtle approach. Like this one."

That hellish hologram changed yet again, and Sherak felt herself go ocher as she saw her own world from space. But it wasn't current imagery. These were ancient Survey Command images, from the Hegemony's very first contact with Tairyon, that she'd had no idea was in the Hegemony database for these creatures to capture.

The hologram zoomed in on another city, far smaller and even more primitive than the human cityscapes had been. Animal-drawn carts creaked along its streets. Smoke rose from chimneys. Hammers clanged on anvils as craftsmen produced swords and daggers, knives, agricultural implements. Children ran in and out between the statues in the town square, playing some elaborate game with hoops and balls, while shoppers chaffered for goods in the marketplaces and primitive music rose from street musicians.

"I'm sure you recognize it, First Minister," Howell said softly. "This is Tairys, four hundred and forty-three Standard Years ago. And these—" he never looked away from Sherak as the hologram zoomed in on the craftsmen, the street musicians "—are the ancestors of the 'nuisance animals.'"

Somehow, Sherak pulled her eyes away from those images, swiveled them to the human.

"Of course," it said, "this was recorded before your people—with the Hegemony's blessing—released your genetic weapon, wasn't it? Before you reduced their mental capacity to a shadow of what it had been. Before they forgot how to work in bronze and iron. How to farm. Before they could barely remember how to—what was it you said?—'chip flint and tie it to the end of a stick,' I think?

"And before ninety-plus percent of their entire pre-contact planetary population died of starvation, of disease, from exposure, from freezing to death in the winter, because they could no longer maintain their civilization and the Iron Age 'technology' that supported it."

The human's eyes bored into her, and Sherak needed no guide to human expressions to feel its fury.

"That . . . that was done centuries ago," she said finally. "We needed the space, and . . . and they were occupying it. We didn't kill them, the way the Shongairi would've done! We only . . . only culled the herd, reduced it to a level—a *self-sustaining* level!—that created the space we needed, as well. It may have been . . . harsher than other methods, but that all happened long, long ago! No living Liatu had anything to do with it. It's not like the nuisance animals even *remember* any of that!"

"And after all, they were only *Untermenschen*," the human said softly. "Who were they to stand in the way of the Liatu's sacred quest for *lebensraum*?"

"I'm afraid your software didn't translate two of those words," Sherak said a bit hesitantly.

"It doesn't matter." Howell shook its head again. "It's not as if the reference would have any meaning for your species even if you understood the words' definitions. But understand *this*, First Minister. The Hegemony's been doing this, or things just like it, to any species that got in its way for over *seventy-four thousand* Standard Years. God only knows how many other Tairyonians, how many Farshus, how many Gyrdari you and your sanctimonious, oh-so-noble Hegemony have raped and enslaved or simply murdered over that incredible length of time. *You* sure as hell don't have a clue, and you don't give a single good goddamn about it, either.

"Well, *we* do. We've been on the receiving end of the Hegemony's benevolent policy towards inconveniently located sentient species. We've found plenty of other examples of it in your own database, as well. And we've decided it has to stop."

"What?" Sheer astonishment startled the one-word question out of Sherak, and Howell's mouth moved in an inscrutable expression she suspected she wouldn't have liked if she'd understood it.

"We've decided it has to stop," it repeated. "Someone has to *put* a stop to it. And that 'someone,' First Minister Sherak, Second Hatched of Your Brood, Daughter of Ursahl, of the Line of Sercom, is *us*."

Sherak stared at him, and then flushed deep coral in incredulous amusement. This creature—this creature which had just confirmed that it came from a single star system, which hadn't even had *spaceflight* twenty years ago—thought it could threaten the entire Hegemony?!

"You're insane," she told it. "The Hegemony's maintained Galactic peace for seventy-five thousand Standard Years. Yes, a few primitive species may have been . . . pushed aside in the process, but most of them didn't even know what to do with the planets they had. And for all those years, the Hegemony you're so busy denigrating has prevented the clashes between *advanced* races that could have sterilized entire star systems! It has scores of member species, inhabiting hundreds—*thousands*—of developed worlds! You . . . you 'humans' may have learned a few technological tricks after defeating somebody like the *Shongairi*, but we aren't all feckless incompetents like them. If you're serious about challenging the power of the entire Hegemony, of actually *threatening* the Founders and the other senior Galactics, they'll crush your miserable little star system like the insignificant sea slugs you are."

"That's as may be, First Minister. But whatever the rest of the Hegemony may be capable of, *it's not here*," Howell said, and the curve of its mouth sharpened.

Sherak froze, and the alien's head bobbed in another of those too-loose nods.

"Our mission—and Admiral Swenson's starships—*is* here . . . and so is your entire system's population. Given those circumstances, do you *really* want to find yourself in a shooting incident with the navy of a species which saw half its total population slaughtered in a kinetic bombardment your Hegemony authorized?"

Sherak stared at him. Too much had come at her too quickly. The notion that a primitive species could acquire even the basics of advanced technology, far less improve upon it, was too preposterous for her to truly internalize. Even accepting the intellectual possibility was all but impossible; actually *believing* it. . . .

And if these "humans" thought they could convince her they truly cared about other species, that they were prepared to challenge the Hegemony out of some warped, misplaced sense of outrage over something like the *nuisance animals*, they were fools. Perhaps revenge might motivate them. *That* she could believe. And how bitterly, poisonously ironic was it that the bestial, flesh-eating Shongairi should be the ones to awaken and enable an even less sane, even more aggressive species and loose it upon the galaxy like some pestilent disease?

There could be only one response to them, and in the fullness of time, she knew the Hegemony would visit that response upon them. But mad as this Howell might be, it did have at least one point.

It and its starships *were* here, and even though it had to be bluffing about its willingness to massacre an entire planet inhabited by one of the Founders, it might actually be sufficiently crazed to carry out its insane threat.

"What, exactly, do you want of me and the Liatu in this star system?" she asked at last.

"What I want is for you to surrender the system to me," Howell said. "I want your military forces to stand down, immediately. I want the System Gyrtoma's delegates to formally cede sovereignty over the system to the Terran Alliance. I want the system's industrial capacity surrendered to us. And—" its mouth shaped another of those curves "—my medical personnel intend to *reverse* the genetic damage your ancestors inflicted upon Tairys's legitimate owners."

Sherak blinked. No species in recorded history had ever issued demands remotely like that to *any* of the Galactics, far less to one of the Founders! It was unthinkable.

Yet this creature, this Howell—it *had* issued those demands, and whatever else these humans might be, it was clear they were dangerous. It was even possible they might be able to defeat Navy Commander Segmar's warships and orbital defenses, despite their massive armament. Even if they couldn't actually vanquish Segmar's forces, they might still inflict an enormous amount of damage before they themselves were destroyed. But she couldn't just roll belly-up and accede to its preposterous demands. Give up a star system which had belonged to her own species for over four hundred Standard Years? There was no way she could do that! And even beyond the consequences for her, for all of her species here in this star system, these humans had to be stopped. If she simply gave them what they wanted, it could only embolden them, and Entropy only knew what they might demand *next*!

But she couldn't tell it that. Not yet, at any rate.

"Those are ... extreme demands, Ambassador Howell," she said, finally. "I can't possibly respond to them without at the very least discussing them with all of my ministers. For that matter, even assuming my ministers were prepared to accede to your ... impertinent ultimatum, we'd have to convince the Gyrtoma. And before we could do *that*, we'd have to communicate it to our population at large, give all of our people an opportunity to voice *their* opinions to their Gyrtoma delegations."

"I didn't expect an immediate response," Howell said. "In fact, I anticipated almost exactly what you've just said. So feel free to return to the planet and discuss it with whomever you wish. I'll give you four of your weeks—thirty-two planetary days—to reach your decision."

Sherak flushed orange-red under the lash of its cool, dismissive tone.

"And what," she asked icily, "do you intend to do if we reject your arrogant demands?"

"Why, in that case," the alien told her, "we'll take a page from the Hegemony's book. We'll *compel* you to accept them. However . . . forcefully that requires."

COUNCIL CHAMBER,
PALACE OF GOVERNMENT,
CITY OF ITHYRA,
PLANET TAIRYS,
TAIRYON SYSTEM,
419.9 LY FROM EARTH,
NOVEMBER 22, YEAR 42 TE.

And then they said they would *compel* us to do so! As if some just-hatched beings could talk to one of the Founders that way!" Sherak's eyes swiveled to take in the council members. Anger predominated, shading toward the pure orange of contempt, but there was also the gray of uneasiness and anxiety. She focused on Third Minister Lyralk, who was completely gray.

"What? Don't tell me you think they can actually beat us!" she barked.

"I'm disquieted by the two additional ships you saw on your way to meeting with the humans," Lyralk said. "If there are two we didn't see before . . . might there be others that we also haven't seen?"

Sherak swiveled an eye toward Segmar.

"What do you think? Is it possible?"

"Possible? Yes, it's *possible*, but I find it highly unlikely. Until recently—according to them, anyway—they didn't even *have* space flight. Frankly, I doubt that. I think it's far more likely that it's some sort of . . . psychological ploy, designed to panic us into simply giving in. In any case, it's ridiculous to think they have all sorts of wonderful, secret technology beyond what we've already encountered! As I said in our very first meeting, the laws of physics apply to everyone, and I find it unlikely that they have additional ships beyond the ones we've seen." He bobbed a shrug. "To have even what they have indicates that the Shongairi—or someone—must have colluded with them somehow."

"I have noted the Shongairi's possible collusion with the humans," High Ghyrcolar Ithral, Second Hatched of Her Brood, Daughter of Arsal, of the Line of Regam, said frostily. As Chief Justice, law enforcement was under her purview. "I assure you that I will be sending communications to the Hegemony Council to look into that."

"Still," Lyralk said, "there may be additional ships in the system. While my advisors believe we can handle the ships we've seen—even with the two new ones—if there were many more, system defense might become . . . problematical."

"You're right, of course," Sherak said. "We need to know the answer to that before we make any plans." Both her eyes swiveled to Segmar. "Which takes us back to the original question. Are there additional human ships in the system, and what are you doing to determine the answer to that?"

"The new arrays are almost finished in the outer system," Segmar replied. "I should have additional information in the next three or four days. In the interim, though, I have a preliminary finding that we hope to be able to confirm once the rest of the array is installed."

"Enough with the disclaimers," Sherak said, her hide turning amber. "What have you found?"

"In speaking with System Surveillance Commander Urdia, we've decided that the humans are trapping their electromagnetic and thermal signatures somehow."

"Can we do that?" Fourth Minister Gortuni asked.

"Well, no, we can't," Segmar admitted, going maroon.

"So how are we going to find them?" Sherak asked.

"Simply trapping their signature isn't enough," Segmar said. "They can't allow it to build up forever—they have to have an outlet for it, or eventually they'd explode. We just need to find the outlet."

"And you think you have that?"

Segmar bobbed a small nod. "We do. Urdia had the out-system arrays turned to face the inner system. Their initial findings were . . . inconclusive, but the first of the new platforms are online, and they confirm Urdia's initial suspicions. The humans appear to be radiating their signatures toward the outer system. Although our current equipment is rudimentary for this task, we'll be able to get better data in the next several days and determine exactly how many ships the humans have. We'll also be able to fix their positions."

"So what are we going to do about the human's demands?" High Ghyrcolar Ithral asked. "If I recall correctly, they said we were to surrender the system, all of our military capabilities, and our industrial capacity. And that they then intend to reverse the genetic modification of the nuisance animals and hand our entire world over to *them*."

Sherak clamped down on her bioluminescence, unwilling to give Ithral the pleasure of seeing how much she was getting under Sherak's hide. *Even in a crisis, Ithral can't resist the opportunity to irritate me.*

"We're not going to do anything, for now," she said after a moment, forcing herself to show the orange of contempt. "I told them we'd need time to give our people an opportunity to voice their opinions—"

"You are going to do that, aren't you?" Ithral interrupted.

"Of course not," Sherak replied. "The rank and file are no more prepared to deal with the demands of this situation than the nuisance animals are." An eye turned to track Segmar. "We're going to use the time to find where the humans are; then, once we have them fixed, we will destroy them."

"And if it turns out we can't find them or there are more of them than we know about?" Fourth Minister Gortuni asked.

"Then we'll regather here for another session to determine our way forward. Until we have all the information, though, there's no need to waste time on possibilities that are unlikely to happen."

"And surrendering to the humans?" Ithral asked.

"Is one of those possibilities that are unlikely," Sherak replied. She owned a lot of the system's industrial capacity, and she'd fling herself into Entropy before she gave it over to the humans. "And with that, we are adjourned." As the council began leaving, she added, "System Medical Director Mynsorlas? A moment of your time, please?"

Mynsorlas, Third Hatched of Her Brood, Daughter of Jorsali, of the Line of Manikar, turned and approached Sherak. She started to say something, but Sherak held up her hand until the rest of the council—*and especially Ithral*—had left. Then she bobbed a small nod to the system medical director.

"I figured you'd like to discuss the possibility of reversing the damage to the nuisance animals. Of course it is possible—" Mynsorlas stopped speaking when Sherak began laughing. "What's so funny?" Mynsorlas asked.

"Reversing what was done to the nuisance animals is the furthest thing from my mind," Sherak said, her hide orange. "The humans are a minor pest, and they'll be gone soon. This planet is ours, and it will *remain* ours. I have no intention of going anywhere or ceding it to anyone, much less the stupid nuisance animals around here."

Her hide darkened.

"You talk about reversing what was done to the nuisance animals. That is *never* going to happen. Not while I'm First Minister, anyway." Both her eyes swiveled to the door, then back to the doctor. "No. What I need is actually more of an insurance policy. . . ."

COUNCIL CHAMBER,
PALACE OF GOVERNMENT,
CITY OF ITHYRA,
PLANET TAIRYS,
TAIRYON SYSTEM,
419.9 LY FROM EARTH,
NOVEMBER 26, YEAR 42 TE.

Thank you all for coming," First Minister Sherak said. Four days had passed since the council's last meeting in this chamber. "Navy Commander Segmar has some information he wishes to share." He'd already shared it with Sherak, of course, or he would *never* have gotten the chance to address the council.

Segmar bobbed a small nod, his hide a bright violet.

"As we've discussed, we've set up additional reconnaissance capabilities in the asteroid belt and outer system to determine where the human ships were hiding. Our new arrays are complete, and I'm happy to inform the Council that *we've found them!*"

"That's good news, Segmar," Sherak said. "What can you tell us about them?"

"As we expected, the humans are radiating their ships' electronic and thermal signatures toward the outer system. We now have the capability to find, locate to a precise position, and then track each ship as it maneuvers." His hide lost some of its coloration. "That's the good news. The bad news is that we've also confirmed that the two additional ships that were seen during the First Minister's flight to the human ships are truly there. They do exist."

"But you have them?" Fourth Minister Gortuni asked. "You're sure?"

"Yes, Minister," Segmar replied. "It's as we expected. The humans can prevent their signatures from escaping to the front of them, but we're easily able to see them from an entire hemisphere behind them, basically aft of midships. Obviously, they have some sort of shield in front of them that prevents us from seeing them. That's useful information, because it essentially means they have to stay in place to keep the shield between us. If they were to turn, we would be able to see them from the planet."

"There are six ships, though," Sherak said. "You're sure."

Segmar allowed a small sigh to slip from his breathing slits. "We're as sure as we can be that there are only six ships in the human formation. Is it possible there are additional ships on the other side of the system, positioned so as to keep their emissions pointed away from the planet and our new sensors? Yes, but we feel that possibility is low. If they had additional ships, they would be with the formation for mutual defense."

"Is there any way to be more certain of their exact positions?"

"Yes, First Minister. We can launch additional recon drones, now that we know where they are, to verify their position and ensure there are no other ships present."

"Good. Please do so." Sherak bobbed a nod. "The question then, is—even with their improved technology—can you still beat them?"

"We believe so," Segmar replied. "Orbital Command Commander Horkan and I have discussed this exhaustively with our staffs, and we feel that the combination of his twelve defensive platforms and my ten dreadnoughts can defend the planet against them. Are the human ships large? Yes, they are, but much of that space has to be taken up with the drives they needed to get here and other peripheral equipment. Their technology isn't that much better than ours—it can't be—and we make up in numbers and total tonnage what we may lack in technology."

"This is wonderful news," Sherak said, her hide blue. "Thank you for your presentation." Her eyes turned to sweep the rest of the council, as her hide shifted to orange. "See? It's as I suspected. We would've wasted all that time planning for contingencies that were unlikely to happen. I propose we show these humans what happens when you challenge a Founding member of the Galactic Union."

A chorus of approval met her proposal, but Fifth Minister Sordal raised a hand.

"Yes," Sherak asked, somewhat contemptuously, of the only male on the council.

"There are a lot of unknowns in this plan," Sordal said. "We don't know for sure that we've found all the human ships. We think we have . . . but we don't *know*. Similarly, we don't know how good their technology is. We think ours is good enough to defeat them, but once again, we don't know."

"Is there a point in all of that, somewhere?" Sherak asked.

"Yes, First Minister, there is. We currently have three courier craft in-system. In the event of a human attack, I would propose sending them to Erquoid. Regardless of what happens here, the Hegemony Council needs to be aware of what the humans are doing so it can respond appropriately."

"I think that makes sense," Ithral added.

Of course you *would.* Sherak bobbed the smallest of nods. She had what she wanted and was prepared to be magnanimous.

"Fine." One eye swiveled to Segmar. "Make it so, and ensure they have whatever protection they need to get past the humans."

"Yes, First Minister."

Sherak's eyes took in the council at large.

"And, with that, I think we're finished here."

G ot another flight incoming, Sir," Petty Officer Troutman announced over the neural link, and Lieutenant Heideman opened his eyes, pulling out of the paperwork he'd been updating via his own link to look at the visual display.

"Got it, Amelia," he acknowledged, and shook his head.

"This makes number seven since I came on watch, Sir," Troutman observed.

"Yep."

Heideman watched as the fresh clutch of Liatu recon drones streaked towards 2nd Fleet's units. They were less stealthy, especially under power, than their PUN counterparts. They were also shorter ranged, but they were actually about fifteen percent better in both categories than the matching Shongair systems had been. The tradeoff which gave them enough endurance to be useful as remote sensor platforms meant their maximum acceleration rate was a paltry eight thousand gravities, however, only about eighty percent of a standard Hegemony shipkiller. At that rate, it would have taken them almost twenty-eight minutes to reach the human ships. Unfortunately for the Liatu—

"Take this batch with the gamma array," he said.

"Gamma shell, aye, Sir," Troutman acknowledged. She entered commands through her neural link, then sat back. "Gamma array enabled," she announced.

Four minutes later, the Liatu drones entered the gamma drones' defensive zone, still well over 1.7 million kilometers short of *Inexorable* . . . and died there. Just like every single one of their predecessors had done, although the range to Admiral Swenson's battle squadrons at intercept varied, depending upon which drone array her missile defense officers used to pick off any given flight.

"They're using up a *lot* of RDs, Sir," Troutman observed as the incoming icons disappeared from the plot.

"They probably have a lot of them *to* use up," Heideman replied.

"You think it's eventually going to dawn on the Froggies that they aren't getting any of them close enough to spot us?"

"That I can't tell you." Heideman shrugged, closing his eyes to return to his paperwork. "I suppose it's possible they think their birds are stealthier than they actually are and genuinely hope they'll eventually sneak one past us. The loss rate ought to suggest they're wrong about that, but they probably figure they might as well expend them as hang on to them. For that matter, they may figure that analyzing where we picked them off will at least give them a solid read on the volume of space we're defending."

"Lotsa luck with *that* one, too, Sir," Troutman said sardonically, and Heideman snorted. The reason they were using different defensive arrays to pick off each drone flight was to prevent the Liatu from doing exactly that.

"Well, admittedly, anybody smart enough to pour piss out of a boot would make that a little difficult for them," he acknowledged after a moment. "On the other hand, it certainly does look like the Admiral and Commander Lopez nailed it. They've been so convinced of their own invincibility for so long, they haven't spent any time even trying to learn how to think outside the box." He shrugged again. "If I had to guess, their Book probably says 'launch recon drones,' so they launch recon drones."

"This is *so* gonna suck for them," Troutman said in a tone of pronounced satisfaction.

"Looks that way," Heideman agreed. "And now, if you'll just keep an eye on things, I've got to get these damned reports done by end of watch."

"On it, Sir."

. . . . .

"SO YOU AND the Admiral are satisfied, Tiff?" Judson Howell asked across the dining room table.

"I think the Admiral's position is that any flag officer who's actually *satisfied* before going into action is an idiot, Dad," Captain Howell replied with a crooked smile. "Still, I'd have to say we're feeling . . . *reasonably confident*, let's say."

"And she's 'confident'—*you're* confident—they still don't have a hard headcount on her ships?"

"As confident as we can be," Tifton said a bit more soberly. "Obviously, we can't be a hundred percent certain of anything like that. But we *did* show them *Neumolimyy* and *La Yarham* when Sherak was out here. They never got a peek at the rest of Vice Admiral Shinobu's squadron before *Neumolimyy* and *La Yarham* brought their smart skins back up and 'disappeared,' but they definitely saw the two of them, as planned."

He shrugged, and Howell nodded. The PUN's nanotech "smart skin" hull appliques were designed to absorb the entire electromagnetic spectrum, including visible light. And they were also designed to completely and accurately reproduce whatever someone might have seen looking through the volume they occupied.

"We *are* the next best thing to certain—I'm talking ninety-nine-point-nine percent sure, in this case—that they've never gotten a drone overflight past our interception shells. That means they haven't been able to get a sensor above us, between us and the transport echelon."

He raised an eyebrow, and Howell nodded again. The transports, the industrial ships, and the freighters supporting 2nd Fleet were parked in a polar position due "north" of the primary, fifteen light-minutes above the plane of the star system's ecliptic.

"Assuming we're right, and they haven't been able to do that," his son continued, "they haven't seen anything from the rest of Shinobu's ships or from CruRon Five or CruRon Three. It's entirely possible—in fact, Hector Lopez and I are taking it as a given—that they've been driving any passive sensors they might have had out-system of us hard ever since they realized we were here. And the Admiral's obliged them by radiating our signatures—*some* of our signatures—directly outward, straight at them. So, by now, they've probably confirmed to their own satisfaction that *Neumolimyy* and *La Yarham* were really there, not just some sort of ghosts produced by our EW systems. And if they have, it's likely they're confident they've located everything we brought to the party. Which means they're significantly underestimating the odds against them." He grimaced. "They're underestimating the *tonnage* odds badly enough,

Dad. I doubt they have a clue, even now, of how badly they're underestimating the technological odds."

"Good." Howell picked up his iced tea glass and sipped from it. "A part of me wishes they'd been smart enough to just throw in the towel, and maybe they would've been, if we'd shown them all of Admiral Swenson's ships from the get-go. I doubt they would have, though. Hell, I would've doubted that even before we got here, before I had a chance to sit down across from Sherak and realize how totally, utterly clueless she is about why anyone might possibly object to what the Liatu did to the Tairyonians. But she genuinely is, and the Hegemony's hubris—its sheer *arrogance*—is a terminal condition." He shook his head. "And if the Liatu are that frigging stupid, then so be it."

"I wish it hadn't come to this, too," Sarah Howell sighed, as she scooped a second serving of green beans onto her plate. "I *hate* the thought of where it's going to end."

"I know you do, Honey." Howell captured her hand in his and squeezed for a moment. "And under other circumstances, I'd agree with you." He shook his head. "But not under these. It doesn't have to happen if they don't choose to be stupid after all, but you and I both know they will. And like Dave Dvorak's always said, stupidity is its own reward."

Sarah looked at her husband, her gray eyes somber, and he squeezed her hand again.

"I think Dad's right, Mom," Tifton said quietly. She looked at him, and he shrugged. "Anybody with a gram of common sense who's seen *Inexorable* should be able to figure out that he really, really doesn't want Admiral Swenson pissed with him. We may not have given Sherak and Hyrak the guided tour, but they saw enough to know we're way ahead of them technologically. Heck—" around his mother, Captain Howell tended to use rather milder expletives than in her absence "—Navy Commander Segmar and his people should have known that before Sherak ever came aboard, if only because they can't even *see* us unless we let them!"

"I'm pretty sure they *do* know that," Sarah said. "Or that they would, if they'd only admit it to themselves."

"And the fact that they won't—or can't—admit it is the reason there's no way we can avoid this," Howell said. "And, I'm sorry, Honey, but it doesn't really break my heart."

His voice turned harder on the last sentence, and Sarah gazed at him.

She understood her husband almost too well, she sometimes thought. And she knew exactly what he was thinking at that moment.

The Planetary Union had chosen Tairyon for the first point of contact with any Galactic beyond the Shongair for a lot of reasons. Most of those reasons were the result of coldly logical analysis. Some of them weren't, and she knew that for her husband, what the Liatu had done to the Tairyonians weighed at least as heavily as—indeed, probably more heavily than—any of those logical analyses.

The rest of the human race saw Judson Howell as a larger-than-life, heroic character, and she already knew that was how history would record him. And history would be right. She knew that, too. But she was the woman who loved him, and she knew that despite the chilled steel strength of his convictions, he was still only a man. She'd held him in the night as Governor of North Carolina while he'd wept over the mega-deaths he'd been unable to prevent. She'd seen his grim determination to resist the Shongair invasion to the last, even when he knew Thikair had begun preparing the bioweapon to kill them all and that he couldn't stop it in the end. She'd watched him as President of the Planetary Union, fighting for the strength and the mental integrity to set aside his passionate hatred for the Shongairi who'd wreaked such carnage upon his people and his planet. She'd seen him *find* that strength and integrity and genuinely endorse Dave Dvorak's mission to the Shong System. But she also knew what that had cost him.

Judson Howell had his own illusions. One of them was that he operated on the basis of coldly pragmatic logic, and logic and pragmatism did play an enormous part in his thinking. But what made him who he truly was, what had transformed him into the figure which could unify an entire planet—an entire species—had nothing to do with pragmatism. *That* had come from his sheer unflinching, unyielding moral integrity. His compassion. His inability to *not* stand up for the victimized, the broken. The abused. His belief in an adult's responsibility to do what he knew was *right,* whatever the cost. He made mistakes—she'd seen that more clearly than almost anyone else, as well. But when he did, and when he recognized that he had, he moved heaven and earth to correct them.

And when that moral integrity, that sense of responsibility, was married to logic and pragmatism, when they reinforced one another rather than conflicting with one another, it transformed him into Juggernaut, and God help anything that got in his way to doing that "right thing" that drove his unstoppable progress.

The Howell Doctrine came from that marriage of pragmatism and morality. It came from his understanding that the Hegemony would never tolerate a species as dedicated to change as humanity. For him, the possibility of the Galactics finding somebody else, somebody more powerful than the Shongairi, to conquer humanity, force Dvorak's "monkey boys and girls" into the static Hegemony mold, was almost as unacceptable as the far more likely probability that the Hegemony Council would simply sign off on a quiet little planetary genocide. And because he understood that, because that was unacceptable, the only *pragmatic* alternative was the creation of the Terran Alliance.

All of that was true, but it was his burning, bone-deep outrage at all the other "quiet little planetary genocides" and their like that had given him the blazing, almost messianic drive to push the Alliance into existence against all odds. And what the Liatu had done to the Tairyonians was the perfect example of the actions, the policies, the casual ruthlessness and callous brutality, that fired that outrage. He'd *known* what they'd done before he ever came here. Now that he'd actually seen it, observed it in all its horrific details, he could not—*would* not—tolerate its continuation.

And he was right. The entire purpose of the Howell Doctrine was to draw a line in the stars. To tell the Hegemony that its days of chewing up the "lesser species" and spitting out the splinters were over. And that made the Tairyon System the perfect place to begin drawing that line. It would be at least seventy-five years before the Council discovered what had happened here. It would almost certainly be a lot longer than that, actually, with the Planetary Union Navy playing spider-in-the-web, picking off each Hegemony starship as it arrived. But eventually—and sometime quite soon, on the scale of the Hegemony's enormous, glacial existence—the Council *would* find out. And when that day came, this star system would serve as the iron proof of what the Terran Alliance truly stood for.

It was unlikely the other Galactics would understand that any more than Sherak could grasp the reason for Howell's outrage over the Liatu's treatment of the "nuisance animals." But humanity would. And the other members of that future Terran Alliance would. And that mattered far more than whether or not the Hegemony ever understood, because it was what would touch that Alliance with the same flame of moral integrity and sense of justice that infused the man Sarah Howell loved.

It was only that she dreaded the price he would pay. That he'd already paid, yes, but the future prices, as well.

"I know it doesn't break your heart," she told him now. "And to tell the truth, it doesn't break mine, either. But it's going to be ugly, Judson. We all know that."

"Yes, it is," he agreed. "And maybe one day, years from now, I'll be less 'okay' about the number of Liatus who are about to die of terminal stupidity. But this isn't that day, Sarah. Even if I wanted to, I can't *let* it be that day. When the Hegemony finds out about this, maybe a couple of centuries from now, we need them to understand that we were able to do this to their best hardware *now*, less than fifty Earth Years after we first gained access to their tech base. We need them to sweat bullets at the mere thought of what we might have learned and applied to our combat capabilities in those intervening centuries. And we need to be able to point to Tairyon and the Tairyonians as proof we mean what we say about not resisting them solely out of self-interest but also out of our certainty that there's a better way to interact with 'lesser species' than the ones they've chosen. And the very best—maybe the only—way for us to accomplish those objectives is to take advantage of the Liatu's willingness to be our example for the other 'Founders.'"

"And for ourselves," she said. "Don't try to pretend that isn't just as important to you. To us." She shook her head. "To prove we meant it when we said we wouldn't stand for the Hegemony's policies. And to take that first step on the path that will *commit* us all to stay the course, because if there'd been even the most remote chance the Hegemony might have left us alone, or even offered us membership, despite our inventiveness, it won't now. It can't."

"If I'd thought there ever was any chance of either of those things, that might worry me," Howell said. "But there wasn't. So this is my next best shot. Draw our line, and build something so big, so powerful, so *terrifying* to the Hegemony that it doesn't dare cross us."

He looked at her, then glanced at their son before his eyes returned to her face.

"What the Hegemony is forcing us to become saddens me," he admitted. "Maybe it even frightens me a little. But one of the things the Galactics have forgotten, or maybe never understood at all, is that life *is* change. Anything that refuses to change, isn't life, it's stasis, and stasis would be the death of everything that makes us human in the first place."

"Preaching to the choir, Dad." There was a trace of sorrow in Captain Howell's eyes, as well, but there was no hesitation to go with it. "Preaching to the choir."

FIRST MINISTER SHERAK'S OFFICE,
PALACE OF GOVERNMENT,
CITY OF ITHYRA,
PLANET TAIRYS,
TAIRYON SYSTEM,
419.9 LY FROM EARTH,
DECEMBER 26, YEAR 42 TE.

E xcuse me, Domynas."

Sherak swiveled her left eye up from the correspondence on her display as Adjunct Yursak stepped through her office door.

"Yes, Yursak?"

"I'm afraid the human Howell is on the com."

Sherak's right eye joined her left, and her hide took on a slight tinge of gray she wouldn't have let most Liatu see. Then both of her eyes swiveled to the date/time display.

"I see," she said, and air whistled through her breathing slits as she drew a deep breath. "I suppose you'd better put him through."

"At once, Domynas."

Yursak dipped his head, covering his eyes briefly, then withdrew. A moment later, the message center's wallpaper came up on her display. She gazed at it for a maunihirth or two, steeling herself, then touched the "ACCEPT CALL" icon.

The human, Howell, appeared. Behind it, she saw what could only be the command deck of a warship, and she knew the pickup's focus had been widened to make sure she saw it.

"Greetings, First Minister," it said. "Should I assume you have a response to my demands?"

"You do realize," Sherak said coldly, "that whatever you may be in a position to do to my people, here in this star system, the rest of the Hegemony will eventually repay you a thousand times over?"

"Assuming the rest of the Hegemony is as competent and capable as *you* are, I'll await their attempt to do that with confidence." Sherak flushed an angry orange-red at the human's dismissive tone, but it only went on calmly. "And as I believe I've already pointed out to you, the rest of the Hegemony isn't here right now. So, what is your response?"

"I'm sure you already know." Sherak's voice was colder than ever. "We know about your other two ships, and Navy Commander Segmar is prepared to resist you with every weapon we possess. You may have a few technological tricks we don't, but if you enter attack range of this planet, we will rip your ships to pieces. Even if you 'win,' the cost will be terrible, and that doesn't even consider what will happen when the Hegemony Council learns of your actions! So I suggest you think very, very carefully before you fire the first shots of an all-out war between your single miserable species and the entire civilized galaxy."

"Among my people," Howell said, "there's a saying—'you can judge a person by the company he keeps.' That's why we have very little concern over the state of our relations with your own species, since the Liatu are among the scum of the galaxy." His mouth shaped another of those curves. "As for the rest of the Hegemony, we have another saying—'you can tell even more about a person's character by the enemies he makes than by the friends he keeps.' And, *that,* First Minister, is why we don't really care about the enmity of the Galactic Hegemony, either. In fact, we've come to the conclusion that enmity between us and the Hegemony's morally degenerate and intellectually impaired members is not only inevitable but actually constitutes a badge of honor. It's long past time someone proved it's not the arbiter of the galaxy anymore, and we're perfectly ready to accept the job."

Despite herself, Sherak's eyes widened ever so slightly. Deep inside, she'd believed Segmar and Third Minister Lyralk were right. That not even a species as mad as these humans would truly embrace the inevitable self-destruction of a challenge to the entire Hegemony. But now—

"Enjoy your contemplation of what will ultimately happen to us," Howell said before she could get her thoughts back into any sort of order. "I doubt it will be as much consolation as you may think in the next day or two.

"Good day, First Minister."

Very well, Admiral Swenson," Judson Howell said formally, turning from his com terminal as he killed the link to First Minister Sherak. "You're authorized to proceed."

"Yes, Sir!" Francisca Swenson responded, then turned to the circular column at her flag deck's center. Its surface was configured into individual com screens that displayed the faces of every squadron, division, and ship commander of 2nd Fleet. They didn't really need the visual interface, given their neural links, but using their eyes for this particular bit of information flow was a data management tool. Besides, there was something about the human brain that *wanted* to use its eyes.

"All right, Ladies and Gentlemen." Her voice was cold, her blue eyes harder than sapphires. "Operation Downfall is a go."

Those icy eyes turned to Vice Admiral Shinobu Kagehisa, Battle Squadron Fifteen's CO, Vice Admiral Patricio Lopez, who commanded the Fifth Cruiser Squadron, and Vice Admiral Marie-Madeleine Suchet, CruRon Three's CO, and she bared her teeth.

"Uncloak the rest of your ships now," she said. "It's time to let the Froggies see what we've *really* brought to the party."

COMMAND CENTER,
SYSTEM COMMAND ONE,
TAIRYS PLANETARY ORBIT,
TAIRYON SYSTEM,
419.9 LY FROM EARTH,
DECEMBER 26, YEAR 42 TE.

H *orkan!* The humans—!"

Orbital Command Commander Horkan, Third Hatched of His Brood, Son of Masdan, of the Line of Jorik, wheeled towards System Surveillance Commander Urdia. Urdia, *Fourth* Hatched of Her Brood, Daughter of Masdan, of the Line of Jorik, actually. That made her his younger brood mate and closest sibling, which might have explained her omission of his rank and title . . . except for the fact that it was the first time in her entire life that she *had* omitted it on duty.

His eyes swiveled to her face, then went wide as he saw her terrified, stark beige expression. He stared at her, but she only pointed at the tactical plot, and Horkan felt both stomachs drop straight to the deck as his eyes followed that shaky digit.

He and Urdia had conscientiously warned both Segmar and the Council of Ministers that there might still be additional human starships in the system. Yet even as they'd dutifully issued their warnings, neither of them had truly believed it. True, the aliens had intercepted every recon drone short of their known vessels, which had kept any active Liatu sensor out of range. But that couldn't shield them from the additional sensor arrays Urdia had gotten into place around Sembach and Corsalt. Those sharp-eyed platforms had confirmed—finally, once they knew to look in the first place—the presence of all six known human ships, not just the four the aliens had persisted in showing them, and nailed down their positions with absolute accuracy. Urdia's crews had detected the emission signatures—the very *strong* emission signatures, actually—those ships had somehow radiated directly away from Tairys and the weapons platforms and ships in orbit about it. But they'd detected *only* those six emission signatures, and if there'd been another one out there, they would have seen it.

The six stupendous starships the aliens *had* brought along had been more than bad enough for Horkan, of course. He knew the capabilities of his twelve defensive stations, but he also realized those six ships alone massed at least eighty-four percent as much as his entire command. Yet he'd also known that, as Segmar had told Shekhar, unlike his orbital weapons platforms, they had to provide for the enormous mass and volume requirements of their phase-drives, normal-space drives, and particle shield generators. That had to consume at least twenty or twenty-five percent of their volume, which pushed the tonnage imbalance even further in the defenders' favor, and as Segmar had also told the First Minister, there were limits to the degree to which superior weapons could make up for tonnage inferiority. Horkan had been grimly certain that the obscenely inventive humans had far too many nasty tactical surprises in store for them, but given those numbers, he'd also understood the Navy Commander's fierce assertion that the combination of Horkan's OWPs and his own ten dreadnoughts could at least defend the planet against any human attack.

But there weren't six of them, he thought with the crystal clarity of a shock so deep the fear hadn't broken through yet. There were *eight*, and even as he watched them begin to accelerate towards Tairyon orbit, *eighteen* more enemy icons appeared, like curses springing into existence from some Kreptu fairy tale.

At least each of the other eighteen ships was "only" a fifth again the size of one of Navy Commander Segmar's dreadnoughts.

If they can do that, conceal that much of their strength from us, what else can they do?

The thought ran through him like one of the nuisance animals' chipped-flint spearheads, and he felt his hide going white and beige as the shock faded—no, it didn't fade; it simply *receded* from his forebrain—when he realized he was about to find out.

PLANETARY COMMAND BUNKER,
PALACE OF GOVERNMENT,
CITY OF ITHYRA,
PLANET TAIRYS,
419.9 LY FROM EARTH,
DECEMBER 26, YEAR 42 TE.

First Minister Sherak loped out of the subbasement elevator with Yursak at her side.

She knew alarms were blaring, sirens wailing, all across Ithyra and every other town and city on the planet. There were none here, in this brightly lit, wood-paneled corridor where soft music played from hidden speakers, but wall brackets flashed the silent, dark-red equivalent as she hurried down the passageway to the command bunker's open hatch.

Armed Prosesecha sentries saluted as she passed them, and she made herself return the courtesy. But she wasn't really focused on military punctilio at that moment, and she wondered what was going through those guards' minds as they watched her scurrying towards safety.

She was only here because the command bunker had the best communications and control facilities in the entire star system, of course. It was essential that the Council of Ministers maintain that control uninterrupted. That was why Second Minister Hyrak had been ensconced in the backup command bunker on the far side of the city for the last two days, providing what everyone hoped would be an unneeded degree of redundancy. Sherak herself had headed here, for the primary bunker, as soon as the human Howell cut its com link. But she'd barely started down the hallway from her office to the central elevator bank when her aural implants began crackling.

It would have been too much to call Navy Commander Segmar's voice panicked, but not by much.

Twenty-four of them—*twenty-four*! They'd *known* there were only six of them—Segmar's own platforms had *told* them that! Where in Entropy had the others been?! How had they *hidden* them from the Navy's sensors once Segmar and Urdia had figured out what to look for and how?

She didn't know the answers to those questions, but she couldn't deny the flood of dreadful relief she felt as she passed through the hatch into the bunker. The pleasant, rushing song of the entrance chamber's water wall was less soothing than usual, but the knowledge that she was shielded under over four siljeshes of earth and stone—not to mention the entire city of Ithyra—had an undeniably calming effect.

At the moment, the entry hatch—entry hatches, actually; there were no less than five of the sliding, sorljesh-thick, superdense tysian panels—stood open. When they were closed, nothing short of a contact fusion explosion could have breached them.

She passed through the entrance chamber and down the internal passages to the central command station. Third Minister Lyralk was already there, and she pushed up off of her chair as Sherak entered.

"What other surprises have the egg thieves produced?" the First Minister demanded harshly, and Lyralk bobbed an unhappy shrug.

"None . . . yet, Domynas. But given what they've already shown us. . . ."

Her voice trailed off, and Sherak gave her a curt bob of acknowledgment. She circled to her own chair and lowered herself onto it, looking at the enormous ceiling-hung display. At the moment, it mirrored the displays aboard Navy Commander Segmar's flagship and System Command One, and her blood ran cold as a winter's day as she watched those icons accelerating with slow, implacable purpose towards her star system's defenders.

"Com Medical Director Mynsorlas," she said softly to Yursak. "Tell her to prep her nanotech. We may need it after all."

Initial launch point in three minutes, Admiral," Commander Teagan O'Mooney reported, and Francisca Swenson glanced at her operations officer.

The petite, black-haired O'Mooney was a far more dangerous person than her fine-boned, forty-seven-kilo frame, oval face, and high, delicate cheekbones might suggest to the unwary. She *looked*, in fact, like an escapee from an old-fashioned girls' school. What she actually *was,* however, was a coldly logical, highly skilled practitioner of the art of war who calculated odds with the cold precision of an old riverboat gambler. And despite her fragile appearance, the ops officer had an equally cold, focused killer instinct. It was O'Mooney who'd put together 2nd Fleet's attack plan, and she'd taken merciless advantage of both 2nd Fleet's firepower and humanity's technological advantages when she did.

"Their dreadnoughts are moving, Ma'am," Captain Howell said quietly, beside Swenson, and she nodded.

The Liatu had only ten dreadnoughts in-system, and *Inexorable,* alone, out-massed all ten of them by a factor of four. No doubt they'd thought the dozen massive weapons platforms in orbit around Tairys, each of them well over twelve billion metric tons of weapons and defenses, would square the balance against the six superdreadnoughts they'd been allowed to see. In fact, her *eight* superdreadnoughts, alone, out-massed the combined Liatu warships and platforms by over sixty percent. Her two heavy cruiser squadrons added "only" 6.8 billion metric tons to her combined displacement . . . which was just over twice the combined tonnage of Segmar's dreadnoughts. Of course, each of those "cruisers" also out-massed a Liatu dreadnought by almost seventeen percent.

It looked as if the Liatu must have begun to recognize just how badly they'd miscalculated the military balance. The three courier vessels her recon platforms had identified in planetary orbit had begun to accelerate away from Tairys, and the dreadnoughts weren't advancing to attack 2nd Fleet. Instead, they'd fallen in to escort those couriers in what certainly looked like a desperation move to break at least one starship out of the system to carry word to the Hegemony Council in the Erquoid System. She'd expected the couriers to try to escape Tairyon no matter what, but assigning their entire dreadnought force as escorts was an interesting move. Perhaps they genuinely believed the active and passive missile defenses of a solid globe of dreadnoughts could absorb enough of 2nd Fleet's fire for at least one of their messengers to get clear.

If so, they were wrong, she thought with grim satisfaction.

Judson Howell wanted the Liatu defenses smashed, not just broken. He wanted them turned into rubble, and he wanted it done as quickly—and mercilessly—as possible. Swenson was no fonder of massacring hopelessly outclassed foes than the next woman, but she understood the Ambassador's thinking . . . and she agreed with it.

Given the Liatus' intransigence, 2nd Fleet's response was inevitable. Even if Swenson had wanted to avoid this attack—and she didn't—it would have been impossible. The Liatu's defiant gauge had been cast down, and the Terran Alliance had no option but to pick it up, if it meant for the Hegemony to take it seriously. And since they had it to do, anyway, she was totally in favor of shattering the best defense they could mount so utterly and so decisively that neither Sherak and her ministers right here in Tairyon nor the rest of the Hegemony, once word did reach Erquoid, would ever be able to deny or ignore the totality of their defeat.

And, she admitted to herself, thinking about the centuries of nightmare existence to which the Liatu had so casually condemned the Tairyonian "nuisance animals," she couldn't think of a species that better deserved the honor of becoming the Alliance's "teaching moment" for the entire Hegemony.

"Fire Plan Bravo," she said. "I want those dreadnoughts nailed, Teagan."

"Aye, aye, Ma'am," Commander O'Mooney replied. "Retargeting now."

"Very good."

"Put the scare into them," Swenson thought. *You were a racist, slave-owning bastard, Nathan Bedford Forrest, you and your Klan. But you knew how to win battles, didn't you? And I'm going to take a great deal*

of satisfaction in applying your advice to a species a hundred times worse than even you *were.*

"One minute, Ma'am."

"Engage as specified, Commander," Swenson replied calmly.

. . . . .

THE *RELENTLESS-ALPHA* superdreadnoughts and their *Sword-Alpha*-class heavy cruiser consorts reached launch range and 15,732 missiles erupted from them in a single titanic wave. Seventy-five percent of them were Mjölnirs, configured with the laser-rod warheads. Five percent of them were Yúnzhōngzǐ jammers. Another ten percent were Shango decoy missiles, and the final ten percent were Aegis escort missiles, designed to shoot the Mjölnirs through to their targets.

They didn't bring up their drives. They simply coasted outward at the 600 KPS of their grav-driver launchers. A second, identical launch followed forty-five seconds later. Then a third.

In just ninety seconds, the Planetary Union Navy put 47,196 missiles into space, and their drives came up in carefully timed succession, their acceleration rates calculated to fuse all three launches into a single, co-ordinated, time-on-target salvo . . . all of it targeted on the Liatu Defense Force's ten dreadnoughts.

. . . . .

"NAVY COMMANDER—"

"I see it," Segmar, Second Hatched of His Brood, Son of Kalisar, of the Line of Jorik, said heavily.

He glanced at the stupendous orbital fortifications that girdled Tairys in a protective shield, and thought about his cousins, Horkan and Urdia. They would live at least a little longer than he, he thought grimly. It was unlikely it would be for more than a few siltahls. Certainly no more than a stohmahl.

Nor was his ghyrsal the only one today's holocaust was about to gut.

Your fault, a voice said in the back of his brain. *This is all* your *fault. You* knew *these creatures—these humans—had concealed at least some of their number. But you were so damned* proud *when you found the two you knew about, weren't you? And a corner of your brain knew it was possible you still hadn't found all of them, didn't it? But you couldn't admit that, could you? Not even to yourself, you fool! And so you assured the Ministers you could at least maul the humans if they attacked. Well, you were wrong, weren't you?*

At least he wouldn't have to bear the shame of surviving the debacle of his own creation, he thought, watching that unbelievable torrent of missiles bear down upon his flagship and its consorts.

· · · · ·

THERE WERE THIRTEEN starships in the fleeing formation, targeted by over 47,000 missiles, 33,000 of them Mjölnir shipkillers. That was over 2,500 per ship, and they reached the end of their runs sixteen minutes after the third salvo had launched. The Mjölnirs came howling in behind the covering Shango decoys and the Yúnzhōngzǐ jammers, spaced just far enough apart to avoid fratricide when they detonated, and the Aegis escort missiles riding shotgun ripped apart the handful of counter-missiles that actually managed to acquire lock.

A hemisphere of nuclear fusion wrapped itself around the flank of Segmar's formation, hurling brimstone harpoons from the Mjölnirs' lasing rods, and no one on either side would ever know exactly how many hits that fiery hurricane actually scored. It didn't matter. When the glare of explosions faded, there was nothing but a spreading cloud of shredded, half-molten debris which had once been three billion tons of warships . . . and 9,250 Liatu crewmen.

· · · · ·

ORBITAL COMMAND COMMANDER Horkan stared at the plot in numb horror.

His cousin Segmar had been less than the most brilliant male Horkan had ever known, and he'd had a tendency to bluster out a response before he'd truly thought about a question. But he'd deserved better than that.

He gazed at the plot for another few moments, then made himself look away as those demonic human starships spawned yet more missiles.

His brood mate and her surveillance crews had gleaned at least some data on the humans' weapons capabilities. His tactical officers were already frantically programming that data into their computers, re-planning their point defense firing solutions on the fly, and his orbital weapons platforms' defensive armaments were enormously more power-ful than any dreadnought's. They'd do a far better job of degrading the humans' fire, he knew, especially with the new data to help.

It wouldn't be enough.

He watched a fresh wave of missiles building as they belched from the alien starships' launchers. Like the salvo which had killed Segmar, the new missiles' drive activations were staggered so that all of them—and there were almost twice as many, this time—would arrive in a single, irresistible torrent. His counter-missiles might pare away a bit of their strength, whittle their numbers a little. But that battering ram of fire would smash through any frail shield he could erect in its path, and he knew—*knew*—every single one of those missiles would be targeted upon a single weapons platform.

Each of his OWPs massed almost forty times as much as one of Segmar's dreadnoughts had. So it was remotely possible one of them might survive a single salvo even that size.

It couldn't possibly survive two of them.

He watched the human missile drives light off at last, accelerating them across the vast gulf still stretching between them and Tairys. Their launchers had already begun pre-spotting the next massive missile strike, and he wondered how many siltahls of life he still had.

PLANETARY COMMAND BUNKER,
PALACE OF GOVERNMENT,
CITY OF ITHYRA,
PLANET TAIRYS,
TAIRYON SYSTEM,
419.9 LY FROM EARTH,
DECEMBER 26, YEAR 42 TE.

First Minister Sherak stared at the master display and the broken, shattered wreckage of her star system's defenses with sick, hate-filled eyes.

Three of Horkan's OWPs showed the icons of technically intact installations, but that was a lie. Not one of those atmosphere-streaming lumps of debris still possessed a trace of offensive firepower. The human recon platforms parked virtually on top of Tairys, no longer even trying to hide their presence, were obviously close enough to determine that.

Any of the orbital forts, however badly damaged, which still had functional weaponry had been systematically eliminated in much smaller, precisely coordinated missile strikes, at any rate. The humans were obviously making a point by *not* finishing off the remnants of the three that could no longer harm them.

Although, a bitter thought reminded her, *none of the others could have "harmed" them, anyway.*

The humans had never even entered Horkan's effective range.

Orbital Command had fired its own thousands of missiles in reply, anyway. In fact, it had been able to stack salvos even larger than those the humans had fired. But the alien starships had maneuvered with elegant precision, forcing Horkan's tactical officers to expend precious drive endurance just to reach them. By the time any of those hundreds of thousands of missiles actually entered attack range, they were little better than ballistic targets for human missile defenses which were far more effective than anything Navy Commander Segmar's forces could ever have mustered.

The Tairyon System's defenders hadn't scored a single hit against the humans.

Not one.

And now those completely undamaged human warships were settling into orbit around *her* planet.

"First Minister."

Sherak swiveled one eye from the display to Adjunct Yursak.

"Let me guess," she said bitterly. "Howell is on the com."

"I'm . . . afraid so, Domynas." Yursak's hide was an interesting blend of anger's orangey-red, anxiety's gray, and sorrow's green, but he met her gaze levelly.

"Put him through," she said harshly, and the human's hated face replaced the tactical display's bitter icons.

"First Minister," it said.

She still had no clue how to read human expressions, but the satisfaction—and confidence—in its tone came through the translating software perfectly. She glared at it silently, and its shoulders moved.

"By our calculations, your decision against surrendering has already cost well over four hundred thousand Liatu lives. Will it truly be necessary for even more of your people to die before you recognize the inevitable and acknowledge our control of this star system?"

"Do whatever you want with the rest of the system," Sherak told it venomously. "But not a single member of your loathsome, insane species will ever set foot on this planet!"

"Really?" Howell tipped its head to one side and the ridiculous little strips of pelt above its deep-set eyes arched. "And why should I think anything of the sort, First Minister?"

"Because I've taken steps to ensure you won't."

"And those steps would be . . . what, exactly?" The alien's tone of mild interest rasped Sherak's fury on the quick.

"You say you're so concerned about the nuisance animals," she shot back. "That's the entire reason you're here, isn't it? Or that's what you *claim*, anyway. Personally, I think you're lying. You don't *truly* care about the nuisance animals any more than any other species that's actually sentient would. But, assuming there's a shred of truth in your pretense of concern, know this—if you attempt to land on *my* planet, *Ambassador* Howell, every single one of those . . . creatures will be *dead* within four planetary days!"

"Really?" Howell moved its head from side to side in another of those grotesquely flexible human gestures. "I'm not surprised a threat like that would occur to someone—some*thing*—like you." The contempt in its translated tone cut like a knife. "Did you really think this possibility wouldn't suggest itself to us, First Minister? I assume you've had your scientific staff cook up a suitable bioweapon? That *does* seem to be your species' default solution, doesn't it?"

Sherak stiffened internally at the alien's obvious lack of surprise. Assuming that it truly *was* unsurprised, she reminded herself. She still couldn't read its expressions or body language, and it could have instructed its translating software to inject whatever emotions it chose into the Liatu words it produced.

"That's precisely what I've done," she told it, ignoring the contemptuous tone of its last sentence.

"I'm not surprised. It's what the Shongairi planned when we proved a bit too difficult to conquer. We didn't much care for it. In fact, we take the entire notion of things like bioweapons and genetic bombs pretty personally, I'm afraid, First Minister. So if you chose to deploy any such weapon against the Tairyonians, it would be a very bad decision on your part."

"Why?" Sherak spat back. "What do I have to lose? What have you creatures *left* me to lose? So now it's your turn to choose how all of this works out. Either you withdraw from the inner system and allow me to send a message to Erquoid and inform the Hegemony Council of events here, then wait to hear back from it . . . or else I deploy the weapon."

"Really?"

"Try landing a shuttle on this planet and find out," Sherak said flatly.

"If you were to successfully do anything of the sort," Howell said levelly, "I would totally destroy every orbital habitat in the star system. And then I'd carry out a systematic kinetic bombardment of your planetary population enclaves."

"Oh, would you?" Sherak sneered pure orange contempt at him. "Are you really stupid enough to expect me to believe you'd commit an atrocity like that over less than two million primitive creatures barely smart enough to bury their own feces when you know how the Hegemony would inevitably respond in the fullness of time?! Do you truly think *I'm* that gullible and stupid?"

"Actually, I realized long ago that you're far stupider than I initially thought was physically possible," Howell told her. "In fact, given your ongoing delusion that there's some reason I or any other human should give a single solitary damn about the Hegemony's 'inevitable responses' to whatever happens here, I expect any one of the Tairyonians you despise is smarter than you are. But you—and when I say 'you,' I mean *you*, as an individual, specifically—would be very ill-advised to even attempt to carry out your threat."

"And why would *that* be?" Sherak demanded contemptuously.

"Because if you don't order your subordinates to destroy your bio-weapon, without harming a single Tairyonian, within the next five Earth minutes—ah, that would be one of your siltahls, First Minister—you'll die and I'll continue this discussion with Second Minister Hyrak, who I suspect will prove more reasonable after your death. And if she doesn't, there's always *Third* Minister Lyralk. Or Fourth Minister Gortuni. Eventually, I'm sure someone—even a Liatu—will see reason."

"I'm in a concealed location, and—"

"You're in a command bunker seven hundred and fifty meters—four of your siljeshes—under the Palace of Government," Howell interrupted.

Sherak's mouth hung open for a moment. Then she shook off her surprise at the fresh, casually displayed evidence that the human knew far too much about her planet.

"Yes, I am," she said. "And that means I'm directly under the largest city on this planet. You expect me to believe that you'd murder three and a half million Liatus just to kill me? What happens to your high and mighty 'moral' objection to our treatment of the nuisance animals if you do that?"

"To be honest, there's a part of me that could live with killing job lots of Liatus just fine," the human replied coldly. "But I don't like that part very much. It reminds me too much of *you*, First Minister. Fortunately, the problem doesn't arise. I can kill you at any moment I choose without harming a single additional Liatu. I suppose I shouldn't say this, but the fact is that I would truly appreciate the opportunity to demonstrate that. And I will, if you don't immediately give the order to destroy your bioweapon."

"Oh, you will?" Sherak sneered. "Then you'd better do it now, because if you haven't started leaving planetary orbit in the same siltahl you just gave *me*, I'll deploy the weapon. So if you genuinely think you can kill me to stop that, go right ahead and try!"

"Have it your own way," another human voice said, and First Minister Sherak, Second Hatched of Her Brood, Daughter of Ursahl, of the Line of Sercom, lurched up from her chair in shock.

That voice hadn't come over the com. It had come from inside the bunker, from directly *behind* her, and she started to twist around towards it, eyes widening in shock.

She was still rising from her chair when a five-fingered hand—a human hand, its fingertips armed with curved, razor-sharp claws at least a sorljesh long—reached around her and ripped out her throat.

Adjunct Yursak lunged to his own feet, staring in disbelieving horror at the human who'd somehow infiltrated the command bunker without setting off a single alarm and then materialized out of thin air, like the demon in some Kreptu fairy tale, to murder the First Minister before his eyes.

"I think you'd better get Second Minister Hyrak on the com, Adjunct," Pieter Ushakov said across Sherak's still-quivering body.

He flicked her blood from his hand as the talons that had shredded her throat retracted into his fingers, and his blue eyes were frozen ice.

"I'm pretty sure she'll want to talk to Ambassador Howell."

S o the situation dirtside is definitely under control, Mister President," Lieutenant General Palazzola said, winding up his report. "I don't say any of the Froggies are happy about it, because they aren't." He shrugged. "On the other hand, there's not a lot they can do about it."

"Aleandro's right about that, Mister President," Admiral Swenson put in. "And between my boarding parties and Rog's technical people, we have control of their complete orbital infrastructure, as well."

"That's your assessment, too, Rog?" Judson Howell looked across the briefing room table at Director of Industrial Operations Roger Mac-Quarie.

He and MacQuarie had been friends since college. More to the point, for the purposes of this conversation, MacQuarie was the man he'd put in charge of creating the mammoth industrial capacity humanity had built around the starting kernel of the platforms they'd captured from Fleet Commander Thikair.

And he was also the man who'd accompanied the Tairyon Mission for the express purpose of converting the Liatu industrial infrastructure to the service of the Terran Alliance.

"Yes," he said now, and shrugged. "We're still sorting through some of the lower-level command interfaces, but we have complete control of the upper-tier nodes. It's going to be a couple of more weeks—our weeks, not Liatu weeks—before my people are comfortable enough to start rooting out all of the Hegemony's damned software redundancies and introducing something like real efficiency to them, but that's all pretty much routine at this point. It's not like we haven't done it before, after all! And the platforms we brought with us are already deploying. Give me a few months, and we'll have pretty much tripled the system's current capacity."

"Good." Howell smiled nastily. "And you'll have such a good purpose to put it all to!"

An unpleasant chuckle ran around the compartment, and Howell smiled more broadly.

He supposed it was unfortunate that Second Minister Hyrak had proved no more reasonable than her old—and recently deceased—friend Sherak when Adjunct Yursak patched Pieter through to her in the backup command bunker.

It had proved unfortunate for *Hyrak,* at any rate.

For obvious reasons, no Liatu had even suspected the capabilities the "vampires" provided to Howell. They'd never suspected that someone like Pieter didn't need a shuttle to reach their planet's surface, or that his cloud of nanobots could flow invisibly through any command bunker hatch that was left conveniently open for him. If Hyrak had been even a tiny bit more naturally reflective than Sherak, though, it might at least have occurred to her that if the humans could infiltrate one command bunker undetected, there was no reason they couldn't have infiltrated *two* of them.

Unhappily for her, it hadn't. She'd not only rejected Pieter's com message, she'd actually begun issuing the order to deploy the bioweapon.

Until Jasmine Sherman materialized out of the thin air of *her* bunker and presented the same argument against her decision that Pieter had already presented to Sherak.

After which Third Minister Lyralk had been only too eager to order the weapon's destruction and surrender the system.

That had been just under a week ago, and the stunned, shellshocked Liatu were still just beginning to adjust to the tectonic changes sweeping through "their" star system.

Sherak's and Hyrak's actions—and fates—suggested to Howell that even after meeting Sherak, his estimate of Liatu arrogance and hubris had remained too low. He'd come to the conclusion since that it would be almost impossible to *over*estimate those qualities, and it was obvious the Liatu had no intention of abiding by the terms of their surrender unless a boot was kept firmly planted on the backs of their nonexistent necks.

Aleandro Palazzola's three Space Marine divisions, backed by Francisca Swenson's warships, were a very substantial boot, however.

The Tairyon Mission's preliminary planning had always presumed that something very much like the "Battle of Tairys"—although, actually, the "Massacre of Tairys" would be a better name for it—was probably inevitable. And it had also called for Tairyon to be massively fortified against any potential Hegemony counterattack afterward, especially if any Liatu starships had managed to escape with word of what had happened here. None of them had, however, which meant MacQuarie's construction crews would have decades—probably at least a couple of centuries, minimum—to work on those fortifications. Given what human-designed weapons platforms and starships were already capable of, that promised a rude reception should the aforesaid potential counterattack ever materialize.

Of course, quite a bit of that industrial capacity would be doing other things for the next few years, he thought with profound satisfaction.

The Liatus here in Tairyon were only beginning to come to grips with the ways in which their lives were about to change, and he expected them to be very, very unhappy when they realized he'd meant what he'd told Sherak about the Terran Alliance's determination to return Tairys to its proper owners.

His medical teams were already spreading out across the planet, dusting the nomadic Tairyonian bands with the nanotech they'd brought with them from Earth, and early indications were that it might prove even more effective than they'd hoped. The damage to the Tairyonians' cognitive functions was actually the result of the subtle rearrangement of no more than two or three protein analogues on their chromosomes. Repairing that damage for future generations of Tairyonians was straightforward—indeed, child's play for modern medical capabilities. Repairing it in *current* generations had been more problematic, but even the present generation's fully mature adults seemed to be responding well. It would probably be a while before they were prepared for the concept of peaceful interaction with any non-Tairyonian, and the human medical teams were being very, very cautious about attempting to initiate contact, but it was obvious that would be happening even sooner than the original mission planners had dared to hope.

And in the meantime, other humans would be making room for them. Not the way the Liatu had "culled" their own ancestors, although he suspected that relatively few of the Liatus currently living on Tairys would see the Terran Alliance's policy in a favorable light. And in some ways, he couldn't really blame them for that, since every single one of them would be moving to an orbital habitat over the next five local years.

That was almost eleven Earth years, and he really would have preferred to push the transition even faster, get it done and out of the way while the Liatu were still in their present state of shock, unlikely to muster anything but passive resistance. That was as quickly as even Galactic-level technology could produce the habitats that would be required, however. Particularly since he had no intention of simply packing them into their new homes like sardines. He had no objection to—in fact, he firmly supported—the notion of providing them with the orbital equivalent of luxury condominiums, and he'd stressed to MacQuarie's engineers that the Liatu habitats had to be amply provided with the aquatic elements their species craved. But they *would* be moved off the world their ancestors had stolen from its original, brutalized inhabitants.

Humanity had a sufficiently dismal record for its own dealings with indigenous peoples over the centuries. Yet that record paled to insignificance beside the sort of policies Galactics like the Liatu habitually deployed against any species—like the Tairyonians—who got in their way. The Planetary Union was determined to learn from its own ancestors' mistakes and misdeeds and equally determined to hold the Hegemony accountable for its even more egregious crimes.

Howell suspected that General Palazzola's Space Marines might find themselves confronting more than merely passive opposition before the great Liatu migration was complete. In many ways, he actually sympathized. Much as he might despise the Liatus' policy toward the Tairyonians—or "inferior species" in general—and despite the contempt he still felt for Sherak and her minions, he *did* understand that Tairys was the only world its Liatu inhabitants had ever known. That he was evicting them from their own homeworld. And if, at some time in the future, the restored Tairyonians were prepared to allow *any* Liatu to return to the planetary surface, he would applaud their decision. But it must be *their* decision, and he would not put their ability to reclaim their own world at risk by leaving hundreds of millions of Liatus on it while they did it.

It's an imperfect solution, he thought now. *But we live in an imperfect universe, and we aren't the ones who screwed this part of it up.*

"All right," he said out loud. "I think the situation is under control here, and since it is, it's time I headed home to report in." He shook his head. "I've got a pretty fair idea that some of your former fellows are going to be moderately appalled by how we handled this, Arthur!"

"Oh, I think you can take that for granted." Arthur McCabe rolled his eyes. "Dad and I argued enough over what he *thought* we'd be doing once we got here. I guarantee you that he's going to do his best to raise merry hell over what's actually happened. After all, we've clearly just poisoned the well where the possibility of amicable relations with the Liatu are concerned."

"Amicable relations?" Admiral Swenson repeated quizzically, and McCabe snorted.

"Dad is genuinely doing his best to be 'realistic' and 'pragmatic,' Admiral. And I have to say that before Sarth—and before Ambassador Dvorak and Alex got hold of me—I was very much where he is now. For that matter, I wish he was right. The thought of—what was it Sherak called us? One 'miserable little species'?—challenging the entire rest of the galaxy should be more than enough to make *anyone* with a working brain nervous as hell. But I'm afraid this is one of those situations where practical experience makes it impossible for me to pretend we could avoid that even if we wanted to." He looked at Howell. "Ambassador Dvorak's right, Mister President. And so are you. If I'd still doubted that for a second, what we've seen out of the Liatu here in Tairyon would have cured me." He shook his head, his expression grim. "The mere fact that we're what and who we are means conflict with the Hegemony is inevitable. Inescapable. They *can't* let us loose to destabilize their neatly organized arrangements, threaten their technological 'stability.' Trying to avoid that conflict could only put us in an even weaker position to survive it when it comes."

"I know." Howell nodded. "At the same time, I'm trying—we *all* need to try—to avoid taking that so much for granted that we get even more bloody-minded and confrontational than we absolutely have to. That's what quite a few people back home are going to wonder about where our policy—*my* policy, really—here in Tairyon is concerned. Which is why I need to get home and start explaining and, if necessary, justifying it.

"Fernando," he looked at Ambassador Garção, who was about to become *Governor* Garção, "are you ready to take over?"

"I think yes," Garção replied with a shrug. "I know the Liatu will get . . . more restive as their military defeat recedes into memory, but I think Arthur, Kacey, and I can handle it, with Aleandro and Francisca's able assistance."

He smiled at Kacey Zukowski. The former Planetary Union Secretary of War would be remaining behind as Garção's military advisor. Her husband, Donald, would remain with her, as what would amount to Garção's Attorney General. Or his interface into the system's existing Liatu legal structure, anyway.

Howell smiled at Kacey, as well. He knew how competent she was, and he'd be leaving Swenson's entire fleet, minus the transport *Isaac O'Reilly,* as the nucleus of the Tairyon System Defense Force. It would be Kacey's task to integrate the new fortifications and heavily automated warships MacQuarie would be building into something sufficient to break the teeth of any Hegemony effort to reclaim the system. He was confident that any routine Hegemony visit to Tairyon would be drawn into the spider's web the Terran Alliance intended to build out here, but eventually, someone was going to wonder why no one had heard anything from Tairyon in the last couple of centuries. By the time they got around to sending someone to make inquiries, the Alliance would have turned the star system into a fortress fit to sneer at Galactic armadas.

It was unfortunate that something the size of the Hegemony could build *super*-armadas, which meant the odds were still enormously in its favor, assuming it was willing to pay the price. But that was always subject to change, and the arthritic pace of interstellar communications would be completely on the Alliance's side for at least the first several centuries of the inevitable conflict.

"In that case," he said out loud, "I think we probably need to leave in the next few days. Given our generation of Gannon Drive, that should get us home fairly close to the time Dave Dvorak—or a courier from him, at any rate—gets back from the Shong System. I think it would be a very good idea for both 'missions' to report to the Union in the same time window, if we can, since how things worked out here—and on Shongaru—will be sort of fundamental to where the Union and the Alliance goes moving forward."

III

EPILOGUE

J udson Howell looked up as a musical tone chimed. He glanced at
the attention request window which had opened on his display, then
tapped an acceptance.

"Sorry to disturb you, Mister President," Eray Mazahar, *Isaac O'Reilly*'s
captain, said.

"Only tidying up a little more paperwork," Howell replied. "Not like
you're interrupting anything I wouldn't just as soon have interrupted."

"Glad to hear that." Mazahar smiled. "But the reason I screened was
to tell you that we've receipted a personal message for you."

"A personal message?" Howell repeated.

"Yes, Mister President. It just came in."

"Well, that was speedy," Howell said, glancing at the time display.
Isaac O'Reilly had dropped sublight just outside Saturn's orbit, thirty
light-minutes from Sol, barely two hours ago. He'd burst-transmitted
his initial report immediately upon arrival and their current velocity
towards the inner system was 58,000 KPS, but given relative planetary
positions, the big transport was still over forty-five light-minutes from
Earth. He had no doubt that the Department of State had pounced on his
report the instant it reached *Bastion*, the stupendous orbital platform the
PU government called home, but there was no way anyone could actually
have *read* it before comming him back.

"May I ask who it's from?" he asked after a moment.

"Well, yes you may, Mister President!" Mazahar's smile turned considerably broader, almost mischievous. "It's from Ambassador Dvorak."

"From Dave?" Howell sat straighter, smiling back at the captain. "So
he did beat us back! Outstanding. Things must have gone even better
than we'd hoped they might!"

"I think we can take that as a given, Sir." Mazahar shook his head.
"I've never actually met the Ambassador myself, but from everything I've

heard, he wouldn't be here if he didn't figure he'd gotten the Shongairi squared away."

"Exactly what I was thinking." Howell nodded. "And put the message through, please," he said, then sent a quick page to Sarah over his neural link.

"Yes?" she replied.

"Com message from Dave! He and Sharon beat us back. Want to watch it with me?"

"Sure!"

He felt her opening the link into a full two-way, which would let her view and hear Dvorak's message through her husband's eyes and ears, as the wallpaper of a waiting com transmission appeared on the display.

He paused a moment longer, until he was certain Sarah was ready, then opened the message queue.

"Well, *there* you are!" a beaming Dave Dvorak said from the display. "Took you long enough!"

Howell chuckled and shook his head as if the other man could see him.

"Actually," Dvorak's expression turned a bit more serious, "I've scanned your report's precis. Sounds like you guys did a good job, although I'm sure you realize that at least a few people here on *Bastion* will have their knickers in a wad over that whole 'blow the Liatu into dust bunnies' thing. Not as many as would have once, but you *know* you're gonna be hearing about it from some of them.

"Things went pretty well on Shongaru, too. Had a few surprises of our own, of course, and a couple of them are likely to affect the way the Alliance unfolds going forward. I need to talk to you about some of those, but it wouldn't make any sense to try to do it with a ninety-minute turnaround time on transmissions. It's going to take you guys about ten hours to decelerate into Earth orbit, and it's coming up on eleven p.m. here in North Carolina. So, unless you have a better idea, Sharon and I will turn in, then pop up to meet you when you get here. I figure all four of us can hop a shuttle to *Bastion* and I'll spring for breakfast—or whichever meal it'll be by your and Sarah's internal clocks—at O'Malley's. That sound good?"

"Well?" Howell asked over the neural link. "You really want to break bread with those two deadbeats?"

"Oh, that is *so* going to cost you when I tell Sharon you said it!"

"You forget, Dear. I am an unscrupulous, underhanded, duplicitous politician. If you tell her, I'll just lie and deny it."

"And she's married to a previously innocent, honest, and forthright firing range owner whom you personally turned into another unscrupulous, underhanded, duplicitous politician," Sarah retorted. "Which means she'll know you're lying."

"Well, there *is* that," he acknowledged with a chuckle. "But the timing sounds good?"

"It'll be way too late for breakfast, as far as you and I are concerned. But O'Malley's? I don't think we've ever tried anything from their menu that wasn't good. And I've *missed* them. Of course the timing sounds good!"

"Great!" He sent her a mental kiss and tapped the display again.

"Well, the mere thought of seeing you again is obviously intensely distasteful to me," he recorded with a grin. "But, as Sarah has just pointed out, O'Malley's kitchen will make up for a lot. So, *of course* we'll be happy to see you. We'll be past lunchtime, ourselves, but we need to start reintegrating with local clocks anyway, so we'll call it either a really late brunch, given that *some* of us will be lagging a little behind that, or lupper, for those of us running ahead." His grin segued into a warm smile. "It's really good to see you, Dave. We're looking forward to it."

He tapped the "SEND" command, and sat, still smiling, for a minute or two before diving back into his paperwork.

. . . . .

"AMBASSADOR DVORAK'S SHUTTLE is inbound, Mister President," Commander Karuna Jadhav, Eray Mazahar's executive officer, announced. "They'll be docking in Boat Bay Ten in about twenty minutes."

"Thank you, Karuna," Howell told her, and glanced over his shoulder as Sarah stepped into their suite's lounge area. "You ready?"

"Of course *I'm* ready," she replied, and he chuckled. Before he'd become Governor of North Carolina, his wife had been one of the more visible cable news anchors and one of the U.S. news establishment's half-dozen most respected—and trusted—political commentators and analysts. His own political career had put something of a damper on that, since she'd always been careful to avoid even the appearance of partisanship, which was harder to do when her spouse had become one of the country's more visibly rising political stars. But she'd managed somehow to balance her career and her role as First Lady of North Carolina.

Until the Shongair invasion had intervened, at least.

But one of the standing jokes between them—and one which had possessed a great deal of truth—had always been that their joint record for punctuality stood the old sexist stereotype firmly on its head. Sarah Howell couldn't *stand* being late, whether for a personal or a professional occasion, whereas *Judson* Howell's sense of urgency was more on the . . . flexible side, at least where personal schedules were involved.

"All right, I'm coming. I'm coming!" he said, waving her towards the hatch.

"'Bout time," she sniffed as she walked past him, nose elevated.

. . . . .

THE HOWELLS STOOD in the boat bay gallery, waiting while the *Starlander* mated with the docking tube. They watched Dave and Sharon Dvorak crossing through the transparent tube, and Howell's eyebrows rose as he took in the menagerie following at the Dvoraks' heels. He wasn't surprised to see the Sarthian sherhynas—they'd become an inseparable part of the Dvorak clan—but the pair of Shongairi were an unexpected addition.

"Well, I see your mission really was a success, Dave!" he said as both Dvoraks exited the tube.

"And I hear the same thing about yours," Dvorak acknowledged as the two of them exchanged back-thumping hugs while Sharon and Sarah embraced.

"I guess we didn't do *too* badly in Tairyon," Howell conceded with a smile. "Although the truth is, I'm a little surprised I haven't already gotten some flak back from Jolasun. Or from the State Department weenies, anyway."

"What? Just because you basically blew up the entire Liatu presence in the star system?" Dvorak shook his head. "Why could anybody possibly be perturbed over a little thing like that?"

Howell chuckled, just a bit sourly, and Dvorak thumped him on the shoulder again.

"Seriously," he said, "everybody knew long before you guys headed out that something like this was most probably going to happen. To be honest, the fact that you were in charge of the mission made them figure it was even more likely, because everybody knew you weren't going to take any shit off the Liatu after what happened here. And given what we already knew they'd done to the Tairyonians. But you may have noticed that even though everybody knew that, you're still the one they decided to send. So I don't think anyone was all that shocked by the way things worked out."

Howell looked at him for a moment, then nodded.

"Oh, by the way!" Dvorak snapped his fingers with the air of someone who'd just remembered something that had slipped his mind. "Let me introduce you. Judson Howell, this is First Minister Urkal-dur-Dyamir-Hyrtal of the Shongair Empire, currently on sabbatical, and Shathyrakym Yudar-zik-Shayma, Shathyra Haymar's father."

Both Shongairi folded their ears—and bent their heads in a gesture of respect they'd clearly acquired from humanity—as Dvorak introduced them. Howell returned the greeting, although he knew his was a bit stiffer than theirs. The last Shongairi *he'd* seen had been planning to murder the entire human race.

"Turns out Jukaris goes even deeper among the Shongairi than we'd thought," Dvorak said in a much more serious tone. "And there's no way that Haymar—or Yudar, who was Shathyra when Thikair was actually dispatched—would have signed off on his frigging bioweapon. Hell, for that matter, they wouldn't have signed off on those damned kinetic bombardments."

Howell gazed at his old friend for a half-dozen heartbeats, and Dvorak met his eyes levelly. Let him look into his own, see the truth there. And as he saw it, Judson Howell realized that he hadn't truly been as reconciled to altering Vlad Drakulya's plans for Shongaru as he'd told himself he was.

"I'm relieved things worked out in Shong less . . . messily than they did in Tairyon," he said, and he was a little surprised to realize he meant it.

"We had to kill too many of them, anyway," Dvorak said sadly.

"That was *not* your fault, Pack Lord," Shathyrakym Yudar said sternly. "Indeed, all of us realized what restraint you humans were showing. It was the mercy you chose to extend as much as the power you possessed to compel that made Haymar—all of us—your tukarasi."

Dvorak made an uncomfortable gesture, and Howell gave a slow mental nod. It sounded like the Planetary Union had chosen the right men to head both of their missions.

"*Anyway,*" Dvorak said now, "Haymar and Yudar—and Urkal—are all quite smart fellows. And after Haymar and I discussed it, we decided it would be best to bring his dad and Urkal along to handle things at this end while I left him at home on Shongaru, working with Fikriyah to get the entire Empire firmly into harness. By this time, all of the Shongair Empire's member systems will have gotten the word and acknowledged Haymar's submission."

"Really? That's outstanding!"

"Oh, you have no idea." Dvorak smiled a bit evilly. "You see, in addition to all of that, Haymar had this idea. Well, he and Brykira hatched it between them, actually. I didn't much care for where I thought they were headed at first, but after they explained it and we hashed it out, kicked it around a little, I decided it was actually a pretty darn good one. I've already discussed it with Jolasun, and he and the Cabinet think it's a good notion, too! In fact, they think it's an even better one now that they've had time to view your report on Tairyon and see how you handled things out there."

"Well, who am I to disagree, if all of you think it's a good idea, whatever it is," Howell said a bit cautiously. He regarded Dvorak's expression dubiously and found himself wondering, suddenly, if there was a reason Dvorak hadn't already sent him a copy of his own report on the Shong Expedition.

"I am *so* glad you feel that way." Dvorak's smile turned even broader.

"Why?" Howell's tone was distinctly suspicious now.

"You remember way back when I was happily running my little shooting range, living up in my cabin in the mountains, minding my own business? Back before you grabbed me and pretty much drafted me as your Secretary of State, right after Vlad kicked the Puppies' ass and headed for Shong? You remember that dinner party with you and Sarah and Bill Jeffers and how unscrupulous you were? How you took advantage of my weakened state with that bum shoulder of mine? How I really,

really, didn't want the job? Thought I wasn't qualified for it? Tried my damnedest to weasel out of it, but you wouldn't let me? Twisted my arm until you *made* me take it, even *knowing* Sharon was likely to shoot me in both kneecaps if I did? You remember all that?"

"I wouldn't have described it in exactly those words, but, yes, I do recall . . . pressing my argument strongly that evening in Greensboro. Why?" Howell was even more suspicious now.

"Because, Judson, my friend," Dvorak said, "after Jolasun and I discussed Haymar and Brykira's idea, he agreed it was downright brilliant. He's gotten both the Senate and House Committees on Extra-Solar Affairs to sign off on it, too. And *especially* since he read your report, he also agrees with me that there's really only one man who's suited to making it work. So he's got a new job proposal for you, and—" Dvorak threw an arm around his shoulders "—trust me, payback's a bitch . . . Your Majesty."

APPENDIX I:
GLOSSARY

cherjuk—a particularly loathsome and destructive carnivorous sea slug native to the Liatu homeworld.

chighor—a medium-sized feline analog of the Planet Shong, about the size of a large lynx. A crafty hunter known for its ambush skills.

Chir Ghyrhyrma—literally, the "Star Herd;" the Liatu equivalent of an imperial parliament.

chothar—Liatu concept of justice. Literally translated as "balance," it enshrines a draconian eye-for-an-eye mentality.

dahrmyk—a Shongair animal which resembles a large, antler-less stag.

ghyrcolar—Liatu "judging mother." A Liatu judge.

ghyrhyrma—Liatu herd.

ghyrsal—Liatu descent or "family line."

guharnak—literally "nuisance animal." Liatu noun for a genetically damaged Tairyonian whose intelligence has been crippled by the Liatu "genetic bomb" used on his ancestors.

gyrsaris—Liatu "brood mates." Liatus born from the same egg hatching.

gyrthora—Liatu matriarchy; the ghyrhyrma's ruling council of mature mothers.

Gyrtoma—Liatu "Assembly." A local, planetary, or system-wide legislative body.

horkaraha—Liatu concept, usually translated as "potency," which subsumes the *collective* wealth, strength, and/or health of an entire ghyrhyrma.

hurgamyth—Liatu "parting;" the age (two Liatu years; approximately 4.5 Earth Years) at which Liatu children's yurkyria (see below), ends and she/he is moved from her/his biological mother's care into the urcoth (see below).

hykarlu—the Shongair equivalent of an eagle. Also the name of the Imperial Shongair Navy's primary shipkiller missile.

hyrsara—"the superior one." Shongair term for the superior in a Jukaris relationship.

irshika—literally "journey," the Shongair religious pilgrimage to the High Temple of Dainthar on Shongaru.

jukahni—Shongair "honor scars."

Jukaris—"the course of honor," the Shongair equivalent of Bushido.

kairsiak—Liatu ideal, usually translated "attainment" or "fulfillment," which might be better called aggressive (or even over-aggressive) achievement in pursuit of horkaraha (see above).

kyrmath—the fiercest herbivore of Shongaru; the Shongair equivalent of the Cape buffalo.

natho—Shongair "son of."

nathyr—Shongair "daughter of."

Pakyrma—literally "speakers for the pack." The Shongair parliament.

Prosesecha—literally "fighter." Liatu term for any armed, official servant of the government. Roughly equivalent to "gendarme," but also to what a human might consider a soldier or marine, not just a law enforcement officer.

shathyra—literally "master of the pack." The Shongair emperor.

shathyrakym—Shongair emperor emeritus; a former shathyra who has reached mandatory retirement/abdication age and stepped down in favor of his heir.

shyrksu—Shongair equivalent of a peregrine falcon. Also the Imperial Shongair Navy's primary counter-missile.

suukarma—literally, "mercy" in Shongair. Its meanings also include the extension of grace and compassion to a defeated foe.

tharkyr—a Shongair nomad.

Thyrma—literally "lords of the pack." The council of ministers through which the Shathyra rules.

tukaras—"the one who submits." Shongair term for a defeated honor challenger; the approximate equivalent of the hyrsara's (see above) vassal.

tyskar—the Shongair analogue of a great white shark.

urgaro—the most feared predator of Shongaru. A 600-kilo sabretooth analogue.

urcoth—Liatu communal "crèche," where their subsequent care, education, and socialization became the responsibility of the ghyrhyrma.

urmakhis—"the dead who breathe." Shongair term for a Shongair who refuses or evades challenge under Jukaris.

ykarno—a Shongair honor challenge surrogate.

yurkyria—the first two years (4.5 Earth Years) of a Liatu's life, when she/he is nurtured and cared for by her/his biological mother.

APPENDIX II:
THE SHONGAIRI

SHONG SYSTEM

Distance from Sol: 241.5 LY
Primary: F6v
Primary Mass: 1.25 solar masses

System Body		Orbit AU	Orbit LM	Orbit Km	Moons	Grav	Population	Year in Earth Years
Cainharn		0.49	4.10	73,800,000	0	0.26	0	0.34
Mysarg		0.87	7.25	130,500,000	1	0.43	0	0.82
Kryanth		1.21	10.02	180,360,000	2	0.62	761,800	1.33
Shongaru		1.94	16.14	290,520,000	2	0.91	4,712,617,000	2.70
Derinar		3.41	28.32	509,760,000	1	1.12	6,273,050	6.30
	Asteroids	6.26	52.06	937,080,000			817,600	NA
Dainthar	Gas giant	12.04	100.17	1,803,060,000	11		0	41.78
Torlu	Ice giant	23.60	196.30	3,533,400,000	7		0	114.65
Therkai	Ice planet	47.06	391.40	7,045,200,000	0		0	322.83

PLANET SHONGARU

Shongaru is approximately the same size and density as Earth (Earth's circumference is 46,250 kilometers [diameter 14,722 kilometers]; Shongaru's is 42,970 kilometers [diameter 13,678 kilometers]), and its gravity is .98 Earth's. Its rotational period is 23.75 hours and its year is 892 days long (2.42 Earth years; 883.3 Earth days). The Shongair "week" is the "six-day," and its year is divided into 36 months, 28 of 25 days each and 8 of 24 days each. Its average surface temperature is 1.15° Celsius lower than Earth's, but its axial inclination is only 13.7°, and its relatively smaller continents allow for greater oceanic moderation of its seasonal temperatures. There is much less difference between a "continental" and a "coastal" climate on Shongaru.

Shongaru has two moons. Kinsaru, the larger moon is about 18 percent the size of Shongaru and rather smaller, proportionately, than Luna is compared to Earth. Kridohr, the smaller (and outer) moon, is slightly less than half Kinsaru's size.

SHONGAIR PHYSIOLOGY

Physically, Shongair have much in common with Earth's canids. They are proportionately more slender than humans, and rather resemble bipedal coyotes, complete with the deep "V-shaped" chest retained from their quadrupedal ancestors, a sharp and pointy muzzle, and highly expressive ears. They have bushy, foxlike tails, approximately half the length of their torsos, and are proportionately rather longer legged (and armed) than a human. They are toe-walkers; their thumbs are located on the outsides of their hands; they have six fingers (including the thumb) on each hand; their elbows are double-jointed; and their legs bend backward compared to a human's. They are carnivores, not omnivores, and their teeth are poorly suited to chewing vegetable matter. They display significant sexual dimorphism; males average about 152 centimeters (5 feet) in height; females average 121 centimeters (approximately 4 feet).

Shongair "faces" are poorly suited to showing emotion, but their ears are capable of displaying highly nuanced emotions.

Shongair births are normally multiple, with an average "litter" size of three but running as high as six and as low as the occasional singleton.

Natural Shongair lifespans without the antigerone medical therapies of the Hegemony are on the order of 80–90 Earth Years (29–33 Shongair years).

FAMILY AND PACK ORGANIZATION

The "litter mate" relationship is extremely deep among Shongairi, closer even than that of full siblings born in different litters. Shongairi mate for life, and courtship rituals may include rites of challenge (see below) between males competing to woo a female as part of their generally male-dominated cultural matrix. However, females may also challenge one another for the right to be wooed by a specific male. While the challenge process continues to exist, it is very often circumvented or turned into an elaborate courtship play by a couple who have no intention of ending up with anyone else.

Shongair societal and familial organization remains tied to the existence of the pack, which serves the function of clan organizations among other species and cultures. The primeval pack was very small, no more than a dozen or so adults and their young who hunted in common and shared prey. When juveniles attained adulthood they were expected to become tharkyri (nomads) and leave the pack until such time as they could (1) gain acceptance to another pack by right of challenge, (2) establish a new pack built out of other tharkyri, or (3) be taken into an existing pack without challenge as a mate (this option was normally available only to a female tharkyr, but exceptions could be made if a male tharkyr was chosen as mate by a senior [usually widowed] female of the pack). Alternatively, a newly adult Shongair could challenge an adult member of the pack for his or her place. This was uncommon under most circumstances, because it meant that the challenged adult, if defeated, was cast out by the pack, which was tantamount to a sentence of death if the adult was elderly or infirm. If a tharkyr challenged for admission to a new pack and defeated his/her opponent, the defeated Shongair did not necessarily lose pack membership. The pack leader could decree an exemption from loss of membership, but the defeated Shongair became the most junior member of the pack. Because of that, he/she very often chose to become tharkyr, anyway.

Challenges for pack membership sometimes resulted in fights to the death, but that was the very rare exception and more often than not the result of an accident when it occurred. Challenge fights were expected to continue only until one opponent submitted to the other, acknowledging defeat, and there was no dishonor in doing so. One might lose status or place, but one did not lose *honor,* unless it was evident that one had not done one's utmost to achieve victory, first. Elderly Shongairi traditionally left the pack when infirmity made them an increasingly net burden upon the hunters. Some, who possessed extraordinarily useful skill sets (flint knappers, for example) never left because their pack leaders decreed their contributions to the pack as craftsmen or teachers made them too valuable. Other elders, as they felt the time for their departure coming closer, often arranged to be "challenged" by a newly adult tharkyr of the pack in order to permit that tharkyr to remain a part of the pack. This was regarded as an intensely honorable choice upon their part.

As the primeval pack evolved into increasingly sophisticated tool-using cultures and developed increasingly urbanized societies, the *size* of the pack increased. With an agrarian society (although in the case of the Shongair, which centered on the production of meat animals, it might more accurately be described as a ranching society), the pressure to restrict pack size to fit the available hunting range decreased, and juveniles no longer became tharkyri upon achieving adulthood *unless they chose to*. They were no longer *required* to live "packless," but it remained a common practice for young adults—the equivalent of "living on your own and seeing the world" among humans, but with a formal severance of the individual Shongair's affiliation with any pack, which required a successful challenge to gain admission to another.

In modern Shongair society, a Shongair attains his or her majority at age 9 (24.3 in Earth Years) without the ancient tradition of challenge or declaration of adulthood by sire or dam. The tradition of tharkyr remains a vibrant part of Shongair family traditions even today.

NAMING CONVENTIONS

Like most of their societal conventions, the Shongairi's naming practices reflect their ancient hunting pack heritage. Shongairi maintain a "pack" affiliation, although that affiliation's centrality to an individual Shongair's identity has waned over the centuries (see below). Pack affiliation designators go back to the very earliest days of Shongair societal evolution, and those still in use today are the survivors of a multiplicity of designators from times past. There are really only three current pack designators: "ur," "ir," and "zik." Of them all, "zik" is both the least common and the most ancient.

Each child is given a first name at birth, but until they attain their majority (see above), children have no surname. Instead, they are known by a patronymic/matronymic. Males are known as "natho" (son) of their male parent, whereas females are known as "nathyr" (daughter) of their *female* parent. At the time they become adults, they lose the patronymic/matronymic (this stems from the ancient tradition that the tharkyr had no "familial" connection until he/she could win one). When they become engaged or wed, their given names are compounded and connected by "dir" (engaged) or "dur" (married). The married name is normally used only in official pack records.

So the full name of a Shongair named Urmahk, of the Gysar Pack, married to a Shongair named Tyruh would be Urmahk-dur-Tyruh-ir-Gysar. The pack affiliation takes precedence, and since the married name is used only in the rolls of the pack, he would normally be called Urmahk-ir-Gysar. Note that first names normally stand alone in personal address and as part of a military or political title. So if Urmahk commanded a battalion of infantry, he would be known as Battalion Commander Urmahk both in direct address or when referred to in the third person.

SOCIETAL ORGANIZATION

Shongair society evolved from the ancient hunting pack and continues to be dominated by the alpha-beta relationship of the pack. Their social organization is also male-dominated. Although females can rise to leadership positions, this is a relatively recent development (as in within the last 100–150 Earth Years [37–56 Shongair years; 50–75 galactic years]) and remains very much a work in progress. Essentially, female leaders have to be twice as good as their male counterparts.

Shongair society enshrines the custom of "testing," the practice by which leaders can be challenged for their positions. The nature of the test depends upon the nature of the position, and these days, it is seldom as simple as a straight physical combat (although that is an acceptable form of testing, regardless of the position, if both parties agree to it). Any leader may be challenged by a single beta only once per Shongaru year (once every 2.7 Earth Years), and the challenger must earn the right to challenge by defeating any others who might challenge for the same position. Challenges are resolved in order of social status, beginning with the lowest strata of those wishing to challenge. Note that a challenger need not be the *immediate* subordinate of the leader being challenged, although within the military, an individual may be challenged only by a subordinate within two rank levels of his own. Challenges may be resolved through comparative test scores, comparative ability to resolve/solve a problem posed by the *challenged party's* immediate superior, or (quite often for managerial/bureaucratic positions) by comparing the two parties' efficiency in clearing cases, resolving disputes, productivity, etc. (In essence, this must be an apples-to-apples comparison. If an assistant prosecutor challenges the district attorney, for example, the comparison would be the percentage of cases closed and convictions secured. It would not be days on the job, cases investigated, or cases defended.)

Status and position do not *depend* on challenges, however. In the overwhelming majority of cases, they are attained through the same avenues of hard work, success, etc. which would lead to a human's being promoted by his superiors or employer. The right of challenge is a secondary avenue, and until and unless an individual is challenged, his "alpha" status in relationship to his subordinates is assumed and unequivocal. That is, someone who has not challenged and defeated his superior must accept the authority of the superior even if both of them are well aware that the subordinate is the more capable.

JUKARIS

Jukaris ("course of honor") is the Shongair equivalent of Bushido, but while Bushido is actually something of an umbrella term describing a *lot* of variations on the central theme of what might be called Japanese chivalry, Jukaris is a strongly unified concept, with only very minor what might be called "regional" variations among pack groups.

Essentially, Jukaris codifies the challenge and submission mechanism of the Shongairi. It lays down the moral and philosophical justifications for both the right to challenge and the responsibility to submit once dominance has been proven. It has existed since the Shongair Bronze Age, but it is also a living and dynamic philosophical code. Changes in Jukaris come only very, very slowly and are always incremental, but Shongair historians can clearly trace its evolution over their species' recorded history.

Although there has never been a formal, legally binding definition of all Jukaris precepts, it has exerted—and *still* exerts—tremendous influence on Shongair society and the evolution of its legal codes. In that sense, it can be thought of as virtually an "unwritten constitution," since most of its core precepts (as currently understood and accepted) are incorporated into Shongair jurisprudence. It goes deeper than that, however, in that it so permeates Shongair culture that individual Shongairi adhere to it on what amounts to an instinctual level.

Jukaris requires a superior to accept any openly issued, honorable challenge. He (or, increasingly, she) *cannot* decline a challenge properly issued under the stipulations of Jukaris. Nor can anyone else "shortstop" a Jukaris challenge. It is the height of dishonor for a third party to intervene in any way to prevent or impede such a challenge. Jukaris does make provision for the challenged party to respond through a ykarno (champion) under certain specified circumstances. For example, a minor child who has inherited a position within the pack cannot be directly challenged to combat, but that minor child's ykarno (usually an adult male relative) can be challenged in his place. The circumstances under which a ykarno can honorably (and legally) receive a Jukaris challenge are limited and very closely defined, however. To refuse or evade challenge is the most dishonorable act a Shongair can commit. A Shongair who does either of those things is urmakhis, "the dead who breathe" (although the original, literal translation from the ancient Shongairi is much less poetic: an "eater of shit"). No Shongair owes obedience or loyalty to any urmakhis. Indeed, continuing to obey a urmakhis is in itself profoundly dishonorable.

Just as Jukaris requires a superior (hyrsara, literally "the superior one") to accept challenge, it requires the challenger to acknowledge that his challenge has failed and to formally submit if he is defeated. (He becomes tukaras ["the one who submits] and, if the challenge was military or political, the rough equivalent [the equivalency is not exact] of the hyrsara's vassal.) Refusal to acknowledge defeat and submit is just as dishonorable as refusing to accept challenge, and any Shongair who refuses is also urmakhis. He is cast out, cut off from his pack, and stripped of all legal status.

Jukaris prescribes the ritual, formal rules for challenge combat. It also stipulates the non-combat conditions (and resolution mode) under which challenge can be issued: comparative levels of performance when challenging for promotion, for example. It defines the rules for honorable combat—what is acceptable and what is not—and, just as important, it stipulates the obligations of the challenger (or any beta) to fight as completely and as vigorously as he possibly can—his obligation to *force* an alpha to *prove* his dominance. It is cowardly (although it normally falls somewhat short of urmakhis levels of disgrace) to yield before one has been *conclusively* defeated. Indeed, jukahni ("honor scars") earned in a furious, all-out *defeat* are fully as honorable in Shongair eyes as victory. As one famous Shongair warrior philosopher put it: "There is no shame in defeat; there is shame only in craven surrender." But jukahni must be *earned,* or else Jukaris has failed of its purpose of demonstrating the pack alpha's right to his dominance.

RELIGION

The Shongairi are pantheistic. Religious fervor is not part of the Shongair psyche, and they actually make pretty poor fanatics in almost every way.

Dainthar, the supreme deity of the Shongair pantheon, is an idealized Shongair. He is the supreme warrior and supreme hunter, the alpha male of alpha males who created Shongaru as a home for his people and stocked it with all of the food animals they could need. He exemplifies the virtues of strength, duty, and stern compassion.

As Dainthar exemplifies the idealized Shongair male, his mate, Frygahr, is the idealized *female* Shongair. She, too, is a supremely gifted huntress, hunting in cooperation with her mate, but she is also the patroness of hearth, home, and family. Dainthar is more to be feared as a warrior; Frygahr is far more to be feared as an *enemy,* however, because she exemplifies the "mama bear" side of the Shongair family.

Shongaru, the home planet of the Shongair, is also regarded as a deity, the daughter of Dainthar and Frygahr. As Shongaru is regarded as their daughter, all Shongairi revere Shongaru as their "mother," the source of their home and their sustenance. The fashion in which herbivores (and some omnivores) have histories of "overgrazing" their habitats is a horrifying perversion to the Shongair, who have an almost genetic drive, dating from the days when they were strictly hunters, before they had mastered the art of raising domesticated food animals, to conserve their natural habitat.

Shongaru's moons, Kinsaru and Kridohr, are littermates, in Shongair cosmology. Kinsaru is male; Kridohr is his "kid sister."

Derinar, for whom Shong VI is named, is the artisan/smith of the gods. The stars of the heavens are a diadem woven by Derinar for Frygahr at the time she wed Dainthar.

Cainharn is the Shongair devil, the suitor for Frygahr's hand who was bested by Dainthar. Among many other "evil" character traits, Cainharn represents the defeated/bested beta (or alpha) who refuses to submit after being vanquished. According to Shongair religious tradition, Cainharn actually attempted to abduct Frygahr even after she had wed Dainthar, and it was that crime which led to his banishment from "the world above" to the "world below" (hell) in which he reigns supreme but which he cannot leave except very briefly. When he does leave, it is almost always for the purpose of damaging Shongaru or otherwise striking back at / demonstrating his unwillingness to submit in order to spite Dainthar and Frygahr. He is also Dainthar's "enforcer," in some ways, however. The main reason Dainthar allows him to periodically escape hell is to refine the dross, so to speak, of the Shongairi. In that regard, it is his function to find, tempt, corrupt, and bring to shameful defeat the Shongairi who would otherwise corrode the ideals for which Dainthar stands. And when Dainthar, in his role as judge, condemns the unworthy dead to hell, it is Cainharn to whom they must submit, the most shameful fate imaginable, since it means they are submitting to one who refused his own rightful submission.

POLITICAL ORGANIZATION

The Shongair Empire is exactly what the name suggests: an empire. The Shathyra (Emperor; literally "Master of the Pack") exercises direct rule, but he (the shathyra is always male) does so only through the Thyrma (Council of Ministers; literally "Lords of the Pack") and the imperial bureaucracy, and with the advice of the Pakyrma (parliament; literally "Speakers for the Pack"). Imperial law requires the shathyra to step down as emperor at age 36 (87 in Earth Years), at which point he becomes the Shathyrakym (Emperor Emeritus) and is seated in the Thyrma for the remainder of his life. The retirement age *was* 28 (67.7 Earth Years), prior to the acquisition of Galactic medical technology.

The crown descends within the royal family, and the position of the Shathyra himself is not subject to challenge in any form. The right to *assume* the crown, however, is vested in every adult son of the current Shathyra. The male heir to whom the crown ultimately falls *is* determined on the basis of challenge, although that challenge is no longer settled by actual combat. (There have, however, been instances—shameful ones, in Shongair eyes, but some occurring within fairly recent historical memory—in which potential heirs were assassinated by one or more of their siblings.) Under normal circumstances, the "challenge" takes the form of comparison of what one might call the potential candidates' résumés by the Thyrma and the Pakyrma. Generally speaking, the number of candidates is seldom greater than three or four. Less qualified heirs normally withdraw their names from consideration, frequently after spirited horse-trading with the remaining candidates. ("I'll withdraw my name from consideration, in return for your promise to name me Minister of Public Works when/if you assume the crown.")

While the evaluation of potential shathyrai by the Thyrma and Pakyrma is officially based solely on merit, it is obviously more subjective than that, and there have been instances (too many of them, in some Shongairi's eyes) in which the new Shathyra received the crown because he was more charismatic than his fellows or because the Thyrma believed he might be more readily influenced / subtly controlled by his ministers. The eventual recipient of the crown must be approved by a majority vote of both the Thyrma and Pakyrma, although it is rare for the Pakyrma to refuse to confirm the Thyrma's decision. By and large, the system has worked as well over the Shongairi's history as most systems for selecting heads of state.

The Shathyra cannot be challenged for his position, but there is provision for him to be removed from office on the basis of incompetence or violation of the Shongair constitution. As with the United Kingdom, the Shongair constitution is primarily unwritten, aside from a written declaration of the rights of Shongairi which most humans might find surprisingly broad in a society so many of his practices are based in submission and dominance. (This is largely because the human understanding of those terms—submission and dominance—is so different from those of the Shongairi, where there is no opprobrium attached to submission and those in positions of dominance have deep and complex responsibilities to those who have submitted to them.) The constitution depends heavily upon well-understood precedent and tradition, however, and a vigorous tradition of constitutional litigation keeps it alive and well. As a result, the responsibilities, powers, and limitations of Shathyra, Thyrma, and Pakyrma are well understood, and the Shongairi have a better track record than most species of holding those individuals and bodies of individuals to account for violating them.

A Shathyra may be impeached by a three-quarters majority vote of the Pakyrma, and the impeachment can be sustained by a three-quarters majority vote of the Thyrma. If the impeachment succeeds, the deposed Shathyra becomes a private citizen, subject to litigation and challenge, although that is normally a moot point. Only five shathyrai have been removed from office, and all but one of them were removed for mental incompetency or physical incapacity, not crimes against the constitution.

UNITS OF MEASURE

TIME

Shongair unit	Earth equivalent
Dirkar	0.34 Earth seconds
Tiskar	4.12 Earth seconds
Shrekar	49.5 Earth seconds
Myrtahl	9.9 Earth minutes
Yirka	1.98 Earth hours
Day	0.98 Earth days (23.75 hours)

DISTANCE

Shongair unit	Earth metric equivalent	Earth Imperial equivalent
Fyrtarn	0.59 millimeters	0.02 inches
Yirtarn	7.03 millimeters	0.28 inches
Dirtarn	8.43 centimeters	3.32 inches
Tarn	1.01 meters	3.31 feet
Shretarn	12.15 meters	13.29 yards
Myrtarn	145.83 meters	159.48 yards
Sheertarn	1.75 kilometers	1.09 miles
Kholtarn	21.00 kilometers	13.05 miles

MASS

Shongair unit	Metric units	Imperial units
Fyrmerk	0.000004 nanograms	0.00081 grains
Yirmerk	0.000048 microgram	0.0097 grains
Dirmerk	0.0005 milligrams	0.116 grains
Tismerk	0.006 centigrams	1.40 grains
Merk	11.7 decigrams	18.05 grains
Shremerk	14 grams	0.49 ounces
Myrmerk	1.404 kilograms	0.71 pounds
Sheermerk	16.848 kilograms	371.35 pounds
Kholmerk	20,217 kilograms	22.29 tons
Shanmerk	242,611.2 tonnes	267,433.06 tons
Hyrmerk	2,911,334.4 kilotonnes	3,209,196,839.00 tons
Solkmerk	34,936,012.8 megatonnes	38,510,360.64 tons
Tolkmerk	419,232,153.6 gigatonnes	462,124,327.68 tons

APPENDIX III:
THE LIATU, TAIRYON, AND THE TAIRYONIANS

THE LIATU

The Liatu homeworld is about 10% larger but rather less dense than Earth, with a gravity of about 1.15 that of Earth. It orbits its F6 primary at a distance of 15 light-minutes, with a rotational period of 25.3 hours, a solar year 2.21 that of Earth, an axial tilt of 20°, and a surface temperature about 1.5° Celsius higher than Earth's. Its planetary year is 765 planetary days (806.7 Earth days) long, divided into 8-day "weeks" in 15, 51-day months. Only 35% of its surface is covered by water, which gives it a more "continental" climate and means that, despite the fact that its axial tilt is actually less than Earth's, its seasonal climate variations are more extreme.

Liatus are cold-blooded amphibians whose nearest terrestrial equivalent would be extremely large herbivorous frogs. In fact, they resemble American bullfrogs with legs which have evolved to allow them to assume a more upright posture in order to free their hands for tool use when necessary. They have three webbed fingers and an opposable thumb on each hand, and their wedge-shaped, webbed feet are proportionately much longer and (with their toes spread for swimming) far broader than those of humans. They are very strong, fast swimmers, capable of attaining speeds of up to 30 kilometers per hour in water. On land, they travel most comfortably on all fours with a loping, "hopping" gait.

The Liatu have two sexes and are egg-layers, whose females usually produce 7–12 eggs per breeding cycle. Breeding cycles occur about every two Liatu years (about every five Earth Years). Between those cycles, they are infertile. Males grow to an average body length of just under seven feet (typically about 82 inches [208 centimeters]), while female body length is only about 61.5 inches (156.2 centimeters). Even more than the rest of their body form, it is their heads which cause humans to think of them as "froglike." Their large, protuberant eyes allow a very "froglike," independent range of motion, which compensates for the fact that their virtually nonexistent necks permit their heads only very limited mobility. Their skins are "lumpy" looking to a human and they are most comfortable in an environment which allows them to immerse themselves in water on a regular basis or at least maintain a high humidity. Indeed, they are very vulnerable to dehydration if they can't, and their idea of a comfortable conversational nook usually includes something a human might call a "mud wallow." They are capable of going for several days without immersion, but it is uncomfortable for them, and they don't like it. They are bioluminescent and display emotion by changing skin tones.

> Calm, contentment = blue
> Happiness = violet
> Exultation = violet-red
> Amusement = coral
> Frustration = amber
> Contempt = pure orange
> Anger = orange-red
> Confusion = maroon
> Disgust = yellow
> Uneasiness, anxiety = gray
> Fear = ocher/beige
> Sadness = green
> Surprise = white
> Jealousy = chartreuse
> Pride = khaki
> Determination = brown
> Appreciation = puce
> Embarrassment = light green

FAMILY ORGANIZATION

Familial relationships, as most species think of them, are quite weak among Liatu and take second (or third) place in the Liatu concept of "ghyrhyrma," which is most often translated as "herd." In many ways, there is no equivalent at all of the concept of "nuclear family," although the ghyrsal (generally translated as either "descent" or "family line") substitutes for it in many ways.

As the above paragraph suggests, Liatus are strongly herd oriented,

even by Galactic standards. Indeed, in many ways the ghyrhyrma completely substitutes for anything a human would call a family. In their
primitive period, the identity of a Liatu's father was irrelevant and quite
often unknown. The egg-laying mother was also responsible for protecting and guarding the fertilized eggs. She was also then—and remains,
now—the primary custodian of the hatchlings for the yurkyria, their
first two years (roughly 4.5 Earth years) of life, during which she is their
sole supervisor and caregiver, assisted by the gyrthora ("matriarchy"), the
ghyrhyrma's ruling council of mature mothers, who see to the distri-
bution of food and, where necessary, shelter for the young. During that
two-year period, Liatu mothers are very, very close to their offspring
and the hatchlings' love for their mothers is very strong. The young, however, have always been looked upon as a resource of the ghyrhyrma, and
when, after two Liatu years, they reach the age of hurgamyth ("parting"),
they are moved from their mother's care into the urcoth, the communal
"crèche," where their subsequent care, education, and socialization become the responsibility of the ghyrhyrma and not of their parents. The
bond between any Liatu and her/his biological mother remains even after hurgamyth, but it is greatly attenuated, and loyalty to the ghyrhyrma
supersedes it in almost every case. The bond between gyrsaris ("brood
mates," Liatu born of the same egg-hatching) remains close for life, although even that relationship takes second place to an individual's bond
with the ghyrhyrma as a whole.

Despite the communal focus on child-rearing (and, really, possession), the Liatu do recognize ghyrsal, the direct multi-generational line
of descent through the maternal line. Each ghyrsal keeps careful track of
its members' accomplishments and achievements, and status within the
ghyrhyrma is stratified on the basis not just of a Liatu's personal achievements, but also those of her/his line of descent back to the beginnings
of record keeping. The ability to claim membership in a high-profile
ghyrsal is an enormous advantage to any Liatu, especially in a military
or political career. Some ghyrsals are particularly associated with specific
careers, the equivalent, for example, of "military families" which completely dominate the highest ranks of the Liatu military establishment.

The Liatu ghyrhyrma should not be confused with the Hexali zhuheraa
("nest"), although there are certain points of congruence. While the Hexali

regard any individuals of their species (including themselves) as expendable in the interests of the herd/nest, the Liatu do not. An individual Liatu may choose to sacrifice her/himself in the interests of the ghyrhyrma, but they would not be *expected* to do that. Instead the Liatu ideal of kairsiak (which is usually translated "attainment" or "fulfilment" but might be better called "aggressive achievement") calls upon the individual to attain and become all that she/he possibly can. The underlying assumption is that as the ghyrhyrma's members maximize their individual wealth, strength, health, etc., they simultaneously strengthen the ghyrhyrma's *collective* wealth, strength, and/or health (all of which is subsumed under the Liatu term horkaraha [literally "potency"]). By the same token, those who are weak or infirm and depend upon the ghyrhyrma for maintenance and support are seen as a net drain on its collective health, wealth, and strength.

This emphasis on the individual's achievement and the importance of horkaraha are both closely tied up with the Liatu's tradition of very aggressive competition between ghyrhyrmas. Their homeworld has less than half the surface water area of Earth, and the continental interiors are ill-suited to Liatu, so competition for choice coastal and riverine habitat was historically severe, and much of the mindset that engendered remains even today. This is one reason Liatus strike many other species as particularly ruthless and why, even today, they as a society are fully prepared to abandon/write off the equivalent of the weak or infirm (i.e., those who might represent a net negative to the herd's interests). Their technology's productivity has moderated that readiness to some extent because it provides the herd/society with a margin of comfort and survival which is so much greater, but Liatus remain far less concerned about the well-being of individuals than about that of society as a whole.

This readiness to discard the weak even among themselves is even more pronounced where non-Liatu are concerned. They see all other species (the modern-day equivalent of herds) as both inherent competitors and *opportunities*. In that respect, their attitudes are far closer to those which the Hegemony's xenologists assign to carnivores than to herbivores.

NAMING CONVENTIONS

Liatu naming conventions are very simple if a bit cumbersome. A Liatu receives a given name at birth (in pre-technical days, she/he wasn't named until she/he had survived yurkyria, since infant mortality was so high). In addition, she/he receives a number, the order in which she/he hatched from her/his clutch of eggs. This is followed by her/his mother's given name, and then by the ghyrsal to which she/he belongs. The ghyrsal is almost always named for its first known matriarch, although a handful of them are named for the geographical locations where those particular ghyrsals originated.

"Isthar, Fourth Hatched of His Brood, Son of Manucar, of the Line of Treumora" would be a pretty usual Liatu name, which would normally be written "Isthar-4th-Manucar-Treumora." To Liatu in general, he would be known in personal address simply as "Isthar," unless a more precise identification was required. To his gyrsaris (literally, "brood mates"), from the same hatching as himself, he would also be known as "Isthar" or, in more intimate circumstances, as "Fourth." On anything like a formal occasion, or when being introduced to a stranger, his full (and decidedly . . . sonorous) name would invariably be used.

SOCIETAL ORGANIZATION

As Liatu technological capabilities advanced and more complex societies evolved out of the primitive hunter-gatherer equivalent of the Neolithic, males acquired greater status within the ghyrhyrma, but they are still clearly "second-class" citizens. Not because they cannot aspire to high bureaucratic and/or political position and great personal wealth, but because they are still regarded as the most expendable members of the ghyrhyrma. In theory, a single male can fertilize an enormous number of females' eggs, and given the disconnect between the "sperm donor" and the offspring, he is also irrelevant (on an individual basis) to their nurture and upbringing. In the most primitive periods, they were the "gatherers" (the Liatu didn't really have any equivalent of the "hunter" side of "hunter-gatherer") and the defenders of the ghyrhyrma against predation and competing ghyrhyrmas. As their society and tech base developed, they were largely relegated to the tasks which required physical strength and toughness (and expendability). The Liatu male stereotype to this day would be the equivalent of the human "big dumb ox," despite the enormous evolution of their technological capabilities. That stereotype is very often overcome in an individual Liatu's career, but it remains a firmly fixed part of the Liatu's collective conceptualization.

The flip side of that, however, is that the Liatu's military and interstellar exploration command has always been very firmly in the hands of Liatu males. There are virtually *no* females in the Liatu Navy, its ground forces, or its Survey Command, although females do dominate in politics—especially at the highest levels—which means those male-dominated institutions almost always answer to female civilian superiors.

RELIGION

In pre-technic days, the Liatu were shamanistic pantheists. Today, however, they are militantly atheistic (and have been for many terrestrial millennia). They regard belief in any supernatural being as a hallmark of a juvenile, inferior race.

LEGAL SYSTEM

The Liatu legal system applies many personal rights protections to other Liatu, but non-Liatu have no legal status except for that guaranteed/granted to them by specific interstellar agreements. As a member species of the Hegemony, they are required by treaty and interstellar covenant to extend basic rights to all other recognized members of the Hegemony. They are *not* required to extend any legal protections whatsoever to any species which is not a member of the Hegemony, which (in no small part) explains actions like their genetic attack on the Tairyonians. They had no legal obligation *not* to do it, and their philosophy/worldview regarded the Tairyonians as obstacles to the collective ghyrhyrma, which their own moral code required them to neutralize or remove in the most expeditious possible manner. Their membership in the Hegemony represents exactly that same outlook. They did not / do not have the ability to *remove* the other star traveling races of the galaxy, so they entered into a binding legal/political arrangement with them which *neutralized* those other races (and can be manipulated to the Liatu's advantage) to the greatest extent possible.

Among their own, the Liatu legal code enshrines the concept of chothar ("balance"). This is very much an "eye-for-an-eye, tooth-for-a-tooth" idea of judgment. Murderers are put to death (imprisonment is not an option); those who intentionally maim another Liatu are maimed in an identical fashion; those who inadvertently maim another Liatu are allowed/required to make restitution in so far as that is possible and become responsible for any disabilities the injured individual may suffer. There are sometimes exceptions to the requirements of chothar, not so much because of any compassionate concern for the malefactor (although that can and does come into play when sentences are handed down), but because too rigorous an enforcement might undercut the ghyrhyrma's horkaraha.

The concept of trial by jury is not part of Liatu jurisprudence. Neither is the principle of presumed innocence. Instead, the accused is assumed to be *guilty* and must demonstrate his or her innocence to the satisfaction of a ghyrcolar (literally "judging mother") who considers all of the evidence presented by both prosecution and the accused and then renders a verdict. There are several layers to the Liatu court system, and any conviction can be appealed to the next highest level. In the distant past, each ghyrhyrma had its own court system and its ghyrcolars were selected from the gyrthora by its most senior members. As Liatu society matured and evolved, that custom was replaced by an elective process at the lowest levels (the human equivalent of city and county magistrates) and an appointive process at the various appellate levels, based on a nomination and confirmation process. And while ghyrcolar may translate literally as "mother," these days it is not at all unheard of for a male to hold that office.

POLITICAL SYSTEM

The pre-technical Liatu political system was very, very simple: the gyrthora governed.

The gyrthora consisted (in theory) of every female member of the ghyrhyrma who had produced young. In practice, it consisted of the *senior* matriarchs of the ghyrhyrma, and new members were admitted to voting rights strictly on the basis of age as the existing members died or retired (either because of incapacity or because they had chosen to let someone else carry the responsibility while they enjoyed their "golden years"). The size of any given gyrthora was set by its own members and subject to change by majority vote. It could be increased in time of need, and then pruned back (frequently to protect and preserve the power of its existing members) once the period of stress had passed. Like the British

Parliament, the gyrthora could do pretty much anything it wanted: it was executive, legislature, and judiciary in one, and the notion of a written constitution or fundamental body of law which would have precluded its doing whatever it chose to do was not a part of Liatu legal thinking. It still isn't, really.

The same basic structure exists today, although it has become rather more representative in nature. Political leaders are overwhelmingly female and members of their ghyrhyrma's matriarchies (although there are male politicians and males are not legally barred from holding even the highest office). They do not automatically acquire seniority by their age, however. Seniority within their own gyrthoras is often (indeed, generally) a very potent political card or token, but they are elected to office in the Gyrtoma ("Assembly"). There are multiple levels of gyrthoras, from the equivalent of the state level all the way through the planetary level to that of the Chir Ghyrhyrma (literally, the "Star Herd"). The Chir Ghyrhyrma is a voluntary association of Liatu star systems, although it would be completely willing to compel association from any Liatu system which didn't fall into line voluntarily. The Chir Gyrtoma is the equivalent of an imperial parliament, and aside from the scope of agreed-upon traditions (which, admittedly, carry a great deal of weight in Liatu thinking), there are literally no limitations upon the Chir Gyrtoma's power. There is not, and never has been, a Liatu equivalent of a crowned, hereditary monarch. In more primitive days, the most senior matriarch of the gyrthora exercised many of the powers of a monarch, but she was always a *limited* monarch, and her "monarchial" powers passed to a successor solely on the basis of age (seniority) and not of family line.

The same tradition carries over to the Chir Ghyrhyrma in that there is no monarch or popularly elected president equivalent. Instead, the elected member of the Chir Gyrtoma who can put together a majority to support her/his candidacy becomes first minister (prime minister) and combines the offices of head of state and head of government in her/his own person. The subordinate members of her/his Toma (cabinet) serve at her/his pleasure, and do not require confirmation to office in the Toma by the Chir Gyrtoma. However, any member of the Chir Gyrtoma may move to deprive a Toma minister (or several of them) of office in the equivalent of a "no-confidence vote." It requires a 60% majority of the Chir Gyrtoma to carry such a vote, and if it looks like that super majority is likely to be found, the first minister will usually require the resignation of the minister(s) facing recall rather than risk the fall of her/his entire government.

For obvious reasons (like the fact that it requires decades, at the very least, to travel between the star systems of the Chir Ghyrhyrma), most member systems have a very high degree of autonomy, especially in terms of local affairs. In the case of well-established colony systems (those with populations in the several millions range), a system Gyrtoma functions for internal affairs exactly as the Chir Gyrtoma functions for the entire empire. In colony systems which have not yet attained that level of population, government is exercised not by elected representatives, but by appointed governors or viceroys, selected by the first minister and (in this case) confirmed by the Chir Gyrtoma. In systems with sufficient population to elect their own Gyrtoma, the imperial administration functions on a parallel track, controlling the administration and function of imperial organs and institutions. For example, the appointed governor would be the civilian commander of any of the Liatu Navy's forces stationed in her/his star system. The system Gyrtoma might elect to raise and organize the equivalent of a system Coast Guard, but it would have no control over vessels falling under the command of the Liatu Navy. The appointed governor is also responsible for the equivalent of collecting the imperial taxes, which are not monetary but based on labor and resources assessed against the star system on the basis of its population and wealth by the Chir Gyrtoma. (Actually, by the current first minister, but let's not quibble here.)

In truth, the Chir Ghyrhyrma makes very little effort to dictate to its member star systems. It is concerned with protecting and promoting the interests of the entire Liatu species and, because of that, exercises a very tight control over interstellar commerce, travel, exploration, and military projection. It doesn't really care what star systems separated by light-years do internally, *as long as nothing they do threatens the imperial system.* Should any star system embark on a course of action which the Chir Gyrtoma believed threatened the collective power and security of

the Chir Ghyrhyrma, the imperial government would be absolutely ruthless in bringing the recalcitrant star system to heel.

UNITS OF MEASURE

TIME

Liatu unit	Earth equivalent
Sorlhirth	0.19 seconds
Maurihirth	2.27 seconds
Maunihirth	27.25 seconds
Siltahl	5.45 minutes
Stohmahl	1.09 hours
Day	1.05 days (25.3 hours)

DISTANCE

Shongair unit	Earth metric equivalent	Earth Imperial equivalent
Quijesh	0.75 millimeters	0.0295 inches
Hirikjesh	9 millimeters	0.354 inches
Sorljesh	10.8 centimeters	4.252 inches
Jesh	1.3 meters	4.265 feet
Maunijesh	15.6 meters	17.060 yards
Siljesh	187.2 meters	204.724 yards
Shrevjesh	2.246 kilometers	1.395 miles
Sarukjesh	26.956 kilometers	16.749 miles

MASS

Liatu	Metric units	Imperial units
Quimerk	43.4 centigrams	0.667 grains
Hirikmerk	52.08 decigrams	8.006 grains
Sorlmerk	6.25 decagrams	96.25 grains
Maurimerk	7.5 hectograms	2.645 ounces
Merk	0.9 kilograms	1.984 pounds
Maunimerk	10.8 kilograms	23.809 pounds

Liatu	Metric units	Imperial units
Silmerk	129.6 kilograms	285.719 pounds
Shrevmerk	1,555.2 kilograms	1.714 tons
Sarukmerk	18,662 kilograms	20.571 tons
Hirumerk	223,944 kilograms	246.856 tons
Tolmmerk	2,687,328 kilograms	2,962.272 tons
Motokmerk	32,247,936 kilograms	35,547.264 tons
Mershmerk	386,975,232 kilograms	426,567.175 tons

THE TAIRYON SYSTEM

Distance from Sol: 490.3 LY

Distance from Liatu System: 449.3 LY

Primary: F7

Primary Mass: 1.20 Solar masses

System body	Orbit AU	Orbit LM	Orbit km	Moons	Grav	Earth masses	Population	Year in Earth Years
Crusai	0.13	1.10	19,802,647.41					
Doltaar	1.19	9.90	178,223,826.71				900,000,000	
Tairys	2.07	17.19	309,461,371.84	1	1.17	1.1		2.72
Asteroids	4.42	36.71	660,868,351.38					
Sembach	8.59	71.42	1,285,731,889.29		2.6	312.1*		
Corsalt	17.04	141.62	2,549,500,842.36		1.8	95.4*		
Torla	34.02	282.72	5,089,640,433.21		1.12	17*		

*Gas giants

The Tairyon homeworld orbits its F7 primary at 17.19 light-minutes, just inside the outer edge of the star's liquid water zone. It has a particularly active CO_2 cycle, which makes its surface temperature only a bit less than 1.0° Celsius lower than Earth's (which makes it chilly by the Liatu's cold-blooded standards), and its axial tilt is 19°. Its seasonal variation is somewhat less than Earth's, but its lower average temperature produces cold winters, by human (or Liatu) standards, and its icecaps are rather larger than Earth's. On the other hand, two-thirds of its surface is water (a much higher percentage than on the Liatu home-world), which also helps ameliorate seasonal climate variations, and its planetary day length (25.4 hours) and year (927 local days [992.8 Earth days]) is a comfortable fit for them.

The Tairyonians themselves are bisexual mammal analogues who bear live young and resemble Terran eastern gorillas, with powerful arms that are proportionately longer than their legs. Their natural skin color is a light gray, covered by gorilla-like pelts in shades ranging from an almost sandy brown to black. They are omnivores but prefer a diet rich in meats. They have five-fingered hands (four fingers and an opposable thumb), but move most comfortably in a gorilla-like posture. Their knuckles have "pads" which allow them to fold their fingers under and cover even rough terrain in quadrupedal mode without damaging their hands. While they carry their heads in a more upright posture and have much less pronounced or-bital ridges, which minimizes the "beetle brow" of the gorilla, they do, in-deed, hugely resemble gorillas. They are also very large, like their terrestrial counterparts: males average 1.9 meters (6'3") in an upright position with an arm span of up to 2.7 meters (8'10") and an average body weight of approx-imately 272 kilograms (600 pounds). Sexual dimorphism is pronounced; females average approximately 75% of the male's size and weight (142 cm [4'8"] and 204 kilograms [450 pounds]).

Prior to the arrival of the Liatu (and their genetic bomb), Tairyonian intelligence was approximately equal to that of humans, and although they were rather less inventive/innovative than humans, they were above the average for the Galactics in that respect. They had evolved written languages, agriculture, and city building, and they worked skillfully in copper, bronze, and iron. In many ways, their technology and social or-ganization were comparable to those of the Roman Republic at the time of the dissolution of the Latin League (roughly 340 BC).

Since the damage of the genetic bomb, they have lost virtually all of those skills and dropped to an intelligence which would be considered Extremely Low on human intelligence scales. They use spoken language (although it is rudimentary), are still capable of constructing crude weap-ons and tools out of flint, and they are still fire users. With those exceptions, they are at very much the "technological" level of their terrestrial gorilla counterparts. Like gorillas, they live in family bands led/ruled by the dominant male, who must be prepared to defend his position and all of whom are eventually deposed by a (usually) younger, stronger challenger. Most Tairyonians (including the dominant male) normally mate for life, and the dominant male's mate is the matriarch of the band and essentially manages the "domestic side" of the band's affairs.

The natural Tairyonian lifespan, assuming adequate medical technology, would be about 90–95 Earth Years. Given their extraordinarily primitive "tech base," the actual average lifespan for a male is only about 50 EY. The average is somewhat lower than that among females, because of deaths in childbirth. That is the *average,* however, accounting for childhood mortality (*not* abandoned children; see paragraph below), accidental death, etc. Assuming that a Tairyonian doesn't die from one of those causes, a male may live as many as 70–75 Earth Years, while females who don't die in childbirth will live an additional 5–10 Earth Years.

One of the greatest tragedies of their genetic damage is that just over 10% of all Tairyonian pregnancies end in multiple birth, but they no longer have the technological capability to support the additional children. Twins can usually (but, unfortunately, far from always) be supported by a single nursing mother, and additional young can sometimes be adopted by other lactating females, but all too often, they must choose which child will be abandoned to die. A total of 6.5% of all births are twins; 2.7% are triplets, so the toll this has taken on generation after generation of Tairyonians has been grievous indeed.

CULTURE

The Tairyonians' culture is . . . minimal. Human Neolithic culture was primitive, without any sort of advanced knowledge technology, etc., but it was still the product of human beings with human-level IQs. Tairyonian "civilization" simply doesn't exist. Each family band is its own tribe, although there is a sort of extended clan structure in which multiple families may form the same band, but because of their lack of any established agricultural structure, those bands are very small—no more than 100–150 adult individuals, maximum—because they subsist entirely as hunter-gatherers.

They are also nomadic, following the herds of prey animals, which means each band requires a relatively large range. Because preserving that range is essential to survival, clashes between bands are not at all uncommon and have often ended in the extermination of one of the competing bands. In such cases, the survivors (or, at least, the surviving females and young) are often incorporated into the victorious band, although if the victorious band is already straining the limits of its hunting range, all of the losing band's members are likely to be killed and, if not killed, are certain to be driven off.

When a family band grows too large to sustain itself on the available range (or when climatic change or overhunting means that range can no longer support a band its size), the dominant male generally divides the band by compelling selected family units to split off into a smaller band which then departs / is driven off to find its own range. Such subsidiary bands' existence is always precarious until/unless they can locate a range of their own not already dominated by a stronger band. Sometimes one or more subsidiary bands encounter one another and amalgamate into a new, larger band. On other occasions, a subsidiary band may encounter an established band which through sickness or accident has declined in numbers. In such cases, the subsidiary band may be adopted by the established band which sees the newcomers as badly needed reinforcements.

Although it varies somewhat from band to band, male children are normally considered adults when they reach their full growth, which occurs around the age of 7 (19 Earth Years), although most of them will still have some "filling out" to do. Females are considered adult when they begin menstruation (around age 6 [16 Earth Years]).

RELIGION

There is no formal Tairyonian religion. As a rule, Tairyonians see themselves as inhabiting a world which abounds in spirits and ghosts, most of them malevolent. The Liatu occupiers of their world are uniformly regarded as demons and devils.

Most family bands have the equivalent of shamans, individual Tairyonians who seem to have a better "ear" for the unseen spirits around them. Those shamans are generally advisors to their bands' dominant males, and the real basis for their positions is that they possess higher than average IQs/intelligence/wisdom and often suggest smart moves on the part of the band—time to move on because it looks like we may have floods, I see that the local lichens we harvest are being decimated by some fungus, I don't like the looks of the neighboring band, etc. Rather than explain the reasoning/logic behind the suggestion (a task to which both their language and their fellow Tairyonians' intelligence are ill-suited), their advice is cloaked in a "the spirits tell me" mode.

LANGUAGES AND NAMING CONVENTIONS

Because of the damage of the genetic bomb and the nine hundred years of isolation following the devastating collapse of their Iron Age civilization, the Tairyonians' languages (of which there were several) shattered along with everything else. Most of the family bands continue to share a very limited vocabulary of "root words" with other bands descended from speakers of their ancestors' language groups, as well as a very rudimentary form of those languages' original grammar, but there is far less similarity and "bleeding over" among Tairyonian languages and dialects than was the case on Earth. To an extent, this is because the Tairyonians lack anything like organized trade networks. Family bands whose ranges abut one another (and who don't see one another as threats to their own territories) often conduct simple barter-based trade exchanges, but neither their civilization's technology nor their own degraded intelligence permit anything much more complex than that.

Like every other aspect of their genetic bomb–crippled society, Tairyonian naming conventions are very "basic," and the damage to their language and language skills only emphasizes that tendency.

Within a given family band, the band's elders are most often known by the skills which make them elders in the first place. For example, a band's senior flint knapper might be known as "Arrow Maker," which would generally be shortened to simply "Arrow." The most skilled hunter or scout might be simply "Hunter" or "Best Hunter." Beyond that, Tairyonians are most often named by their mothers for something she associates with them. For example, a child with blue or gray eyes (which are vanishingly rare) might be called "Sky," or a child who is exceptionally nimble might be called "Dodger." It is not at all unusual for a child to be known simply as "Boy" or "Girl" (usually with the father's or mother's name attached) until and unless they "earn" a new name. Thus a male child whose father is a flint knapper might be known as "Arrow Maker's Boy" or female child whose mother is a skilled potter (the Tairyonians have lost the art of working metals or kiln-firing pottery but they still make crude vessels out of clay or carved wood) might be "Clay Shaper's Girl." Because their ability to support large family units is so limited, it is unusual for a single mated pair to have more than two children at any given moment, in which case "Younger" might be attached to the younger child's name if both of them are male or both of them are female.

CONTACT WITH THE LIATU

The (extremely limited) good news for the Tairyonians is that the amphibian Liatu aren't really interested in the interiors of Tairys' continents.

Despite their high birth rate and the fact that they've been in possession of the star system for almost 900 Earth Years, the system's total Liatu population in it is only about one billion, since the original colonizing population was so small. Of that total, approximately 10% (roughly 100,000,000) live in/on orbital habitats and industrial platforms. A percentage of those—possibly as high as a third—live there because they actually prefer artificial environments; the majority are there because that's where their "jobs" are and/or because the local Gyrtoma requires them to spend some time there providing essential service functions in order to "earn" a spot on the planetary surface.

Of the 900,000,000+/-Liatu on the planet, 99.9% live within 100 kilometers of a seacoast, lake, or major river. There *are* a handful of Liatu settlements / small population centers in the continental interiors, but they exist only to serve some special need. A very few of them are what you might call "tourist traps"—small Liatu towns located at the Tairys equivalent of the Grand Canyon or a similar "natural attraction." (Despite the lower average temperature of the planet, there is nothing remotely resembling a Liatu "ski lodge.")

Because of that, contact between Tairyonians and the Liatu is much more limited than one might assume. It usually occurs when a family band strays into one of those coastal areas the Liatu have claimed for themselves. The Liatu are quite ruthless, however, about driving off bands, even in the continental interiors, if there is some reason for them to establish one of those settlements / small population centers of theirs.

ABOUT THE AUTHORS

DAVID WEBER is the most popular living author of military science fiction. Aside from the Safehold series beginning with *Off Armageddon Reef,* he is also known for the *New York Times* bestselling Honor Harrington series, the most recent of which was *Uncompromising Honor.* He lives in South Carolina.

CHRIS KENNEDY is a former school principal and naval aviator. His self-published novels include the Occupied Seattle military fiction duology, the Theogony and Codex Regius science fiction trilogies, and the War for Dominance fantasy series.